CLASSIC
SCIENCE
FICTION
STORIES

First published in 2011 by Miles Kelly Publishing Ltd
Harding's Barn, Bardfield End Green, Thaxted, Essex, CM6 3PX, UK

2 4 6 8 10 9 7 5 3 1

PUBLISHING DIRECTOR Belinda Gallagher
CREATIVE DIRECTOR Jo Cowan
EDITORS Carly Blake, Ned Miles
SENIOR DESIGNER Simon Lee
IMAGE MANAGER Liberty Newton
PRODUCTION MANAGER Elizabeth Collins
REPROGRAPHICS Stephan Davis

ISBN 978-1-84810-477-8

Printed in China

British Library Cataloguing-in-Publication Data
A catalogue record for this book is available from the British Library

ACKNOWLEDGEMENTS

The Time Machine (first published by William Heinemann, London, 1895) and *The War of the Worlds* (first published by
William Heinemann, London, 1898) reproduced by permission of A P Watt Ltd on behalf of The Literary Executors
of the Estate of H G Wells

Beachhead from *Strangers in the Universe* (first published by Simon & Schuster, New York, 1956) reproduced by
permission of Pollinger Limited and the Estate of Clifford Simak

The publishers would like to thank the following artists who have contributed to this book:
Si Clark/The Bright Agency, Malcolm Davis/The Bright Agency, Oliver Frey/Temple Rogers,
Arthur Haas/The Bright Agency, Andrew McGeachy, Keith Page/The Bright Agency, Mike Saunders

All other artwork from the Miles Kelly Artwork Bank

The publishers would like to thank the following sources for the use of their photographs:
Dreamstime.com Cover Philcold; 65 Jakelv7500
Shutterstock.com 35(t) SerrNovik, (m) Nancy A Thiele; 79 Shawn Hine; 85 prudkov; 93(frame) diak, Image
Focus; 95 mirkos; 99 dundanim; 100 argus; 102–103 plavusa87; 130 Ralf Juergen Kraft; 136 Jan Kaliciak;
142–143 Bertrand Benoit; 158–159 medvedeff; 159 Igor Plotnikov; 162 Igor Plotnikov; 166 Igor Plotnikov; 170 Igor
Plotnikov; 179 Gl0ck; 180–181 Emelyanov; 182–183 Emelyanov; 185 billyhoiler; 186 Emelyanov; 187 Emelyanov;
195 Digital Media Pro; 197 Markus Gann; 256 Eky Studio; 260 Andrii Muzyka; 307(monitor) kbgen, Phecsone;
309 andreiuc88; 318 Richard J Ashcroft; 324 2happy; 324–325 javarman; 326–327 Luis Amaral; 411 Roman Sigaev;
415 Anteromite; 443 Jakub Krechowicz; 495 crop; 503 Ivan Cholakov Gostock-dot-net; 506 italianestro;
509 Mushakesa; 510 greglith

All other photographs are from:
digitalSTOCK, digitalvision, John Foxx, PhotoAlto, PhotoDisc, PhotoEssentials, PhotoPro, Stockbyte

Every effort has been made to acknowledge the source and copyright holder of each picture.
Miles Kelly Publishing apologises for any unintentional errors or omissions.

Made with paper from a sustainable forest

Self-publish your
children's book

buddingpress.co.uk

www.mileskelly.net   info@mileskelly.net

www.factsforprojects.com

CLASSIC
SCIENCE
FICTION
STORIES

COMPILED BY TIG THOMAS

Miles
KeLLy

OUT OF THIS WORLD

THINKING TIME

THE MIND OF
THE SCIENTIST

THE OTHER

FUTURE IMPERFECT

FOREWORD

ALIENS, SPACESHIPS, TIMESLIPS, a dying sun, intergalactic warfare, modified humans — science fiction invents life as it might be in a slightly altered world. It looks into the future, down the microscope and out to other galaxies. Sometimes a previous era's science fiction has even become our reality (look out for Mark Twain inventing the Internet in 1898). It is always exciting, sometimes chilling, occasionally hilarious. Many great writers have dipped their pens into the bubbling, mutating ink of the sci-fi pool and produced spectacular writing. Set phasers to stun and enjoy the ride.

BEACHHEAD

1951

CLIFFORD D SIMAK

THERE WAS NOTHING, absolutely nothing, that could stop a human planetary survey party. It was a highly specialized unit created for and charged with one purpose only… to establish a bridgehead on an alien planet, to blast out the perimeters of that bridgehead and establish a base where there would be some elbow-room. Then hold that elbow-room against all corners until it was time to go.

After the base was once established, the brains of the party got to work. They turned the place inside out. They put it on tape and captured it within the chains of symbols they scribbled in their field books. They pictured it and wrote it and plotted it and reduced it to a neat assembly of keyed and symbolic facts to be inserted in the galactic files.

If there was life, and sometimes there was, they prodded it to get reaction. Sometimes the reaction was extremely violent and other times it was much more dangerously subtle. But there were ways in which to handle both the violent and the subtle, for the legionnaires and their robotics were trained to a razor's edge and knew nearly all the answers.

As we were saying, there was nothing in the universe, so far known, that could stop a human survey party.

Tom Decker sat at his ease in the empty lounge and swirled the ice in the highball glass, well contented, watching the first of the robots emerge from the bowels of the cargo space. They dragged a conveyor belt behind them as they emerged and Decker, sitting idly, watched them drive supports into the ground and rig up the belt.

A door clicked open back of Decker and he turned his head. "May I come in, sir?" Doug Jackson asked.

"Certainly," said Decker.

Jackson walked to the great curving window and looked out. "What does it look like, sir?" he asked.

Decker shrugged. "Another job," he said. "Six weeks. Six months. Depends on what we find." Jackson sat down beside him. "This one looks tough," he said. "Jungle worlds always are a bit meaner than any of the others."

Decker grunted at him. "A job," he said. "That's all. Another job to do. Another report to file. Then they'll either send out an exploitation gang or a pitiful bunch of bleating colonists."

"Or," said Jackson, "they'll file the report and let it gather dust for a thousand years or so."

"They can do anything they want," Decker told him. "We turn it in. What someone else does with it after that is their affair, not ours."

They sat quietly, watching the six robots roll out the first of the packing-cases, rip off its cover and unpack the seventh robot, laying out his various parts neatly in a row in the tramped-down, waist-high grass. Then, working as a team, with not a single fumble, they put No. 7 together, screwed his brain case into his metal skull, flipped up his energizing switch and slapped the breastplate home.

No. 7 stood groggily for a moment. He swung his arms uncertainly, shook his head from side to side. Then, having oriented himself, he stepped briskly forward, helped the other six heave the packing box containing No. 8 off the conveyor belt.

"Takes a little time this way," said Decker, "but it saves a lot of space. Have to cut our robot crew in half if we didn't pack them at the end of every job. They stowaway better."

He sipped at his highball speculatively. Jackson lit a cigarette.

"Some day," said Jackson, "we're going to run up against something that we can't handle."

Decker snorted.

"Maybe here," insisted Jackson, gesturing at the nightmare jungle world outside the great curved sweep of the vision plate.

"You're a romanticist," Decker told him shortly. "In love with the unexpected. Besides that, you're new. Get a dozen trips under your belt and you won't feel this way."

"It could happen," declared Jackson.

Decker nodded, almost sleepily. "Maybe," he said. "Maybe it could, at that. It never has, but I suppose it could. And when it does, we take it on the lam. It's no part of our job to fight a last ditch battle. When we bump up against something that's too big to handle, we don't stick around. We don't take any risks."

He had another sip.

"Not even calculated risks," he said.

The ship rested on the top of a low hill, in a small clearing masked by tall grass, sprinkled here and there with patches of exotic flowers. Below the hill a river flowed sluggishly, a broad expanse of chocolate-coloured water moving in a sleepy tide through the immense, vine-entangled forest.

As far as the eye could see the jungle stretched away, a brooding darkness that even from behind the curving quartz of the vision plate seemed to exude a heady, musty scent of danger that swept up over the grass-covered hilltop. There was no sign of life, but one knew, almost instinctively, that sentiency lurked in the buried pathways and tunnels of the great tree-land.

Robot No. 8 had been energized and now the eight split into two groups, ran out two packing boxes at a time instead of one. Soon there were twelve robots and then they formed themselves into three groups.

"Like that," said Decker, picking up the conversation where they had left it lying. He gestured with his glass, now empty. "No calculated risks. We send the robots first. They unpack and set up their fellows. Then the whole gang turns to and uncrates the machinery and sets it up and gets it operating. A man doesn't even put his foot on the ground until he has a steel ring around the ship to give him protection."

Jackson sighed. "I guess you're right," he said. "Nothing can happen. We don't take any chances. Not a single one."

"Why should we?" Decker asked. He heaved himself out of the chair, stood up and stretched. "Got a job or two to do," he said. "Last minute checks and so on."

"I'll sit here for a while," said Jackson. "I like to watch. I'm new to this. It is fascinating."

"You'll get over that," said Decker, "in another twenty years."

In his office, Decker lifted the sheaf of preliminary reports off his desk and ran through them slowly, checking each one carefully, filing away in his mind the basic facts of the world outside.

He worked stolidly, wetting a big, blunt thumb against his out-thrust tongue to flip the report pages off the top of the neat stack and deposit them, in not so neat a pile to his right, face downward.

Atmosphere – pressure slightly more than Earth. High in oxygen content. Gravity – a bit more than Earth. Temperature – hot. Jungle worlds always were. There was a breeze outside now, he thought. Maybe there'd be a breeze most of the time. That would be a help. Rotation – thirty-six hour day.

Radiation – none of local origin, but some hard stuff getting through from the sun. He made a mental note: Watch that!

Bacterial and virus count – as usual. Lots of it. Apparently, not too dangerous. Not with every single soul hypoed and immunized and hormoned to his eyebrows. But you never can be sure, he thought. Not entirely sure. No calculated risks, he had told Jackson. But here was a calculated risk, and one you couldn't do a single thing about. If there was a bug that picked you for a host and you weren't loaded for bear to fight him, you took him on and did the best you could.

Life factor – lot of emanation. Probably the vegetation, maybe even the soil, was crawling with all sorts of loathsome life. Vicious stuff, more than likely. But that was something that you took care of as a matter of routine. No use taking any chances. You went over the ground even if there was no life… just to be sure there wasn't.

A tap came on the door and he called out for the man to enter.

It was Captain Carr, commander of the Legion unit.

Carr saluted snappily. Decker did not rise, made his answering salute a sloppy one on purpose. No use, he told himself, letting the fellow establish any semblance of equality, for there was no such equality in fact. A captain of the Legion did not rank with the commandant of a galactic survey party.

"Reporting, sir," said Carr. "We are ready for a landing."

Decker rumbled at him. "Fine, Captain. Fine."

What was the matter with the fool? The Legion always was ready, always would be ready – that was no more than tradition. Why carry out such an empty, stiff formality?

But it was the nature of a man like Carr, he supposed. The Legion, with its rigid discipline, with its ancient pride of service and tradition, attracted men like Carr, was a perfect finishing school for accomplished martinets.

Tin soldiers, Decker thought, but accomplished ones. As hard-bitten a gang of fighting men as the galaxy had ever known. They were drilled and disciplined to a razor's edge, serum- and hormone-injected against all known diseases of an alien world, trained and educated in alien psychology and strictly indoctrinated with high survival characteristics, which stood up under even the most adverse circumstances.

"We shall not be ready for some time, Captain," Decker said. "The robots have just started their uncrating."

"Very well," said Carr. "We await your orders, sir."

"Thank you, Captain," Decker told him, making it quite clear that he wished he would get out. But when Carr turned to go, Decker called him back.

"What is it, sir?" asked Carr.

"I've been wondering," said Decker. "Just wondering, you understand. Can you imagine any circumstance which might arise that the Legion could not handle?"

Carr's expression was a pure delight to see. "I'm afraid, sir," he said, "I don't understand your question." Decker sighed. "I didn't think you would," he said.

Before nightfall the full working force of robots had been uncrated and had set up some of the machines, enough to establish a small circle of alarm posts around the ship.

A flame thrower burned a barren circle on the hilltop, stretching five hundred feet around the ship. A hard-radiations generator took up its painstaking task, pouring pure death into the soil. The toll must have been terrific. In some spots the ground virtually boiled as the dying life forms fought momentarily and fruitlessly to escape the death that cut them down.

The robots rigged up huge batteries of lamps that set the hilltop ablaze with a light as bright as day and the work went on.

As yet no human had set foot outside the ship.

Inside the ship the robot stewards set up a table in the lounge so that the human diners could see what was going on outside.

The entire company, except for the legionnaires, who stayed in quarters, had gathered for the meal when Decker came into the room.

"Good evening, gentlemen," he said. He strode to the table's head and the others ranged themselves along the sides. He sat down and there was a scraping of drawn chairs as the others took their places.

He clasped his hands in front of him and bowed his head and parted his lips to say the customary words. And then he halted even as he spoke and when the words did come they were different than the ones he had said by rote a thousand times before.

"Dear Father, we are Thy servants in an unknown land and there is a deadly pride upon us. Teach us humility and lead us to the knowledge, before it is too late, that men, despite their far travelling and their mighty works, still are as children in Thy sight. Bless the bread we are about to break, we beg Thee, and keep us forever in Thy compassion. Amen."

He lifted his head and looked down the table. Some of them, he saw, were startled. The others were amused.

They wonder if I'm cracking, he thought. They think the Old Man's breaking up. And that may be true, for all I know. Although I was all right until this afternoon. All right until young Doug Jackson...

Platters and plates were being passed up and down the table's length and there was the commonplace, homely clatter of silverware and china.

"This looks an interesting world, sir," said Waldron, the anthropologist. "Dickson and I were up in observation just before the sun set. We thought we saw something down by the river. Some sort of life."

Decker grunted, scooping fried potatoes out of the bowl on to his plate. "Funny if we don't run across a lot of life here. The radiation wagon stirred up a lot of it when it went over the field today."

"What Waldron and I saw," and Dickson, "looked humanoid."

Decker squinted at the biologist. "Sure of that?" he asked.

Dickson shook his head. "The seeing was poor. Could not be absolutely sure. Seemed to me there were two or three of them. Matchstick men."

Waldron nodded. "Like a picture a kid would draw," he said. "One stroke for the body. Two strokes each for arms and legs. A circle for a head. Angular. Ungraceful. Skinny."

"Graceful enough in motion, though," said Dickson. "When they moved they went like cats. Flowed, sort of."

"We'll know plenty soon enough," Decker told them, mildly. "In a day or two we'll flush them."

Funny, he thought. On almost every job someone popped up to report he had spotted humanoids. Usually there weren't any. Usually it was just imagination. Probably wishful thinking, he told himself, the yen of men far away from their fellow men to find in an alien place a type of life that somehow seemed familiar.

Although the usual humanoid, once you met him in the flesh, turned out to be so repulsively alien that alongside him an octopus would seem positively human.

Franey, the senior geologist, said, "I've been thinking about those mountains to the west of us, the ones we caught sight of when we were coming in. Had a new look about them. New mountains are good to work in. They haven't worn down, easier to get at whatever's in them."

"We'll lay out our first survey lines in that direction," Decker told him.

Outside the curving vision plate the night was alive with the blaze of the batteries of lights. Gleaming robots toiled in shining gangs. Ponderous machines lumbered past. Smaller ones scurried like frightened beetles. To the south, great gouts of flame leaped out and the sky was painted red with the bursts of a squad of flame throwers going into action.

"Chewing out a landing field," said Decker. "A tongue of forest juts out there. Absolutely level ground. Like a floor. Won't take a great deal of work to turn it into a field."

The stewards brought coffee and brandy and a box of good cigars. Decker and his men settled back in their chairs, taking life easy, watching the work going on outside the ship.

"I hate this waiting," Franey said, settling down comfortably to his cigar.

"Part of the job," said Decker. He poured more brandy into his coffee.

By dawn the last machines were set up and either had been moved out to their assigned positions or were parked in the motor pool. The flamers had enlarged the burned-over area and three radiation wagons were busy on their rounds. To the south, the airfield had been finished and the jets were lined up and waiting, in a plumb-straight line.

Some of the robots, their work done for the moment, formed themselves in solid ranks to shape a solid square, neat and orderly and occupying a minimum of space. They stood there in the square, waiting against the time when they would be needed, a motor pool of robots, a reservoir of manpower.

Finally the gang-plank came down and the legionnaires marched out in files of two, with clank and glitter and a remorseless precision that put all machines to shame. There were no banners and there were no drums, for these were useless things and the Legion, despite its clank and glitter, was an organization of ruthless efficiency.

The column wheeled and became a line and the line broke up and the platoons moved out toward the planet-head perimeter.

There machine and legionnaire and robot manned the frontier Earth had set up on an alien world.

Busy robots staked out and set up an open-air pavilion of canvas that rippled in the breeze, set up tables and chairs beneath the shading canvas, moved out a refrigerator filled with refreshments, with extra ice compartments.

Finally it was safe and comfortable for ordinary men to leave the shelter of the ship.

Organization, Decker told himself – organization and efficiency and leaving not a thing to chance. Plug every loophole before it was a loophole. Crush possible resistance before it could become resistance. Gain absolute control over a certain number of square feet of planet and operate from there.

Later, of course, there were certain chances taken; you couldn't eliminate them all. There would be field trips and even with all precautions that robot and machine and legionnaire could offer, there would be certain risks. There would be aerial mapping and surveys, and these, too, would have elements of chance, but with those elements reduced to the very minimum.

And always there would be the base – an absolutely safe and impregnable base to which a field party or a survey flight could retreat, from which reinforcements could be sent out or counter-action taken.

Foolproof, he told himself, as foolproof as it could be made.

He wondered briefly what had been the matter with him the night before. It had been that young fool, Jackson, of course – a capable biochemist possibly, but certainly the wrong kind of man for a job like this. Something had slipped up; the screening board should have stopped a man like Jackson, should have spotted his emotional instability. Not that he could do any actual harm of course, but he could be upsetting. An irritant, said Decker. That's what he is – just an irritant.

Decker laid an armful of paraphernalia on the long table underneath the gay pavilion. From it he selected a rolled-up sheet of map paper, unrolled it, spread it flat and thumb-tacked it at all four corners. On it a portion of the river and the mountains to the west had been roughly penciled in. The base was represented by a crossed-through square – but the rest of it was blank. But it would be filled in; as the days went by it would take on shape and form.

From the field to the south, a jet whooshed up into the sky, made a lazy turn and straightened out to streak toward the west. Decker walked to the edge of the pavilion's shade and watched it as it dwindled out of sight. That would be Jarvis and Donnelly, assigned to the preliminary survey of the southwest sector between the base and the western mountains.

Another jet rose lazily, trailing its column of exhaust, gathered speed and sprang into the sky. Freeman and Johns, he thought.

Decker went back to the table, pulled out a chair and sat down. He picked up a pencil and tapped it idly on the almost-blank map paper. Behind his back he heard another jet whoom upward from the field.

He let his eyes take in the base. Already it was losing its raw, burned-over look. Already it had something of the look of Earth about it, of the efficiency and common sense and get-the-job-done attitude of the men of Earth.

Small groups of men stood about the base talking. One of them, he saw, was squatted on the ground, talking things over with three squatting robots. Others walked about, giving orders, planning, sizing up the situation.

Decker grunted with satisfaction. A capable gang of men, he

thought. Most of them would have to wait around to really get down to work until the first surveys came in, but even while they waited they would not be idle.

They'd take soil samples and test them. The life that swarmed in the soil would be captured and brought in by grinning robots and the squirming, vicious things would be pinned down and investigated – photographed, X-rayed, dissected, analyzed, observed, put through reaction tests. Trees and plants and grasses would be dug for a look at soil strata. The river's water would be analyzed. Seines would dredge up some of the life it held. Wells would be driven to establish water tables.

All of this here, at the moment, while they waited for the first preliminary flights to bring back data that would pinpoint other areas worthy of investigation.

Once those reports were in, the work would be started in dead earnest. Geologist and mineral men would probe into the planet's hide. Weather observation points would be set up. Botanists would take far-ranging check samples. Each man would do the work for which he had been trained. Field reports would pour back to the base, there to be correlated and fitted into the picture.

Work then, work in plenty. Work by day and night. And all the time the base would be a bit of Earth, a few square yards held inviolate against all another world might muster.

Decker sat easily in his chair and felt the breeze that came beneath the canvas, a gentle breeze that ruffled through his hair, rattled the papers on the table and twitched the tacked-down map. It was pleasant here, he thought. But it wouldn't stay pleasant long. It almost never did.

Some day, he thought, I'll find a pleasant planet, a paradise planet where the weather's always perfect and there's food for the picking of it and natives that are intelligent to talk with and companionable in other ways – and I will never leave it. I'll refuse to leave when the ship is ready to cast off. I'll live out my days in a fascinating corner of a lousy galaxy – a galaxy that is gaunt with hunger and mad with savagery and lonely beyond all that can be said of loneliness.

He looked up from his reverie and saw Jackson standing at the pavilion's edge, watching him. "What's the matter, Jackson?" Decker asked with sudden bitterness. "Why aren't you…"

"They're bringing in a native, sir," said Jackson, breathlessly. "One of the things Waldron and Dickson saw. The robots caught him, sir."

The native was humanoid, but he was not human.

As Waldron and Dickson had said, he was a matchstick man, a flesh and blood extension of a drawing a four-year-old might make. He was black as the ace of spades and he wore no clothing, but the eyes that looked out of the pumpkin-shaped head at Decker were bright with a light that might have been intelligence.

Decker tensed as he looked into those eyes. Then he looked away, saw the men standing silently around the pavilion's edge, silent and waiting, tense as he was.

Slowly, Decker reached out his hand to one of the twin headsets of the mentograph. His fingers closed over it and for a moment he felt a vague, but forceful reluctance to put it on his head. It was disturbing to contact, or attempt to contact, an alien mind. It gave one a queasy feeling in the pit of the stomach. It was a thing, he thought, that man never had been intended to do – an experience that was utterly foreign to any human background.

Decker lifted the headset slowly, fitted it over his skull, made a sign toward the second set. For a moment the alien eyes watched him, the creature standing erect and motionless.

Courage, thought Decker. Raw and naked courage, to stand here in this suddenly unfamiliar environment that had blossomed almost overnight on familiar ground, to stand here motionless and erect, surrounded by creatures that must look as if they had dropped from some horrific nightmare.

The humanoid took one step closer to the table, reached out a hand and took the headset. Fumbling with its unfamiliarity, he clamped it on his head. And, never for a moment, did the eyes waver from Decker's eyes, always alert and watchful.

Decker forced himself to relax, tried to force his mind into an attitude of peace and calm. That was a thing you had to be careful of. You couldn't scare the critters – you had to lull them, quiet them down, make them feel your friendliness. They would be upset and humpy – a sudden thought, even a

28

suggestion of human brusqueness would wind them up tighter than a drum.

There was intelligence here, he told himself, being careful to keep his mind unruffled – a greater intelligence than one would think looking at the creature. Intelligence enough to know that he should put on the headset – guts enough to do it.

He caught the first faint mental whiff of the matchstick man and the pit of his stomach contracted suddenly and there was an ache around his belly. There was nothing in the thing he caught, nothing that could be put in words, but there was an alienness, as a smell is alien. There was a non-human connotation that set one's teeth on edge. He fought back the gagging blackness of repulsive disgust that sought to break the smooth friendliness he held within his mind.

"We are friendly," Decker forced himself to think. "We are friendly. We are friendly. We are friendly. We are..."

"You should not have come," said the thought of the matchstick man.

"We will not harm you," Decker thought. "We are friendly. We will not harm you. We will not harm you..."

"You will never leave," said the humanoid.

"Let's be friends," thought Decker. "Let's be friends. We have gifts. We will help you. We will..."

"You should not have come," said the matchstick thought. "But since you are here, you can never leave." Humour him, Decker told himself. Humour him. Humour him.

"All right, then," he thought. "We will stay. We will stay and we will be friendly. We will stay and teach you. We will give you the things we have brought for you and we will stay with you."

"You will not leave," said the matchstick man's thought, and there was something so cold and logical and matter-of-fact about the way the thought was delivered that Decker went cold.

The humanoid meant it… meant every word of the thing he said. He was not being dramatic, nor was he blustering… and neither was he bluffing. He actually thought that the humans would not leave, that they would not live to leave the planet.

Decker smiled softly to himself.

"You will die here," said the humanoid thought.

"Die?" asked Decker. "What is die?"

The matchstick man's thought was pure disgust. Deliberately, he reached up and took off the headset, laid it carefully back upon the table. Then he turned and walked away and not a man made a move to stop him.

Decker took off his headset, slammed it on the tabletop. "Jackson," he said, "pick up a phone and tell the Legion to let him through. Let him leave. Don't try to stop him." He sat limply in his chair and looked at the ring of faces that was watching him.

Waldron asked, "What is it, Decker?"

"He sentenced us to death," said Decker. "He said he would not allow us to leave the planet. He said that we would die here."

"Strong words," said Waldron.

"He meant them," Decker said.

He lifted a hand, flipped it wearily. "He doesn't know, of course," he said. "He really thinks that he can stop us leaving. He thinks that we will die."

It was an amusing situation, really. That a naked humanoid should walk out of the jungle and threaten to kill a human survey party. That he should really think that he could do it. That he should be positive about it.

But there was not a single smile on any of the faces that looked at Decker.

"We can't let it get us," Decker said.

"Nevertheless," Waldron declared, "we should take all precautions."

Decker nodded. "We'll go on emergency alert immediately," he said. "We'll stay that way until we're sure... until we're..."

He halted angrily. Sure of what? Sure that an alien savage who wore no clothing, who had not a sign of culture about him could wipe out a group of humans protected by a ring of steel, held within a guard of machines and robots and a group of fighting men who knew all there was to know concerning the refinement of dealing out swift and merciless extermination to anything that moved against them? Ridiculous?

Of course it was ridiculous! And yet the eyes had held intelligence. The being had had not only intelligence, but courage. He had stood within a circle of what to him were alien beings and he had not flinched. He had faced the unknown and said what there was to say and then had walked away with a dignity any human would have been proud to wear. He had known that the alien beings within the confines of the base were not of his own planet, for he had said they should not have come and his thought had implied that he was aware they were not of this world of his. He had understood that he was supposed to put on the headset, but whether that was an act more of courage than of intelligence one would never know – for you could not know if he had realized what the headset had been for. Not knowing, the naked courage of clamping it to his head was of an order that could not be measured.

"What do you think?" Decker asked Waldron.

"We'll have to be careful," Waldron told him evenly. "We'll have to watch our step. Take all precautions now that we are warned. But there's nothing to be scared of, nothing we can't handle."

"He was bluffing," Dickson said. "Trying to scare us into leaving."

Decker shook his head. "I don't think he was," he said. "I tried to bluff him and it didn't work. He's just as sure as we are."

The work went on.

There was no attack.

The jets roared out and thrummed away, mapping the land. Field parties went out, cautiously. They were flanked by robots and by legionnaires and preceded by lumbering machines that knifed and tore and burned a roadway through even the most stubborn of the terrain they went up against. Radio weather stations were set up at distant points, and at the base the weather tabulators clicked off the data that the stations sent back.

Other field parties were flown into the special areas pinpointed for more extensive exploration and investigation.

And nothing happened.

The days went past.

The weeks went past.

The machines and robots watched and the legionnaires stood ready and the men hurried with their work to get off the planet.

A bed of coal was found and mapped. An iron range was discovered. One area in the mountains to the west crawled with radioactive ores. The botanists found twenty-seven species of edible fruits. The base swarmed with animals that had been trapped as specimens and remained as pets.

And a village of the matchstick men was found. It wasn't much of a place. Its huts were primitive. Its sanitation was non-existent. Its people were peaceful. Decker left his chair under the pavilion to lead a party to the village.

The party entered cautiously, weapons ready, but being very careful not to move too fast, not to speak too quickly, not to make a motion that might be construed as hostile.

The natives sat in their doorways and watched them. They did not speak and they did not move. They simply watched the humans as they marched to the centre of the village.

There the robots set up a table and placed a mentograph upon it. Decker sat down in a chair and put one of the headsets on his skull. The rest of the party drew up into a line and waited.

Decker waited and the others waited and the natives sat in their doorways watching. They waited for an hour and not a native stirred. None came forward to put on the other headset. Decker waved his hand wearily, took off the headset. "It's no use," he said. "It won't work. Go ahead and take your pictures. Do anything you wish. But don't disturb the natives. Don't touch a single thing." He took a handkerchief out of his pocket and mopped his steaming face.

Waldron came and leaned on the table. "What do you make of it?" he asked.

Decker shook his head. "It haunts me," he said. "There's just one thing that I am thinking. It must be wrong. It can't be right. But I thought of it and I can't get rid of it."

"Sometimes that happens," Waldron said. "No matter how

illogical a thing may be, it sticks with a man, like a burr inside his brain."

"I thought," said Decker, "that they have told us all that they have to tell us. That they have nothing more they wish to say to us."

"That's what you thought," said Waldron.

Decker nodded. "A funny thing to think," he said. "Out of clear sky. And it can't be right."

"I don't know," said Waldron. "Nothing's right here. Notice that they haven't got a single iron tool. Not a single scrap of metal in evidence at all. Their cooking untensils are stone, a sort of funny stuff like soapstone. What few tools they have are stone."

"And yet," Decker told him, "they're intelligent. Look at their eyes. Intelligence there if you ever saw it. And that fellow who came into the base. He knew what to do with the headset. He knew that we didn't belong on the planet."

Waldron sucked thoughtfully at a back tooth. "We better be getting back to base," he said. "It's getting late."

He held his wrist in front of him.

"My watch has stopped," he said. "What time do you have, Decker?"

Decker's arm came up and Waldron heard the sharp gasp of his breath. Slowly, Decker raised his head, looked at the other man."

"My watch has stopped, too," he said, and his voice was scarcely louder than a whisper.

For a moment they were graven images, eyes matching eyes, and then Waldron jerked his head away.

"Assemble,' he shouted. "Back to the base. Quick!"

The men came running. The robots fell into place. The column marched away. The natives sat in their doorways and watched them leave.

Decker sat in his camp chair and listened to the canvas of the pavilion snapping softly in the wind, alive in the wind, talking and laughing to itself. The lantern, hung on the ring above his head, swayed gently and cast fleeting shadows that seemed at times to be the shadows of living, moving things. A robot stood quietly by one of the pavilion poles.

Stolidly Decker reached out a finger and stirred the little pile of wheels and springs that lay upon the table.

Sinister, he thought.

Sinister and queer.

The guts of watches, lying on the table.

Not of two watches alone, not only his and Waldron's watches, but many other watches from the wrists of other men. All of them silent, stilled in their task of marking time.

Night had fallen hours before, but the base still was astir with activity that was at once feverish and furtive. Men moved about in the shadows and crossed the glaring patches of brilliance shed by the banks of lights set up by the robots many weeks before. Watching them, one would have sensed that they moved with a haunting sense of doom — and would have known as well that they knew, deep in their inmost hearts, that there was no doom to fear. No definite thing that one could put a finger on and say this is the thing to fear. No direction that one could point and say doom lies out there, waiting to leap upon us.

Just one small thing.

Watches had stopped running.

And that was a simple thing for which there must be some simple explanation.

Except, thought Decker, on an alien planet no occurrence, no accident or incident, can be regarded as a simple thing for which a simple explanation must necessarily be anticipated.

For the matrix of cause and effect, the mathematics of chance, may not hold true on alien planets as they hold true on Earth.

There was one rule, Decker thought grimly.

One rule: Take no chances.

That was the one safe rule to follow, the only rule to follow.

Following it, he had ordered all field parties back to base, ordered the crew to prepare the ship for emergency take-off, had alerted the robots to be ready at an instant to get the machines aboard – to even desert the machines and leave without them if circumstances should dictate that such was necessary.

Having done that, there was no more to do but wait. Wait until the field parties came back from their advance camps. Wait until some reason could be assigned to the failure of the watches.

It was not a thing, he told himself, that should be allowed to panic one. It was a thing to recognize, not to disregard. It was a thing which made necessary a certain number of precautions, but it was not a thing that should make one lose all sense of proportion.

You could not go back to Earth and say: "Well, you see, our watches stopped and so…" A footstep sounded and he swung around in his chair. It was Jackson.

"What is it, Jackson?" Decker asked.

"The camps aren't answering, sir," said Jackson. "The operator has been trying to raise them and there is no answer... not a single peep."

Decker grunted. "Take it easy," he said. "They will answer. Give them time."

He wished, even as he spoke, that he could feel some of the assurance that he tried to put into his voice. For a second, a rising terror mounted in his throat and he choked it back.

"Sit down," he said. "We'll sit here and have a beer and then we'll go down to the radio shack and see what's stirring." He rapped on the table. "Beer," he said. "Two beers."

The robot standing by the pavilion pole did not answer.

He made his voice louder.

The robot did not stir.

Decker put his fists upon the table and tried to rise, but his legs suddenly were cold and had turned to water and he could not raise himself. "Jackson," he panted, "go and tap that robot on the shoulder. Tell him we want some beer."

He saw the fear that whitened Jackson's face as he rose and moved slowly forward. Inside himself, starting in the pit of his belly and rising to worry at his throat, he felt the same whiplash terror that Jackson must have felt.

Jackson stood beside the robot and reached out a hesitant hand, tapped him gently on the shoulder, tapped him harder – and the robot fell flat upon his face!

Feet hammered across the hard packed earth, heading toward the pavilion. Decker jerked himself around, sat four-square and solid in his chair, waiting.

It was MacDonald, chief engineer.

He stopped at the table's edge and gripped its boards with two grimy hands. His face was twisted as if he were about to weep.

"The ship, sir. The ship…"

Decker nodded, almost idly. "I know, Mr. MacDonald. The ship won't run."

MacDonald gulped. "The big stuff's all right, sir. But the little gadgets… the injector mechanism, the…" He stopped and stared at Decker. "You knew," he said. "How did you know?"

"I knew," said Decker, "that it would come some day. Not like this, perhaps. But in any one of several ways. I knew that the days would come when our luck would run too thin, when we'd cover all the possibilities but the one that we could not suspect and that, of course, would be the one that would ruin us."

He was thinking, the natives had no metal. No sign of any metal in their camp at all. Their dishes were soapstone and they wore no ornaments. Their implements were stone. And yet they were intelligent enough, civilized enough, cultured enough, to have fabricated metal. For there was metal here… a great deposit of it in the western mountains. They tried, perhaps, many centuries ago. Had fashioned metal tools and metal ornaments and had them go to pieces underneath their fingers after a few short weeks.

Waldron came into the pavilion on cat-like feet.

"The radio's dead," he said, "and the robots are dying like flies. The place is littered with them, just so much scrap steel."

Decker nodded. "The little stuff, the finely fabricated will go first," he said. 'Like watches and radio innards and robot brains and injector mechanisms. After that it will be the big stuff. The ship will melt into a heap of slag."

"The native told us," Waldron said, "when you had him up here. 'You will never leave,' he said."

"We didn't understand," said Decker. "We thought he was threatening us and we knew that we were too big, too well guarded for any threat of his to harm us. He wasn't threatening us at all, of course. He was just telling us. Warning us, maybe, although even then it might have been too late. He might even have felt sorry for us."

He made a hopeless gesture with his hand. "What is it?" he asked.

"No one knows," said Waldron, quietly. "Not yet at least. We may find out later, but it won't help us any. A microbe, maybe. A virus. Something that eats iron after it has been subjected to heat or alloyed with other metals. Something that won't tolerate alloyed metal on the planet. It doesn't go for iron ore. If it did, that deposit we found would have been gone long ago. Possibly the radioactive ore as well."

"How does it survive?" asked Decker. "Without stuff to eat, how does it live?"

"I wouldn't know," said Waldron. "It might not be a metal-eating organism at all. It might be something else. Something in the atmosphere."

"We tested the atmosphere."

But, even as the words left his mouth, Decker saw how foolish they were. They had tested the atmosphere, but how could they have detected something they had never run across before? Man's yardstick was limited – limited to the things he knew about, limited by the circle of his own experience.

He guarded himself against the obvious and the imaginable. He could not guard himself against the unknowable or the unimaginable.

Decker stood up and saw Jackson standing by the pavilion pole, with the robot stretched out at his feet, his metal hide gleaming in the shine of the swaying lantern.

"You have your answer," he told the biochemist. "Remember that first day. You talked with me in the lounge."
Jackson nodded. "I remember, sir," he said. His voice was quiet.

And suddenly, Decker realized, the entire base was quiet.

A gust of wind came out of the jungle and rattled the canvas and set the lantern to swaying violently. Now, for the first time since they had landed, he caught in the wind the alien smell of an alien world.

A MARTIAN ODYSSEY

1934

STANLEY G WEINBAUM

JARVIS STRETCHED HIMSELF as luxuriously as he could in the cramped general quarters of the *Ares*.

"Air you can breathe!" he exulted. "It feels as thick as soup after the thin stuff out there!" He nodded at the Martian landscape stretching flat and desolate in the light of the nearer moon, beyond the glass of the port.

The other three stared at him sympathetically – Putz, the engineer, Leroy, the biologist, and Harrison, the astronomer and captain of the expedition. Dick Jarvis was chemist of the famous crew, the *Ares* expedition, first human beings to set foot on the mysterious neighbour of the earth, the planet Mars. This, of course, was in the old days, less than twenty years after the mad American Doheny perfected the atomic blast at the cost of his life, and only a decade after the equally mad Cardoza rode on it to the moon. They were true pioneers, these four of the *Ares*. Except for a half-dozen moon expeditions and the ill-fated de Lancey flight aimed at the seductive orb of Venus, they were the first men to feel other gravity than earth's, and certainly the first successful crew to leave the earth-moon system. And they deserved that success when one considers the difficulties and discomforts – the months spent in acclimatization chambers back on earth, learning to breathe the air as tenuous as that of Mars, the challenging of the void in the tiny rocket driven by the cranky reaction motors of the twenty-first century, and mostly the facing of an absolutely unknown world.

Jarvis stretched and fingered the raw and peeling tip of his frostbitten nose. He sighed again contentedly.

"Well," exploded Harrison abruptly, "are we going to hear what happened? You set out all shipshape in an auxiliary rocket, we don't get a peep for ten days, and finally Putz here picks you out of a lunatic ant-heap with a freak ostrich as your pal! Spill it, man!"

"According to orders," he said, "I watched Karl here take off toward the North, and then I got into my flying sweat-box and headed South. You'll remember, Cap – we had orders not to land, but just scout about for points of interest. I set the two cameras clicking and buzzed along, riding pretty high – about two thousand feet – for a couple of reasons. First, it gave the cameras a greater field, and second, the under-jets travel so far in this half-vacuum they call air here that they stir up dust if you move low. So, with the speed and the altitude and the blurring caused by the under-jets, the seeing wasn't any too good. I could see enough, though, to distinguish that what I sailed over was just more of this grey plain that we'd been examining the whole week since our landing — same blobby growths and the same eternal carpet of crawling little plant-animals, or biopods, as Leroy calls them. So I sailed along, calling back my position every hour as instructed, and not knowing whether you heard me."

"I did!" snapped Harrison.

"A hundred and fifty miles south," continued Jarvis imperturbably, "the surface changed to a sort of low plateau, nothing but desert and orange-tinted sand. I figured that we were right in our guess then, and this grey plain we dropped on was really the Mare Cimmerium, which would make my orange desert the region called Xanthus. If I were right, I ought to hit another grey plain, the Mare Chronium in another couple of hundred miles, and then another orange desert, Thyle I or II. And so I did."

"Putz verified our position a week and a half ago!" grumbled the captain. "Let's get to the point."

"Coming!" remarked Jarvis. "Twenty miles into Thyle —

believe it or not – I crossed a canal!"

"Putz photographed a hundred! Let's hear something new!"

"And did he also see a city?"

"Twenty of 'em, if you call those heaps of mud cities!"

"Well," observed Jarvis, "from here on I'll be telling a few things Putz didn't see!" He rubbed his tingling nose, and continued. "I knew that I had sixteen hours of daylight at this season, so eight hours – eight hundred miles – from here, I decided to turn back. And right there, Putz's pet motor quit! The atomic blast got weak. I started losing altitude right away, and suddenly there I was with a thump right in the middle of Thyle! Smashed my nose on the window, too!" He rubbed the injured member ruefully.

"I could have fixed!" exclaimed the engineer. "I bet it vas not serious."

"Probably not," agreed Jarvis sarcastically. "Only it wouldn't fly. Nothing serious, but I had my choice of waiting to be picked up or trying to walk back – eight hundred miles, and perhaps twenty days before we had to leave! Forty miles a day! Well," he concluded, "I chose to walk. Just as much chance of being picked up, and it kept me busy."

"We'd have found you," said Harrison.

"No doubt. Anyway, I rigged up a harness from some seat straps, and put the water tank on my back, took a cartridge belt and revolver, and some iron rations, and started out."

"Water tank!" exclaimed the little biologist, Leroy. "She weigh one-quarter ton!"

"Wasn't full. Weighed about two hundred and fifty pounds earth-weight, which is eighty-five here. Then, besides, my own personal two hundred and ten pounds is only seventy on Mars, so, tank and all, I grossed a hundred and fifty-five, or fifty-five pounds less than my everyday earth-weight. I figured on that when I undertook the forty-mile daily stroll. Oh — of course I took a thermo-skin sleeping bag for these wintry Martian nights.

"Off I went, bouncing along pretty quickly. Eight hours of daylight meant twenty miles or more. It got tiresome, of course — plugging along over a soft sand desert with nothing to see, not even Leroy's crawling biopods. But an hour or so brought me to the canal — just a dry ditch about four hundred feet wide, and straight as a railroad on its own company map.

"There'd been water in it sometime, though. The ditch was covered with what looked like a nice green lawn. Only, as I approached, the lawn moved out of my way!"

"Eh?" said Leroy.

"Yeah, it was a relative of your biopods. I caught one — a little grass-like blade about as long as my finger, with two thin, stemmy legs."

"He is where?" Leroy was eager.

"He is let go! I had to move, so I ploughed along with the

walking grass opening in front and closing behind. And then I was out on the orange desert of Thyle again.

"I plugged steadily along, cussing the sand that made going so tiresome, and, incidentally, cussing that cranky motor of yours, Karl. It was just before twilight that I reached the edge of Thyle, and looked down over the grey Mare Chronium. And I knew there was seventy-five miles of *that* to be walked over, and then a couple of hundred miles of that Xanthus desert, and about as much more Mare Cimmerium. Was I pleased? I started cussing you fellows for not picking me up!"

"We were trying, you sap!" said Harrison.

"That didn't help. Well, I figured I might as well use what was left of daylight in getting down the cliff that bounded Thyle. I found an easy place, and down I went. Mare Chronium was just the same sort of place as this — crazy leafless plants and a bunch of crawlers; I gave it a glance and hauled out my sleeping bag. Well, I was just about to turn in when suddenly I heard the wildest sort of shenanigans! There was a racket like a flock of crows eating a bunch of canaries — whistles, cackles, caws, trills and what have you. I rounded a clump of stumps, and there was Tweel!"

"Tweel?" said Harrison, and "Tveel?" said Leroy and Putz.

"That freak ostrich," explained the narrator. "At least, Tweel is as near as I can pronounce it without sputtering. He called it something like 'Trrrweerrlll.'"

"What was he doing?" asked the Captain.

"He was being eaten! And squealing, of course, as anyone would."

"Eaten! By what?"

"I found out later. All I could see then was a bunch of black ropy arms tangled around what looked like, as Putz described it to you, an ostrich. I wasn't going to interfere, naturally; if both creatures were dangerous, I'd have one less to worry about."

"But the bird-like thing was putting up a good battle, dealing vicious blows with an eighteen-inch beak, between screeches. And besides, I caught a glimpse or two of what was on the end of those arms!" Jarvis shuddered. "But the clincher was when I noticed a little black bag or case hung about the neck of the bird-thing! It was intelligent!

That or tame, I assumed. Anyway, it clinched my decision. I pulled out my automatic and fired into what I could see of its antagonist.

"There was a flurry of tentacles and a spurt of black corruption, and then the thing, with a disgusting sucking noise, pulled itself and its arms into a hole in the ground. The other let out a series of clacks, staggered around on legs about as thick as golf sticks, and turned suddenly to face me. I held my weapon ready, and the two of us stared at each other.

"The Martian wasn't a bird, really. It wasn't even bird-like, except just at first glance. It had a beak all right, and a few feathery appendages, but the beak wasn't really a beak. It was somewhat flexible; I could see the tip bend slowly from side to side; it was almost like a cross between a beak and a trunk. It had four-toed feet, and four fingered things – hands, you'd have to call them, and a little roundish body, and a long neck ending in a tiny head – and that beak. It stood an inch or so taller than I, and – well, Putz saw it!"

The engineer nodded. "*Ja!* I saw!"

Jarvis continued. "So – we stared at each other. Finally the creature went into a series of clackings and twitterings and held out its hands toward me, empty. I took that as a gesture of friendship."

"Perhaps," suggested Harrison, "it looked at that nose of yours and thought you were its brother!"

"Huh! You can be funny without talking! Anyway, I put up my gun and said 'Aw, don't mention it,' or something of the sort, and the thing came over and we were pals.

"By that time, the sun was pretty low and I knew that I'd

better build a fire or get into my thermo-skin. I decided on the fire. I picked a spot at the base of the Thyle cliff, where the rock could reflect a little heat on my back. I started breaking off chunks of this desiccated Martian vegetation, and my companion caught the idea and brought in an armful. I reached for a match, but the Martian fished into his pouch and brought out something that looked like a glowing coal; one touch of it, and the fire was blazing – and you all know what a job we have starting a fire in this atmosphere!

"And that bag of his!" continued the narrator. "That was a manufactured article, my friends; press an end and she popped open – press the middle and she sealed so perfectly you couldn't see the line.

"Well, we stared at the fire a while and I decided to attempt some sort of communication with the Martian. I pointed at myself and said 'Dick'; he caught the drift immediately, stretched a bony claw at me and repeated 'Tick.' Then I pointed at him, and he gave that whistle I called Tweel; I can't imitate his accent. Things were going smoothly; to emphasize the names, I repeated 'Dick,' and then, pointing at him, 'Tweel.'

"There we stuck! He gave some clacks that sounded negative, and said something like 'P-p-p-proot.' And that was just the beginning; I was always 'Tick,' but as for him – part of the time he was 'Tweel,' and part of the time he was 'P-p-p-proot,' and part of the time he was sixteen other noises!

"We just couldn't connect. I tried 'rock,' and I tried 'star,' and 'tree,' and 'fire,' and Lord knows what else, and try as I would, I couldn't get a single word! Nothing was the same for two successive minutes, and if that's a language, I'm an alchemist!

Finally I gave it up and called him Tweel, and that seemed to do.

"But Tweel hung on to some of my words. He remembered a couple of them, which I suppose is a great achievement if you're used to a language you have to make up as you go along. But I couldn't get the hang of his talk; either I missed some subtle point or we just didn't *think* alike – and I rather believe the latter view.

"I've other reasons for believing that. After a while I gave up the language business, and tried mathematics. I scratched '2+2=4' on the ground, and demonstrated it with pebbles. Again Tweel caught the idea, and informed me that three plus three equals six. Once more we seemed to be getting somewhere.

"So, knowing that Tweel had at least a grammar school education, I drew a circle for the sun, pointing first at it, and then at the last glow of the sun. Then I sketched in Mercury, and Venus, and Mother Earth, and Mars, and finally, pointing to Mars, I swept my hand around in a sort of inclusive gesture to indicate that Mars was our current environment. I was working up to putting over the idea that my home was on the earth.

"Tweel understood my diagram all right. He poked his beak at it, and with a great deal of trilling and clucking, he added Deimos and Phobos to Mars, and then sketched in the earth's moon!

"Do you see what that proves? It proves that Tweel's race uses telescopes – that they're civilized!"

"Does not!" snapped Harrison. "The moon is visible from here as a fifth magnitude star. They could see its revolution with the naked eye."

"The moon, yes!" said Jarvis. "You've missed my point. Mercury isn't visible! And Tweel knew of Mercury because he placed the Moon at the *third* planet, not the second. If he didn't know Mercury, he'd put the earth second, and Mars third, instead of fourth! See?"

"Humph!" said Harrison.

"Anyway," proceeded Jarvis, "I went on with my lesson. Things were going smoothly, and it looked as if I could put the idea over. I pointed at the earth on my diagram, and then at myself, and then, to clinch it, I pointed to myself and then to the earth itself shining bright green almost at the zenith.

"Tweel set up such an excited clacking that I was certain he understood. He jumped up and down, and suddenly he pointed at himself and then at the sky, and then at himself and at the sky again. He pointed at his middle and then at Arcturus, at his head and then at Spica, at his feet and then at half a dozen stars, while I just gaped at him. Then, all of a sudden, he gave a tremendous leap. Man, what a hop! He shot straight up into the starlight, seventy-five feet if an inch! I saw him silhouetted against the sky, saw him turn and come down at me headfirst, and land smack on his beak like a javelin! There he stuck square in the centre of my sun-circle in the sand – a bull's eye!"

"Nuts!" observed the captain. "Plain nuts!"

"That's what I thought, too! I just stared at him open-mouthed while he pulled his head out of the sand and stood up. Then I figured he'd missed my point, and I went through the whole blamed rigamarole again, and it ended the same way, with Tweel on his nose in the middle of my picture!"

"Maybe it's a religious rite," suggested Harrison.

"Maybe," said Jarvis dubiously. "Well, there we were. We could exchange ideas up to a certain point, and then – blooey! Something in us was different, unrelated; I don't doubt that Tweel thought me just as screwy as I thought him. Our minds simply looked at the world from different viewpoints, and perhaps his viewpoint is as true as ours. But – we couldn't get together, that's all. Yet, in spite of all difficulties, I *liked* Tweel, and I have a queer certainty that he liked me."

"Nuts!" repeated the captain. "Just daffy!"

"Yeah? Wait and see. A couple of times I've thought that perhaps we – " He paused, and then resumed his narrative. "Anyway, I finally gave it up, and got into my thermo-skin to sleep. The fire hadn't kept me any too warm, but that damned sleeping bag did. Got stuffy five minutes after I closed myself in. I opened it a little and bingo! Some eighty-below-zero air hit my nose, and that's when I got this pleasant little frostbite to add to the bump I acquired during the crash of my rocket.

"I don't know what Tweel made of my sleeping. He sat around, but when I woke up, he was gone. I'd just crawled out of my bag, though, when I heard some twittering, and there he came, sailing down from that three-storey Thyle cliff to alight on his beak beside me. I pointed to myself and toward the north, and he pointed at himself and toward the south, but when I loaded up and started away, he came along.

"So the two of us plugged along across the Mare Chronium. Same sort of place as this – same crazy plants and same little green biopods growing in the sand, or crawling out of your way. We talked – not that we understood each other, you know, but just for company. I sang songs, and I suspect Tweel did too; at least, some of his trillings and twitterings had a subtle sort of rhythm.

"Then, for variety, Tweel would display his smattering of English words. He'd point to an outcropping and say 'rock,' and point to a pebble and say it again; or he'd touch my arm and say 'Tick,' and then repeat it. He seemed terrifically amused that the same word meant the same thing twice in succession, or that the same word could apply to two different objects. It set me wondering if perhaps his language wasn't like the primitive speech of some earth people. No word for food or water or man – words for good food and bad food, or rain water and sea water, or strong man and weak man – but no names for general classes. But that wasn't the case with Tweel; it was just that we were somehow mysteriously different – our minds were alien to each other. And yet – we *liked* each other! In fact, I'm not so sure but that he couldn't teach our highly praised human intelligence a trick or two. Oh, he wasn't an intellectual superman, I guess; but don't overlook the point that he managed to understand a little of my mental workings, and I never even got a glimmering of his."

"Well, we plugged along across the Mare Chronium all that

day, and all the next. Mare Chronium – Sea of Time! Say, I was willing to agree with Schiaparelli's name by the end of that march! Just that endless plain of weird plants, and never a sign of any other life. It was so monotonous that I was even glad to see the desert of Xanthus toward the evening of the second day.

"I was fair worn out, but Tweel seemed as fresh as ever, for all I never saw him drink or eat. I think he could have crossed the Mare Chronium in a couple of hours with those block-long nose dives of his, but he stuck along with me. I offered him some water once or twice; he took the cup from me and sucked the liquid into his beak, and then carefully squirted it all back into the cup and gravely returned it.

"Just as we sighted Xanthus, or the cliffs that bounded it, one of those nasty sand clouds blew along, not as bad as the one we had here, but mean to travel against. I pulled the transparent flap of my thermo-skin bag across my face and managed pretty well, and I noticed that Tweel used some feathery appendages growing like a moustache at the base of his beak to cover his nostrils, and some similar fuzz to shield his eyes."

"He is a desert creature!" exclaimed the little biologist, Leroy.
"Huh? Why?"

"He drink no water – he is adapt' for sandstorm – "

"Proves nothing! There's not enough water to waste anywhere on this desiccated pill called Mars. We'd call all of it desert on earth, you know." He paused. "Anyway, after the sandstorm blew over, a little wind kept blowing in our faces, not strong enough to stir the sand. But suddenly things came drifting along from the Xanthus cliffs – small, transparent spheres, for all the world like glass tennis balls! But light — they were almost light enough to float even in this thin air — empty, too; at least, I cracked open a couple and nothing came out but a bad smell. I asked Tweel about them, but all he said was 'No, no, no,' which I took to mean that he knew nothing about them. So they went bouncing by like tumbleweeds, or like soap bubbles, and we plugged on toward Xanthus. Tweel pointed at one of the crystal balls once and said 'rock,' but I was too tired to argue with him. Later I discovered what he meant.

"We came to the bottom of the Xanthus cliffs finally, when there wasn't much daylight left. I decided to sleep on the plateau if possible; anything dangerous, I reasoned, would be more likely to prowl through the vegetation of the Mare Chronium than the sand of Xanthus. Not that I'd seen a single sign of menace, except the rope-armed black thing that had trapped Tweel, and apparently that didn't prowl at all, but lured its victims within reach. It couldn't lure me while I slept, especially as Tweel didn't seem to sleep at all, but simply sat patiently around all night. I wondered how the creature had managed to trap Tweel, but there wasn't any way of asking him. I found that out too, later; it's devilish!

"However, we were ambling around the base of the Xanthus barrier looking for an easy spot to climb. At least, I was. Tweel could have leaped it easily, for the cliffs were lower than Thyle — perhaps sixty feet. I found a place and started up, swearing at the water tank strapped to my back — it didn't bother me except when climbing — and suddenly I heard a sound that I thought I recognized!

"You know how deceptive sounds are in this thin air. A shot

sounds like the pop of a cork. But this sound was the drone of a rocket, and sure enough, there went our second auxiliary about ten miles to westward, between me and the sunset!"

"Vas me!" said Putz. "I hunt for you."

"Yeah; I knew that, but what good did it do me? I hung on to the cliff and yelled and waved with one hand. Tweel saw it too, and set up a trilling and twittering, leaping to the top of the barrier and then high into the air. And while I watched, the machine droned on into the shadows to the south.

"I scrambled to the top of the cliff. I was bitterly disappointed by the failure to attract attention. I pulled out my thermo-skin bag and crawled into it, as the night chill was already apparent. Tweel stuck his beak into the sand and drew up his legs and arms and looked for all the world like one of those leafless shrubs out there. I think he stayed that way all night."

"Protective mimicry!" exclaimed Leroy. "See? He is desert creature!"

"In the morning," resumed Jarvis, "we started off again. We hadn't gone a hundred yards into Xanthus when I saw something queer! This is one thing Putz didn't photograph, I'll wager!

"There was a line of little pyramids — tiny ones, not more than six inches high, stretching across Xanthus as far as I could see! Little buildings made of pygmy bricks, they were, hollow inside and truncated, or at least broken at the top and empty. I pointed at them and said 'What?' to Tweel, but he gave some negative twitters to indicate, I suppose, that he didn't know. So off we went, following the row of pyramids because they ran north, and I was going north.

"Man, we trailed that line for hours! After a while, I noticed

another queer thing: they were getting larger. Same number of bricks in each one, but the bricks were larger.

"By noon they were shoulder high. I looked into a couple – all just the same, broken at the top and empty. I examined a brick or two as well; they were silica, and old as creation itself!"

"How you know?" asked Leroy.

"They were weathered – edges rounded. Silica doesn't weather easily even on earth, and in this climate – !"

"How old you think?"

"Fifty thousand – a hundred thousand years. How can I tell?

The little ones we saw in the morning were older — perhaps ten times as old. Crumbling. How old would that make *them*? Half a million years? Who knows?" Jarvis paused a moment. "Well," he resumed, "we followed the line. Tweel pointed at them and said 'rock' once or twice, but he'd done that many times before. Besides, he was more or less right about these.

"Anyway, we plugged along across Xanthus and in about the middle of the afternoon, something else queer happened. The pyramids ended."

"Ended!"

"Yeah; the queer part was that the last one — and now they were ten-footers — was capped! See? Whatever built it was still inside; we'd trailed 'em from their half-million-year-old origin to the present.

"Tweel and I noticed it about the same time. I yanked out my automatic (I had a clip of Boland explosive bullets in it) and Tweel, quick as a sleight-of-hand trick, snapped a queer little glass revolver out of his bag. It was much like our weapons, except that the grip was larger to accommodate his four-taloned hand. And we held our weapons ready while we sneaked up along the lines of empty pyramids.

"Tweel saw the movement first. The top tiers of bricks were heaving, shaking, and suddenly slid down the sides with a thin crash. And then — something — something was coming out!

"A long, silvery-grey arm appeared, dragging after it an armoured body. Armoured, I mean, with scales, silver-grey and dull-shining. The arm heaved the body out of the hole; the beast crashed to the sand.

"It was a nondescript creature — body like a big grey cask,

arm and a sort of mouth-hole at one end; stiff, pointed tail at the other — and that's all. No other limbs, no eyes, ears, nose — nothing! The thing dragged itself a few yards, inserted its pointed tail in the sand, pushed itself upright, and just sat.

"Tweel and I watched it for ten minutes before it moved. Then, with a creaking and rustling like — oh, like crumpling stiff paper — its arm moved to the mouth-hole and out came a brick! The arm placed the brick carefully on the ground, and the thing was still again.

"Another ten minutes — another brick. Just one of Nature's bricklayers. I was about to slip away and move on when Tweel pointed at the thing and said 'rock'! I went 'huh?' and he said it again. Then, to the accompaniment of some of his trilling, he said, 'No — no — ,' and gave two or three whistling breaths.

"Well, I got his meaning, for a wonder! I said, 'No breath?' and demonstrated the word. Tweel was ecstatic; he said, 'Yes, yes, yes! No, no, no breet!' Then he gave a leap and sailed out to land on his nose about one pace from the monster!

"I was startled, you can imagine! The arm was going up for a brick, and I expected to see Tweel caught and mangled, but — nothing happened! Tweel pounded on the creature, and the arm took the brick and placed it neatly beside the first. Tweel rapped on its body again, and said 'rock,' and I got up nerve enough to take a look myself.

"Tweel was right again. The creature was rock, and it didn't breathe!"

"How you know?" snapped Leroy, his black eyes blazing interest.

"Because I'm a chemist. The beast was made of silica! There

must have been pure silicon in the sand, and it lived on that. Get it? We, and Tweel, and those plants out there, and even the biopods are *carbon* life; this thing lived by a different set of chemical reactions. It was silicon life!"

"Anyhow, there the thing was, alive and yet not alive, moving every ten minutes, and then only to remove a brick. Those bricks were its waste matter. See, Frenchy? We're carbon, and our waste is carbon dioxide, and this thing is silicon, and *its* waste is silicon dioxide – silica. But silica is a solid, hence the bricks. And it builds itself in, and when it is covered, it moves over to a fresh place to start over. No wonder it creaked! A living creature half a million years old!"

"How you know how old?" Leroy was frantic.

"We trailed its pyramids from the beginning, didn't we? If this weren't the original pyramid builder, the series would have ended somewhere before we found him, wouldn't it? – ended and started over with the small ones. That's simple enough, isn't it?

"But he reproduces, or tries to. Before the third brick came out, there was a little rustle and out popped a whole stream of those little crystal balls. They're his spores, or eggs, or seeds – call 'em what you want. They went bouncing by across Xanthus just as they'd bounced by us back in the Mare Chronium.

"Lord! That queer creature! Do you picture it? Blind, deaf, nerveless, brainless – just a mechanism, and yet – immortal! Bound to go on making bricks, building pyramids, as long as silicon and oxygen exist, and even afterwards it'll just stop. It won't be dead. If the accidents of a million years bring it its food again, there it'll be, ready to run again, while brains and civilizations are part of the past. He paused again. "Well," he resumed, "Tweel and I left the pyramid creature and ploughed along through Xanthus. I was tired and a little disheartened by Putz's failure to pick me up, and Tweel's trilling got on my nerves, as did his flying nosedives. So I just strode along without a word, hour after hour after hour across that monotonous desert.

"Toward mid-afternoon we came in sight of a low dark line on the horizon. I knew what it was. It was a canal; I'd crossed it in the rocket and it meant that we were just one-third of the way across Xanthus. Pleasant thought, wasn't it? And still, I was keeping up to schedule.

"We approached the canal slowly; I remembered that this one was bordered by a wide fringe of vegetation and that Mud-heap City was on it.

"I was tired, as I said. I kept thinking of a good hot meal, and then from that I jumped to reflections of how nice and home-like even Borneo would seem after this crazy planet, and from that, to thoughts of little old New York, and then to thinking about a girl I know there – Fancy Long. Know her?"

"Vision entertainer," said Harrison. "I've tuned her in. Nice blonde – dances and sings on the *Yerba Mate* hour."

"That's her," said Jarvis ungrammatically. "I know her pretty well – just friends, get me? – though she came down to see us off in the *Ares*. Well, I was thinking about her, feeling pretty lonesome, and all the time we were approaching that line of rubbery plants.

"And then – I said, 'What 'n Hell!' and stared. And there she was – Fancy Long, standing plain as day under one of those crack-brained trees, and smiling and waving just the way I remembered her when we left!"

"Now you're nuts, too!" observed the captain.

"Boy, I almost agreed with you! I stared and pinched myself and closed my eyes and then stared again – and every time, there was Fancy Long smiling and waving! Tweel saw something, too; he was trilling and clucking away, but I scarcely heard him. I was bounding toward her over the sand, too amazed even to ask myself questions.

"I wasn't twenty feet from her when Tweel caught me with one of his flying leaps. He grabbed my arm, yelling, 'No – no – no!' in his squeaky voice. I tried to shake him off – he was as light as if he were built of bamboo – but he dug his claws in and yelled. And finally some sort of sanity returned to me and I stopped less than ten feet from her. There she stood, looking as solid as Putz's head!"

"Vot?" said the engineer.

"She smiled and waved, and waved and smiled, and I stood there dumb as Leroy, while Tweel squeaked and chattered. I *knew* it couldn't be real, yet – there she was!

"Finally I said, 'Fancy! Fancy Long!' She just kept on smiling and waving, but looking as real as if I hadn't left her thirty-seven million miles away.

"Tweel had his glass pistol out, pointing it at her. I grabbed his arm, but he tried to push me away. He pointed at her and said, 'No breet! No breet!' and I understood that he meant that the Fancy Long thing wasn't alive. Man, my head was whirling!

"Still, it gave me the jitters to see him pointing his weapon at her. I don't know why I stood there watching him take careful aim, but I did. Then he squeezed the handle of his weapon; there was a little puff of steam, and Fancy Long was gone! And in her place was one of those writhing, black, rope-armed horrors like the one I'd saved Tweel from!

"The dream-beast! I stood there dizzy, watching it die while Tweel trilled and whistled. Finally he touched my arm, pointed at the twisting thing, and said, 'You one-one-two, he one-one-two.' After he'd repeated it eight or ten times, I got it. Do any of you?"

"*Oui!*" shrilled Leroy. "*Moi – je le comprends!* He mean you think of something, the beast he know, and you see it! *Un chien* – a hungry dog, he would see the big bone with meat! Or smell it – not?"

"Right!" said Jarvis. "The dream-beast uses its victim's longings and desires to trap its prey. The bird at nesting season would see its mate; the fox prowling for its own prey would see a helpless rabbit!"

"How'd your friend know?" asked the captain abruptly.

"Tweel? I wonder! I couldn't ask him. But it's just another proof that his intelligence is equal to ours or greater."

"He's daffy, I tell you!" said Harrison. "What makes you think his intellect ranks with the human?"

"Plenty of things! First, the pyramid-beast. He hadn't seen one before; he said as much. Yet he recognized it as a dead-alive automaton of silicon."

"He could have heard of it," objected Harrison. "He lives around here, you know."

"Well how about the language? I couldn't pick up a single idea of his and he learned six or seven words of mine. And do you realize what complex ideas he put over with no more than those six or seven words? The pyramid-monster — the dream-beast! In a single phrase he told me that one was a harmless automaton and the other a deadly hypnotist. What about that?"

"Huh!" said the captain.

"*Huh* if you wish! Could you have done it knowing only six words of English? Could you go even further, as Tweel did, and tell me that another creature was of a sort of intelligence so different from ours that understanding was impossible — even more impossible than that between Tweel and me?"

"Eh? What was that?"

"Later. The point I'm making is that Tweel and his race are worthy of our friendship. Somewhere on Mars — and you'll find I'm right — is a civilization and culture equal to ours, and maybe more than equal. And communication is possible between them and us; Tweel proves that. It may take years of patient trial, for their minds are alien, but less alien than the next minds we encountered – if they *are* minds."

"The next ones? What next ones?"

"The people of the mud cities along the canals." Jarvis frowned, then resumed his narrative. "I thought the dream-beast and the silicon-monster were the strangest beings conceivable, but I was wrong. We left the dream-beast dying, dragging itself back into its hole, and we moved toward the canal. There was a carpet of that queer walking-grass scampering out of our way, and when we reached the bank, there was a yellow trickle of water flowing. The mound city I'd noticed from the rocket was a mile or so to the right and I was curious enough to want to take a look at it.

"A hundred yards from the city we crossed a sort of road – just a hard-packed mud trail, and then, all of a sudden, along came one of the mound builders!

"Man, talk about fantastic beings! It looked rather like a barrel trotting along on four legs with four other arms or tentacles. It had no head, just body and members and a row of eyes completely around it. The top end of the barrel-body was a diaphragm stretched as tight as a drum head, and that was all. It was pushing a little coppery cart and tore right past us like the proverbial bat out of Hell. It didn't even notice us, although I thought the eyes on my side shifted a little as it passed.

"A moment later another came along, pushing another empty cart. Same thing – it just scooted past us. Well, I wasn't going to be ignored by a bunch of barrels playing train, so when the third one approached, I planted myself in the way – ready to jump, of course, if the thing didn't stop.

"But it did. It stopped and set up a sort of drumming from the diaphragm on top. And I held out both hands and said, 'We are friends!' And what do you suppose the thing did?"

"Said, 'Pleased to meet you,' I'll bet!" suggested Harrison.

"I couldn't have been more surprised if it had! It drummed on its diaphragm, and then suddenly boomed out, 'We are v-r-r-riends!' and gave its pushcart a vicious poke at me! I jumped aside, and away it went while I stared dumbly after it.

"A minute later another one came hurrying along. This one didn't pause, but simply drummed out, 'We are v-r-r-riends!' and scurried by. How did it learn the phrase? Were all of the creatures in some sort of communication with each other? Were they all parts of some central organism? I don't know, though I think Tweel does.

"Anyway, the creatures went sailing past us, every one greeting us with the same statement. It got to be funny; I never thought to find so many friends on this God-forsaken ball! Finally I made a puzzled gesture to Tweel; I guess he understood, for he said, 'One-one-two – yes! – two-two-four – no!' Get it?"

"Sure," said Harrison, "It's a Martian nursery rhyme."

"Yeah! Well, I was getting used to Tweel's symbolism, and I figured it out this way. 'One-one-two – yes!' The creatures were intelligent. 'Two-two-four – no!' Their intelligence was not of our order, but something different and beyond the logic of two and two is four. Maybe I missed his meaning. Perhaps he meant that their minds were of low degree, able to figure out the simple things – 'One-one-two – yes!' – but not more difficult things – 'Two-two-four – no!' But I think from what we saw later that he meant the other.

"After a few moments, the creatures came rushing back – first one, then another. Their pushcarts were full of stones, sand, chunks of rubbery plants, and such rubbish as that. They droned out their friendly greeting, which didn't really sound so friendly, and dashed on. The third one I assumed to be my first acquaintance and I decided to have another chat with him. I stepped into his path again and waited.

"Up he came, booming out his 'We are v-r-r-riends' and stopped. I looked at him; four or five of his eyes looked at me. He tried his password again and gave a shove on his cart, but I stood firm. And then the – the dashed creature reached out one of his arms, and two finger-like nippers tweaked my nose!"

"Haw!" roared Harrison. "Maybe the things have a sense of beauty!"

"Laugh!" grumbled Jarvis. "I'd already had a nasty bump and a mean frostbite on that nose. Anyway, I yelled 'Ouch!' and jumped aside and the creature dashed away; but from then on, their greeting was 'We are v-r-r-riends! Ouch!' Queer beasts!

"Tweel and I followed the road squarely up to the nearest mound. The creatures were coming and going, paying us not the slightest attention, fetching their loads of rubbish. The road simply dived into an opening, and slanted down like an old mine, and in and out darted the barrel-people, greeting us with their eternal phrase.

"I looked in; there was a light somewhere below, and I was curious to see it. It didn't look like a flame or torch, you understand, but more like a civilized light, and I thought that I might get some clue as to the creatures' development. So in I went and Tweel tagged along, not without a few trills and twitters, however.

"The light was curious; it sputtered and flared like an old arc light, but came from a single black rod set in the wall of the corridor. It was electric, beyond doubt. The creatures were fairly civilized, apparently.

"Then I saw another light shining on something that glittered and I went on to look at that, but it was only a heap of shiny sand. I turned toward the entrance to leave, and the Devil take me if it wasn't gone!

"I suppose the corridor had curved, or I'd stepped into a side passage. Anyway, I walked back in that direction I thought we'd come, and all I saw was more dimlit corridor. The place was a labyrinth! There was nothing but twisting passages running every way, lit by occasional lights, and now and then a creature running by, sometimes with a pushcart, sometimes without.

"Well, I wasn't much worried at first. Tweel and I had only come a few steps from the entrance. But every move we made after that seemed to get us in deeper. Finally I tried following one of the creatures with an empty cart, thinking that he'd be going out for his rubbish, but he ran around aimlessly, into one passage and out another. When he started dashing around a pillar like one of these Japanese waltzing mice, I gave up, dumped my water tank on the floor, and sat down.

"Tweel was as lost as I. I pointed up and he said 'No – no – no!' in a sort of helpless trill. And we couldn't get any help from the natives. They paid no attention at all, except to assure us they were friends – ouch!

"Lord! I don't know how many hours or days we wandered around there! I slept twice from sheer exhaustion; Tweel never seemed to need sleep. We tried following only the upward corridors, but they'd run uphill a ways and then curve downwards. The things never noticed us at all, except, as I say, to greet us with 'We are v-r-r-riends! Ouch!' They seemed to have no home-life of any sort, but just scurried around with their pushcarts, bringing in rubbish. And finally I discovered what they did with it.

"We'd had a little luck with a corridor, one that slanted upwards for a great distance. I was feeling that we ought to be close to the surface when suddenly the passage debouched into a domed chamber, the only one we'd seen. And man! – I felt like dancing when I saw what looked like daylight through a crevice in the roof.

"There was a – a sort of machine in the chamber, just an enormous wheel that turned slowly, and one of the creatures was in the act of dumping his rubbish below it. The wheel ground it with a crunch – sand, stones, plants, all into powder that sifted away somewhere. While we watched, others filed in, repeating the process, and that seemed to be all.

"Then I saw something else. There was something beyond the wheel, something shining on a sort of low pedestal. I walked over; there was a little crystal about the size of an egg. The light from it stung my hands and face, almost like a static discharge, and then I noticed another funny thing. Remember that wart I had on my left thumb? Look!" Jarvis extended his hand. "It dried up and fell off – just like that! And my abused nose – say, the pain went out of it like magic! The thing had the property of hard X-rays or gamma radiations, only more so; it destroyed diseased tissue and left healthy tissue unharmed!

"I was thinking what a present *that'd* be to take back to Mother Earth when a lot of racket interrupted. We dashed back to the other side of the wheel in time to see one of the pushcarts ground up. Some suicide had been careless, it seems.

"Then suddenly the creatures were booming and drumming all around us and their noise was decidedly menacing. A crowd of them advanced toward us; we backed out of what I thought was the passage we'd entered by, and they came rumbling after us, some pushing carts and some not. Crazy brutes! There was a whole chorus of 'We are v-r-r-riends! Ouch!' I didn't like the 'ouch'; it was rather suggestive.

"Tweel had his glass gun out and I dumped my water tank for greater freedom and got mine. We backed up the corridor with the barrel-beasts following – about twenty of them. Queer thing – the ones coming in with loaded carts moved past us inches away without a sign.

"Tweel must have noticed that. Suddenly, he snatched out that glowing coal cigar-lighter of his and touched a cart-load of plant limbs. Puff! The whole load was burning – and the crazy beast pushing it went right along without a change of pace! It created some disturbance among our 'V-r-r-riends,' however – and then I noticed the smoke eddying and swirling past us, and sure enough, there was the entrance!

"I grabbed Tweel and out we dashed and after us our twenty pursuers. The daylight felt like Heaven, though I saw at first glance that the sun was all but set, and that was bad, since I couldn't live outside my thermo-skin bag in a Martian night – at least, without a fire.

"And things got worse in a hurry. They cornered us in an

angle between two mounds, and there we stood. I hadn't fired nor had Tweel; there wasn't any use in irritating the brutes. They stopped a little distance away and began their booming about friendship and ouches.

"Then things got still worse! A barrel-brute came out with a pushcart and they all grabbed into it and came out with handfuls of foot-long copper darts – sharp-looking ones – and all of a sudden one sailed past my ear – zing! And it was shoot or die then.

"We were doing pretty well for a while. We picked off the ones next to the pushcart and managed to keep the darts at a minimum, but suddenly there was a thunderous booming of 'v-r-r-riends' and 'ouches,' and a whole army of 'em came out of their hole.

"Man! We were through and I knew it! Then I realized that Tweel wasn't. He could have leaped the mound behind us as easily as not. He was staying for me!

"Say, I could have cried if there'd been time! I'd liked Tweel from the first, but whether I'd have had gratitude to do what he was doing – suppose I *had* saved him from the first dream-beast – he'd done as much for me, hadn't he? I grabbed his arm, and said 'Tweel,' and pointed up, and he understood. He said, 'No – no – no, Tick!' and popped away with his glass pistol.

"What could I do? I'd be a goner anyway when the sun set, but I couldn't explain that to him. I said, 'Thanks, Tweel. You're a man!' and felt that I wasn't paying him any compliment at all. A man! There are mighty few men who'd do that.

"So I went 'bang' with my gun and Tweel went 'puff' with his, and the barrels were throwing darts and getting ready to rush us,

and booming about being friends. I had given up hope. Then suddenly an angel dropped right down from Heaven in the shape of Putz, with his under-jets blasting the barrels into very small pieces!

"Wow! I let out a yell and dashed for the rocket; Putz opened the door and in I went, laughing and crying and shouting! It was a moment or so before I remembered Tweel; I looked around in time to see him rising in one of his nosedives over the mound and away.

"I had a devil of a job arguing Putz into following! By the time we got the rocket aloft, darkness was down; you know how it comes here – like turning off a light. We sailed out over the desert and put down once or twice. I yelled 'Tweel!' and yelled it a hundred times, I guess. We couldn't find him; he could travel like the wind and all I got – or else I imagined it – was a faint trilling and twittering drifting out of the south. He'd gone, and damn it! I wish – I wish he hadn't!"

The four men of the *Ares* were silent – even the sardonic Harrison. At last little Leroy broke the stillness.

"I should like to see," he murmured.

"Yeah," said Harrison. "And the wart cure. Too bad you missed that; it might be the cancer cure they've been hunting for a century and a half."

"Oh, that!" muttered Jarvis gloomily. "That's what started the fight!" He drew a glistening object from his pocket.

"Here it is."

LEAVING FOR THE MOON

1865 FROM **FROM THE EARTH TO THE MOON**

JULES VERNE

Three scientists — two Americans and a Frenchman — have undertaken to fly to the Moon in their creation, a bullet-shaped projectile fired from a hole in the Earth by igniting a giant explosion underneath it. This extract begins with the nervous time as they prepare to take their flight.

FROM 10 P.M. TO 10 46' 40"

THE MOMENT THAT THE GREAT CLOCK belonging to the works at Stony Hill had struck ten, Barbican, Ardan and M'Nicholl began to take their last farewells of the numerous friends surrounding them. The two dogs intended to accompany them had been already deposited in the Projectile. The three travellers approached the mouth of the enormous cannon, seated

themselves in the flying car, and once more took leave for the last time of the vast throng standing in silence around them. The windlass creaked, the car started, and the three daring men disappeared in the yawning gulf.

The trap-hole giving them ready access to the interior of the Projectile, the car soon came back empty; the great windlass was presently rolled away; the tackle and scaffolding were removed, and in a short space of time the great mouth of the Columbiad was completely rid of all obstructions.

M'Nicholl took upon himself to fasten the door of the trap on the inside by means of a powerful combination of screws and bolts of his own invention. He also covered up very carefully the glass lights with strong iron plates of extreme solidity and tightly fitting joints.

Ardan's first care was to turn on the gas, which he found burning rather low; but he lit no more than one burner, being desirous to economize as much as possible their store of light and heat, which, as he well knew, could not at the very utmost last them longer than a few weeks.

Under the cheerful blaze, the interior of the Projectile looked like a comfortable little chamber, with its circular sofa, nicely padded walls, and dome shaped ceiling.

All the articles that it contained, arms, instruments, utensils, etc., were solidly fastened to the projections of the wadding, so as to sustain the least injury possible from the first terrible shock. In fact, all precautions possible, humanly speaking, had been taken to counteract this, the first, and possibly one of the very greatest dangers to which the courageous adventurers would be exposed.

Ardan expressed himself to be quite pleased with the appearance of things in general.

"It's a prison, to be sure," said he "but not one of your ordinary prisons that always keep in the one spot. For my part, as long as I can have the privilege of looking out of the window, I am willing to lease it for a hundred years. Ah! Barbican, that brings out one of your stony smiles. You think our lease may last longer than that! Our tenement may become our coffin, eh? Be it so."

Barbican, having made sure by personal inspection that everything was in perfect order, consulted his chronometer, which he had carefully set a short time before with Chief Engineer Murphy's, who had been charged to fire off the Projectile.

"Friends," he said, "it is now twenty minutes past ten. At 10 46' 40" precisely, Murphy will send the electric current into the gun-cotton. We have, therefore, twenty-six minutes more to remain on Earth."

"Twenty-six minutes and twenty seconds," observed Captain M'Nicholl, who always aimed at mathematical precision.

"Twenty-six minutes!" cried Ardan, gaily. "An age, a cycle, according to the use you make of them. In twenty-six minutes how much can be done! The weightiest questions of warfare, politics, morality, can be discussed, even decided, in twenty-six minutes. Twenty-six minutes well spent are infinitely more valuable than twenty-six lifetimes wasted.'

"Ardan," interrupted Barbican, "after a very little while we shall have plenty of time for philosophical disputations. Just now let us think of something far more pressing."

"More pressing! what do you mean? are we not fully prepared?"

"Yes, fully prepared, as far at least as we have been able to foresee. But we may still, I think, possibly increase the number of precautions to be taken against the terrible shock that we are so soon to experience."

"What? Have you any doubts whatever of the effectiveness of your brilliant and extremely original idea? Don't you think that the layers of water, regularly disposed in easily-ruptured partitions beneath this floor, will afford us sufficient protection by their elasticity?"

"I hope so, indeed, my dear friend, but I am by no means confident."

"He hopes! He is by no means confident! Listen to that, Mac! Pretty time to tell us so! Let me out of here!"

"Too late!" observed the Captain quietly. "The trap-hole alone would take ten or fifteen minutes to open."

"Oh then I suppose I must make the best of it," said Ardan, laughing. "All aboard, gentlemen! The train starts in twenty minutes!"

"In nineteen minutes and eighteen seconds," said the Captain, who never took his eye off the chronometer.

The three travellers looked at each other for a little while, during which even Ardan appeared to become serious. After another careful glance at the several objects lying around them, Barbican said, quietly:

"Everything is in its place, except ourselves. What we have now to do is to decide on the position we must take in order to neutralize the shock as much as possible. We must be particularly careful to guard against a rush of blood to the head."

"Correct!" said the Captain.

"Suppose we stood on our heads, like the circus tumblers!" cried Ardan, ready to suit the action to the word.

"Better than that," said Barbican; "we can lie on our side. Keep clearly in mind, dear friends, that at the instant of departure it makes very little difference to us whether we are inside the bullet or in front of it. There is, no doubt, *some* difference," he added, "but it is exceedingly little."

"Thank heaven for the *some*!" interrupted Ardan, fervently.

"Don't you approve of my suggestion, Captain?" asked Barbican.

"Certainly," was the hasty reply. "That is to say, absolutely. Seventeen minutes twenty-seven seconds!"

Three mattresses, thick and well wadded, spread on the disc forming the false bottom of the Projectile, were arranged in lines whose parallelism was simply perfect. But Ardan would never think of occupying his until the very last moment. Walking up and down, with the restless nervousness of a wild beast in a cage, he kept up a continuous fire of talk.

"Ten, forty-two, ten!" repeated M'Nicholl, as mechanically as if it was the chronometer itself that spoke.

"Four minutes and a half more," said Barbican.

"Oh! four and a half little minutes!" went on Ardan. "Only think of it! We are shut up in a bullet that lies in the chamber of a cannon nine hundred feet long. Underneath this bullet is piled a charge of 400 thousand pounds of gun-cotton, equivalent to 1600 thousand pounds of ordinary gunpowder! And at this very instant our friend Murphy, chronometer in hand, eye on dial, finger on discharger, is counting the last seconds and getting ready to launch us into the limitless regions of planetary — ”

“Ardan, dear friend,” interrupted Barbican, in a grave tone, “a serious moment is now at hand. Let us meet it with some interior recollection. Give me your hands, my dear friends.”

“Certainly,” said Ardan, with tears in his voice, and already at the other extreme of his apparent levity.

The three brave men united in one last, silent, but warm and impulsively affectionate pressure.

“And now, great God, our Creator, protect us! In Thee we trust!” prayed Barbican, the others joining him with folded hands and bowed heads.

“Ten, forty-six!” whispered the Captain, as he and Ardan quietly took their places on the mattresses.

Only forty seconds more!

Barbican rapidly extinguishes the gas and lies down beside his companions.

The deathlike silence now reigning in the Projectile is interrupted only by the sharp ticking of the chronometer as it beats the seconds.

Suddenly, a dreadful shock is felt, and the Projectile, shot up by the instantaneous development of 200,000 millions of cubic feet of gas, is flying into space with inconceivable rapidity!

What had taken place within the Projectile? What effect had been produced by the frightful concussion? Had Barbican’s ingenuity been attended with a fortunate result? Had the shock been sufficiently deadened by the springs, the buffers, the water layers, and the partitions so readily ruptured? Had their combined effect succeeded in counteracting the tremendous violence of a velocity of 12,000 yards a second, actually sufficient to carry them from London to New York in six minutes? These, and a hundred other questions of a similar nature were asked that night by the millions who had been watching the explosion from the base of Stony Hill. Themselves they forgot altogether for the moment; they forgot everything in their absorbing anxiety regarding the fate of the daring travellers. Had one among them been favoured with a glimpse at the interior of the projectile, what would he have seen?

Nothing at all at first, on account of the darkness; except that the walls had solidly resisted the frightful shock. Not a crack, nor a bend, nor a dent could be perceived; not even the slightest injury had the admirably constructed piece of mechanical workmanship endured. It had not yielded an inch to the enormous pressure, and, far from melting and falling back to Earth, as had been so seriously apprehended, in showers of blazing aluminium, it was still as strong in every respect as it had been on the very day that it left the Cold Spring Iron Works, glittering like a silver dollar.

Of real damage there was actually none, and even the disorder into which things had been thrown in the interior by the violent shock was comparatively slight. A few small objects lying around loose had been furiously hurled against the ceiling, but the others appeared not to have suffered the slightest injury. The partitions beneath the disc having been ruptured, and the water having escaped, the false floor had been dashed with tremendous violence against the bottom of the Projectile, and on this disc at this moment three human bodies could be seen lying perfectly still and motionless.

Were they three corpses? Had the Projectile suddenly become a great metallic coffin bearing its ghastly contents through the air with the rapidity of a lightning flash?

In a very few minutes after the shock, one of the bodies

stirred a little, the arms moved, the eyes opened, the head rose and tried to look around. Finally, with some difficulty, the body managed to get on its knees. It was the Frenchman! He held his head tightly squeezed between his hands for some time as if to keep it from splitting. Then he felt himself rapidly all over, cleared his throat with a vigorous "hem!" listened to the sound critically for an instant, and then said to himself in a relieved tone, but in his native tongue:

"One man all right! Call the roll for the others!"

He tried to rise, but the effort was too great for his strength. He fell back again, his brain swimming, his eyes bursting, his head splitting. His state very much resembled that of a young man waking up in the morning after his first tremendous 'spree'.

Lying quietly on his back for a while, he could soon feel that the circulation of his blood, so suddenly and violently arrested by the terrific shock, was gradually recovering its regular flow; his heart grew more normal in its action; his head became clearer, and the pain less distracting.

"Time to call that roll," he at last exclaimed in a voice with some pretensions to firmness; "Barbican! MacNicholl!"

He listens anxiously for a reply. None comes. "Call that roll again!" he mutters in a voice far less assured than before; "Barbican! MacNicholl!"

The same fearful unearthly stillness.

He contrived without much difficulty to get on his feet. Balancing himself then for a moment, he began groping about for the gas. But he stopped suddenly.

"Hold on a minute!" he cried; "before lighting this match, let us see if the gas has been escaping. Setting fire to a mixture of air and hydrogen would make a pretty how-do-you-do! Such an explosion would infallibly burst the Projectile, which so far seems all right, though I'm blest if I can tell whether we're moving or not."

He began sniffing and smelling to discover if possible the odour of escaped gas. He could not detect the slightest sign of anything of the kind. At the touch of the match, the gas burst into light and burned with a steady flame. Ardan immediately bent anxiously over the prostrate bodies of his friends. They lay on each other like inert masses, M'Nicholl stretched across Barbican.

Ardan first lifted up the Captain, laid him on the sofa, opened his clenched hands, rubbed them, and slapped the palms vigorously. Then he went all over the body carefully, kneading it, rubbing it, and gently patting it. In such intelligent efforts to restore suspended circulation, he seemed perfectly at home, and after a few minutes his patience was rewarded by seeing the Captain's pallid face gradually recover its natural colour, and by feeling his heart gradually beat with a firm pulsation.

At last M'Nicholl opened his eyes, stared at Ardan for an instant, pressed his hand, looked around searchingly and anxiously, and at last whispered in a faint voice:

"How's Barbican?"

"Barbican is all right, Captain," answered Ardan quietly, but still speaking French. "I'll attend to him in a jiffy. He had to wait for his turn. I began with you because you were the top man. "

In less than thirty seconds more, the Captain not only was able to sit up himself, but he even insisted on helping Ardan to lift Barbican, and deposit him gently on the sofa.

The poor President had evidently suffered more from the concussion than either of his companions. As they took off his coat they were at first terribly shocked at the sight of a great patch of blood staining his shirt bosom, but they were inexpressibly relieved at finding that it proceeded from a slight contusion of the shoulder, little more than skin deep.

Every approved operation that Ardan had performed for the Captain, both now repeated for Barbican, but for a long time with nothing like a favourable result.

M'Nicholl interrupted himself every moment to lay his ear on the breast of the unconscious man. At first he had shaken his head quite despondingly, but by degrees he found himself more and more encouraged to persist.

"He breathes!" he whispered at last.

At last, Barbican suddenly opened his eyes, started into an upright position on the sofa, took his friends by the hands, and, in a voice showing complete consciousness, demanded eagerly:

"Ardan, M'Nicholl, are we moving?"

His friends looked at each other, a little amused, but more perplexed. In their anxiety regarding their own and their friend's recovery, they had never thought of asking such a question. His words recalled them at once to a full sense of their situation.

"We may be lying fifty feet deep in a Florida marsh, for all I know," observed M'Nicholl.

"Or, likely as not, in the bottom of the Gulf of Mexico," suggested Ardan.

"Suppose we find out," observed Barbican, jumping up to try, his voice as clear and his step as firm as ever.

But trying is one thing, and finding out another. Having no

means of comparing themselves with external objects, they could not possibly tell whether they were moving, or at an absolute standstill. Though our Earth is whirling us continually around the Sun at the tremendous speed of 500 miles a minute, its inhabitants are totally unconscious of the slightest motion. It was the same with our travellers. Through their own personal consciousness they could tell absolutely nothing. Were they shooting through space like a meteor? They could not tell. Had they fallen back and buried themselves deep in the sandy soil of Florida, or, still more likely, hundreds of fathoms deep beneath the waters of the Gulf of Mexico? They could not form the slightest idea.

Listening evidently could do no good. The profound silence proved nothing. The padded walls of the Projectile were too thick to admit any sound whether of wind, water, or human beings. Barbican, however, was soon struck forcibly by one circumstance. He felt himself to be very uncomfortably warm, and his friend's faces looked very hot and flushed. Hastily removing the cover that protected the thermometer, he closely inspected it, and in an instant uttered a joyous exclamation.

"Hurrah!" he cried. "We're moving! There's no mistake about it. The thermometer marks 113 degrees Fahrenheit. Such a stifling heat could not come from the gas. It comes from the exterior walls of our Projectile, which atmospheric friction must have made almost red hot. But this heat must soon diminish, because we are already far beyond the regions of the atmosphere, so that instead of smothering we shall be shortly in danger of freezing."

"What?" asked Ardan, much bewildered. "We are already far

beyond the limits of the terrestrial atmosphere! Why do you think so?"

"For a very simple reason," said Barbican, pointing to the chronometer, "it is now more than seven minutes after 11. We must, therefore, have been in motion more than twenty minutes. Consequently, unless our initial velocity has been very much diminished by the friction, we must have long before this completely cleared the fifty miles of atmosphere enveloping the Earth."

"Correct," said the Captain, cool as a cucumber, because once more in complete possession of all his senses, "but how much do you think the initial velocity to have been diminished by the friction?"

"By a third, according to my calculations," replied Barbican, "which I think are right. Supposing our initial velocity, therefore, to have been 12,000 yards per second, by the time we quitted the atmosphere it must have been reduced to 8,000 yards per second. At that rate, we must have gone by this time — "

"Friend Michael, you say we're moving?"

"Yes."

"In consequence of the explosion?"

"Certainly!"

"Which must have been attended with a tremendous report?"

"Of course!"

"Did you hear that report, friend Michael?"

"N — o," replied Ardan, a little disconcerted at the question. "Well, no; I can't say that I did hear any report."

"It's a fact!" exclaimed Barbican, puzzled, but not bewildered. "Why did we not hear that report?"

"Too hard for me," said Ardan. "Give it up!"

The three friends gazed at each other for a while with countenances expressive of much perplexity. Barbican appeared to be the least self-possessed of the party. It was a complete turning of the tables from the state of things a few moments ago. The problem was certainly simple enough, but for that very reason the more inexplicable. If they were moving the explosion must have taken place; but if the explosion had taken place, why had they not heard the report?

Barbican's decision soon put an end to speculation.

"Conjecture being useless," said he, "let us have recourse to facts. First, let us see where we are. Drop the deadlights!"

This operation, simple enough in itself and being immediately undertaken by the whole three, was easily accomplished. The screws fastening the bolts by which the external plates of the deadlights were solidly pinned, readily yielded to the pressure of a powerful wrench. The bolts were then driven outwards, and the holes which had contained them were immediately filled with solid plugs of India rubber. The bolts once driven out, the external plates dropped by their own weight, turning on a hinge, like portholes, and the strong plate-glass forming the light immediately showed itself. A second light exactly similar, could be cleared away on the opposite side of the Projectile; a third, on the summit of the dome, and a fourth, in the centre of the bottom. The travellers could thus take observations in four different directions, having an opportunity of gazing at the firmament through the side lights, and at the Earth and the Moon through the lower and the upper lights of the Projectile.

Ardan and the Captain had commenced examining the floor,

previous to operating on the bottom light. But Barbican was the first to get through his work at one of the side lights, and M'Nicholl and Ardan soon heard him shouting:

"No, my friends!" he exclaimed, in tones of decided emotion; "we have *not* fallen back to Earth; nor are we lying in the bottom of the Gulf of Mexico. No! We are driving through space! Look at the stars glittering all around! Brighter, but smaller than we have ever seen them before! We have left the Earth and the Earth's atmosphere far behind us!"

93

"Hurrah! Hurrah!" cried M'Nicholl and Ardan, feeling as if electric shocks were coursing through them, though they could see nothing, looking down from the side light, but the blackest and profoundest obscurity.

Barbican soon convinced them that this pitchy blackness proved that they were not, and could not be, reposing on the surface of the Earth, where at that moment, everything was illuminated by the bright moonlight; also that they had passed the different layers of the atmosphere, where the diffused and refracted rays would be also sure to reveal themselves through the lights of the Projectile. They were, therefore, certainly moving. No doubt was longer possible.

"It's a fact!" observed the Captain, now quite convinced.

Ardan, taking off his hat, made a profound bow to both of his companions, without saying a word. After indulging in silent wonder for a minute or two, he joined his companions who were now busy looking out at the starry sky.

"Where is the Moon?" he asked. "How is it that we cannot see her?"

"The fact of our not seeing her," answered Barbican, "gives me very great satisfaction in one respect; it shows that our Projectile was shot so rapidly out of the Columbiad that it had not time to be impressed with the slightest revolving motion – for us a most fortunate matter. As for the rest – see, there is *Cassiopeia*, a little to the left is *Andromeda*, further down is the great square of *Pegasus*, and to the southwest *Fomalhaut* can be easily seen swallowing the *Cascade*. All this shows we are looking west and consequently cannot see the Moon, which is approaching the zenith from the east. Open the other light – But hold on! Look here! What can this be?"

The three travellers, looking westwardly in the direction of *Alpherat*, saw a brilliant object rapidly approaching them. At a distance, it looked like a dusky moon, but the side turned towards the Earth blazed with a bright light, which every moment became more intense. It came towards them with prodigious velocity and, what was worse, its path lay so directly in the course of the Projectile that a collision seemed inevitable. As it moved onward from west to east, they could easily see that

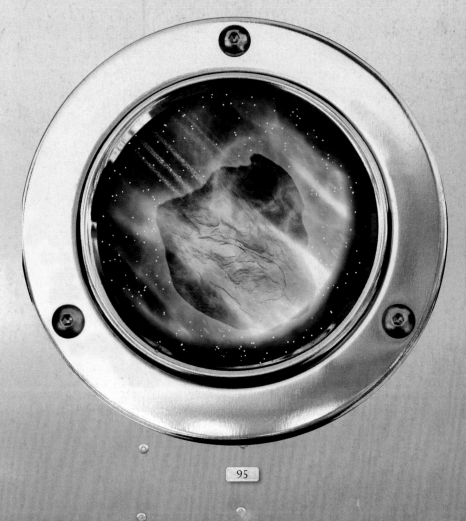

it rotated on its axis, like all heavenly bodies. In fact, it somewhat resembled a moon on a small scale, describing its regular orbit around the Earth.

"*Mille tonerres!*" cried Ardan, greatly excited; "what is that? Can it be another projectile?" M'Nicholl, wiping his spectacles, looked again, but made no reply. Barbican looked puzzled and uneasy. A collision was quite possible, and the results, even if not frightful in the highest degree, must be extremely deplorable. The Projectile, if not absolutely dashed to pieces, would be diverted from its own course and dragged along in a new one in obedience to the irresistible attraction of this furious asteroid.

Barbican fully realized that either alternative involved the complete failure of their enterprise. He kept perfectly still, but, never losing his presence of mind, he curiously looked on the approaching object with a gladiatorial eye, as if seeking to detect some unguarded point in his terrible adversary.

Nearer and nearer it came, but without noise, without sparks, without a trail, though its lower part was brighter than ever. Its path lying little above them, the nearer it came the more the collision seemed inevitable. Imagine yourself caught on a narrow railroad bridge at midnight with an express train approaching at full speed, its reflector already dazzling you with its light, the roar of the cars rattling in your ears, and you may conceive the feelings of the travellers. At last it was so near that the travellers started back in affright, with eyes shut, hair on end, and fully believing their last hour had come.

In an instant all was over. The velocity of the Projectile was fortunately great enough to carry it barely above the dangerous point; and in a flash the terrible bolide disappeared rapidly several hundred yards beneath the affrighted travellers.

"Good bye! And may you never come back!" cried Ardan, hardly able to breathe. "It's perfectly outrageous! Not room enough in infinite space to let an unpretending bullet like ours move about a little without incurring the risk of being run over by such a monster as that! What is it anyhow? Do you know, Barbican?"

"I do," was the reply.

"Of course, you do! What is it that he don't know? Eh, Captain?"

"It is a simple bolide, but one of such enormous dimensions that the Earth's attraction has made it a satellite."

"What!" cried Ardan, "another satellite besides the Moon? I hope there are no more of them!"

"They are pretty numerous," replied Barbican; "but they are so small and they move with such enormous velocity that they are very seldom seen. Petit, the Director of the Observatory of Toulouse, who these last years has devoted much time and care to the observation of bolides, has calculated that the very one we have just encountered moves with such astonishing swiftness that it accomplishes its revolution around the Earth in about three hours and 20 minutes!"

"Whew!" whistled Ardan, "where should we be now if it had struck us!"

"You don't mean to say, Barbican," observed M'Nicholl, "that Petit has seen this very one?"

"So it appears," replied Barbican.

"And do all astronomers admit its existence?" asked the Captain.

"Well, some of them have their doubts," replied Barbican —

"If the unbelievers had been here a minute or two ago," interrupted Ardan, "they would never express a doubt again."

"If Petit's calculation is right," continued Barbican, "I can even form a very good idea as to our distance from the Earth."

"It seems to me Barbican can do what he pleases here or elsewhere," observed Ardan to the Captain.

"Let us see, Barbican," asked M'Nicholl; "where has Petit's calculation placed us?"

"The bolide's distance being known," replied Barbican, "at the moment we met it we were a little more than five thousand miles from the Earth's surface."

"Five thousand miles already!" cried Ardan, "why we have only just started!"

"Let us see about that," quietly observed the Captain, looking at his chronometer, and calculating with his pencil. "It is now ten minutes past 11; we have therefore been 23 minutes on the road. Supposing our initial velocity of 10,000 yards or nearly seven miles a second, to have been kept up, we should by this time be about 9,000 miles from the Earth; but by allowing for friction and gravity, we can hardly be more than 5,500 miles. Yes, friend Barbican, Petit does not seem to be very wrong in his calculations."

But Barbican hardly heard the observation. He had not yet answered the puzzling question that had already presented itself to them for solution; and until he had done so he could not attend to anything else.

"That's all very well and good, Captain," he replied in an absorbed manner, "but we have not yet been able to account for a very strange phenomenon. Why didn't we hear the report?"

No one replying, the conversation came to a standstill, and Barbican, still absorbed in his reflections, began clearing the second light of its external shutter. In a few minutes the plate dropped, and the Moon beams, flowing in, filled the interior of the Projectile with her brilliant light. The Captain immediately put out the gas, from motives of economy as well as because its glare somewhat interfered with the observation of the interplanetary regions.

The Lunar disc struck the travellers as glittering with a splendour and purity of light that they had never witnessed before. The beams, no longer strained through the misty atmosphere of the Earth, streamed copiously in through the glass and coated the interior walls of the Projectile with a brilliant silvery plating. The intense blackness of the sky enhanced the dazzling radiance of the Moon. Even the stars blazed with a new and unequalled splendour, and, in the absence of a refracting atmosphere, they flamed as bright in the close proximity of the Moon as in any other part of the sky.

"How they're gazing at her this very moment from Stony Hill!" said the Captain at last to break the silence.

"By Jove!" cried Ardan. "It's true! Captain you're right. We were near forgetting our dear old Mother, the Earth. What ungrateful children! Let me feast my eyes once more on the blessed old creature!"

Barbican, to satisfy his companion's desire, immediately commenced to clear away the disc which covered the floor of the Projectile and prevented them from getting at the lower light. A round hole about a foot and a half in diameter appeared, bored through the floor of the Projectile. It was closed by a circular pane of plate-glass, which was about six inches thick, fastened by a ring of copper. Below, on the outside, the glass was protected by an aluminium plate, kept in its place by strong bolts and nuts. The latter being unscrewed, the bolts slipped out by their own weight, the shutter fell, and a new communication was established between the interior and the exterior.

Ardan knelt down, applied his eye to the light, and tried to look out. At first everything was quite dark and gloomy.

"I see no Earth!" he exclaimed at last.

"Don't you see a fine ribbon of light?" asked Barbican, "right beneath us? A thin, pale, silvery crescent?"

"Of course I do. Can that be the Earth?"

"*Terra Mater* herself, friend Ardan. That fine fillet of light, now hardly visible on her eastern border, will disappear altogether as soon as the Moon is full. Then, lying as she will be between the Sun and the Moon, her illuminated face will be turned away from us altogether, and for several days she will be involved in impenetrable darkness."

"And that's the Earth!" repeated Ardan, hardly able to believe his eyes, as he continued to gaze on the slight thread of silvery white light, somewhat resembling the appearance of the 'Young May Moon' a few hours after sunset.

Whilst the travellers were profoundly absorbed in the contemplation of this wondrous sight, a sparkling shower of shooting stars suddenly flashed over the Earth's dark surface, making it for a moment as bright as the external ring. Hundreds of bolides, catching fire from contact with the atmosphere, streaked the darkness with their luminous trails, overspreading it occasionally with sheets of electric flame. The Earth was just then in her perihelion, and we all know that the months of November and December are so highly favourable to the appearance of these meteoric showers that at the famous display of November, 1866, astronomers counted as many as 8,000 between midnight and four o'clock.

For hours they continued to gaze with indescribable interest on the faintly luminous mass so easily distinguishable among the other heavenly bodies. Jupiter blazed on their right, Mars flashed his ruddy light on their left, Saturn with his rings looked like a round white spot on a black wall; even Venus they could see almost directly under them, easily recognizing her by her soft, sweetly scintillant light. But no planet or constellation possessed any attraction for the travellers, as long as their eyes could trace that shadowy, crescent-edged, diamond-girdled, meteor-furrowed spheroid, the theatre of their existence, the home of so many undying desires, the mysterious cradle of their race!

Meantime the Projectile cleaved its way upwards, rapidly, unswervingly, though with a gradually retarding velocity. As the Earth sensibly grew darker, and the travellers' eyes grew dimmer, an irresistible somnolency slowly stole over their weary frames. The extraordinary excitement they had gone through during the last four or five hours, was naturally followed by a profound reaction.

"Captain, you're nodding," said Ardan at last, after a longer silence than usual; "the fact is, Barbican is the only wake man of the party, because he is puzzling over his problem. As we are asleep let us be asleep!"

So saying he threw himself on the mattress, and his companions immediately followed the example.

They had been lying hardly a quarter of an hour, when Barbican started up with a cry so loud and sudden as instantly to awaken his companions.

The bright moonlight showed them the President sitting up in his bed, his eye blazing, his arms waving, as he shouted in a tone reminding them of the day they had found him in St. Helena wood.

"*Eureka*! I've got it! I know it!"

"What have you got?" cried Ardan, bouncing up and seizing him by the right hand.

"What do you know?" cried the Captain, stretching over and seizing him by the left.

"The reason why we did not hear the report!"

"Well, why did not we hear it!" asked both rapidly in the same breath.

"Because we were shot up 30 times faster than sound can travel!"

THE CYCAP NOTEBOOKS

2011

STEPHEN JAMES

CHAPTER 1

YOU – WHOEVER YOU MIGHT BE — will so not believe this. I hardly believe it myself, but I keep mentally pinching myself and I am awake, am functioning normally, am still Danny Reed, still live at Mulberry Farm, Wistone, Suffolk, England. I still brush my teeth, eat Shredded Wheat at breakfast, go to the loo and tease my eleven-year-old sister Dot. I'm at Wistone County High — the world's worst school, don't understand a word Miss Pitt says, and come home and get told to cheer up or sit up or buck up or wake up. And yet since yesterday everything is different — for always.

On Sunday there was a violent summer storm that came from nowhere with a wind that nearly ripped off the roof and a thunderclap that made Mum's cups and saucers on the kitchen shelves rattle. Yesterday was a day off school. Something about teacher training – and how Miss Pitt needs it! The weather yesterday was breezy and bright – 20°C, 30 percent chance of precipitation.

I put my binoculars, notebook, some fodder and a cold drink in my rucksack and set off with Rabid for a walk up round the set-aside and into the copse. I was hoping to see the jays and their chicks and check out the badgers. Up on the top field I could see the rooftop of the farm, and hear Dad's Chase tractor farting away in the lower barley field. No sign of the jays. I swept the valley with the binoculars for signs of our adopted heron, but if it was not airborne it was impossible to spot. It can stay as still as a stick. Saw a fox dart into a hedge and jotted in my notebook. 'Fox 8:20 a.m., farm-side of copse.' All right, so I am a bit of a nature freak. I keep notes of where and when I see animals and plants and make drawings and photographs of them. Doesn't make me a complete geek does it? I play Playstation games too, and probably have some habits as revolting as yours.

I trudged into the soggy copse towards the badger set. Rabid is 50 percent dog, 50 percent JCB. He just loves to dig. He has a nose like an aardvark's. My parents call him Fidget, but understandably he doesn't respond to this insulting name. When I take him for walks and he's off the lead I shout 'Rabid dog! Rabid dog!' Gets the attention of other dog walkers.

I knew something was different as I entered the copse but I couldn't quite pinpoint what. It was the daylight – there was more of it. The big old oak that had apparently stood since the time of Shakespeare was on its side. It had a white scar down its middle where I guessed the lightning had struck. Its huge roots had been wrenched from the ground as the tree tipped over. That, sadly, was where the badger set had been.

Rabid had obviously found something because he was making those little whistling and whining sounds, a sure sign that some serious tunnelling was about to start. I supposed he'd got a scent of a dead badger killed when the oak fell.

Dirt was flying everywhere by the time I got near him and his nose was whistling like a kettle. His claws were scraping on something white – I caught glimpses of something like a large white bowl, which his claws were sliding off. He put his dirty muzzle into the hole he'd made to get his jaws on the lip of the bowl and then jumped back as though he'd just been stung by a scorpion. Rabid turned his head at an angle and thrust his ears forward, trying to work out what had just happened. A low menacing growl bubbled in his throat.

I got my fingers under the edge of the bowl and heaved it out of its shallow grave. If it were a bowl it was unlike any that I'd ever set eyes on, more like an ancient Egyptian headpiece with an elongated neck cover. It was the purest white. The muddy soil just fell off with a brush of my sleeve. Rabid was jumping vertically and barking like a mad thing — very much the brave dog now.

I sat on a tree stump and inspected this weird find. Who buried it, why and when? How did it get under a tree hundreds of years old? Didn't look especially valuable. The outside was totally smooth and made of plastic or something similar. A cross between plastic and porcelain, it had virtually no weight. It was strangely warmish. The inside was white too, with two bumps about where your temples would go if you were to put it on your head, which would need to be quite big too — about the size of a pumpkin. But you weren't there, were you. So I brushed out the soil and put it on my head instead.

Bad move, Danny, bad move. There was a low humming sound, so low I felt it more than heard it. I could feel the thing move! I swear it moved somehow. I quickly snatched it off and threw it away from me and stared in disbelief at Rabid. He tilted his head and panted back as though to say 'What did I tell you, dumbo?'

Do you know the feeling when you are about to do something really stupid and a voice whispers: 'You are about to do something really stupid aren't you? Go on then — do it'? So I picked up the pudding bowl, headpiece, helmet thing again and stared at it, felt inside with my hand and felt nothing, put its outside to my ear and heard nothing, listened to my inner warning voice, ignored it and put the thing back on my head.

Again that low, low hum. And it sort of shuddered. It quickly (too quickly) got smaller. I could feel it moulding itself to the shape of my head! I went to take it off, but it was now formed around my jaw and under the back of my skull. There was not even room for my fingernails to go under the lip. The helmet fitted as tightly as a surgical glove.

I could feel the panic break over me in a cold wave. This horrendous thing was permanent – like a new head. Stupid thoughts ran through it – how would it go down at Wistone County High? Would my parents even recognize me? The cold wave quickly became a heat wave. I felt tears well up and a single sob escaped. I held my new smooth head in my hands and wept like a small kid. In my profound dejection I had failed to notice the fact that even though my ears were completely covered I could still hear perfectly Rabid's pathetic tiny whines. And somewhere between my ears, in the middle of my brain it seemed, I could hear the deep, dark hum that I heard when I first picked up the headpiece before stupidly, stupidly, stupidly wearing it. I concentrated on this hum and to my amazement it formed an image in my brain like a ball of creamy light bobbing on an inky blue sea. And now I had two images in my head – in one was the copse, the view through the trees down to my house and Rabid. In the other was the bobbing ball in its lake of blueness.

As I 'focused' on the bobbing ball, the hum changed note. And by moving my 'eyes' I could move the ball around on the screen inside my head. I could move it up out of its blue sea and into the 'sky' or below and under the 'waves', or left or right. After a little practice I was able to make it bounce off towards a distant horizon and almost disappear or come back rushing towards me until its glowing creaminess filled my entire head.

The change in pitch of the humming sound was what I now gave my attention to. When I relaxed it went to its low

background hum like a large, distant generator. When I mentally grabbed hold of the hum and focused on the light ball, I could move them both – light ball and hum together. It was like tuning a radio into a station and its range of sound was enormous. I steered the light ball and its sounds in every direction and near and far. For one spooky moment it crossed a point where a noise almost like a voice came and went. I tried to find this point again – it was somewhere just above the 'waves' and if the ball was the size of a football then about 30 metres away. I put the ball roughly there and moved it around and caught clips of voices, words like 'There. No. Where… have it, no, near, there,' and realized suddenly that these words were my thoughts, but not in my voice! I held the ball in the same place and deliberately thought a certain word to try out this strange mental microphone. 'Hello,' I thought, and 'Hello,' I heard in a calm, featureless voice. This was instantly followed by 'Hello,' in a different voice, a soothing voice, a woman's voice, a bit like my mum's – in fact EXACTLY like my mum's.

By now I was certain that I'd gone insane. I was sitting on a log wearing a funny hat talking in my head to my mum.

'Help me,' I thought to myself. And the Mum voice came back with this extraordinary message.

'Danny, relax. Do not be afraid. You are not insane and you are not in danger.' This was my mum soothing me when I'd hurt myself.

'I will now slow down your heart rate to make you feel calm. There, that's better.' And it was. 'I have used your memory and your language and have borrowed a voice you feel comfortable with. You may choose a different voice after this introduction.' By now I was certain I was dreaming. Yet there was Rabid still looking at me and panting hard, there was the gap through the trees and the roof of my house, there was the smell of leaf mould and the mocking gluck, gluck, gluck of a green woodpecker. There was Mum talking again.

'Welcome, Danny. I am Simla, your guide and pilot. You are now connected to Cycap Control where all coordinates for Space and Time are stored. As you have never used Cycap or a Cycap Capsule before, I will teach you how to use the controls and help you navigate SpaceTime. But first, I can sense you are anxious about the fitting of the Cycap Capsule.'

"Dead right," I said out loud. "How do I get this… this Cycap thing off my head?"

'You must simply see it, Danny. Just see it getting bigger and see yourself lifting it off your head. I will be waiting for you on your return.'

CHAPTER 2

LATER: The Cycap thing came off just as Mum — I mean the voice — had said it would. I imagined pumping it up like a football with a bicycle pump and the thing just loosened and I could take it off. If you think I was feeling fine about everything by then, I need to explain something. I felt as fine as you do in one of those dreams where you walk into your classroom having forgotten to wear anything below the waist, or as fine as you might feel after being told by your PE teacher that you're a pathetic bag of pig's offal (Mr Henderson), or as fine as you might feel when the Year 10 hardnuts barge you into a hedge (Chris Beaumont and his gang who call themselves 'The Squad').

No, I didn't feel fine at that point. I wanted to scrape a hole under the fallen oak with my bare hands and bury this thing that had confirmed that I was not just different from everybody, but that I was a total weirdo. I knew I had a good imagination, sure, but I didn't think it would ever completely take me over. So I walked away from the Cycap and shouted back at it: "I'm not bloody stupid and I'm not bloody mad," and added for good measure, "You're a pathetic bag of pig's offal!" All this aggression made Rabid (from a safe distance) start up his poor excuse for a bark — it's a sort of strangled yelp with a wheeze at the end, and every time he does it he lifts vertically off the ground as though his little jumps made the bark more threatening.

I swept the fields below through the binoculars and noted '9:05 a.m., usual boring crows. Nothing else.' I sat on a tuft of grass and felt in my rucky for some food. The Bovril sandwich was wet cardboard, but I swallowed it down. Some 20 metres behind me the Cycap was where I'd thrown it, waiting quietly for me to pick it up and bring it to life. I resisted its magnetism – for the best part of a minute.

'Welcome back Danny,' my mum said.

'Ummm… hi. Can we, can you change the voice? It's a bit, you know, weird, having Mum's voice talking to me.'

'You can change it, Danny. Just think of a voice you like and imagine how the voice sounds.'

I thought for a while of my favourite TV programme, Match Magic, and someone with *almost* the same voice as Lenni Gallagher, the ex-England striker who fronted the show, said to me: 'Is this the voice you'd like?'

"That's just amazing," I said. I noticed that Rabid shot off home as soon as I put the headpiece on again, so I was quite alone.

'We'll start with a short lesson in synaptics,' the almost-Lenni said. 'But first, I need to do a full scan. Now relax, Danny, and think of something unstimulating.'

I thought for a moment of the things that bored me most – French with Mrs Mountjoy, Maths with Mr Amos, and cleaning my room.

I began to sense a light behind my eyes that slowly grew brighter until the brightness was almost painful. Suddenly it was gone. Lenni Gallagher spoke, but this time *exactly* like himself and I don't just mean the sound. I mean the cheeky, cheery guy using his kind of words and everything. His personality.

'I have just had a good look at your brain, Danny. Everything seems normal enough. Weight: 1.3 kilos, 1.9 percent of your body weight, 1.7 litres of brain matter, 102 billion neurons and roughly ten times that number of synapses. That's pretty high.'

'Is that good?' I asked.

'That's good. So is your cognition. Your ability to learn will peak in fifteen months at 27 percent.'

'That doesn't sound good,' I said.

'It's pretty good. With the right stimulation and exercise we can get it higher though – much higher. Your retention is only average. You are being selective about what to remember and what to forget and you are forgetting too much.'

'Like maths,' I said.

'Especially that. But that is for another session. I have devised an exercise for you.'

In my mind I saw the ball again, but this time it was a Premier League type football and the inky sea had been replaced with a perfect football pitch with eleven players in Manchester United strip. I support Arsenal! I merely thought this thought and there was the Arsenal team trotting out onto the pitch. This was a video game without any controls or screen except my mind. I saw what I had to do as the ball was passed expertly from Man U player to Man U player. I haven't spent (at a good guess because I like to work these things out) about 80 solid days out of the last three years playing football video games without some benefit. I admit that some of those 80 hours might have been used more constructively towards my GCSE course work (especially geography). But if you are really quite good at a subject – like FIFA World Cup for instance – why shouldn't this be a GCSE subject? To my mind being good at FIFA World Cup is a life skill and just as important as geography. My parents have friends round and they play cards. For hours! Then they moan at me for… anyway.

I got the hang of this mind-FIFA pretty quickly (after the first game went Man U 12–1 Arsenal). I don't know how much time passed before Lenni said: 'Isn't it time you thought about going home for lunch?' I looked at my watch and got two shocks at once. The first was that it was just after 12 p.m. and two hours had gone in a minute it seemed. The second was that I caught a glimpse of my reflected face in the watch glass. It was my normal head except my hair was a bit flattened. Where was the headpiece? Lenni was instantly there with the answer to my unspoken question.

'Cycap is designed so that the wearer looks normal. Much more than 99 percent of an atom is empty space. Inner space if you like. Cycap design uses that inner space to make the headpiece insubstantial. Not just invisible, but undetectable.'

"Bloody hell!" I said.

I decided that I would give it the ultimate test – soup and sandwiches with Mum and Dad.

CHAPTER 3

I COULD see Mum clearly from the top of the hill above our house. Usually I could hardly see the house from there, but my vision had improved. I realized the strangest thing – I could zoom in! Mum was wearing her green apron with flowers on. I could zoom in on the flowers from over a kilometre away. She was looking worried and I realized why. There was Rabid at her feet barking wheezily. Rabid never returned home without me. I could hear his bark as though he was right beside me. I started to laugh at my newfound powers. I waved at Mum and shouted: "Mum! Over here! Mum!" But she couldn't see me, let alone hear me. But the soup smelled good. This was getting freakier by the minute. I could smell the soup! It was leek and potato.

"Danny, for goodness sakes boy, you frightened me nearly to death. Fidget comes home with his tail between his legs. Why did he come home without you? And you don't answer when I ring your mobile. First there's no signal and then it goes straight to answerphone. I sent Dad up to look for you and he comes back saying: 'He'll be okay. He'll just be watching birds or muntjac or something and the time just passes.' 'So why's Fidget back then?' I ask him and he says: 'Because that dog is plain stupid, that's why.' For goodness sakes Danny."

I took the punishment. I couldn't help wondering why, though, that whenever my mum rings my mobile I rarely hear it, yet whenever Sanjay calls me (usually a question on which homework is due because he never ever writes anything down, or a technical question on Call of Duty) I hear it first ring.

All was quickly forgiven. As we're having the soup around the kitchen table I said to Mum: "Delicious soup, Mum. I could smell it from miles away. Must be the nutmeg you put in." Her expression goes from looking pleased, to drop-jawed surprise. I never say anything about the food she puts in front of me except 'I can't stand smoked haddock,' or 'liver and bacon makes me want to vomit,' or 'Has this got garlic in it? I hate garlic.'

While Mum is still recovering I say to Dad: "Is the tractor all right, Dad?"

"What d'you mean, is it all right?"

"Well, it was blowing out some white smoke."

"So?"

"I just wondered if the plugs might need replacing." I looked at my soup spoon and took a slurp knowing Dad was staring at me and his jaw was on the table like Mum's.

My sister Dot, who's 13 and a bit daft, is following the exchanges like someone watching tennis with their mouth open.

"You been using Mum's Eternity again?"

I made a quick exit to my room before they could frame a sentence. You see Cycap was able to analyze literally anything I thought about. Me question: 'What's that smell?' Cycap answer: 'Leek and potato soup with rosemary and nutmeg.' Me question: 'I wonder why the tractor is making white smoke instead of black.' Cycap answer: 'Plugs need replacing, petrol contamination or injector problem.' And the quite bizarre thing was that my own parents and sister didn't see or even suspect that I might be wearing an invisible mind-enhancing supercomputer from an alien world.

Lying on my bed I noticed the weather had changed. The wind was chucking rain against the window. I felt really cosy and warm and safe. I wondered why I felt so good and sure enough, back came an answer in a voice as quiet as a thought.

'This is rest time. Your brain has had to absorb a lot in the last few hours so Cycap is putting you in recovery mode. It has analyzed your brain chemistry and adjusted the levels of Serotonin, Gaba and Tyrophane. This is making you feel good and relaxed. I am going to tell you a bedtime story, Danny, after which you will enjoy a deep sleep.'

I pulled the duvet around myself and snuggled up just like I did when mum told me a story when I was four years old. Managed not to put my thumb in my mouth though.

'A long time ago, in a galaxy far away,' the soft voice began, and I settled down for Star Wars being told to me by a voice inside my own head, but that was not to be the story. Cycap was just revealing it had a sense of humour. 'There was a race of beings who looked very much like humans. We shall call them the Hajaan and their planet, Nem,' the voice continued. 'The Hajaan were very advanced, but very lonely. Their scanners told them that life existed all over the Universe, but not in their galaxy, not any more. Their belief was that all life should come together for the greatest good of Universal Existence. Without life, they believed, the Universe would collapse into itself. Life, they believed, should seek life, in whatever form.

'They built starships of great power. Of the hundreds of billions of galaxies in the Universe, they carefully selected a few thousand – the galaxies from which the strongest signals were returned, confirming the presence of life.

'A million Hajaans were chosen to become Seekers. This was a thing of great honour for them. Seekers were the very cream of Hajaan youth – physically strong and with minds like shining stars. They would learn to master the Cycap – the Cycap was the Hajaans' most brilliant piece of technology among many brilliant inventions. It was a mind, a transport device, a survival suit, a communicator, a whole small world that could fit on a Hajann head. It was a way of bringing together those life forms that were sprinkled throughout space and time.

'The scientists and astronomers on your planet think in straight lines. They imagine space as infinitely long and infinitely wide. But our scientists realized it was more complicated. Imagine space as a length of rope made of billions of strands, each infinitely long and each a universe. Now knot that length of rope into a vast complex ball. Although each strand is still the same length, some strands are touching others. Universes are criss-crossing universes. The trick was to jump from one universe to another and that required extremely good timing.

'There was a special day. The Hajaans called it 'Day One'. By their calculations it happened once every Pulse. Space and time was a living entity, they believed, and their instruments detected a Pulse every kamath (in Earth rotations – 2057 years). A kamath was approaching and this was the perfect time to launch the Great Search.

One of the Seekers was called Baahan. Like his million fellow Seekers, he was honoured to have been chosen, but heart-broken to leave his family and his planet, Nem. The kamath arrived with accelerating speed for Baahan. He said his goodbyes and stepped proudly aboard one of the starships.'

In my head appeared a number of images. There was Nem, set in an alien sky with a distant huge flash that I took to be the star in their solar system. And an image of the starship. It was a huge structure – like a block of flats floating through space, flanked by giant engines. Another being inside a starship – like a scene inside the spacecraft in one of the Alien movies I thought. I felt Baahan's pride and anguish. I realized that the Cycap was giving me Bahaan's emotions.

'In a minute you will fall asleep and during your sleep Cycap will upload information in your brain that will help you understand what is happening to you. Now you must sleep. Brammanamfiossumnaaaa…'

120

When I opened my eyes it was still daylight, but I knew it was the next day. I'd slept for 17 solid hours! Missed tea, TV and an hour's worth of Conquer the Dead 2. But I felt great. Hungry enough to eat the duvet, but great. I always remember my dreams. This one was crystal clear and was about finding an alien helmet up in the copse that spoke in the voice of Lenni Gallagher and had amazing powers.

'Good morning, Danny,' Lenni Gallagher said softly.

CHAPTER 4

To the outside it would have seemed like just another Tuesday morning. There was me waiting for the 562 bus at the bottom of our driveway, watching the cars and lorries go past while wearing an alien headpiece. I reckon that the expressions on the drivers' faces might have been no different if the Cycap had been visible. They were all in their get-to-work mode: tuned to Radio 2, focused on their own world of worries, seeing a kid waiting at a bus stop with a part of their minds that registered very little. 'Was that boy wearing a ceramic bowl on his head that speaks to him with the voice of a well-known football commentator? Traffic seems quite light today.'

The number 562 bus has a bit of a reputation. Chris Beaumont and The Squad always occupy the back quarter. When I say 'occupy' I mean it in the sense of an invading army. By the time the bus gets to me, the front half is always full which means I have no choice but to get into range of The Squad and their latest form of torture. For a good two weeks they found it hilarious to flick the back of my head and when I looked round they would all be looking at the ceiling in a pose of innocence. Beaumont invented some other really comical stunts, like letting off a stink bomb and saying loudly:

"Driver, sir – Danny Reed has farted again. Can you stop the bus, please? We're all dying back here." The driver ignored them and their gasping and coughing. The bus eventually arrived at school and The Squad rushed down the bus, each of them pinching their noses with one hand, leaving the other free to swipe me on the back of the head.

Everyone on the 562 was put on detention following the driver's report to the head teacher, Mrs Rindell, she with her pinched features and straw-coloured hair always tied in a bun. Beaumont had already been to see her to explain that I'd let off the stink bomb in some ridiculous vendetta against him and his friends.

That happened a few weeks ago – in a galaxy far, far away, or so it now seems. So, travel a million or so light years back to this Tuesday morning I'm telling you about and there I am sitting on the 562 in my usual exposed seat with The Squad behind me and the taunts just starting.

"No farting today, Reed."

"He doesn't need to. He stinks anyway."

"Yeah, I can smell cabbages. Rotten cabbages."

I didn't say anything, but I felt a sort of charge building up in me, like the static in that Wimshurst machine in the science lab before the contacts were placed close together and the spark flew.

As always I just stared out of the window and saw my own reflection in the glass and smeared mud. In the reflection I saw Buckley, one of The Squad's meanest recruits, come up behind me ready to slap my head or flick my ear. His hand went back and came down in an arc towards my head, but it never made contact. It skidded off about a centimetre above my scalp with a tiny crackle. Buckley let out a cry of pain and puzzlement.

"Whaaa...," was all he said.

I heard Beaumont say to Buckley: "You wuss," and I was aware that he was now behind me with his hand ready to strike.

Somehow I knew how to increase the intensity of the 'charge', and with Beaumont's attempted blow I heard a much louder crackle as his hand struck down into an invisible layer of fired up electrons. There was a girly yelp of pained surprise. When he recovered he was able to whimper: "You're a... a devil. There's something wrong with you, Reed," and then pathetically, "and you hurt my hand."

I slowly got out of my seat and turned to face them. They were all wide-eyed and slightly huddled together on the back seat – their place of power. I felt powerful myself, like never before in my life. I kept my eyes unwaveringly on Beaumont and stood right in front of him. I quickly flicked my hand in front of his face and made a noise like: 'Dzzzz!' He yelped again, though I hadn't touched him. I leaned right up to his blackhead-studded face and said: "Wuss!" and then went back to my seat.

"You just wait Reed," he managed. "You just wait." They always say that for some reason.

Tuesdays were normally rubbish days. Double maths to start. I'm all right at maths. Well, average – predicted grade C. Mr Amos is white-haired and a bit mad. No one messes about with him though, so he usually gets good results. He writes equations on the whiteboard that seem as easy to understand as Chinese to me. I normally copy them down and then work through them when I get home. In this lesson it was as though he was writing basic sentences in plain English. I saw the right side of the equation before he wrote it.

"So," he was saying as he wrote a long series of numbers, letters and symbols, brackets and horizontal lines, "write down this equation and let me have your answers in your exercise books for next week along with three more sets starting on page 53 in your textbooks. You may use calculators."

"Seventeen," I said – it just popped out of my mouth, or my head.

Mr Amos turned round from the blackboard and looked over his black, thick-framed glasses at me. There was a long pause. He turned back to the whiteboard and studied it as if there was some secret message there that gave away the answer to the simpletons he was forced to teach.

"How did you work that out, Reed?"

"I just saw the answer, sir."

"Where did you see the answer? I haven't finished writing the equation," Amos turned back to the board again looking for the number 17. It wasn't there.

"It's the square root of 289, sir, and you get the 289 by…"

"Yes, I know how you get to 289 thank you very much, Reed."

There was a titter around the class.

"Be quiet," he roared, his pasty skin reddening up. "You'll see me afterwards, Reed."

Amos set me triple homework going right up to page 56. That was all right by me. I realized it would take me no time at all with the equations all being written in plain language. Nothing simpler. It was while I was talking to Amos that the shaking started. I was shivering uncontrollably, but I wasn't cold. In fact, I felt just fine.

"What's wrong, Reed? Why are you shaking, boy?" Amos said,

peering at me through those thick lenses.

"I'm all right sir, honestly," I said.

"Go and see the nurse. Tell her I sent you." Amos was okay really.

I didn't see the nurse – instead, I just asked Lenni, my on-board, in-head nurse and teacher, what was going on.

'You are not very fit, Danny.' Lenni explained as though he was talking to a player on the England bench. 'Your muscle tone is poor. I am exercising your muscles to bring them up to standard. You'll need to eat lots of protein over the next few days.'

By midday I was ravenous. I ate my packed lunch of Marmite and cheese sandwiches, hardly noticing them go down. I then went to the school canteen and got a plate heaped with pasta and something they laughingly call 'Bolognaise sauce'.

Afternoon classes started with science. It was all too easy, like they were giving me Year 7 stuff to do, but easier. I kept my mouth shut though – I could see where this would go otherwise.

I should have done the same in French. Mrs Mountjoy was scary. It was conversation as always on a Tuesday.

"Comment allez-vous, Danny?

"Tres bien, madame, merci."

She seemed encouraged by this unusual fluency and said, in French of course: "And did you have a good weekend?"

In French I replied: "Yes, thank you very much. It was an amazing weekend as it happens."

"Why is that?" Mrs Mountjoy said, her eyes widening with my relatively unstoppable chatter. I could sense the rest of the class exchanging glances, mouths opening in 'o's of shock.

Mrs Mountjoy's delight was almost uncontainable. She lit up during our conversation and clapped her little pink hands together as I completed every sentence with the verb forms and tenses correctly, uttered in an accent that was pretty much native to Paris itself. It was as though I'd seen the error of my ways by the light of her teaching skills. I was her prodigy, sacre bleu! I was her French-speaking wayward son, returned gloriously to the fold. For one terrible moment I thought she was going to clasp me to her plentiful breast. The rest of the lesson passed with her hardly taking her eyes off me in an adoring sort of way. As we left she pulled me to one side and pressed a fat book into my hand. It was called *A la recherche du temps perdu* by Marcel Proust that she sometimes read from to everyone's complete incomprehension.

"You're ready for Marcel, Danny," she said almost tearfully. "You'll love him, I know you will."

Over the next week I had more conversations with Lenni. I asked him/it, as I was sitting in my bedroom, if this was all delusional. 'Am I schizophrenic? Because that would explain everything – voices in my head talking to me.'

'You are not suffering from schizophrenia, Danny, or delusions, though it's a sensible question for someone in your situation to ask. I think it's time for a small demonstration. We need to go outside for this.'

In the farmyard at the front of the house Lenni said: 'How far do you think you can throw a stone, Danny? Could you throw one over the roof of that barn on the hillside, for instance?'

'No way! It's got to be half a kilometre.'

'It's 516 metres. Pick up a stone and throw it. Make it land on the roof of that barn.'

'I told you, it's way too far – ten times too far,' I said.

'Indulge me, please.'

I picked up a stone the size and shape of a chicken's egg shaking my head. Here I was, being told to do daft things by my imaginary friend, Lenni Gallagher. I was clearly nuts. I sighed in resignation, weighed the heft of the stone in my hand, drew back my arm and let fly with everything I had. I watched it form a perfect and physically impossible parabola rising some hundreds of metres in the air, and saw it fall and bounce on the roof of the old barn, shattering a slate. A second later I heard the clatter as the sound came back. Dad rushed out of the barn a moment later looking round with his hands on his hips. I could imagine his bewilderment and swearing.

'That stone was no delusion, Danny,' Lenni said in my head. 'The Cycap has been building up your muscles and metabolism. Your body strength is up 812 percent, your reaction time is up 387 percent, and you are now using an additional 28 percent of your brain capacity.'

I couldn't deny it. I felt fitter and looked stronger. Mum couldn't believe how I'd shaped up in the last few days. And my mind felt like it was turbo-charged. Maths, science, languages – they were all a doddle.

'You are being made ready, Danny.'

'Ready for what?' I asked.

'Ready for a journey.'

CHAPTER 5

"WHY are you being so nice to me, Danny? It's really creepy."
This was my sister Dot's reaction to my newly discovered ability
to be pleasant and personable. Not only had my muscles and my
intellect grown, but my 'nice' quotient had gone up dramatically.
I found I could smile more, have meaningful conversations, be
interested in what people had to say – even care about what
they said.

I had, I supposed, grown up in a matter of weeks and I was
beginning to quite like the person I'd become. I did have a
strange fondness for the old, that is, younger Danny – that head-
bowed, spotty, mumbling, moody, irritable kid I used to be. But
he'd left.

"You're my sister and I like you. So why shouldn't I be nice to
you?"

"That's just weird. Mum, isn't Danny weird? And how come
you don't have spots all of a sudden?"

"He's growing up, love. And he's quickly turning into a
handsome young man," she said, and then to herself she added,
"And goodness, how quickly."

"That's just weird," Dot said.

The original voice of the Cycap, who had introduced 'herself' as
Simla, spoke to me as I snuggled down for a deep and peaceful
sleep. The voice lulled me so that I didn't know if I slept or was
just sleepy. The story of the Hajaans continued.

'Bahaan spent eight Nem years aboard the starship with over
a thousand other Hajaan Seekers all on similar missions. One by

one their numbers were reduced as they set off from the starship, each tasked with seeking and recording life forms throughout the Universe.

Reports were received from some successful searches. Your own galaxy revealed rich clusters of life. There was the planet we called Goraanst (which means 'symphony' in Hajaan) that was inhabited by immensely tall glass-like columns, heptagonal in section and emitting the most musical of sounds. The columns grew from minerals deep in the planet's crust and they communed with each other by, to Hajaan ears at least, sublime musical sounds. From the diminutive planet Fanuum (meaning 'speck') came a report of life forms not so very different from our own – humanoids with a culture and technology similar to that of your ancient Greece. There was one major difference – the Fanuumians were tiny versions of humans, only 20 centimetres tall. As for the Hajaan Seeker who reported from the planet Baansh – sadly she did not survive long. The dominant life form was like a massive sea-anemone that slid slowly over land. It was armed with hundreds of crystalline harpoons on tethers that it shot

131

into anything worth eating. Its hapless prey were dragged into the creature's stomach and slowly dissolved by gastric acids.

'Bahaan at last reached the coordinates for the planet where he would conduct his search for life. The one designated for him was the third in its solar system and was located in the second quadrant of the M52 spiral galaxy – the planet known as Earth.

I saw in my head a vision of Bahaan – slim, muscular and entirely human in appearance. I saw him slide from a chute out of the starship into a star-filled sky. He was inside a transparent egg-shaped vessel, ending in a nose-cone that I recognized easily as the Cycap itself. He sped towards a distant blue planet that I knew to be Earth and entered its atmosphere in a burst of light.

'This was more than two thousand Earth years ago,' Simla continued. 'Bahaan lived among Earth's peoples and travelled widely. He became a legend. But he knew he had to return to the starship with his precious findings about a planet that teemed with the life that Hajaans sought so keenly. When the appointed day came to rendezvous with the starship, Bahaan was ready, but the starship never arrived. Years earlier it had been evaporated in a neutron stream from an advanced and wholly aggressive civilization on the furthermost reaches of your galaxy. Bahaan, marooned on Earth, lived out his life here. Before he died, he buried his Cycap deep in the ground where it remained until you came along. It wanted to be discovered. It announced its whereabouts with resonances and signals. It split the tree, not the lightning. You didn't find the Cycap – it found you.'

I spent the next few weeks trying to find the right words and the right moment. I imagined the conversation. 'Mum, Dad, Dot –

there's something I have to tell you. You see it is the time of the kamath and I have been chosen to stand in for Bahaan who was sent as a Seeker from the planet Nem. He died two thousand years ago and his Seeker starship is going to return to this solar system and I am to rendezvous with it in space. How do I think I'm going to do that? That's a good question. I have on my head a Cycap. No, of course you can't see it – it's invisible! And this Cycap can create a protective forcefield around me and project me into space.'

You see my problem. Mum, Dad, Dot – I perfectly understand why you would never believe me. I am not mad. I love all of you and I am going to miss you forever. But I have to do this. I really do. So I have made this diary and called it the Cycap Notebooks. In two days I am to return to the copse and stand in the clearing. I'll leave these notebooks for you and I will set up the video camera to record what happens. Then you'll see I'm not mad – just very, very lucky. Look after Rabid for me.

Danny xxx

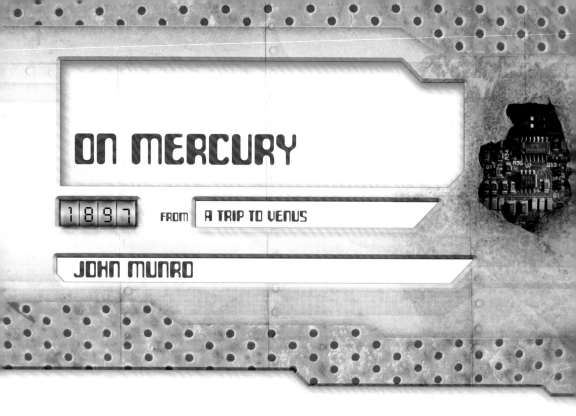

ON MERCURY

1897 FROM A TRIP TO VENUS

JOHN MUNRO

Mr Carmichael has developed a means of travelling in a spaceship, which he calls a 'car'. He, his daughter and two colleagues – Professor Gazen and the other who is narrating the story – have first visited Venus and have now moved on to Mercury.

IT WAS BROAD DAY when I awoke, and oppressively warm in the little cabin.

Apparently there was nobody in the car but myself. Wondering, and perhaps a trifle uneasy at the dead stillness, I dressed rapidly and went outside.

The air was excessively hot, moist and sultry as before a thunderstorm. Black boulders and crags, speckled with lichens and carpeted with coarse herbage, shut out the prospect on every side but one, where the edge of the platform on which the car was resting ran along the sky.

I was looking away over a vast plain towards a distant range of volcanic mountains. A broad river wound through the midst between isolated volcanoes curling with smoke, or expanded into marshy lakes, on the margin of which living monsters were splashing in the mud or soaring into the air.

"Gazen, Gazen! Hallo there! Hallo!" I shouted.

There was no response, and the dead silence that swallowed up my voice was awful. I shouted again at the very pitch of my voice, and this time an answering cry came to my relief. On turning in the direction from which it proceeded, I observed Professor Gazen coming slowly towards me round a mass of turreted rocks.

Just at that moment we were startled by a piercing shriek from behind the crags, and rushing, or rather bounding forward, saw a sight that made our very blood run cold.

A flying monster with enormous bat-like wings and hanging legs was evidently swooping down on Miss Carmichael as she stood beside her easel on the brow of the cliff.

"Run for your life!" roared Gazen, dashing towards her with frantic speed.

Alas! She did not hear him, or else she was fascinated by the approaching horror, and rooted to the spot. He was still several hundred yards from her, but owing to the feebleness of gravity on the planet he was so preternaturally light and nimble that he might have covered the distance in a minute or so, had he been more accustomed to control his limbs, and the ground been smoother. As it was he leaped high into the air, and rebounded

from the stones like a rubber ball, at the risk of spraining his ankles or breaking his neck, while brandishing his arms, and firing his pistol to frighten away the monster.

Too late. The huge leathery wings of the dragon overshadowed the shrinking form of the girl, and the talons of its drooping feet caught in her dress. She made one desperate, but futile effort to free herself from its terrible clutch, and was borne away over the abyss of the valley as easily as a lamb is carried by an eagle.

"Oh, Heaven!" cried Gazen, stopping with a gesture of despair.

He was deeply moved, and pale as death; but he did not altogether lose his head.

What was to be done?

"The car – the car!" he exclaimed. "We must follow her in the car. Keep your eye on the beast while I go for it."

Carmichael was fast asleep in his cabin, after his long weary vigil during the passage from Venus, but the car was quickly put in motion, and I jumped on board just as it cleared the brink of the precipice.

The dragon, which had the start of us by a mile or more, was apparently steering for the mountains on the other side of the valley. Notwithstanding its enormous bulk and the dead weight hanging from its claws, it flew with surprising speed, owing to the weakness of gravity and the vast spread of its wings.

I shall never forget that singular chase, which is probably unparalleled in the history of the universe. A prey to anxiety, we did not properly observe the marvellous aspect of the country beneath us and still we could not altogether blind ourselves to it.

Mountainous quadrupeds or lizards crashing and tearing through their branches — one of them at least six hundred feet in length, with a ridgy back and long spiky tail, dragging on the ground, a baleful green eye, and a crooked mouth full of horrid fangs, which made it look the very incarnation of cruelty and brute strength — gigantic alligators and crocodiles resting motionless in the shallows, with their snouts high in the air — hideous toads or suchlike forbidding reptiles, many with tusks like the walrus, and some with glorious eyes, crouching on the banks or waddling in the reeds, and so enormous as to give variety to the landscape — volcanic craters, with red-hot lava simmering in their depths — while over all great dragons and other bat-like animals were flitting through the dusky atmosphere like demons in a nightmare.

Little by little we gained upon our quarry, but being afraid to run him too close for fear that he might drop his victim, we kept at a safe distance behind him, yet within rifle range, and near enough to make a prompt attack when he should settle on the ground.

At length we reached the other side of the valley, and found to our intense satisfaction that the monster was making for a rocky ledge on the shoulder of an extinct volcano, where we could see the yawning mouth of what appeared an immense cavern.

"That is probably his den," said Gazen, who was now as collected as I have ever seen him.

The event showed that his surmise was correct, for soon after

he had spoken the dragon uttered a startling cry — a kind of squawk like that of a drake, but much louder, hoarser, shriller — and alighted on the ground.

"There is not a moment to lose," said Gazen. "We must attack him before he enters the cave."

Certainly the darkness inside the cavern would give the beast a great advantage, and although we might succeed in killing him, we could scarcely hope to find Miss Carmichael alive. Was she alive now? I had my doubts, but I kept them to myself. Since she had been carried away she had not given the smallest sign of life, not even when the dragon settled.

We might have fought the creature from the air, but we had decided to assail him on the solid ground, because we should thus be able to scatter and take him in the flank, if not in the rear.

While Carmichael landed his car the astronomer and I kept a sharp watch on the beast, all ready to fire at the first movement that seemed to threaten the safety of the young girl, who was lying motionless at the bottom of a slope which led up to the mouth of the cavern. Freed from his burden, the dragon now stood erect, and a more awful monster it would be difficult to conceive.

I have called him a dragon, but he was not at all like the dragons of our imagination. With his great bullet head and prick ears, his beetling

139

brows and deep sunken eyes, his ferocious mouth and protruding tusks, his short thick neck and massive shoulders, his large, gawky and misshapen trunk, coated with dingy brown fur, shading into dirty yellow on the stomach, his stout, bandy legs armed with curving talons, and his huge leathern wings hanging in loose folds about him, he looked more like an imp of Satan than a dragon.

Hitherto he had not appeared to notice his pursuers; but now that he was freer to observe, the grating of the car upon the rocks caught his attention. He turned quickly and stared at the apparition of the vessel, which must have been a strange object to him; but he did not seem to take alarm. It was the gaze of a jaguar or a tiger who sees something curious in the jungle – vigilant and deadly if you like, but neither scared nor fierce.

We lost no time in sallying forth, all three of us, armed with rifle, cutlass and revolver. Mr Carmichael in the middle, I on the lower, and Gazen on the upper side, or that nearest to Miss Carmichael. The rocks around were slippery, and the sickening stench of rotting skeletons made our very gorge rise. Suddenly a loud squeaking in the direction of the cave arrested us, and before we had recovered from our surprise, nearly a dozen young dragons, each about the size of a man, tumbled hastily down the slope, and rushed upon the lifeless form of Miss Carmichael.

"Great Scott, there's the whole family," muttered Gazen between his teeth, at the same time bringing his rifle to the shoulder, and firing in quick succession.

The foremost of the family, which had already flung itself upon the prey, was seen to spring head over heels into the air, and fall back dead; another lay writhing in agony upon the ground, and uttering strangely human shrieks; whilst the others, terrified by the noise, turned and fled back helter-skelter to the cave.

The old one, roused to anger by the injury done to his offspring, snarled ferociously at his enemies and, drawing himself to his full height, made a furious dash for Gazen.

Our rifles cracked again and again. The monster started as he felt the shots and halted, glaring from one to another of us like a man irresolute. Purple streams were gushing from his head and sides. He attempted to fly and ran towards the brink of the ledge, but ere he could gain sufficient impetus to launch himself into the air. He staggered and fell heavily to the ground, with his broken wings beneath him.

Gazen flew towards Miss Carmichael, and bent over her.

"Is she alive?" enquired Carmichael, in breathless and trembling accents.

"Yes, thank God," responded Gazen fervently as he raised her hand to his lips and kissed them.

There were tears of joy in his eyes, and I knew then what I had long suspected, that he loved her.

Suddenly a loud croak in the distance caused us to look up, and we beheld another dragon on the wing, coming rapidly towards us from a pass among the mountains. There was not a moment to be lost. Gazen took Miss Carmichael in his arms and we all hurried on board the car, eager to escape from this revolting spot.

THE cloudy surface of Mercury now lay far beneath us, and the glowing disc of the sun, which appeared four or five times larger than it does on the earth, had taken a bluish tinge — a proof that we had reached a very great altitude.

"What a magnificent 'sun-spot'!" exclaimed the professor in a tone of admiration. "Just take a peep at it."

I placed my eye to the telescope, and saw the glowing surface of the disc resolved into a marvellous web of shining patches on a dimmer background, and in the midst a large blotch.

"Have you been able to throw any fresh light on these mysterious 'spots'?" I enquired.

"I am more than ever persuaded they are breaks in the photosphere caused by eruptions of heated matter, chiefly gaseous from the interior — eruptions such as this might give rise to craters like that of the Moon, were the sun cooler.."

While Gazen was yet speaking we both became sensible of a stillness in the car.

The machinery had ceased to vibrate.

"Is there anything wrong, Carmichael?" asked Gazen through the speaking tube.

There was no response.

"I say, Carmichael, is anything the matter?" he reiterated in a louder tone.

Still no answer.

We were now thoroughly alarmed, and though it was against the rules, we descended into the machinery room. The cause of Carmichael's silence was only too apparent. We saw him lying on the floor beside his strange machine, with his head leaning against the wall. There was a placid expression on his face, and he appeared to slumber, but we soon found that he was either in a faint or dead.

Gazen went and called Miss Carmichael.

She had been resting in her cabin after her trying experience with the dragon, and although most anxious about her father and far from well herself, she behaved with calm self-possession.

"I think the heat has overcome him," she said after a quick examination; and truly the cabin was insufferably hot, thanks to the machinery and the fervid rays of the sun.

We could not open the scuttles and admit fresh air, for there was little or none to admit.

"I shall try oxygen," she said on reflecting a moment.

Accordingly, she and I administered oxygen gas from one of our steel bottles to his lungs by means of a makeshift funnel applied to his mouth. In some fifteen or twenty minutes he began to show signs of returning animation, and soon afterwards, to our great relief, he opened his eyes.

At first he looked about him in a bewildered way, and then he seemed to recollect his whereabouts. After an ineffectual attempt to speak and move his limbs, he fixed his eyes with a meaning expression on the engines.

We had forgotten their stoppage. Miss Carmichael sprang to investigate the cause.

"They are jammed," she said after a short inspection. "The essential part is jammed with the heat. Whatever is to be done?"

We stared at each other blankly as the terrible import of her words came home to us. Unless we could start the machines again, we must inevitably fall back on Mercury. Perhaps we were falling now!

We endeavoured to think of a ready and practicable means of cooling the engines, but without success. The water and oil on board was lukewarm. None of us knew how to make a freezing mixture even if we had the materials; our stock of liquid air had long been spent.

Miss Carmichael tried to make her father understand the difficulty in hopes that he would suggest a remedy, but all her efforts were in vain. Carmichael lay with his eyes closed in a kind of lethargy or paralysis.

"Perhaps, when we are falling through the planet's atmosphere," said I, "if we open the scuttles and let the cold air blow through the room, it will cool the engines."

"I'm afraid there will not be time," replied Gazen, shaking his head, "we shall fall much faster than we rose. The friction of the air against the car will generate heat. We shall drop down like a meteoric stone and be smashed to atoms."

"We have parachutes," said Miss Carmichael, "do you think

we shall be able to save our lives?"

"I doubt it," answered Gazen sadly. "They would be torn and whirled away."

"So far as I can see there is only one hope for us," said I. "If we should happen to fall into a deep sea or lake, the car would rise to the surface again."

"Yes, that is true," responded Gazen; "the car is hollow and light. It would float. The water would also cool the machines and we might escape."

The bare possibility cheered us with a ray of hope.

"If we only had time, my father might recover, and I believe he would save us yet," said Miss Carmichael.

"I wonder how much time we have," muttered Gazen.

"We can't tell," said I. "It depends on the height we had reached and the speed we were going at when the engines stopped. We shall rise like a ball thrown into the air and then fall back to the ground."

"I wonder if we are still rising," remarked Gazen. "Let us take a look at the planet."

"Don't be long," pleaded Miss Carmichael, as we turned to go. "Meanwhile, I shall try and bring my father round."

On getting to the observatory, we consulted the atmospheric pressure gauge and found it out of use, a sign that we had attained an altitude beyond the atmosphere of Mercury, and were now in empty space.

We turned to the planet, whose enormous disc, muffled in cloud, was shining lividly in the weird sky. At one part of the limb, a range of lofty mountain peaks rose above the clouds and chequered them with shadow.

Fixing our eyes upon this landmark we watched it with bated breath. Was it coming nearer, or was it receding from us? That was the momentous question.

My feelings might be compared to those of a prisoner at the bar watching the face of the juryman who is about to deliver the verdict.

After a time – I know not how long but it seemed an age – the professor exclaimed,

"I believe we are still rising."

It was my own impression, for the peak I was regarding had grown as I thought smaller, but I did not feel sure, and preferred to trust the more experienced eyes of the astronomer.

"I shall try the telescope," he went on, "we are a long way from the planet."

"How far do you think?"

"Many thousand miles at least."

"So much the better. We shall get more time."

"Humph! prolonging the agony, that's all. I begin to wish it was all over."

Gazen directed his instrument on the planet and we resumed our observations.

"We are no longer rising," said Gazen after a time. "I suppose we are near the turning-point."

As a prisoner scans the countenance of the judge who is about to pronounce the sentence of life or death, I scanned the cloudy surface underneath us to see if I could discover any signs of an ocean that would break our fall, but the vapours were too thick and compact.

"Strange!" muttered Gazen by-and-by, as if speaking to himself.

"What is strange?"

"We are neither rising nor falling now. We don't seem to move."

"Impossible!"

"Nevertheless, it's a fact," he exclaimed at the end of some minutes. "The focus of the telescope is constant. We are evidently standing still."

"Hurrah!"

"What can it mean?" cried Gazen.

"Simply this," said I joyfully. "We have reached the 'dead-point' where the attraction of Mercury on the car is balanced by the attraction of the sun. It can't be anything else."

"Wait a minute," said Gazen, making a rapid calculation. "Yes, yes, probably you are right. I did not think we had come so far; but I had forgotten that gravitation on Mercury is only half as strong as it is on the earth or Venus. Let us go and tell Miss Carmichael."

We hurried downstairs to the engine room and found her kneeling beside her father, who was no better.

She did not seem much enlivened by the good news.

"What will that do for us?" she enquired doubtfully.

"We can remain here as long as we like, suspended between the sun and Mercury," replied Gazen.

"Is it better to linger and die in a living tomb than be dashed to pieces and have done with it?"

"But we shall gain time for your father to recover."

"I am afraid my father will never recover in this place. The heat is killing him. Unless we can get further away from the sun he will die, I'm sure he will."

An idea flashed into my head.

"Look here," said I to Gazen, "you remember our conversation in your observatory one day on the propelling power of rockets – how a rocket might be used to drive a car through space?"

"Yes, but we have no rockets."

"No, but we have rifles, and rifle bullets fired from the car, though not so powerful, will have a similar effect."

"Well?"

"The car is now at rest in space. A slight impulse will direct it one way or another. Why should we not send it off in such a way that, in falling towards Mercury, it will not strike the planet, but circle around it; or if it should fall towards the surface, will do so at a great slant and allow the atmosphere to cool the engines sufficiently."

"Let me see," said Gazen, drawing a diagram in his notebook and studying it attentively. "Yes, there is something in that. It's a forlorn hope at best, but perhaps it's our only hope. If we could only get into the shadow of the planet we might be saved."

As delay might prove fatal to Carmichael, and since it was uncertain whether he could right the engines and get them functional in their present situation, we decided to act on the suggestion without loss of time. Gazen and I calculated the positions of the rifles and the number of shots to be fired in order to give the required impetus to the car. The engine-room, being well provided with scuttles, was chosen as the scene of our operations. A brace of magazine rifles were fixed through two of the scuttles in such a way that the recoil of the shots would urge the car in an oblique direction backwards, so as to clear or almost clear the planet, allowance being made for the forward motion of the latter in its orbit. Needless to say, the barrel of each rifle was packed round so as to keep the air in the car from escaping into space.

At a given signal the rifles were discharged simultaneously by Gazen and myself. There was very little noise, but the car trembled with the shock and Carmichael, still lethargic, opened his eyes.

Had it produced the desired effect? We could not tell without an appeal to the telescope.

"I'll be back in a moment," cried Gazen, springing upstairs to the observatory.

"Do you feel any better, father?" enquired Miss Carmichael, laying her cool hand on the invalid's fevered brow.

He winked and tried to nod in the affirmative. "Were you asleep, father? Did the shock rouse you?"

He winked again.

"Do you know what we are doing?" Before he could answer the foot of Gazen sounded on the stair. He had left us with an eager, almost confident eye. He came back looking grave in the extreme.

"We are not falling towards Mercury," he said gloomily. "We are rushing to the sun!"

I cannot depict our emotion at this awful announcement, which changed our hopes into despair. A vision of the car, plunging through an atmosphere of flame, into the fiery entrails of the sun, flashed across my excited brain, and then I seemed to lose the power of thought.

"Out of the frying-pan, into the fire," said I at last, in

frivolous reaction.

"His will be done!" murmured Miss Carmichael, instinctively drawing closer to her father, who seemed to realize our jeopardy.

"We must look the matter in the face," said Gazen, with a sigh.

"What a death!" I exclaimed. "To sit and watch the vast glowing furnace that is to swallow us up come nearer and nearer, second after second, minute after minute, hour after hour."

"The nearer we approach the sun, the faster we shall go," said Gazen. "The heat will stifle us. It will be all over in a few hours."

What a death! To see, to feel ourselves roasting as in an oven. It was too horrible.

"Are you certain there is no mistake?" I asked at length.

"Quite," replied Gazen. "Come and see for yourself."

We had all but gained the door when Miss Carmichael followed us.

"Professor," she said, with a tremor in her voice and a look of supplication in her eyes, "you will come back soon – you will not leave us long."

"No, my darling – I beg your pardon," answered Gazen, obeying the impulse of his heart. "God knows I would give my life to save you if I could."

In another instant he had locked her in his arms.

I left them together and ascended to the observatory, where Gazen soon afterwards rejoined me.

"I'm the happiest man alive," said he, with a beaming countenance. "Congratulate me. I'm betrothed to Miss Carmichael."

I took his proffered hand, scarcely knowing whether to laugh or cry.

"It seems to me that I have found my life in losing it," he continued with a grim smile. "Saturn! What a courtship is ours — what an engagement!"

I wrung his hand in silence.

"Now let us take a look through the telescope," he went on, wiping his eyes, and adjusting the instrument. "You will see how soon it gets out of focus. We are flying from Mercury, my friend, faster and faster."

It was true.

"But I don't understand how that should be," said I. "The firing ought to have had a contrary effect."

"The rifles are not to blame," answered Gazen. "If we had used them earlier we might have saved ourselves. But all the time that we were discussing ways and means and making our preparations to shoot, we were gradually drifting towards the sun without knowing it. We overlooked the fact that the orbit of Mercury is very far from circular, and that he is now moving further away from the sun every instant. As a consequence his attractive power over the car is growing weaker and weaker every moment. The car had reached the 'dead-point' where the attractive powers of the sun and planet over it just balanced each other; but as that of the planet grew feebler the balance turned, and the car was drawn with ever accelerating velocity towards the sun."

"Like enough."

So this was the end! After all our care and forethought, after all our struggles, after all our success, to perish miserably like

moths in a candle, to plunge headlong into that immense
conflagration as a vessel dives into the ocean and is never heard
of more! Not a vestige of us, not even a charred bone to tell the
tale. Our friends at home when they admired the sun would they
ever fancy that it was our grave – ever dream that our ashes
were whirling in its flames. The cry of Othello, in his despair,
which I had learned at school, came back to my mind – 'Blow
me about in winds! Roast me in sulphur! Wash me in steep-
down gulfs of liquid fire!'

Regrets, remorse and bitter reflections overwhelmed me.
Why had we come to Mercury? Why had we endeavoured to do
so much? What folly had drawn me into this mad venture at all?
Why had we attempted to approach so near the sun, daring the
heat, which had jammed our engines and disabled our best
intellect; risking the powerful attraction that was hurrying us to
our doom?

Suddenly a peculiar thrill shook the car. With a bounding
heart I started to my feet and dashed into the engine-room. It
was true then. Yes, it was true. The engines were at work, and
we were saved!

We owed our salvation to Mr Carmichael. The firing of our
magazine rifles, followed by the news of our perilous situation,
had roused him from his lethargy. Although still unable to speak,
he had contrived by means of his eyes to make his daughter
understand that he wished another dose of oxygen. When she
was about to administer it, he called her attention to the fact
that in expanding as it issued from the cylinder, the gas became
very cold. She caught his meaning instantly, and on applying the
gas to the sensitive parts of the machinery had succeeded in

cooling and releasing them.

It seems that Carmichael, in order to save time, had been working the engines at an unusually high speed, which, together with the heat of the sun, had caused them to jam. Their enforced rest had of itself allowed them to cool somewhat, and by reducing the speed until we reached a cooler region, they did not stick again.

CARMICHAEL recovered from his illness, and the journey to the earth was accomplished without accident. We landed safely on some undiscovered islands in the Arctic Circle, and after a flying visit to the North Pole in the vicinity, we bore away for England, keeping high over the sea to escape notice. Going southward we passed through all sorts of weather, thick snow, hurricanes, fog and so forth; but it made no difference to us.

The first sign of man we saw was a ship rolling in a storm off the Hebrides; but apparently she was not in distress, else we should have gone to her succour. How easy with such a car to rescuc lives and property from sinking ships, and even patrol the seas in search of them!

The sun was setting in purple and gold as we approached the English coast, and although at our elevation we were still in sunshine, the twilight had begun to gather over the distant land. The first sound we heard was the moaning of the tide along the shore, and the mournful sighing of the wind among the trees. Hills, fields and woods lay beneath us like a garden in miniature. The lamps and fires of lonely villages and farmhouses twinkled like glow-worms in the dusk. A railway train, with its white puff of smoke and lighted carriages, seemed to be crawling like a fiery caterpillar along the ground; but in a few moments we had left it far behind. As it grew darker and darker we descended nearer to the surface. A herd of sheep stood huddled on the grass, and stared at us; a flock of geese ran cackling into a farmyard; the watch-dog barked and tugged furiously at his chain; a little boy screamed with fright.

"That sounds homely," said the professor to Miss Carmichael and myself, who were standing with him on the gallery outside the car. "It's the sweetest music I've heard for many a day. Venus was a charming place, but I for one am glad to get home again."

Yes, I too felt a deep and tranquil pleasure in returning to the familiar scenes and the beloved soil of my infancy.

"I should like to go back to Venus," said Miss Carmichael. "We can go there now at any time."

"Of course we can," replied Gazen, "and to Mars as well. Your father's invention opens up a bewildering prospect of complications in the universe. So long as each planet was isolated and left to manage its own affairs, the politics of the solar system were comparatively simple; but what will they be when one globe interferes with another?"

"Father was talking of that very matter the other night," said Miss Carmichael, "and he declared that rather than see any harm come, he would keep his invention a secret — at all events for a thousand years longer."

We had glided rapidly across the Black Country, with its furnaces and forges blazing in the darkness, and now the dull red glow of the metropolis was visible on the horizon. Half an hour later we descended in the garden of Carmichael's cottage, and found everything as snug as when we had left it.

Leaving my fellow travellers there, I took the train for London, and was driven to my club where I intended to sleep. It was a raw wet evening, and in spite of a certain joy at being home again, I could not help feeling that my heart was no longer here, but on another planet.

In the smoking-room of the club the first person I saw was my friend the Viscount, who was sitting just where I had left him on the night we started for Venus, with his glass of toddy before him, and a cigar between his lips.

"Hallo!" he exclaimed. "Haven't seen you for some time – must be nearly two months. Been abroad? You look brown."

"Yes."

"Well, suppose we finish our game of chess."

"With pleasure."

"You remember the wager – a thousand to a hundred sovereigns that I win."

He was the better player, and although I had a slight advantage in the game as it stood, I was by no means certain of winning, especially as I was tired and sleepy; but ever since my sojourn in Venus, my intellect had been unusually clear and active. I played as I had never played before, and in three moves had won the wager.

"That will pay my travelling expenses," said I, pocketing his cheque.

I have only to add that Professor Gazen and Miss Carmichael are about to be married. For myself, as soon as the ceremony is over I shall return to Venus.

SULTANA'S DREAM

1905

ROKHEYA SHEKHAWAT HOSSEIN

*The zenana was a secluded set of rooms in an Indian household where the
women lived, out of sight of any men. Women who were kept from the sight
of men were described as being 'in purdah'. Such women would wear a veil
if they went out — their faces would only be seen by other women and by
very close male relatives.*

ONE EVENING I was lounging in an easy chair in my
bedroom and thinking lazily of the condition of Indian
womanhood. I am not sure whether I dozed off or not. But, as
far as I remember, I was wide awake. I saw the moonlit sky
sparkling with thousands of diamond-like stars, very distinctly.

All on a sudden a lady stood before me; how she came in,
I do not know. I took her for my friend, Sister Sara.

"Good morning," said Sister Sara. I smiled inwardly as I knew it was not morning, but starry night. However, I replied to her, saying, "How do you do?"

"I am all right, thank you. Will you please come out and have a look at our garden?"

I looked again at the moon through the open window, and thought there was no harm in going out at that time. The men-servants outside were fast asleep just then, and I could have a pleasant walk with Sister Sara.

When walking I found to my surprise that it was a fine morning. The town was fully awake and the streets alive with bustling crowds. I was feeling very shy, thinking I was walking in the street in broad daylight, but there was not a single man visible.

Some of the passers-by made jokes at me. Though I could not understand their language, yet I felt sure they were joking. I asked my friend, "What do they say?"

"The women say that you look very mannish."

"Mannish?" said I,

"What do they mean by that?"

"They mean that you are shy and timid like men."

"Shy and timid like men?" It was really a joke. I became very nervous when I found that my companion was not Sister Sara, but a stranger. Oh, what a fool had I been to mistake this lady for my dear old friend, Sister Sara.

She felt my fingers tremble in her hand, as we were walking hand in hand.

"What is the matter, dear?" she said affectionately.

"I feel somewhat awkward," I said in a rather apologizing tone, "as being a purdahnishin woman I am not accustomed to walking about unveiled."

"You need not be afraid of coming across a man here. This is Ladyland, free from sin and harm. Virtue herself reigns here."

By and by I was enjoying the scenery. Really it was very grand. I mistook a patch of green grass for a velvet cushion. Feeling as if I were walking on a soft carpet, I looked down and found the path covered with moss and flowers.

"How nice it is," said I.

"Do you like it?" asked Sister Sara. (I continued calling her 'Sister Sara' and she kept calling me by my name).

"Yes, very much; but I do not like to tread on the tender and sweet flowers."

"Never mind, dear Sultana; your treading will not harm them – they are street flowers."

"The whole place looks like a garden," said I admiringly. "You have arranged every plant so skillfully."

"Your Calcutta could become a nicer garden than this if only your countrymen wanted to make it so."

"They would think it useless to give so much attention to horticulture, while they have so many other things to do."

"They could not find a better excuse," she said with a smile.

I became very curious to know where the men were. I saw more than a hundred women while walking there, but not a single man.

"Where are the men?" I asked her.

"In their proper places, where they ought to be."

"Pray let me know what you mean by 'their proper places'."

"Oh, I see my mistake, you cannot know our customs, as you were never here before. We shut our men indoors."

"Just as we are kept in the zenana?"

"Exactly so."

"How funny," I burst into a laugh. Sister Sara laughed too.

"But dear Sultana, how unfair it is to shut in the harmless women and let loose the men."

"Why? It is not safe for us to come out of the zenana, as we are naturally weak."

"Yes, it is not safe so long as there are men about the streets, nor is it so when a wild animal enters a marketplace."

"Of course not."

"Suppose, some lunatics escape from the asylum and begin to do all sorts of mischief to men, horses and other creatures; in that case what will your countrymen do?"

"They will try to capture them and put them back into their asylum."

"Thank you! And you do not think it wise to keep sane people inside an asylum and let loose the insane?"

"Of course not!" I said laughing lightly.

"As a matter of fact, in your country this very thing is done! Men, who do or at least are capable of doing no end of mischief, are let loose and the innocent women shut up in the zenana! How can you trust those untrained men out of doors?"

"We have no hand or voice in the management of our social affairs. In India, man is lord and master, he has taken to himself all powers and privileges and shut up the women in the zenana."

"Why do you allow yourselves to be shut up?"

"Because it cannot be helped as they are stronger than women."

"A lion is stronger than a man, but it does not enable him to dominate the human race. You have neglected the duty you owe to yourselves and you have lost your natural rights by shutting your eyes to your own interests."

"But my dear Sister Sara, if we do everything by ourselves, what will the men do then?"

"They should not do anything, excuse me; they are fit for nothing. Only catch them and put them into the zenana."

"But would it be very easy to catch and put them inside the four walls?" said I. "And even if this were done, would all their business – political and commercial – also go with them into the zenana?"

Sister Sara made no reply. She only smiled sweetly. Perhaps she thought it useless to argue with one who was no better than a frog in a well.

By this time we had reached Sister Sara's house. It was situated in a beautiful heart-shaped garden. It was a bungalow with a corrugated iron roof. It was cooler and nicer than any of our rich buildings. I cannot describe how neat and how nicely furnished and how tastefully decorated it was.

We sat side by side. She brought out of the parlour a piece of embroidery work and began putting on a fresh design.

"Do you know knitting and needle work?"

"Yes; we have nothing else to do in our zenana."

"But we do not trust our zenana members with embroidery!" she said laughing, "as a man has not patience enough to pass thread through a needlehole even!"

"Have you done all this work yourself?" I asked her pointing to the various pieces of embroidered teapoy cloths.

"Yes."

"How can you find time to do all these? You have to do the office work as well? Have you not?"

"Yes. I do not stick to the laboratory all day long. I finish my work in two hours."

"In two hours! How do you manage? In our land the officers – magistrates, for instance – work seven hours daily."

"I have seen some of them doing their work. Do you think they work all the seven hours?"

"Certainly they do!"

"No, dear Sultana, they do not. They dawdle away their time in smoking. Some smoke two or three cheroots during the office time. They talk much about their work, but do little. Suppose one cheroot takes half an hour to burn off, and a man smokes twelve cheroots daily; then you see, he wastes six hours every day in sheer smoking."

We talked on various subjects, and I learned that they were not subject to any kind of epidemic disease, nor did they suffer from mosquito bites as we do. I was very much astonished to hear that in Ladyland no one died in youth except by rare accident.

"Will you care to see our kitchen?" she asked me.

"With pleasure," said I, and we went to see it. Of course the men had been asked to clear off when I was going there. The kitchen was situated in a beautiful vegetable garden. Every creeper, every tomato plant was itself an ornament. I found no smoke, nor any chimney either in the kitchen – it was clean and bright; the windows were decorated with flower gardens. There was no sign of coal or fire.

"How do you cook?" I asked.

"With solar heat," she said, at the same time showing me the pipe, through which passed the concentrated sunlight and heat. And she cooked something then and there to show me the process.

"How did you manage to gather and store up the sun-heat?" I asked her in amazement.

"Let me tell you a little of our past history then. Thirty years ago, when our present Queen was thirteen years old, she inherited the throne. She was Queen in name only, the Prime Minister really ruling the country.

"Our good Queen liked science very much. She circulated an order that all the women in her country should be educated. Accordingly, a number of girls' schools were founded and supported by the government. Education was spread far and wide among women. And early marriage also was stopped. No woman was to be allowed to marry before she was twenty-one. I must tell you that, before this change we had been kept in strict purdah."

"How the tables are turned," I interposed with a laugh.

"But the seclusion is the same," she said. "In a few years we had separate universities, where no men were admitted."

"In the capital, where our Queen lives, there are two universities. One of these invented a wonderful balloon, to which they attached a number of pipes. By means of this captive balloon which they managed to keep afloat above the cloud-land, they could draw as much water from the atmosphere as they pleased. As the water was incessantly being drawn by the university people no cloud gathered and the ingenious Lady Principal stopped rain and storms thereby."

"Really! Now I understand why there is no mud here!" said I. But I could not understand how it was possible to accumulate water in the pipes. She explained to me how it was done, but I was unable to understand her, as my scientific knowledge was very limited. However, she went on.

"When the other university came to know of this, they became exceedingly jealous and tried to do something more extraordinary still. They invented an instrument by which they could collect as much sun-heat as they wanted. And they kept the heat stored up to be distributed among others as required.

"While the women were engaged in scientific research, the men of this country were busy increasing their military power. When they came to know that the female universities were able to draw water from the atmosphere and collect heat from the sun, they only laughed at the members of the universities and called the whole thing 'a sentimental nightmare'!"

"Your achievements are very wonderful indeed! But tell me, how you managed to put the men of your country into the zenana. Did you entrap them first?"

"No."

"It is not likely that they would surrender their free and open air life of their own accord and confine themselves within the four walls of the zenana! They must have been overpowered."

"Yes, they have been!"

"By whom? By some lady-warriors, I suppose?"

"No, not by arms."

"It cannot be. Men's arms are stronger than women's. Then?"

"By brain."

"Even their brains are bigger and heavier than women's. Are they not?"

"Yes, but what of that? An elephant also has got a bigger and heavier brain than a man has. Yet man can enchain elephants and employ them, according to their own wishes."

"Well said, but tell me please, how it all actually happened. I am dying to know it!"

"Women's brains are somewhat quicker than men's. Ten years ago, when the military officers called our scientific discoveries 'a sentimental nightmare', some of the young ladies wanted to say something in reply to those remarks. But both the Lady Principals restrained them and said they should reply not by word, but by deed, if ever they got the opportunity. And they had not long to wait for that opportunity."

"How marvellous!" I heartily clapped my hands. "And now the proud gentlemen are dreaming sentimental dreams themselves.

"Soon afterwards certain persons came from a neighbouring country and took shelter in ours. They were in trouble having committed some political offence. The king, who cared more for power than for good government, asked our kind-hearted Queen to hand them over to his officers. She refused, as it was against her principle to turn out refugees. For this refusal the king declared war against our country.

"Our military officers sprang to their feet at once and marched out to meet the enemy. The enemy, however, was too strong for them. Our soldiers fought bravely, no doubt. But in spite of all their bravery the foreign army advanced step by step to invade our country.

"Nearly all the men had gone out to fight; even a boy of sixteen was not left home. Most of our warriors were killed, the rest driven back and the enemy came within twenty-five miles of the capital.

"A meeting of a number of wise ladies was held at the Queen's palace to advise as to what should be done to save the land. Some proposed to fight like soldiers; others objected and said that women were not trained to fight with swords and guns, nor with any weapons. A third party regretfully remarked that they were hopelessly weak of body.

"'If you cannot save your country for lack of physical strength,' said the Queen, 'try to do so by brain power.'

'There was a dead silence for a few minutes. Her Royal Highness said again, 'I must commit suicide if the land and my honour are lost.'

"Then the Lady Principal of the second university (who had collected sun-heat), who had been silently thinking during the consultation, remarked that they were all but lost, and there was little hope left for them. There was, however, one plan which she would like to try, and this would be her first and last efforts. If she failed in this, there would be nothing left but to commit suicide. All present solemnly vowed that they would never allow themselves to be enslaved, no matter what happened.

"The Queen thanked them heartily, and asked the Lady Principal to try her plan. The Lady Principal rose again and said, 'before we go out the men must enter the zenanas. I make this prayer for the sake of purdah.'

"'Yes, of course,' replied Her Royal Highness.

"On the following day the Queen called upon all men to retire into zenanas for the sake of honour and liberty. Wounded and tired, they took that order rather for a boon! They bowed low and entered the zenanas without uttering a single word of protest. They were sure that there was no hope for this country at all.

"Then the Lady Principal with her two thousand students marched to the battlefield, and arriving there directed all the rays of the concentrated sunlight and heat towards the enemy.

"The heat and light were too much for them to bear. They all ran away panic-stricken, not knowing in their bewilderment how to counteract that scorching heat. When they fled away leaving their guns and other ammunitions of war, they were burnt down by means of the same sun-heat. Since then no one has tried to invade our country any more."

"And since then your countrymen never tried to come out of the zenana?"

"Yes, they wanted to be free. Some of the police commissioners and district magistrates sent word to the Queen to the effect that the military officers certainly deserved to be imprisoned for their failure; but they never neglected their duty and therefore they should not be punished and they prayed to be restored to their respective offices.

"Her Royal Highness sent them a circular letter intimating to them that if their services should ever be needed they would be sent for, and that in the meanwhile they should remain where they were. Now that they are accustomed to the purdah system and have ceased to grumble at their seclusion, we call the system 'Mardana' instead of 'zenana'."

"But how do you manage," I asked Sister Sara, "to do without the police or magistrates in case of theft or murder?"

"Since the 'Mardana' system has been established, there has been no more crime or sin; therefore we do not require a policeman to find out a culprit, nor do we want a magistrate to try a criminal case."

"That is very good, indeed. I suppose if there was any dishonest person, you could very easily chastise her. As you gained a decisive victory without shedding a single drop of blood, you could drive off crime and criminals too without much difficulty!"

"Now, dear Sultana, will you sit here or come to my parlour?" she asked me.

"Your kitchen is not inferior to a queen's boudoir!" I replied with a pleasant smile, "but we must leave it now; for the gentlemen may be cursing me for keeping them away from their duties in the kitchen so long." We both laughed heartily.

"How my friends at home will be amused and amazed, when I go back and tell them that in the far-off Ladyland, ladies rule over the country and control all social matters, while gentlemen are kept in the Mardanas to mind babies, to cook and to do all sorts of domestic work; and that cooking is so easy a thing that it is simply a pleasure to cook!"

"Yes, tell them about all that you see here."

"Please let me know, how you carry on land cultivation and how you plough the land and do other hard manual work."

"Our fields are tilled by means of electricity, which supplies motive power for other hard work as well, and we employ it for our aerial conveyances too. We have no railroad nor any paved streets here."

"Therefore neither street nor railway accidents occur here," said I. "Do not you ever suffer from a lack rainwater?" I asked.

"Never since the 'water balloon' has been set up. You see the big balloon and pipes attached thereto. By their aid we can draw as much rainwater as we require. Nor do we ever suffer from flood or thunderstorms. We are all very busy making nature yield as much as she can. We do not find time to quarrel with one another as we never sit idle. Our noble Queen is exceedingly fond of botany; it is her ambition to convert the whole country into one grand garden."

"The idea is excellent. What is your chief food?"

"Fruits."

"How do you keep your country cool in hot weather? We regard the rainfall in summer as a blessing from Heaven."

"When the heat becomes unbearable, we sprinkle the ground with plentiful showers drawn from the artificial fountains. And in cold weather we keep our room warm with sun-heat."

She showed me her bathroom, the roof of which was removable. She could enjoy a shower bath whenever she liked, by simply removing the roof (which was like the lid of a box) and turning on the tap of the shower pipe.

"You are a lucky people!" I said. "You know no want. What is your religion, may I ask?"

"Our religion is based on Love and Truth. It is our religious duty to love one another and to be absolutely truthful. If any person lies, she or he is..."

"Punished with death?"

"No, not with death. We do not take pleasure in killing a creature of God, especially a human being. The liar is asked to leave this land for good and never to come to it again."

"Is an offender never forgiven?"

"Yes, if that person repents sincerely."

"Are you not allowed to see any man, except your own relations?"

"No one except sacred relations."

"Our circle of sacred relations is very limited; even first cousins are not sacred."

"But ours is very large; a distant cousin is as sacred as a brother."

"That is very good. I see purity itself reigns over your land. I should like to see the good Queen, who is so wise and far-sighted and who has made all these rules."

"All right," said Sister Sara.

Then she screwed a couple of seats onto a square plank. To this plank she attached two smooth and well-polished balls. When I asked her what the balls were for, she said they were hydrogen balls and they were used to overcome the force of gravity. The balls were of different capacities to be used according to the different weights desired to be overcome. She then fastened to the air-car two wing-like blades, which she said were worked by electricity. After we were comfortably seated she touched a knob and the blades began to whirl, moving faster and faster every moment. At first we were raised to the height of about six or seven feet and then off we flew. And before I could realize that we had commenced moving, we reached the garden of the Queen.

My friend lowered the air-car by reversing the action of the machine, and when the car touched the ground the machine was stopped and we got out.

I had seen from the air-car the Queen walking on a garden path with her little daughter (who was four years old) and her maids of honour.

"Halloo! You here!" cried the Queen addressing Sister Sara. I was introduced to Her Royal Highness and was received by her cordially without any ceremony.

I was very much delighted to make her acquaintance. In the

course of the conversation I had with her, the Queen told me that she had no objection to permitting her subjects to trade with other countries. "But," she continued, "no trade was possible with countries where the women were kept in the zenanas and so unable to come and trade with us. Men, we find, are rather of lower morals and so we do not like dealing with them. We do not covet other people's land, we do not fight for a piece of diamond though it may be a thousand-fold brighter than the Koh-i-Noor, nor do we grudge a ruler his Peacock Throne. We dive deep into the ocean of knowledge and try to find out the precious gems, which nature has kept in store for us. We enjoy nature's gifts as much as we can."

After taking leave of the Queen, I visited the famous universities, and was shown some of their manufactories, laboratories and observatories.

After visiting the above places of interest we got again into the air-car, but as soon as it began moving, I somehow slipped down and the fall startled me out of my dream. And on opening my eyes, I found myself in my own bedroom still lounging in the easy-chair!

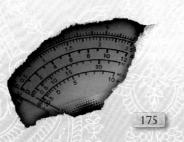

THINKING TIME

TIME AFTER TIME

2 0 1 1

STEPHEN JAMES

MALLORY EASED BACK in one of the spongy, moulded seats of the shuttle. Beside him the outer walls of the Cosmotron12 Collider slid past. He was travelling along a short section of the 54 kilometres of tubing that completed the structure. He'd been round the entire perimeter many times, never failing to marvel at its colossal size and to imagine the vast mass of Earth's crust above his head. This was the third generation of particle accelerator and it had already raised high expectations. Mallory was determined that his particular brainchild would not disappoint a world crying out for something spectacular – something to justify the monumental effort the Collider12 represented.

Of course, he knew he was one of many responsible for the

Cosmotron12 – hundreds of technicians, scientists and engineers had laboured the best part of fifteen years to make this happen. The cost in effort, lives and euros was of giddying proportions. Yet, when he thought about his own small but special contribution, that amazing by-product of the whole Cosmotron12 programme that he and only he had anticipated, he couldn't help feeling that he was perched on a pyramid of heroic achievement. A warm glow of satisfaction pulsed inside him. The glow intensified when he thought about how Professor Hatsek had railed and fumed against his entire project.

Professor Hatchet, Mallory liked to call him. The old guy sat there opposite him in the weekly committee meetings on Practice and Safety, looking like a wizened version of Einstein, but without the great man's humour. "You continue with this mad scheme Mallorwy and you will bwing the whole Cosmotwon12 programme into disrepute. You must not play dice with these forces." Strange how he could sometimes pronounce his 'r's and sometimes not.

Mallory spoke to the rest of the committee at that last, brittle meeting, avoiding the professor's glare: "There are no dice involved – just science. As the professor knows only too well, I predicted the phenomenon of Time Skip before the Cosmotron12 was even built. In a paper in *Nature* four years ago..."

"Please, please – not that damn paper. How many times must we hear about that paper!" Hatsek looked as though he'd swallowed something very bitter.

"Four years ago," Mallory persisted still engaging with anyone in the committee who would catch his eye except Hatsek, "I calculated that if a particle vortex of sufficient speed and power could be created, there would be a discernible distortion of time to anything within this vortex. A Time Skip."

Mallory didn't much care for the term 'Time Skip' anymore, but the media had invented the term finding his own scientific labels too hard going – like his 'non-linear temporal anomaly' for example. So Time Skip had stuck. And that's what the public wanted – a Time Skip of 193.488 seconds into the future meant more to them than all the other abstract demands made of the Cosmotron12. The man and woman in the street didn't give a moment's thought to quantum mechanics or supersymmetry or quark gluon plasma or weak and strong nuclear forces, but tell them that the Cosmotron12 could give them a glimpse into the future and they were yours. The military bigwigs were putty in your hands as well, of course. They hung around the Cosmotron12 Programme like hungry dogs waiting for a juicy morsel to fall off the laboratory bench – might there be a ray or beam or energy pulse that would magically obliterate their enemies? No? Shame. What a waste of all those billions. But wait! You say you have something that can skip time and allow us to see three minutes into the future? Surely, that would give us an edge. Possibly see the enemy manoeuvre before they knew it themselves. Wonderful! Let's increase the research budget. Let's double it!

So, while the military brains fantasized about weapons, the general public imagined holidays into their own futures and the theorists pored over the mathematical implications of the phenomenon, Mallory quietly planned his next audacious step.

There was one question that everyone wanted the answer to. It was more important than 'How big is the Universe?' Even more important to people than 'How did the Universe begin?' The question Mallory intended to answer was the one that everyone had asked since primitive man had evolved the ability to imagine beyond the immediate necessities of food and shelter. As the millennia rolled on they sought the answer from their shamans, witchdoctors, oracles, prophets and holy men. It was the one question that none of them could answer with any real certainty. Until Mallory, Mallory hoped.

The shuttle whispered to a halt and Mallory stepped from it

directly into the research centre that was his subterranean home-from-home. Time stopped strangely still here. There was no daylight of course, and the lab technicians and fellow researchers worked when they felt like it, so all sense of a daily routine was lost. It was 5:12 a.m. and there were several people already at work in the centre. Van Zandt, grossly overweight, but a brilliant physicist, was wearing falling-down jeans and a t-shirt bearing the message: *WARNING Eating Chocolate Makes Your Clothes Shrink*. Mallory brushed his brow with a finger by way of a greeting to Van Zandt.

"How's it hanging, time bandit?" Van Zandt said as usual in his harsh Terminator-ese.

Mallory smiled again and tipped an imaginary hat.

Van Zandt's particular obsessional research focused on the speed of light. He was challenging its 'artificial limit' as he called it. The Vortex accelerated particles to within a fraction of a second of this artificial limit. The constraints arising from Einstein's imperative – that $E=mc^2$, which strictly denied the possibility of mass travelling beyond the speed of light, was not a definitive barrier to Van Zandt, it was merely a theoretical limit and a challenge. Mallory's work was in the fine band of physics that focused on sub-light speed particle behaviour – just before Einstein's titanic equation came to bear. The Vortex would add a 'whip-crack' to the particles at their previously maximum speed and within that spinning core time itself would undergo distortion.

Like most brilliant people, Van Zandt was certifiably mad.

"Have you heard of Universalism?" Van Zandt once asked Mallory over their sandwich 'lunch' (it was just after midnight).

Mallory inwardly sighed. "No, I don't remember that I have heard of Universalism."

"Well, that's a shame. But I'm not surprised, because I only recently invented it. We all need a God, and mine is the Universe. Hence Universalism. You have to see the Universe as a concept, a God-like entity. We are all made up from its component parts, so we are all part of it. We can't see it or understand it, but we can feel it. We are as connected to it as a proton in an atom is connected to a molecule. Think about it."

And Mallory did so.

Mallory's lab office was directly conjoined with the Particle Vortex Chamber, to give it its full name. His lab office was his inner sanctum, while the chamber was the altar of his work. It was where he offered up his learning and where it was greedily accepted or spat out with disdain. So persuasive had been the arguments in his *Nature* paper (though he said it himself), so irreducible, that for him to be denied a lab office directly connected to the chamber would have been an insult. He had conceived the chamber, had moulded it from a visionary moment during a dream. It was a 'night-gift', something passed on to him the night his father died as Mallory lay weeping in his bed. He imagined himself, as he slept or half-slept, following the spirit of his father down through caverns of rock and twisting tubes of ice into a glorious vault of light – the junction of souls. There he touched his father's cold temple with his own outstretched finger and felt a charge of energy, a stab of life.

He remembered, as he rocked back and forth in his chair in the lab office, the vortex chamber's gradual birthing. He had watched the gantry cranes gently shift the sections of tubing containing the colossal electromagnets with such admirable and patient precision. The vortex chamber was a beautifully engineered doughnut. You entered its centre from below and sealed yourself in with a whine of servomotors closing the steel trapdoor. The chamber was a smooth cylinder at the very heart of the doughnut big enough for one person and a small lab bench. It was grafted onto the outer walls of the Massive Collider like a pimple on a blue whale. The particles, just as they neared the finishing line of their 54-kilometre race through the Collider, were sucked into the vortex and accelerated towards their own oblivion.

There had been over thirty test runs now and each time the plates that recorded the traces of the particles – the very moment they collided with their destination – showed nothing.

But how could particles die? How could they be and then not be within a sealed tubular world from which nothing escaped? Where could they go? It all fitted his own theory, he finally realized. Those super-accelerated particles did not evaporate, did not just vanish. No. They moved into another plane. They moved into a future.

Mallory encrypted the final details of his plan on his laptop.

August 13th

1. *Use cameras to record what happens in the VC during a 3-minute event*

   The VC is equipped with 4 high-speed cameras. Each of these is connected to a monitor in the central lab and everything is recorded automatically once the VC is entered. The next VC test is in five days. I will set up an event that lasts three minutes (193.488 secs) and observe.

2. *Find 'assistant' for the trial*

   Van Zandt is flaky, but earnest. His 'Universalism' theory makes him a good contender. Jerry Wong would do it once he understood the science, but he is highly ethical and just might blow the whistle. What about Galina? She is a total pragmatist – no emotional baggage etc.

3. *Method of 'exit'*

   Guns are out – where would I find a gun? And messy. Drugs are difficult to get hold of and get past security. Doctor Weber – might he help? Probably not, bit of a stuffed shirt. Whole place is humming with high voltage currents. I need to tap into some of the feed cables – possibly the camera circuits. Need at least 100mA to cause definite fibrillation. I can make a simple cardiac catheter. Yes – electricity should be the means.

4. *Decide on a date for the trial – Sept 4th?*

   A test is scheduled for that date. Strangely it is the anniversary of Dad's death.

5. *Secrecy*

   I must keep this absolutely quiet or the fools like Prof Hatchet will see me barred from the VC. When I have the evidence at the end of the trial, I will go public and enjoy watching Hatchet eat his words.

6. *Check will*

On August 18th, the day before the scheduled date for the next Vortex Chamber test, Mallory booked access to the chamber.

There was a motive beyond setting up the experiment. He took the opportunity to 'check' the automatic cameras and arranged with Jean Rebauld, the chief lab technician, for them to be switched off. He had in his tool case a two-metre length of cabling ending in an exposed live wire poking through a sticky pad, an electrical junction box and some insulating tape. While the cameras were switched off he unscrewed the glass panel behind which was one of the cameras. He felt behind the camera and breathed a small sigh of relief when he found the electric cable had plenty of slack. Working quickly, he snipped the cable, bared the wires with his electrician's pliers and, using the junction box, added the length of cable he'd brought with him to the circuit. He coiled this up and hid it behind the camera and then screwed back the glass panel. Mallory then set up his four Time Skip Demos ready for the next day. He then left the chamber making sure he spoke airily to Rebauld and reminded him to reconnect the camera circuit.

Twenty-four hours later he was seated in the viewing room in front of the monitors. Also in the room was his nemesis,

Professor Hatsek, who stared stonily at the backs of his hands. Karl Van Zandt was there: "I've put 100 euros on this working Mallory. Don't let me down, now."

Hatsek sniffed with disgust. "Science is not a matter of bets," he said.

"All life is a gamble last time I checked," Van Zandt chuckled.

Galina Madorf and Tomas Korne, both committee members, made up the rest of the observation team. Galina, a petite blonde with crystalline blue eyes, finely chiselled features and almost translucent skin, was an expert on dark matter – a vast proportion of the Universe about which mankind could only guess, a bit like Galina herself. Everyone down here was an expert on something, Mallory thought. Tomas Korne, though was an expert on just about nothing and everything. He ran the show. He was le Directeur. He wore sharp suits at all times. He wore red-framed oval glasses that said 'I'm stylish, I'm eccentric, and I'm very, very rich'. He was a financial alchemist. He looked at pure science and found ways of turning it into pure gold. Mallory didn't trust him. No one did. After this little puppet show, if everything went well, Korne would be onto his pals in Washington talking 'applications', 'revenue streams', and 'investment returns'. "Can we get on with this?" Hatsek sighed. "I have a very full day."

It was 18:42 hours. How could Hatsek have a full day left at a quarter to seven in the evening? In a few minute's time, by pure coincidence, there would be a full moon rising above a horizon few of them witnessed these days, or these nights, immured as they were in their troglodyte underworld.

"I think we are about ready," Mallory said quietly, stifling the nervousness that nearly choked him. The display on the wall showed the Massive Collider data. The 54 kilometres of steel and titanium gut was beginning its electromagnetic peristalsis. Huge amounts of energy were flowing through its metallic musculature. That thrumming murmur and vibration familiar to all the scientists in the observation room was now starting its gentle upward rise, measured and calibrated in those rows of figures displayed in every lab and office in the complex.

In five seconds the energy levels would reach criticality and the particle mass would be sent on its way and arrive at the Vortex Chamber almost instantaneously. Mallory concentrated his focus on the lab rat known as Roadkill, the unwitting and all-important biological experiment. The camera was zoomed in on the unsuspecting rodent, one of four experiments that Mallory had set up to run simultaneously: a digital clock; a four-minute electric fuse connected to a halogen bulb; a family video (it was of him playing beach cricket with his father when he was nine); and the rat.

Roadkill was doing what he loved most – eating. He was holding up his tiny rat hands to his mouth as though shocked at something he'd just seen, nibbling the sunflower seed they held.

The counter read, 3, then 2 then 1. There was a whoop of excitement from Korne and a grunt of disappointment from Hatsek. Galina said slowly "Oh… my… God!" while Van Zandt giggled like a chimp.

Mallory was concentrating on the monitor that showed Roadkill. The rat had vanished! Mallory shot forward in his chair not daring to believe his eyes. The camera zoomed out revealing the whole cage and there was Roadkill again in a near corner, this time contentedly scratching his little furry stomach. Mallory was aware that a huge half moon of a smile was stretching across his face – he was looking at Roadkill three minutes into the rat's future. He felt a slap on his back and Van Zandt said, "You have just demonstrated a piece of scientific magic, but more important – I am 100 euros better off!" and the overweight physicist gave him a bear hug, squashing Mallory up against his pot belly and sweaty t-shirt.

Korne approached Mallory not knowing whether to come from the right or left and finally gave Mallory a quick self-conscious hug. "Magnificent! Quite magnificent! We must now go full clappers on this project." Korne had never quite mastered English idioms. Hatsek had mysteriously disappeared. Mallory wondered to himself if the Prof was now scratching his little furry parts and nibbling on a seed.

The other three experiments had been equally successful. The family video had skipped 193 seconds – Mallory's dad was now licking an ice cream and laughing silently to the camera, his mouth a halo of yellow cream. The halogen bulb burned brightly three minutes ahead of 'real' time and the digital clock skipped from 17:06:38 to 17:09:59.

But Mallory's demonstration had not yet finished. "It's not over you know," he said quietly, almost triumphantly, to those remaining in the viewing room. "The particles are still circling in the vortex. Please, sit down and watch what happens when the vortex slows down." He nodded towards the Cosmotron12 timer. "26 seconds to go." He felt like a showman. What had Van Zandt said? 'Scientific magic'. Yes, exactly – he was a magician with a group of open-mouthed children in his thrall. The seconds slowly ran down as though held back by a time distortion of their own: 16… 15… 14. This was the moment when theory and reality had their own massive collision, 9… 8… 7. It was one thing to pull a rabbit from a hat, or a rat called Roadkill from the present, but 3… 2… 1… the room was suddenly very quiet. The Cosmotron12 had stopped.

A feeling of great achievement warmed the small of his back as he pored over the video playbacks that evening. An endorphin-rush perhaps – though biochemistry was not his field. He felt that warmth increase each time he played back those last moments. Precisely 193.488 seconds after the visceral hum of the Cosmotron12 subsided, the four experiments magically, beautifully and predictably reversed. The clock flipped back to its earlier time, the electronic fuse began its countdown to ignition, there was Dad, once again playing cricket (and not scoffing ice cream) and Roadkill was feeding his face with those nimble little paws. Everything restored to normality with the world still turning gracefully on its axis. If only Roadkill could talk what wonderful things he might have to say, Mallory mused. And a time skip of three minutes to a rat was the human equivalent of one and a quarter hours.

'Human equivalent' – the thought had Mallory slewing sideways into another wide-awake reverie. He spoke out loud a conversation with himself. He did this when troubled or when trying to solve a scientific problem.

Forget about the other experiments. They proved that Roadkill was not a fluke. Let's just think about what happened to a living animal. It skipped into its own future by three minutes. When Cosmotron12 stopped, it skipped back with no apparent ill effects. Anything that happened during those three minutes was 'lost' time. Would Roadkill then live through the lost time or could it be infinitely random and varied? Was Roadkill able to choose where he went in the cage, whether he ate or scratched or slept or whatever ratty decisions he might make? Or were his actions programmed by... by what? Mallory wondered. By an unchangeable future? By something people might call fate? There was only one way to find out.

Most of the people who worked at Cosmotron12 stayed in a hotel a few kilometres away, but a few lived in their basic 'apartments' underground within the complex. Mallory was one of these. And so was Galina. He took a deep breath and called her at her apartment. He was not very good at this he realized. Way out of practice. She picked up.

> *Hello?*
> *Galina — it's Tom Mallory. I er... I wondered. I was wondering if you... whether you might...*
> *Go for a drink?*
> *Yes, exactly. A drink.*
> *At the Hadron bar? In about an hour?*
> *Yes. Perfect. In an hour.*
> *I'll see you then, Tom.*
> *Perfect. See you then.*

THE SECOND EXPERIMENT

He'd put his cards on the table with Galina while they sipped drinks at the Hadron bar. All, that is, except one particular card. He hadn't told her about the additional feature of his experiment that included a length of electrical cable as part of the equipment. Galina knew perfectly well that the committee strictly forbade any experimentation with Cosmotron12 that involved human life or, for that matter, its counterpart. He could not risk her reporting back to the committee. After the experiment anything that happened prior to it would not much matter. After it the world would be forever changed.

He and Galina arrived in the shuttle as they had planned a little after 3:00 a.m. The laboratory complex was deserted. Even Van Zandt was absent. The monitoring team for the routine collider run at 4:00 a.m. would start arriving in half an hour's time. There was no Vortex Chamber activities scheduled for today, so Mallory hoped the lab would remain quiet. A fluorescent tube was flickering. He made a mental note that it needed replacing. Strange, Mallory wondered, that his brain should register a malfunctioning light bulb when he was on the brink of something so momentous.

"You understand what you have to do? It's important that there is a witness to what happens to me. Video can be tampered with. You need to write down your observations."

"Just like any experiment, Tom. I do know what to do. I am a scientist, remember. Quite a good scientist actually."

"Yes, of course. I'm sorry," Mallory said. "Just a bit nervous."

"Understandably," Galina said, showing in her voice a hint of an emotion she was not famous for.

"But remember to go on recording everything – especially during the three minutes after the time skip and at exactly the 193 second mark.

"At 4:00 a.m., when the collider run starts, you will video me from all four cameras as well as observe me through the chamber window." Mallory knew that his 'secondary' experiment would be revealed to Galina by then, but there would be nothing she could do. The chamber was sealed and the collider process was unstoppable. All she could do was watch.

From Galina Madorf's notebooks:
03:24 a.m. Tom enters the VC, closes the trapdoor and connects himself to the sensors. He looks nervous. Heart monitor is showing a pulse rate of 162, but that's to be expected – he is about to try to project himself into the future, after all. Skin sensors show increased perspiration. That is obvious just by looking at him. He has beside him the digital clock used in the previous experiment, the electronic fuse connected to the halogen bulb, and the video of himself and his father playing on the beach. The only thing missing is the rat, Roadkill. Tom is standing in for Roadkill. 04:00 a.m. I can hear the collider starting up. Tom can hear it too. He looked at me and gave me a wink. I am beginning to realize the enormity of what he's doing. This is science as it should be – confrontation of scientist with the utterly unknown. Am I falling in love with him?

In The Vortex Chamber Mallory felt as if he was standing under a waterfall with the deafening roar and crushing weight of speeding particles. Suddenly, there was silence – a huge and bottomless pit of silence. He checked himself quickly – everything seemed in order. He looked up to the observation window. Galina looked worried. The halogen bulb glowed brightly, his father was eating ice cream and his clock showed 04:03:15 while hers read 04:00:02. There was very little time. Mallory took a screwdriver from his pocket, unscrewed the glass panel in front of one of the four video cameras and withdrew the cabling he'd previously hidden with its live wire protruding through a sticky pad. He glanced up at Galina. She was frowning in confusion that turned to disbelief as he mouthed 'Goodbye,' to her and pressed the cable end to his chest.

He died quickly and painfully, his brain yielding to its oxygen starvation with fanatical reluctance. There were random memories as the synapses sparked in their death throes: eating burnt toast, jumping into a swimming pool, grazing his knee. Hundreds of these memories flicked on and flicked off and then there was darkness, but not a black darkness. It was more a suffusion of purples and crimsons that gradually coalesced into a weak glow. He felt no panic, just a deep, deep restfulness. He did not think as he had nothing with which to think. He simply 'was'. A pinpoint of light formed in the purple glow and slowly grew in size and brightness. It moved towards him or he to it. Finally, finally, he was engulfed.

04:01:35 Tom, what have you done? You silly, silly man. I tried to open the trap door, but it is locked from inside. Tom is lying on the floor of the chamber. He is unconscious. I think he might be... he electrocuted himself with a wire taken from behind one of the glass panels. He must have planned this. To see what happens when he dies and then to cheat death by skipping back to the present. We are nearly at the 193-second point. Tom just stood up as though nothing had happened to him.

04:00 I can hear collider starting up. Tom can hear it too. He looked at me and gave me a wink. I am beginning to realize the enormity of what he is doing. This is science as it should be — confrontation of scientist with the utterly unknown. Am I falling in love with him?

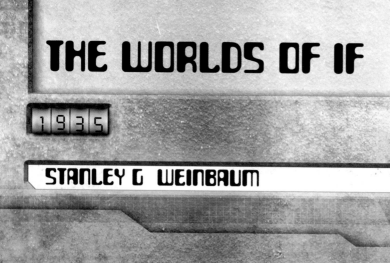

THE WORLDS OF IF

1935

STANLEY G WEINBAUM

I **STOPPED** on the way to Staten Island Airport to call up, and that was a mistake, doubtless, since I had a chance of making it otherwise. But the office was affable. "We'll hold the ship five minutes for you," the clerk said. "That's all we can do."

So I rushed back to my taxi and we spun off to the third level and sped across the Staten Bridge like a comet treading a steel rainbow. I had to be in Moscow by evening, by eight o'clock in fact, for the opening of bids on the Ural Tunnel. The Government required the personal presence of an agent of each bidder, but the firm should have known better than to send me, Dixon Wells, even though the N J Wells Corporation is, so to speak, my father. I have a – well, an undeserved reputation for being late to everything; something always comes up to prevent me from getting anywhere on time. It's never my fault; this time it was a chance encounter with my old physics professor, old Haskel van Manderpootz. I couldn't very well just say hello and goodbye to him; I'd been a favourite of his back in the college days of 2014.

I missed the airliner, of course. I was still on the Staten Bridge when I heard the roar of the catapult and the Soviet rocket Baikal hummed over us like a tracer bullet with a long tail of flame.

We got the contract anyway; the firm wired our man in

Beirut and he flew up to Moscow, but it didn't help my
reputation. However, I felt a great deal better when I saw the
evening papers; the Baikal, flying at the north edge of the
eastbound lane to avoid a storm, had locked winds with a British
fruitship and all but a hundred of her five hundred passengers
perished in the crash. I had almost become 'the late Mr Wells' in
a grimmer sense.

I'd made an engagement for the following week with old van
Manderpootz. It seems he'd transferred to NYU as head of the
department of Newer Physics – that is, of Relativity. He
deserved it; the old chap was a genius if ever there was one, and
even now, eight years out of college, I remember more from his
course than from half a dozen in calculus, steam and gas,
mechanics, and other hazards on the path to an engineer's
education, So on Tuesday night I dropped in an hour or so late,
to tell the truth, since I'd forgotten about the engagement until
mid-evening.

He was reading in a room as disorderly as ever. "Humph!" he
granted. "Time changes everything but habit, I see. You were a
good student, Dick, but I seem to recall that you always arrived
in class toward the middle of the lectures."

"I had a course in East Hall just before," I explained. "I
couldn't seem to make it in time."

"Well, it's time you learned to be on time," he growled. Then
his eyes twinkled. "Time!" he said. "The most fascinating word in
the language. Here we've used it five times (there goes the sixth
time – and the seventh!) in the first minute of conversation; each
of us understands the other, yet science is just beginning to learn
its meaning. Science? I mean that I am just beginning to learn."

I sat down. "You and science are synonymous," I grinned. "Aren't you one of the world's outstanding physicists?"

"One of them!" he snorted. "One of them! And who are the others?"

"Oh, Corveille and Hastings and Shrimski – "

"Bah! Would you mention them in the same breath with the name of van Manderpootz? A pack of jackals, eating the crumbs of ideas that drop from my feast of thoughts! Had you gone back into the last century, now – had you mentioned Einstein and de Sitter – there, perhaps, are names worthy to rank with (or just below) van Manderpootz!"

I grinned again in amusement. "Einstein was considered pretty good, wasn't he?" I remarked. "After all, he was the first to tie time and space to the laboratory. Before him they were just philosophical concepts."

"He didn't!" rasped the professor. "Perhaps, in a dim, primitive fashion, he showed the way, but I – I, van Manderpootz – am the first to seize time, drag it into my laboratory, and perform an experiment on it."

"Indeed? And what sort of experiment?"

"What experiment, other than simple measurement, is it possible to perform?" he snapped.

"Why – I don't know. To travel in it?"

"Exactly."

"Like these time machines that are so popular in the current magazines? To go into the future or the past?"

"Bah! Many bahs! The future or the past – *pfui*! It needs no van Manderpootz to see the fallacy in that. Einstein showed us that much."

"How? It's conceivable, isn't it?"

"Conceivable? And you, Dixon Wells, studied under van Manderpootz!" He grew red with emotion, then grimly calm. "Listen to me. You know how time varies with the speed of a system – Einstein's relativity."

"Yes."

"Very well. Now suppose then that the great engineer Dixon Wells invents a machine capable of travelling very fast, enormously fast, nine-tenths as fast as light. Do you follow? Good. You then fuel this miracle ship for a little jaunt of a half-million miles, which, since mass (and with it inertia) increases according to the Einstein formula with increasing speed, takes all the fuel in the world. But you solve that. You use atomic energy. Then, since at nine-tenths light-speed, your ship weighs about as much as the Sun, you disintegrate North America to give you sufficient motive power. You start off at that speed, a hundred and sixty-eight thousand miles per second, and you travel for two hundred and four thousand miles. The acceleration has now crushed you to death, but you have penetrated the future." He paused, grinning sardonically. "Haven't you?"

"Yes."

"And how far?"

I hesitated.

"Use your Einstein formula!" he screeched. "How far? I'll tell you. One second!" He grinned triumphantly. "That's how possible it is to travel into the future. And as for the past – in the first place, you'd have to exceed light-speed, which immediately entails the use of more than an infinite number of horsepowers. We'll assume that the great engineer Dixon Wells solves that little problem too, even though the energy output of the whole Universe is not an infinite number of horsepowers. Then he applies this more than infinite power to travel at two hundred and four thousand miles per second for ten seconds. He has then penetrated the past. How far?"

Again I hesitated.

"I'll tell you. One second!" He glared at me. "Now all you have to do is to design such a machine, and then van Manderpootz will admit the possibility of travelling into the future – for a limited number of seconds. As for the past, I have just explained that all the energy in the Universe is insufficient for that."

"But," I stammered, "you just said that you – "

"I did not say anything about travelling into either the future or the past, which I have just demonstrated to you to be impossible – a practical impossibility in the one case and an absolute one in the other."

"Then how do you travel in time?"

"Not even van Manderpootz can perform the impossible," said the professor, now faintly jovial. He tapped a thick pad of typewriter paper on the table beside him. "See, Dick, this is the world, the Universe." He swept a finger down it. "It is long in time, and," – sweeping his hand across it – "it is broad in space, but," – now jabbing his finger against its centre – "it is very thin in the fourth dimension. Van Manderpootz takes always the shortest, the most logical course. I do not travel along time, into past or future. No. Me, I travel across time, sideways!"

I gulped. "Sideways into time! What's there?"

"What would naturally be there?" he snorted. "Ahead is the

future; behind is the past. Those are real, the worlds of past and future. What worlds are neither past nor future, but contemporary and yet – extemporal – existing, as it were, in time parallel to our time?"

I shook my head.

"Idiot!" he snapped. "The conditional worlds, of course! The worlds of 'if'. Ahead are the worlds to be; behind are the worlds that were; to either side are the worlds that might have been – the worlds of if!"

"Eh?" I was puzzled. "Do you mean that you can see what will happen if I do such and such?"

"No!" he snorted. "My machine does not reveal the past nor predict the future. It will show, as I told you, the conditional worlds. You might express it, by 'if I had done such and such, so and so would have happened.' The worlds of the subjunctive mode."

"But – are those – worlds of if – real?"

"Real? What is real? They are real, perhaps, in the sense that two is a real number as opposed to V-2, which is imaginary. They are the worlds that would have been if – do you see?"

I nodded. "Dimly. You could see, for instance, what New York would have been like if England had won the Revolution instead of the Colonies."

"That's the principle, true enough, but you couldn't see that on the machine. Part of it, you see, is a Horsten psychomat (stolen from one of my ideas, by the way) and you, the user, become part of the device. Your own mind is necessary to furnish the background. For instance, if George Washington could have used the mechanism after the signing of peace, he could have seen what you suggest. We can't. You can't even see what would have happened if I hadn't invented the thing, but I can. Do you understand?"

"Of course. You mean the background has to rest in the past experiences of the user."

"You're growing brilliant," he scoffed. "Yes. The device will show ten hours of what would have happened if – condensed, of course, as in a movie, to half an hour's actual time.'

"Say, that sounds interesting!"

"That," said the professor grandly, "is van Manderpootz's great contribution to human happiness. 'Of all sad words of tongue or pen, the saddest are these: It might have been!' True no longer, my friend Dick. Van Manderpootz has shown that the proper reading is, 'It might have been – worse!'"

It was very late when I returned home, and as a result, very late when I rose, and equally late when I got to the office. My father was unnecessarily worked up about it, but he exaggerated when he said I'd never been on time. He forgets the occasions when he's awakened me and dragged me down with him. Nor was it necessary to refer so sarcastically to my missing the Baikal; I reminded him of the wrecking of the liner, and he responded heartlessly that if I'd been aboard, the rocket would have been late, and so would have missed colliding with the fruitship. It was likewise superfluous for him to mention that when he and I had tried to snatch a few weeks of golfing in the mountains, even the spring had been late. I had nothing to do with that.

"Dixon," he concluded, "you have no conception whatever of time. None whatever."

The conversation I had with van Manderpootz recurred to me. I was impelled to ask, "And have you, sir?"

"I have," he said grimly. "I most assuredly have. Time," he said oracularly, "is money."

You can't argue with a viewpoint like that.

But those aspersions of his rankled, especially that about the Baikal. Tardy I might be, but it was hardly conceivable that my presence aboard the rocket could have prevented the catastrophe. It irritated me; in a way, it made me responsible for the deaths of those unrescued hundreds among the passengers and crew, and I didn't like the thought.

Of course, if they'd waited an extra five minutes for me, or if I'd been on time and they'd left on schedule instead of five minutes late, or if – if!

If! The word called up van Manderpootz and his subjunctivisor – the worlds of 'if', the weird, unreal worlds that existed beside reality, neither past nor future, but contemporary, yet extemporal. Somewhere among their ghostly infinities existed one that represented the world that would have been had I made the liner. I had only to call up Hasket van Manderpootz, make an appointment, and then – find out.

Yet it wasn't an easy decision. Suppose – just suppose that I found myself responsible – not legally responsible, certainly; there'd be no question of criminal negligence, or anything of that sort – not even morally responsible, because I couldn't possibly have anticipated that my presence or absence could weigh so heavily in the scales of life and death, nor could I have known in which direction the scales would tip. Just – responsible; that was all. Yet I hated to find out.

I hated equally not finding out. Uncertainty has its pangs too, quite as painful as those of remorse. It might be less nerveracking to know myself responsible than to wonder, to waste thoughts in vain doubts and futile reproaches. So I seized the visiphone, dialled the number of the University and at length gazed on the broad, humorous, intelligent features of van Manderpootz, dragged from a morning lecture by my call.

I was all but prompt for the appointment the following evening, and might actually have been on time but for an unreasonable traffic officer who insisted on booking me for speeding. At any rate, van Manderpootz was impressed.

"Well!" he rumbled. "I almost missed you, Dixon. I was just going over to the club, since I didn't expect you for an hour. You're only ten minutes late."

I ignored this. "Professor, I want to use your – uh – your subjunctivisor."

"Eh? Oh, yes. You're lucky, then. I was about to dismantle it."

"Dismantle it! Why?"

"It has served its purpose. It has given birth to an idea far more important than itself. I shall need the space it occupies."

"But what is the idea, if it's not too presumptuous of me to ask?"

"It is not too presumptuous. You and the world which awaits it so eagerly may both know, but you bear it from the lips of the author. It is nothing less than the autobiography of van Manderpootz!" He paused impressively.

I gaped. "Your autobiography?"

"The world, though perhaps unaware, needs it. I shall detail my life, my work. I shall reveal myself as the man responsible for the three years' duration of the Pacific War of 2004.

"You?"

"None other. Had I not been a loyal Netherlands subject at that time, and therefore neutral, the forces of Asia would have been crushed in three months instead of three years. The subjunctivisor tells me so; I would have invented a calculator to forecast the chances of every engagement; van Manderpootz would have removed the hit or miss element in the conduct of war." He frowned solemnly. "There is my idea. The autobiography of van Manderpootz. What do you think of it?"

I recovered my thoughts. "It's – uh – it's colossal!" I said vehemently. "I'll buy a copy myself. Several copies. I'll send 'em to my friends. But – couldn't I see your subjunctivisor before it's dismantled to make way for the greater work?"

"Ah! You wish to find out something?"

"Yes, professor. Do you remember the Baikal disaster of a week or two ago? I was to have taken that liner to Moscow. I just missed it." I related the circumstances.

"Humph!" he grunted. "You wish to discover what would have happened had you caught it, eh? Well, I see several possibilities. Among the world of 'if' is the one that would have been real if you had been on time, the one that depended on the vessel waiting for your actual arrival, and the one that hung on your arriving within the five minutes they actually waited. In which are you interested?"

"Oh – the last one." That seemed the likeliest. After all, it was too much to expect that Dixon Wells could ever be on time, and as to the second possibility – well, they hadn't waited for me, and that in a way removed the weight of responsibility.

"Come on," rumbled van Manderpootz. I followed him across

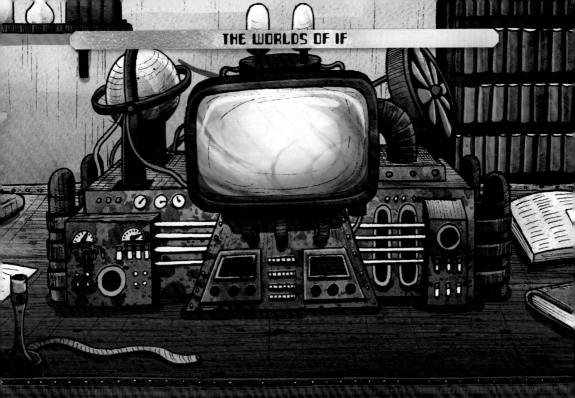

to the Physics Building and into his littered laboratory. The device still stood on the table and I took my place before it, staring at the screen of the Horsten psychomat. I waved a signal to van Manderpootz, the thing clicked, and the subjunctivisor was on.

The grassless clay of the field appeared. It is a curious thing about the psychomat that you see only through the eyes of your image on the screen. It lends a strange reality to the working of the toy; I suppose a sort of self-hypnosis is partly responsible.

I was rushing over the ground towards the glittering, silver-winged projectile that was the Baikal. A glowering officer waved me on, and I dashed up the slant of the gangplank and into the ship; the port dropped and I heard a long 'whew!' of relief.

"Sit down!" barked the officer, gesturing toward an

unoccupied seat. I fell into it; the ship quivered under the thrust of the catapult, grated harshly into motion, and then was flung bodily into the air. The blasts roared instantly, then settled to a more muffled throbbing, and I watched Staten Island drop down and slide back beneath me. The giant rocket was under way.

"Whew!" I breathed again. "Made it!" I caught an amused glance from my right. I was in an aisle seat; there was no one to my left, so I turned to the eyes that had flashed, glanced, and froze staring.

It was a girl. Perhaps she wasn't actually as lovely as she looked to me; after all, I was seeing her through the half-visionary screen of a psychomat. I've told myself since that she couldn't have been as pretty as she seemed, that it was due to my own imagination filling in the details. I don't know; I remember only that I stared at curiously lovely silver-blue eyes and velvety dark- brown hair, and a small amused mouth, and an impudent nose. I kept staring until she flushed.

"I'm sorry," I said quickly. "I – was startled."

There's a friendly atmosphere aboard a trans-oceanic rocket. The passengers are forced into a crowded infirmary for anywhere from seven to twelve hours, and there isn't much room for moving about. Generally, one strikes up an acquaintance with his neighbours; introductions aren't at all necessary, and the custom is simply to speak to anybody you choose – something like an all-day trip on the railroad trains of the last century, I suppose. You make friends for the duration of the journey, and then, nine times out of ten, you never hear of your travelling companions again.

The girl smiled. "Are you the individual responsible for the delay in starting?"

I admitted it. "I seem to be chronically late. Even watches lose time as soon as I wear them."

She laughed. "Your responsibilities can't be very heavy."

We talked. Her name, it developed, was Joanna Caldwell, and she was going as far as Paris. She was an artist, or hoped to be one day, and of course there is no place in the world that can supply both training and inspiration like Paris. So it was there she was bound for a year of study, and despite her demurely humorous lips and laughing eyes, I could see that the business was of vast importance to her. I gathered that she had worked hard for the year in Paris, had scraped and saved for three years as fashion illustrator for some woman's magazine, though she couldn't have been many months over twenty-one. Her painting meant a great deal to her, and I could understand it. I'd felt that way about polo once.

So, we were sympathetic spirits from the beginning. I knew that she liked me, and it was obvious that she didn't connect Dixon Wells with the N J Wells Corporation. And as for me – well, after that first glance into her silver eyes, I simply didn't care to look anywhere else. The hours seemed to drip away like minutes while I watched her.

You know how those things go. Suddenly I was calling her Joanna and she was calling me Dick, and it seemed as if we'd been doing just that all our lives. I'd decided to stop over in Paris on my way back from Moscow, and I'd secured her promise to let me see her. She was different, I tell you; cool and humorous, yet sympathetic and serious, and as pretty as a Majolica figurine.

We could scarcely realize it when the steward passed along to take orders for luncheon. Four hours out? It seemed like forty minutes. And we had a pleasant feeling of intimacy in the discovery that both of us liked lobster salad and detested oysters. It was another bond; I told her whimsically that it was an omen, nor did she object to considering it so.

Afterwards we walked along the narrow aisle to the glassed-in observation room up forward. It was almost too crowded for entry, but we didn't mind that at all, as it forced us to sit very close together. We stayed long after both of us had begun to notice the stuffiness of the air.

It was just after we had returned to our seats that the catastrophe occurred. There was no warning save a sudden lurch, the result, I suppose, of the pilot's futile last-minute attempt to swerve – just that and then a grinding crash and a terrible sensation of spinning, and after that a chorus of shrieks that were like the sounds of a battle.

It was a battle. Five hundred people were picking themselves up from the floor, were trampling each other, milling around, being cast helplessly down as the great rocket-plane, its left wing but a broken stub, circled downward towards the Atlantic.

The shouts of officers sounded and a loudspeaker blared. "Be calm," it kept repeating, and then, "There has been a collision. We have contacted a surface ship. There is no danger – There is no danger – "

I struggled up from the debris of shattered seats. Joanna was gone; just as I found her crumpled between the rows, the ship struck the water with a jar that set everything crashing again. The speaker blared, "The lifebelts are under the seats."

I dragged a belt loose and snapped it around Joanna, then

donned one myself. The crowd was surging forwards now, and the tail end of the ship began to drop. There was water behind us, sloshing in the darkness as the lights went out. An officer came sliding by, stooped, and fastened a belt about an unconscious woman ahead of us. "You all right?" he yelled, and passed on without waiting for an answer.

The speaker must have been cut onto a battery circuit. "And get as far away as possible," it ordered suddenly. "Jump from the forward port and get as far away as possible. A ship is standing by. You will be picked up. Jump from the – " It went dead again.

I got Joanna untangled from the wreckage. She was very pale; her silvery-blue eyes were closed. I started dragging her slowly and painfully towards the forward port, and the slant of the floor increased until it was like the slide of a ski-jump. The officer passed by again. "Can you manage her?" he asked, and again dashed away.

I was getting there. The crowd around the port looked smaller, or was it simply huddling closer? Then suddenly, a wail of fear and despair went up, and there was a roar of water. The observation room walls had given. I saw the green surge of waves, and a billowing deluge rushed down upon us. I had been late again.

That was all. I raised shocked and frightened eyes from the subjunctivisor to face van Manderpootz, who was scribbling on the edge of the table.

"Well?" he asked.

I shuddered. "Horrible!" I murmured. "We – I guess we wouldn't have been among the survivors."

"We, eh? We?" His eyes twinkled.

I did not enlighten him.

I thanked him, said goodnight and went dolorously home.

Even my father noticed something queer about me. The day I got to the office only five minutes late, he called me in for some anxious questioning as to my health. I couldn't tell him anything, of course. How could I explain that I'd been late once too often, and had fallen in love with a girl two weeks after she was dead?

The thought drove me nearly crazy. Joanna! Joanna with her silvery eyes now lay somewhere at the bottom of the Atlantic. I went around half dazed, scarcely speaking. One night I actually lacked the energy to go home and sat smoking in my father's big overstuffed chair in his private office until I finally dozed off. The next morning, when old N J entered and found me there before him, he turned pale as paper, staggered, and gasped, "My heart!" It took a lot of explaining to convince him that I wasn't early at the office but just very late going home.

At last I felt that I couldn't stand it. I had to do something – anything at all. I thought finally of the subjunctivisor. I could see – yes, I could see what would have transpired if the ship hadn't been wrecked! I could trace out that weird, unreal romance hidden somewhere in the worlds of 'if'. I could, perhaps, wring a sombre, vicarious joy from the things that might have been. I could see Joanna once more!

It was late afternoon when I went over to van Manderpootz's quarters. He wasn't there; I encountered him finally in the hall of the Physics Building.

"Dick!" he exclaimed. "Are you sick?"

"Sick? No, not physically. Professor, I've got to use your subjunctivisor again. I've got to!"

"Oh – that toy. You're too late, Dick. I've dismantled it. I have a better use for the space."

I gave a miserable groan and was tempted to damn the autobiography of the great van Manderpootz. A gleam of sympathy showed in his eyes, and he took my arm, dragging me into the little office adjoining his laboratory.

"Tell me," he commanded.

I did. I guess I made the tragedy plain enough, for his heavy brows knit in a frown of pity. "Not even van Manderpootz can bring back the dead," he murmured. "I'm sorry, Dick. Take your mind off the affair. Even if my subjunctivisor were available, I wouldn't permit you to use it. That would be but to turn the knife in the wound." He paused. "Try to find something else to occupy your mind. Do as van Manderpootz does. Find forgetfulness in work."

"Yes," I responded dully. "But who'd want to read my autobiography? That's all right for you."

"Autobiography? Oh! I remember. No, I have abandoned that. History itself will record the life and works of van Manderpootz. Now I am engaged in a far grander project."

"Indeed?" I was utterly, gloomily disinterested.

"Yes. Gogli has been here, Gogli the sculptor. He is to make a bust of me. What better legacy can I leave to the world than a bust of van Manderpootz, sculptured from life? Perhaps I shall present it to the city, perhaps to the university. I would have given it to the Royal Society if they had been a little more receptive, if they – if – if!" The last in a shout.

"Huh?"

"If!" cried van Manderpootz. "What you saw in the subjunctivisor was what would have happened if you had caught the ship!"

"I know that."

"But something quite different might really have happened! Don't you see? She – she – where are those old newspapers?"

He was pawing through a pile of them. He flourished one finally. "Here! Here are the survivors!"

Like letters of flame, Joanna Caldwell's name leaped out at me. There was even a little paragraph about it, as I saw once my reeling brain permitted me to read:

'At least a score of survivors owe their lives to the bravery of twenty-eight-year-old Navigator Orris Hope, who patrolled both aisles during the panic, lacing lifebelts on the injured and helpless, and carrying many to the port. He remained on the sinking liner until the last, finally

fighting his way to the surface through the broken walls of the observation room. Among those who owe their lives to the young officer are: Patrick Owensby. New York City; Mrs. Campbell Warren, Boston; Miss Joanna Caldwell, New York City — '

I suppose my shout of joy was heard over in the Administration Building, blocks away. I didn't care; if van Manderpootz hadn't been armoured in stubby whiskers, I'd have kissed him. Perhaps I did anyway; I can't be sure of my actions during those chaotic minutes in the professor's tiny office.

At last I calmed. "I can look her up!" I gloated. "She must have landed with the other survivors, and they were all on that British tramp freighter the Osgood, that docked here last week. She must be in New York — and if she's gone over to Paris, I'll find out and follow her!"

Well, it's a queer ending. She was in New York, but — you see, Dixon Wells had, so to speak, known Joanna Caldwell by means of the professor's subjunctivisor, but Joanna had never known Dixon Wells. What the ending might have been if — if — but it wasn't; she had married Orris Hope, the young officer who had rescued her. I was late again.

PLANETOID 127

1926

EDGAR WALLACE

Three friends, Chap, Elsie and Tim, have been invited to visit Professor Colson, a friend of theirs and Tim's science teacher, who lives in a house with a huge telescope projecting from the roof.

THEY PASSED INTO a wide hall and down a long, broad corridor that was lit on one side by narrow windows through which the girl had a glimpse of a neat courtyard, also surrounded by colourful flowerbeds.

On the other side of the corridor, doors were set at intervals and it was on the second of these that Tim, in passing, read an inscription. It was tidily painted in small, gold lettering:

PLANETOID 127.

"Is that the number of an asteroid?" asked Tim?

"No," said the professor as he opened the door of a large and airy library. "My Planetoid was discovered on a certain 12th of July – 127. And it was not even an asteroid!"

He chuckled.

"Yes, I am interested in asteroids."

His eyes went mechanically to the cornice of the room above the stone fireplace and Tim, looking up, saw that there was a square black cavity in the oaken panelling and wondered what was its significance.

"They are more real and tangible to me than the great planetary masses. Jupiter – a vapour mass; Saturn – a molten mass, yielding the secret of its rings to the spectroscope; Vulcan – no planet at all – between Mercury, which is the nearest planet to the Sun and the Sun itself, there is no planetary body, though some foolish people think there is and have called it Vulcan – "

An elderly footman had appeared in the doorway and the professor hurried across to him. There was a brief consultation and with a word of apology, he went out.

From the black cavity above the fireplace came a thin whine of sound, and then a deafening splutter like exaggerated and intensified 'atmospherics'.

"What is that?" whispered the girl.

Before Tim could answer, the spluttering ceased, and then a soft, sweet voice spoke:

"'Lo... Col–son! *Ja'ze ga shil*? I speak you, Col–son... Planetoid 127... Big fire in my *zehba*... city... big fire..."

There was a click and the voice ceased abruptly, and at that moment Professor Colson came in.

He saw the amazed group staring at the square hole in the

wall, and his lips twitched.

"You heard? I cut off the connection, though I'm afraid I may not get him again tonight."

"Who is he, sir?" asked Tim frowning. "Was that a transmission from any great distance?"

The professor did not answer at once. And then:

"The man who spoke was a man named Colson," he said deliberately; "and he spoke from a distance of one hundred and eighty-six million miles!"

They listened, dumbfounded.

"A hundred and eighty-six million miles?" said Tim incredulously "But, Mr. Colson, that was not your voice I heard?"

He smiled faintly and shook his head.

"That was literally my alter ego – my other self," and then he changed the subject quite abruptly. "Let us have tea," he said, smiling at Elsie.

As they sat at tea, Elsie glanced out admiringly upon the brilliant-hued garden that was visible through the big window, and then she saw something that filled her with astonishment. Two men had come into view round the end of a square-cut hedge. One was a commonplace little fellow. The second was taller and older, and, she judged, of a better class. His long, hawk-like face was bent down towards his companion, and they were evidently talking on some weighty matter.

"By Jove!" said Chap suddenly. "Isn't that Hildreth?"

Mr Colson looked up quickly; his keen blue eyes took in the scene at once.

"Yes, that's Mr Hildreth," he said quietly. "Do you know him?"

"He has often been to our house."

Colson nodded.

"Yes, he is a very important person in the City," he said, with a touch of sarcasm in his voice. "But he is not a very important person here, and I am wondering why he has come again."

He rose quickly and went out of the room, and presently Tim, who was watching the newcomers, saw them turn their heads as with one accord and walk out of sight, evidently towards the professor. When the old man came back there was a faint flush in his cheek and a light in his eye which Tim did not remember having seen before.

"They are returning in half an hour," he said, unnecessarily it seemed, to Elsie.

"We're taking up your valuable time, Mr Colson," she said with a dazzling smile. "I think there's going to be a storm, so we had better get back. Are you coming with us, Tim?"

"Why, surely..." began Chap, but she interrupted him.

"Tim said he had an engagement near and was leaving us here," she said.

Tim had opened his mouth to deny having made any such statement, when a look from her silenced him. A little later, she managed to speak with Tim alone.

"I'm quite sure Mr Colson wants to speak to you," she said; "and if he does, you are not to worry about us."

"But why on earth do you think that?"

"I really don't know." She shook her head. "But I have that feeling. And I'm sure he did not want to see you until those two men came."

How miraculously right she was, was soon proved. As they walked into the garden towards the path leading to the riverside,

Colson said: "Would it be possible for you to come back and spend the night here, Lensman?"

"Why, yes, sir," said Tim in astonishment.

"Return when you can," said Colson in a low voice. "And the sooner the better. There are one or two things that I want to talk over with you – I waited for an opportunity to do so last term, but it never arose."

Tim saw his companions on their way and then he retraced his steps up the hill. He found the professor waiting for him, pacing up and down the garden, his head on his breast, his hands clasped behind him.

"Come back into the library, Lensman," he said – and then, with a note of anxiety in his voice: "You did not see those scoundrels?"

"You mean Dawes and Hildreth?"

"Those are the gentlemen," said the other. "You wouldn't imagine, from my excited appearance when I returned to you, that they had offered me no less than a million pounds. And, by the way, you will be interested to learn that there have been three burglaries in this house during the last month."

Tim gasped. "But surely, sir, that is very serious?"

"It would have been very serious for the burglars if I had, on either occasion, the slightest suspicion that they were in the grounds," said Mr Colson. He led the way into his library.

"I have a secret so profound that I have been obliged to follow the practice of the ancient astronomers."

He pointed through the window to a square stone that stood in the centre of the garden, a stone which the boy had noticed before, though he had dismissed it at once as a piece of meaningless ornamentation.

"That stone?" he asked.

Colson nodded.

"Come, I will show it to you," he said, rising to his feet. He opened a door in what appeared to be the solid wall, and Tim followed him into the garden.

The stone stood upon an ornamental plinth and was carved with two columns of figures and letters.

"But what on earth does that mean?"

"It is a cryptogram," said Mr Colson quietly. "When Huygens made his discovery about Saturn's rings, he adopted this method to prevent himself from being forestalled in the discovery. I have done the same."

His keen ears heard a sound and he pulled out his watch.

"Our friends are here already," he said in a lower voice.

They went back to the library and closed the door, and presently the butler appeared to announce the visitors.

The attitude of the two newcomers was in remarkable contrast. Mr Hildreth was self-assured, a man with the world at his fingertips, and greeted the professor as though he were his oldest friend and had come at his special invitation. Mr Dawes, on the contrary, looked thoroughly uncomfortable.

Tim had a look at the great financier, and he was not impressed. There was something about those hard eyes that was almost repellent.

After perfunctory greetings had passed, there was an awkward pause, and the financier looked at Tim.

"My friend, Mr Lensman, will be present at this interview," said Colson, interpreting the meaning of that glance.

"He is rather young to dabble in high finance, isn't he?" drawled the other.

"Young or old, he's staying," said Colson, and the man shrugged his shoulders.

"I hope this discussion will be carried on in a calm atmosphere," he said. "As your young friend here probably knows, I have made you an offer of a million pounds, on the understanding that you will turn over to me all the information which comes to you by – er – a..." His lip curled. "Mysterious method, into which we will not probe too deeply."

"You might have saved yourself the journey," said Colson calmly. "Indeed, I could have made my answer a little more final, if it were possible; but it was my wish that you should be refused in the presence of a trustworthy witness. I do not want your millions – I wish to have nothing whatever to do with you."

"Be reasonable," murmured Dawes, who took no important part in the conversation.

The old man ignored him, and stood waiting for the financier's reply.

"I'll put it very plainly to you, Colson," said Hildreth, sitting on the edge of the table. "You've cost me a lot of money. I don't know where you get your market 'tips' from, but you're most infernally right. You undercut my market a month ago, and took the greater part of a hundred thousand pounds out of my pocket. I offer to pay you the sum to put me in touch with the source of your information. You have a wireless plant here, and somewhere else in the world you seem to have a miracle-man who seems to be able to foretell the future – with disastrous consequences to myself. I may tell you – and this you will know — that, but for the fact that your correspondent speaks in a peculiar language, I should have had your secret long ago. Now, Mr Colson, are you going to be sensible?"

Colson smiled slowly.

"I'm afraid I shall not oblige you. I know that you have been listening in — I know also that you have been totally baffled. I shall continue to operate in your or any other market, and I give you full liberty to go to the person who is my informant, and who will be just as glad to tell you as he is to tell me, everything he knows."

Hildreth took up his hat with an ugly smile. "That is your last word on it?"

Colson nodded.

"My very last." The two men walked to the door, and turned.

"It is not mine," said Hildreth, and there was no mistaking the ominous note in his tone.

They stood at the window watching the two men until they had gone out of sight, and then Tim turned to his host.

"What does he want really?" he asked.

Mr Colson roused himself from his reverie with a start.

"What does he want? I will show you. The cause of all our burglaries, the cause of this visit. Come with me."

They turned into the passage, and as the professor stopped before the door labelled 'Planetoid 127', Tim's heart began to beat a little faster. Colson opened the door with two keys and ushered him into the strangest room which Tim had ever seen.

A confused picture of instruments, of wires that spun across the room like the web of a spider, of strange little machines which seemed to be endowed with perpetual motion — for they worked all the time – these were his first impressions.

The room was lined with felt, except on one side, where there was a strip of fibrous panelling. Towards this the professor went. Pushing aside a panel, he disclosed the circular door of a safe and, reaching inside his hand, he took out a small red-covered book.

"This is what the burglars want!" he said exultantly. "The Code! The Code of the Stars!"

Tim Lensman could only stare at the professor.

"I don't understand you, Mr Colson," he said, puzzled. "You mean that book is a code... an ordinary commercial code?"

Colson shook his head.

"No, my boy," he said quietly; "that is something more than a code, it is a vocabulary – a vocabulary of six thousand words, the simplest and the most comprehensive language that humanity has ever known! That is why they are so infinitely more intelligent than we," he mused. "I have not yet learned the process by which this language was evolved, but it is certain that it is their universal tongue."

He turned with a smile to the bewildered boy.

"Do you realize," he said as he closed the door, "that there are in this world sounds which never reach the human brain? The lower animals, more sensitive to vibratory waves, can hear noises which are never registered upon the human ear. Suppose somebody was signalling – not from Mars, because there is no analogy to human life on that planet, but from some – some other world, big or little – is it not possible that the sound may be of such a character that not only the ear, even when assisted by the most powerful of microphones, cannot detect, but which no instrument man has devised can translate to an audible key?"

"Do you suggest, sir, that signals of that nature are coming through from outer space?" asked Tim in surprise. And Mr Colson inclined his head.

"Undoubtedly. There are at least three worlds signalling to us," said the science master. "Sometimes the operators make some mechanical blunder, and there is an accidental emission of sound that is picked up on this earth and is credited to Mars. One of the most definite of the three comes from a system which is probably thousands of light-years away. In other words, from a planet that is part of a system beyond our knowledge.

The most powerful telescope cannot even detect the star around which this planet whirls! Another, and fainter, signal comes from an undetected planet beyond the orbit of Neptune."

"But surely life could not exist beyond the orbit of Neptune?" suggested Tim.

"Not life as we understand it," said the professor. "I admit that these signals are faint and unintelligible. But the third planet…"

"Is it your Planetoid 127?" asked Tim eagerly; and Colson nodded.

"I asked you to stay tonight," he said, "because I wanted to tell you something of vital interest to me, if not to science. For the past few months I have been engaged in putting into writing the story of my extraordinary discovery: a discovery made possible by the years of toil I have applied to perfecting the instruments which have placed me in contact with this strange and almost terrifying world."

It seemed as though he were going to continue, and Tim was listening with all ears, but in his definite way the old man changed the subject.

They dined at eight. Neither during the meal nor the period which intervened before bedtime did Mr Colson make any further reference to his discoveries. He disappeared about ten, after showing Tim to his room. The boy was dozing off, when there came a tap at his door.

"Come in, sir," he said, and the professor entered. From his face Tim guessed that something had happened.

He set down the electric lantern he was carrying and came towards the bed. There was a sharp quality in his voice. "Do you remember somebody speaking… the wireless voice? I was not in

the library when the call came through, so I did not hear it distinctly."

"Yes, sir; you told me, it was Colson…"

"I know," said the professor impatiently. "But tell me how he spoke?" His tone was almost querulous with anxiety. "I only heard the end. Was it a gruff voice, rather like mine?"

Tim shook his head.

"No, sir," he said in surprise; "it was a very thin voice, a sort of whine…"

"A whine?" The professor almost shouted the question.

"Yes, sir."

"That is strange," he said, speaking half to himself. "I have been trying to get him all the evening, and usually it is simple. Why should his assistant speak…? I have not heard him for three days. What did he say?"

Tim told him, as far as he could remember, the gist of the message that had come through, and for a long time the professor was silent.

"'He does not speak English very well – the assistant, I mean – and he would find a difficulty in putting into words… you see, our language is very complicated."

He walked slowly to the door and stood for a while, the handle in his hand.

"If anything should happen, you will find my account in the most obvious place." He smiled faintly. "I'm afraid I am not a very good amateur mason…"

With these cryptic words He took his departure. Tim tossed from side to side and dropped into an uneasy doze. He dreamt that he and the professor were stalking through black, illimitable space. Then there was a sharp crash of sound, and Tim sat up in bed. Something had wakened him. In an instant he had slipped out of bed, and had raced out into the corridor. He ran down the stairs, stumbling in the darkness, and presently came to the doors of the library and the room of Planetoid 127.

The library was empty. A quick glance told him that it was not here the professor was to be sought. He had no doubt that in his sleep he had heard the cry of the old man. Trying the door of the Planetoid room, to his consternation he found it was open. Even as he had opened the door he could detect the acrid smell of cordite, and when the light switched on he was not unprepared for the sight which met his eyes An instrument had been overturned; ends of cut wires dangled from roof and wall. But his eyes were for the moment concentrated upon the figure that lay beneath the open safe. It was Professor Colson, and Tim knew instinctively that the old man was dead.

Tim looked over his shoulder to the shivering butler who stood in the doorway. "Get on the telephone to the police," he said; and, when the man had gone, he made a brief examination of the apartment.

One of the heavy shutters that covered the windows had been forced open, and the casement window was ajar. Without hesitation, lightly clothed as he was, Tim jumped through the window onto a garden bed. Which way had the murderer gone? Not to the high road, that was certain. There could only be one avenue of escape, and that was the path that led down to the backwater.

He vaulted up to the windowsill as the shivering butler made his reappearance.

"I've called the police, they're coming up at once," he said.

Stopping only to snatch an electric hand lamp from the hallstand, Tim sped off into the grounds. His progress was painful, for he felt every stone and pebble through the thin soles of his slippers.

Nearer and nearer to the river he came, and presently he heard ahead of him the sound of stumbling footsteps, and challenged his quarry.

"Halt!" he said. The words were hardly out of his mouth when a pencil of flame quivered ahead in the darkness, something whooshed past his head and struck the bole of a tree with a thud. Instantly Tim extinguished his lamp. There was no sound ahead until he heard a splash of water, the hollow sound of feet striking the bottom of a boat, and a faint chug-chug of engines. There was nothing for Tim to do now but to retrace his steps to the house. He came into the room of death to find two police officers in the room. One of them was kneeling by the side of the dead man, the other was keenly surveying the damaged apparatus.

"This is the young gentleman, sir," said the shivering butler, and the officers turned their attention to Tim.

In a few words he described what he had seen, and whilst one of the policemen went to telephone a warning along to the lock-keepers, he gave an account to the other of the events of that night so far as he knew them.

"There have been quite a few burglaries here," said the sergeant. "I shouldn't be surprised if this is the work of the same fellow that tried to do the other jobs. Do you know anything about this?"

He held a sheet of paper to the boy, and Tim took it. It was covered with Colson's fine writing.

"It looks almost as though it were some kind of message he'd been writing down." said the officer. "But who could tell him stuff like that?"

Tim read the message:

"Colson was killed by robbers in the third part of the first division of the day. Nobody knows who did this, but the correctors are searching. Colson said there was a great earthquake in the island beyond the yellow sea. This happened in the sixth division of the day and many were killed. This place corresponds to Japan, but we call it the Island of the Yellow Sea. The great oilfields of the Inland Sea have become very rich, and those who own the fields have made millions in the past few days. There will be…"

Here the writing ended.

"What does he mean by 'Colson was killed in the third division' or whatever it is?" said the dumbfounded policeman. "He must have known he was going to be killed… it certainly beats me."

"It beats me, too," said Tim sadly. "Poor old friend!"

At eleven o'clock came simultaneously Inspector Bennett, from Scotland Yard, and Mr Colson's lawyer: a stout, middle-aged man, who had some information to give.

"Poor Mr Colson always expected such a death. He had made an enemy, a powerful enemy, and he told me only two days ago that this man would stop at nothing."

"Did he give his name?" asked the detective.

Tim waited breathlessly for the answer, but the lawyer shook his head.

"Why did you see him two days ago? On any particular business?"

"Yes," said Mr Stamford, the lawyer. "I came here to make a will, by which this young gentleman was named as Mr Colson's sole heir!"

"Me?" said Tim incredulously. "Surely you must be mistaken Mr Stamford?"

"No, Mr Lensman. Colson had enormous faith in you, and said that he had made a study of your character and was completely satisfied that you could carry on his work. That was the one thing which worried him, the possibility of his life's work being broken off."

Borrowing the old motorcycle of the science master, Tim rode over to Bisham and broke the news to Chap West and his sister. The girl was horrified.

"But, Tim, it doesn't seem possible!" she said. "Why should they do it? The poor old man!"

Tim shook his head. "Something beyond my understanding," he replied. "Mr Colson made a discovery, but what that discovery was we have to learn. One of the last things he told me was that he had written out a full account of his investigations, and I am starting an immediate search for that manuscript."

"Have you any idea what the nature of the discovery was?" asked Chap.

Tim hesitated.

"Yes, I think I have," he said. "Mr Colson was undoubtedly in communication with another planet!"

"Then it was Mars!" cried Chap triumphantly.

"Of course it was not Mars," interrupted his sister scornfully. "Mr Colson told us distinctly that there was no life on Mars."

"Where is it, Tim?" he asked.

"I don't know." Tim shook his head. "I have been questioning his assistants – there were two at the house – but he never took them into his confidence. The only hint they can give me is that when poor Mr Colson was listening in to these mysterious voices he invariably had the receiving gear directed towards the Sun. You know, of course, that he did not use the ordinary aerial, but an apparatus shaped like a convex mirror."

"Towards the Sun?" gasped Chap. "But there can't be any life on the Sun! Why, the temperature of the Sun is umpteen thousand degrees centigrade… and anyway, nobody has ever seen the Sun: you only see the photoscope…"

"All this I know," said Tim, listening patiently, "but there is the fact: the receiving mirror was not only directed towards the Sun, but it moved by clockwork so that it was directed to the Sun at all hours of the day, even when the sky was overcast and the Sun was invisible. I admit that the whole thing sounds incredible, but Colson was not mad. That voice we heard was very distinct."

He went back to the house.

In the weeks which followed the death and funeral of Professor Colson, Tim found every waking minute occupied. He had enlisted the services of the cleverest of scientists, and from the shattered apparatus one of the most brilliant of mechanical minds of the country was rebuilding the broken instruments. Sir Charles Layman, one of the foremost scientific minds in England, had been called into consultation by the lawyer, and to him Tim had related as much as he knew of Professor Colson's secret.

"I knew Colson," said Sir Charles; "he was undoubtedly a genius. But this story you tell me takes us into the realm of fantasy. It isn't possible that life can exist on the Sun; and really, young gentleman, I can't help feeling that you have been deceived over these mysterious voices."

"Then three people were deceived," said Tim firmly. "My friend Chap West and his sister both heard the speaker."

Sir Charles pursed his lips and shook his head.

"It does seem most extraordinary. The mysterious world – where is it? Life in some form may exist on a planetoid, but it is almost certain that these small masses which whirl through space in the zone between Mars and Jupiter are barren globules of rock as dead as the moon and innocent of atmosphere. There are a thousand and one reasons why life could not exist on these planetoids; and of course the suggestion that there can be life on the Sun is preposterous."

Then he asked, with sudden interest:

"Did Professor Colson believe in the existence of Vulcan?"

Tim shook his head. "No, sir, he derided the idea."

"He was right," nodded Sir Charles. "You have found no data, no photographs?"

The word 'photograph' reminded Tim. "Yes, there is a book full of big enlargements, but mostly of a solar eclipse," he said. "They were taken on Friday Island last year."

236

"Would you get them for me?" asked Sir Charles, interested.

Tim went out and returned with a portfolio, which he opened on the table. Sir Charles turned picture after picture without speaking a word, then he laid half a dozen apparently similar photographs side by side and pored over them with the aid of a magnifying glass. They were the conventional type of astronomical photo: the black disc of the moon, the bubbling white edges of the corona; but evidently Sir Charles had seen something else, for presently he indicated a speck with a pen.

"These photographs were taken by different cameras," he said. "And yet they all have this."

He pointed to the pinpoint of white that had escaped Tim's observation. It was so much part of the flame of the corona that it seemed as though it were a spark thrown out by one of those eruptions of ignited gas that flame up from the Sun's surface.

"Surely that is a speck of dust on the negative?" said Tim.

"But it is on all the negatives," said Sir Charles emphatically. "No, I cannot be sure for the moment, but if that is not Zeta or Theta Cankris – it is too large for the star 20 Cankris – then we may be on the way to rediscovering Professor Colson's world! What are your immediate plans?"

"The voice amplifier has been reconstituted," said Tim. "The experts are conducting a test today, though I very much doubt whether they will succeed in establishing communication."

A smile fluttered at the corner of the lawyer's mouth.

"Do you still believe that Mr Colson was in communication with another planet?"

"I'm certain," said Tim emphatically.

He went back to the blue drawing room, and had hardly

entered before Sir Charles came in.

"It is as I thought," said the scientist; "neither Zeta nor Theta! It is, in fact, a distinct body of some kind, and, in my judgment, well outside the orbit of the hypothetical Vulcan. If you look at the back of the photograph..."

He turned it over, and Tim saw that, written in pencil in the microscopic calligraphy of the Professor, were a dozen lines of writing:

"*I knew, of course, that this was a dead world, without any kind of atmosphere or even water. There can be no life there. I made an enlargement by my new process, and this revealed to me a series of flat, rocky valleys.*"

"What the deuce his new process was, heaven only knows!" said Sir Charles in despair. "Poor Colson must have been the most versatile genius the world has known."

Sir Charles waited until the experts had finished the work of reassembling two of the more complicated machines; but, though experimenting until midnight, they could not establish communication, and at last, with a sense of despair, Tim ordered the work to cease for the night.

The whole thing was becoming a nightmare to him. He could not sleep at night. Chap and his sister came over in the morning to assist him in a search, which had gone on ever since the death of Professor Colson.

"We can do no more," said Tim helplessly, "until we have seen the Professor's manuscript. Until then we do not know what we are searching for."

"What about that stone in the garden? Won't that tell you anything?" asked Chap. "I'd like to see it."

They went out into the courtyard
together and stood before the stone in silence.

"Of course, that isn't as difficult as it appears," said Chap, to
whom cryptograms were a passion. "Perhaps, when we find the
sentence, the mystery will be half-solved."

He jotted the inscription down in a notebook, and
throughout the day was puzzling over a solution.

Tim walked to the end of the drive to see his friends off, and
then returned to the study. He was alone in the house now, save
for the servants.

He had taken up his quarters in a spare room immediately

above the library, and for an hour after his visitors had departed he sat on the broad window seat, looking down into the courtyard, now bathed in the faint radiance of the crescent moon. And then – was his eye playing tricks with him? He could have sworn he saw a dark figure melt out of the darkness and move along the shadow of the box hedge.

He pushed open the casement window, but could see nothing. His pulse beat a little quicker as he watched. There was no doubt about it now. In the moonlight the figure was touching the stone, and even as Tim looked the little obelisk fell with a crash.

In a second Tim was out of the room and speeding along the corridor. As he came into view of the figure, it stooped and picked something from the ground.

The manuscript! What a fool he had been! That was where the old man had concealed the story of his discovery! But there was no time for regret: the mysterious visitor had already disappeared into the shadows. Behind him, Tim heard the soft purr of a car engine, and, racing up the slope, he came into view of a red tail light as it disappeared down the broad drive towards the road.

Then he remembered Colson's motorbike, he had left it leaning against the wall. Yes, there it was! He had hardly started the machine going when he heard a crash. The unknown had driven his car through the frail iron gates and was flying along the road to Maidenhead.

The car reached the crest of the hill as Tim came up to its rear, and, heedless of danger, stretched out his hand, and, catching hold of the hood, let the motorbike slip from between his knees.

For a second he held on desperately, his feet swinging in the air, and then, with an effort, he threw his leg over the edge of the hood and dropped breathlessly on to the seat behind the driver. At first the man at the wheel did not realize what had happened, and then, with a yell of rage, he turned and struck blindly at the unauthorised passenger.

The blow missed him by a fraction of an inch, and in another second his arm was around the driver's neck. The car swayed and slowed, and then an involuntary movement of the man revealed the whereabouts of the manuscript. Tim thrust into the inside-pocket and his fingers touched a heavy roll of paper. In a flash the packet was in his hand.

The car was now almost at a standstill, and, leaping over the side, Tim plunged into the hedge by the side of the road. His run home was without event.

There was no sleep for him that night. With successive cups of strong coffee, brought at intervals, he sat poring over the manuscript, page by page, almost incredulous of his own eyes and senses. He had read it again and again until he knew almost every word. Then, locking the papers away in the safe, he walked slowly to the instrument room, and gazed in awe at this evidence of the dead man's genius.

Something within him told him that never in future would human speech pulsate through this network of wires; never again would that strange little amplifier bring within human hearing the thin sounds of space. He turned the switch and set the little machine working; saw the multicoloured lights gleam and glow. But the words that filtered through light and charcoal would, he thought, be dead for everlasting.

His hand had gone out to turn the switch that stopped the machine, when:

"Oh, Colson, why do you not speak to me?"

The voice came from the very centre of the machine. There was no visible microphone. It was as though the lights and the whirling wheels had become endowed with a voice. Tim's heart nearly stopped beating.

"Oh, Colson," wailed the voice, "they are breaking the machines. I have come to tell you this before they arrive. He is dead – he, the master, the wizard, the wonderful man…"

The servant! Mr Colson had told him that it was the servant who had spoken. The astral Colson was dead now. How should he reply?

"Where are you?" he asked hoarsely, but there was no answer, and soon he understood why. Presently:

"I will wait for you to speak. When I hear you I will answer. Speak to me, Colson! In a thousand seconds…"

A thousand seconds! Colson had told him once that wireless waves travel at the same speed as light. Then he was a hundred and eighty million miles away, and a thousand seconds must pass – nearly seventeen minutes – before his voice could reach through space to the man who was listening.

How had he made the machine work? Perhaps the mechanism had succeeded before, but there had been nobody at the other end – wherever the other end might be. And then:

"Oh, Colson, they are here… goodbye!"

There came to him the sound of a queer tap-tap-tap and then a crackle as though of splintered glass, and then a scream, so shrill, so full of pain and horror, that involuntarily he stepped back. Then came a crash, and silence. He waited, hardly daring to breathe, but no sound came. At the end of an hour he turned off the switch and went slowly up to his room.

He awoke to find a youth sitting on the edge of his bed. He was so weary and dulled that he did not recognize Chap, even after he spoke.

"Wake up. I've got some news for you, dear old bird," said Chap. "Hildreth was found just outside Maidenhead, his car broken to bits — they think his steering-wheel went wrong when he was doing sixty an hour. At any rate, he smashed into a tree, and all that's left of his machine is hot iron!"

"Was he killed?"

Chap nodded.

"Completely," he said callously. "And perhaps it's as well for him, for Bennett was waiting at his house to arrest him. Do you know what time it is? It's two o'clock in the afternoon, you lazy devil, and Sir Charles and Stamford want to see you. Sir Charles has a theory..."

Tim swung out of bed and walked to the window, blinking into the sunlit garden.

"All the theories in the world are going to evaporate before the facts," he said. Putting his hand under his pillow, he took out the Professor's manuscript. "I'll read something to you this afternoon.

His breakfast was also his luncheon, but it was not until after the meal was over, and they had adjourned to the library, that he told them what had happened in the night. Bennett, who arrived soon after, was able to fill in some of the gaps of the story.

"Hildreth," he said, "in spite of his wealth and security, was a crook of crooks. He was under the impression that Colson received messages in code and was anxious to get the codebook. By the way, we found the charred remnants of that book in the car. It was burnt out, as you probably know. "

"None of the code remains?" asked Tim anxiously. The detective shook his head.

"No, sir, none. There are one or two words – for instance, 'Zeiith' means 'the Parliamentary system of the third decade', whatever that may mean. It seems an odd sort of code to me."

"That is very unfortunate," said Tim. "I had hoped to devote my time to telling the history of this strange people, and the book would have been invaluable."

"Which people is this?" asked Sir Charles puzzled. "Did our friend get into communication with one of the lost tribes?"

Tim laughed, in spite of himself. "No, sir. I think the best explanation I can offer you is to read Mr Colson's manuscript, which I discovered last night."

"Is it about the planet?" asked Sir Charles quickly, and Tim nodded.

"Then you have discovered it! It is a planetoid…"

Tim shook his head. "No, sir," he said quietly. "It is a world as big as ours."

The scientist looked at him open-mouthed.

"A world as big as ours, and never been discovered by our astronomers? How far away?"

"At its nearest, a hundred and eighty million miles," said Tim.

"Impossible!" cried Sir Charles scornfully. "It would have been detected years ago."

"It has never been detected because it is invisible," said Tim.

"Invisible? How can a planet be invisible?"

"Nevertheless, it is invisible," said Tim. "And now," he said, as he took the manuscript from his pocket, "if you will give me your attention, I will tell you the story of Neo. Incidentally, the cryptogram on the stone reads: 'Behind the Sun is another world!'"

Tim turned the flyleaf of the manuscript and began reading in an even tone.

"My name," the manuscript began "is Charles Royton Colson. In June 1914, my attention was called to a statement made by the Superintendent of the great wireless telegraph station outside Berlin, that he had on three separate occasions taken what he described as 'slurred receptions' from an unknown station. There immediately followed a suggestion that these mysterious dashes and dots had come from Mars. A year later, the wireless station at Cape Cod also reported signals, as did a private station in Connecticut; whilst the Government station at Rio de Janeiro reported that it had heard a sound like 'a flattened voice.' It was obvious that these stories were not inventions, and I set to work. After about six months of hard toil I succeeded in fashioning an instrument which enabled me to test my theories. My main theory was that, if the sound came from another world, it would in all probability be pitched in a key that would be inaudible to human ears. For example, there is a dog whistle which makes no sound that we detect, but which is audible to every dog. My rough amplifier had not been operating for a week when I began to pick up scraps of signals and scraps of words – unintelligible to me, but obviously human speech. Not only was I able to hear, but I was able to make myself heard; and the first startling discovery I made was that it took my voice a thousand and seven seconds to reach the person who was speaking to me.

"After hard experimental work, I succeeded in clarifying the voices, and evidently the person at the other end was as anxious as I to make himself understood and to understand the nature of his unknown correspondent's speech.

"You may imagine what a heartbreaking business it was, with no common vocabulary, invisible to one another, and living possibly in conditions widely different, to make our meaning clear to one another. We made a start with the cardinal numbers, and after a week's interchange we had mastered these. I was then struck with the idea of pouring a glass of water from a tumbler near to my microphone, and using the word 'water'. In half an hour I heard the sound of falling water from the other end and the equivalent word, which will be found in the vocabulary. I then clapped my hands together, and used the word 'hand'. With these little illustrations, which took a great deal of time, began the formation of the dictionary. In the Neo language there are practically no verbs and few adjectives. Very much is indicated by a certain inflexion of voice.

"All the time I was searching the heavens in the vain endeavour to discover the exact location of this world, which was, from the description I had, exactly the same size as ours, and therefore should have been visible. The chief difficulty I had lay in the fact that the voices invariably came from the direction of the Sun. Then came the great eclipse, and, as you know, I went to the South Sea Islands to make observations. It was our good fortune to have fine weather, and at the moment of total eclipse I took several particularly excellent photographs, some of which you will find in the portfolio marked 'L'. In these and photographs taken by other astronomers, you will see, if you make a careful observation, close to the corona, a tiny speck of light, which at first I thought was my world, but which afterwards I discovered was a dead mass of material upon which it was impossible for life to exist.

"One night, when I was turning over the matter in my mind, and examining each photograph in the study of my house on the Thames, the solution flashed on me. This tiny speck, which was not a star, and was certainly not Vulcan, was the satellite of another world, and that world was moving on the same orbit as our own Earth, following exactly the same course, but being, as it was, immediately opposite to us behind the Sun, was never visible! On whatever part of the ellipse we might be, the Sun hid our sister world from us, and that was why the voice apparently came from the Sun, for it was through the solar centre that the waves must pass. Two Earths chasing one another along the same path, never overtaking, never being overtaken,

balancing one another perfectly! It was a stupendous thought!

"I conveyed to my unknown friend, who called himself Colson, though I am under the impression that he probably thought that 'Colson' was the English word for 'scientist' – and I

asked him to make observations. These he sent to me after a few days, confirming my theory. It was after we had begun to talk a little more freely, and my acquaintance with the language had increased so that I could express myself clearly, that it occurred to me there was an extraordinary similarity both in our lives and our environment. And this is the part in my narrative which you will find difficult to believe – I discovered that these two worlds were not only geographically exact, but that the incidents of life ran along on parallel lines. There were great wars in Neo, great disasters, which were invariably duplicated on our Earth, generally from two to three days before or after they had happened in this new world. Men and women were doing in that world exactly as we were doing in ours. There were Stock

Exchanges, railways, aeroplanes, as though twin worlds had produced twin identities; twin inspirations.

"I learnt this first when my friend told me that he had been seeking me for some time. He said that he had had a broken knee some five years ago, and during his enforced leisure he had pointed out the possibility of his having another identity. He said he was frequently feeling that the person he met for the first time was one in reality whom he had seen before; and he was conscious that the thing he did today, he had done a week before. That is a sensation which I also have had, and which every human being has experienced.

"But to go back to the story of his having been laid up with a broken knee. He had no sooner told me this than I realized that I also had had a broken knee – I had a spill on my motorbike – and that I had spent the hours of my leisure pondering the possibility of there being another inhabited planet! In very truth this man was my twin soul: was me, had lived my life, thought my thoughts, performed every action which I performed.

"Then one day my astral friend, Colson, incidentally mentioned that there was great excitement in his town because a man had bought some steel stock which had since risen considerably in price – he mentioned the name – and, glancing through a newspaper, I saw the name of a stock that sounded very similar to that of which he had told me. Moreover, the price was very much as he had mentioned it; and the wild idea occurred to me that if happenings were actually duplicated, I might possibly benefit by my knowledge. With great trepidation I invested the whole of my savings, which were not very considerable, in these shares, and a few days later had the gratification of selling out at a colossal profit. I explained to my friend at the next opportunity what I had done, and he was considerably amused, and afterwards took an almost childish delight in advising me as to the violent fluctuations in various stocks. For years I have bought and sold with considerable benefit to myself. Not only that, but I have been able to warn Governments of impending disasters. I informed the Turkish Government of the great Armenian earthquake, and warned the Lamborn Shipping Company of the terrible disaster which overtook one of their largest liners – though I was not thanked for my pains.

"After this had been going on for some years, I was prepared to learn that my friend had incurred the enmity of a rich man, whom he called Frez on his side, and that this had been brought about unwittingly through me. For this is a curious fact: not everything on this new world is three days in advance of ours. Often it happened that the Earth was in advance, and I was able, in our exchanges, to tell him things that were happening here which had not yet occurred in Neo, with the result that he followed my example, and in the space of a year had become a very rich man.

"Colson, as I called him, had a servant, whose name I have never learnt; he was called the equivalent to 'helper', and I guess, rather than know, that he is a much younger man than my double, for he said that he had been to school as a pupil of Colson's. He too learnt quickly; and if there is any difference in the two worlds, it is a keener intelligence: they are more receptive, quicker to grasp essentials."

Here followed twenty closely written pages of technical

description. Tim folded the manuscript and looked around at the astonished faces. Stamford was the first to break the silence.

"Preposterous!" he spluttered. "Impossible! Absurd! It's a nightmare! Another world – good God!"

"I believe every word of it." It was Sir Charles's quiet voice that stilled the agitated lawyer. "Of course, that is the speck by the side of the corona! Not the world which poor Colson found, but the moon of that world."

"But couldn't it be visible at some time?"

Sir Charles shook his head. "Not if it followed the exact orbit of the Earth and was placed directly opposite – that is to say, immediately on the other side of the Sun. It might overlap at periods, but in the glare of the Sun it would be impossible to see so tiny an object."

He took the manuscript from Tim's hand and read rapidly through the technical description.

"With this," he said, touching the paper, "we shall be able to get into communication with these people. If we only had the vocabulary!" he groaned.

"I am afraid you will never hear from Neo again, sir," said Tim quietly, and told of that brief but poignant minute of conversation he had had before the cry of the dying servant, and the crash of broken instruments, had brought the voice to an abrupt end.

After the lawyer and the scientist had departed, he went with Elsie into the instrument room, and they gazed in silence upon the motionless apparatus.

"The link is broken," he said at last; "it can never be forged again, unless a new Colson arrives on both Earths."

She slipped her arm in his.

"Aren't you glad?" she asked softly. "Do you want to know what will happen tomorrow or the next day?"

He shivered. "No. I don't think so. But I should like to know what will happen in a few years' time, when I'm a little older and you're a little older."

"Perhaps we'll find a new world of our own," said Elsie.

THE TIME TRAVELLER

1895 FROM THE TIME MACHINE

H G WELLS

AND THE DOOR opened wider, and the Time Traveller stood before us. I gave a cry of surprise. "Good heavens, man! What's the matter?" cried the Medical Man, who saw him next. And the whole tableful turned towards the door.

He was in an amazing plight. His clothes were dusty and dirty, and smeared with green down the sleeves; his hair disordered, and as it seemed to me greyer — either with dust and dirt or because its colour had actually faded. His face was ghastly pale; his chin had a brown cut on it — a cut half-healed; his expression was haggard and drawn, as by intense suffering. For a moment he hesitated in the doorway, as if he had been dazzled by the light. Then he came into the room. He walked with just such a limp as I have seen in footsore tramps. We stared at him in silence, expecting him to speak.

He said not a word, but came painfully to the table, and made a motion towards the wine. The Editor filled a glass of champagne, and pushed it towards him. He drained it, and it seemed to do him good: for he looked round the table, and the ghost of his old smile flickered across his face.

"What on earth have you been up to, man?" said the Doctor. The Time Traveller did not seem to hear.

"Don't let me disturb you," he said, with a certain faltering articulation. "I'm all right." He stopped, held out his glass for more, and drank it down in one. "That's good," he said. His eyes grew brighter, and a faint colour came into his cheeks. His glance flickered over our faces with a certain dull approval, and then went round the warm and comfortable room. Then he spoke again, still as it were feeling his way among his words. "I'm going to wash and dress, and then I'll come down and explain things… Save me some of that mutton. I'm starving for a bit of meat."

He looked across at the Editor, who was a rare visitor, and hoped he was all right. The Editor began a question. "Tell you presently," said the Time Traveller. "I'm – funny! Be all right in a minute."

He put down his glass, and walked towards the staircase door. Again I remarked his lameness and the soft padding sound of his footfall, and standing up in my place, I saw his feet as he went out. He had nothing on them but a pair of tattered, blood-stained socks. Then the door closed upon him. I had half a mind to follow, till I remembered how he detested any fuss about himself. For a minute, perhaps, my mind was wool-gathering. Then, "Remarkable Behaviour of an Eminent Scientist," I heard the Editor say, thinking (as is his habit) in headlines. And this brought my attention back to the bright dinner -table.

"What's the game?" said the Journalist. "Has he been doing the Amateur Cadger? I don't follow." I met the eye of the Psychologist, and read my own interpretation in his face. I thought of the Time Traveller limping painfully upstairs. I don't think anyone else had noticed his lameness.

The first to recover completely from this surprise was the Medical Man, who rang the bell – the Time Traveller hated to have servants waiting at dinner – for a hot plate. At that the Editor turned to his knife and fork with a grunt, and the Silent

Man followed suit. The dinner was resumed. Conversation was exclamatory for a little while, with gaps of wonderment; and then the Editor got fervent in his curiosity. "Does our friend eke out his modest income with a crossing? or has he his Nebuchadnezzar phases?" he inquired.

"I feel assured it's this business of the Time Machine," I said, and took up the Psychologist's account of our previous meeting. The new guests were frankly incredulous. The Editor raised objections.

"What was this time travelling? A man couldn't cover himself with dust by rolling in a paradox, could he?" And then, as the idea came home to him, he resorted to caricature. Hadn't they any clothes-brushes in the Future? The Journalist too, would not believe at any price, and joined the Editor in the easy work of heaping ridicule on the whole thing. They were both the new kind of journalist – very joyous, irreverent young men. "Our Special Correspondent in the Day After Tomorrow reports," the Journalist was saying – or rather shouting – when the Time Traveller came back. He was dressed in ordinary evening clothes, and nothing save his haggard look remained of the change that had startled me.

"I say," said the Editor hilariously, "these chaps here say you have been travelling into the middle of next week!"

The Time Traveller came to the place reserved for him . He smiled, in his old way. "Where's my mutton?" he said. "What a treat it is to stick a fork into meat again!"

"Story!" cried the Editor.

"Story be damned!" said the Time Traveller. "I want something to eat. I won't say a word until I get some peptone into my arteries. Thanks. And the salt."

"One word," said I. "Have you been time travelling?"

"Yes," said the Time Traveller, mouth full, nodding his head.

"I'd give a shilling a line for a verbatim note," said the Editor. The Time Traveller pushed his glass towards the Silent Man and rang it with his fingernail; at which the Silent Man, who had been staring at his face, started convulsively, and poured him wine. The rest of the dinner was uncomfortable. For my own part, sudden questions kept on rising to my lips, and I dare say it was the same with the others. The Journalist tried to relieve the tension by telling anecdotes of Hettie Potter. The Time Traveller devoted his attention to his dinner, and displayed the appetite of a tramp. The Medical Man smoked a cigarette, and watched the Time Traveller through his eyelashes. The Silent Man seemed even more clumsy than usual, and drank champagne with regularity and determination out of sheer nervousness. At last the Time Traveller pushed his plate away, and looked round us.

"I suppose I must apologize," he said. "I was simply starving. I've had a most amazing time." He reached out his hand for a cigar, and cut the end. "But come into the smoking room. It's too long a story to tell over greasy plates." And ringing the bell in passing, he led the way into the adjoining room.

"You have told Blank, and Dash, and Chose about the machine?" he said to me, leaning back in his easychair and naming the three new guests.

"But the thing's a mere paradox," said the Editor.

"I can't argue tonight. I don't mind telling you the story, but I can't argue. I will," he went on, "tell you the story of what has happened to me, if you like, but you must refrain from interruptions. I want to tell it. Badly. Most of it will sound like lying. So be it! It's true – every word of it, all the same. I was in my laboratory at four o'clock, and since then… I've lived eight days… such days as no human being ever lived before! I'm nearly worn out, but I shan't sleep till I've told this thing over to you. Then I shall go to bed. But no interruptions! Is it agreed?"

"Agreed," said the Editor, and the rest of us echoed 'Agreed.' And with that the Time Traveller began his story as I have set it forth. He sat back in his chair at first, and spoke like a weary man. Afterwards he got more animated. In writing it down I feel with only too much keenness the inadequacy of pen and ink – and, above all, my own inadequacy – to express its quality. You read, I will suppose, attentively enough; but you cannot see the speaker's white, sincere face in the bright circle of the little lamp, nor hear the intonation of his voice. You cannot know how his expression followed the turns of his story! Most of us hearers were in shadow, for the candles in the smoking-room had not been lit, and only the face of the Journalist and the legs of the Silent Man from the knees downward were illuminated. At first we glanced now and again at each other. After a time we ceased to do that, and looked only at the Time Traveller's face.

"I have already told you of the sickness and confusion that comes with time travelling. And this time I was not seated properly in the saddle, but sideways and in an unstable fashion. For an indefinite time I clung to the machine as it swayed and vibrated, quite unheeding how I went, and when I brought myself to look at the dials again I was amazed to find where I had arrived. One dial records days, and another thousands of days, another millions of days, and another thousands of millions. Now, instead of reversing the levers, I had pulled them over so as to go forward with them, and when I came to look at these indicators I found that the thousands hand was sweeping round as fast as the seconds hand of a watch – into futurity.

"As I drove on, a peculiar change crept over the appearance of things. The palpitating greyness grew darker; then – though I was still travelling with prodigious velocity – the blinking succession of day and night, which was usually indicative of a

slower pace, returned, and grew more and more marked. This puzzled me very much at first. The alternations of night and day grew slower and slower, and so did the passage of the sun across the sky, until they seemed to stretch through centuries. At last a steady twilight brooded over the Earth, a twilight only broken now and then when a comet glared across the darkling sky. The band of light that had indicated the Sun had long since disappeared; for the Sun had ceased to set — it simply rose and fell in the west, and grew ever broader and more red. All trace of the moon had vanished. The circling of the stars, growing slower and slower, had given place to creeping points of light. At last, some time before I stopped, the Sun, red and very large, halted motionless upon the horizon, a vast dome glowing with a dull heat, and now and then suffering a momentary extinction. At one time it had for a little while glowed more brilliantly again, but it speedily reverted to its sullen red heat. I perceived by this slowing down of its rising and setting that the work of the tidal drag was done. The Earth had come to rest with one face to the sun, even as in our own time the moon faces the earth. Very cautiously, for I remembered my former headlong fall, I began to reverse my motion. Slower and slower went the circling hands until the thousands one seemed motionless and the daily one was no longer a mere mist upon its scale. Still slower, until the dim outlines of a desolate beach grew visible.

"I stopped very gently and sat upon the Time Machine, looking round. The sky was no longer blue. North eastward it was inky black, and out of the blackness shone brightly and steadily the pale white stars. Overhead it was a deep Indian red and starless, and south eastward it grew brighter to a glowing scarlet where, cut by the horizon, lay the huge hull of the sun, red and motionless. The rocks about me were of a harsh reddish colour, and all the trace of life that I could see at first was the intensely green vegetation that covered every projecting point on their southeastern face. It was the same rich green that one sees on forest moss or on the lichen in caves: plants which like these grow in a perpetual twilight.

"The machine was standing on a sloping beach. The sea stretched away to the south-west, to rise into a sharp bright horizon against the wan sky. There were no breakers and no waves, for not a breath of wind was stirring. Only a slight oily swell rose and fell like a gentle breathing, and showed that the

eternal sea was still moving and living. And along the margin where the water sometimes broke was a thick incrustation of salt – pink under the lurid sky. There was a sense of oppression in my head, and I noticed that I was breathing very fast. The sensation reminded me of my only experience of mountaineering, and from that I judged the air to be thinner than it is now.

"Far away up the desolate slope I heard a harsh scream, and saw a thing like a huge white butterfly go slanting and fluttering up into the sky and, circling, disappear over some low hillocks beyond. The sound of its voice was so dismal that I shivered and seated myself more firmly upon the machine. Looking round me again, I saw that, quite near, what I had taken to be a reddish mass of rock was moving slowly towards me. Then I saw the thing was really a monstrous crab-like creature. Can you imagine a crab as large as yonder table, with its many legs moving slowly and uncertainly, its big claws swaying, its long antennae, like carters' whips, waving and feeling, and its stalked eyes gleaming at you on either side of its metallic front? Its back was corrugated and ornamented with ungainly lumps, and a greenish incrustation blotched it here and there. I could see the many palps of its complicated mouth flickering and feeling as it moved.

"As I stared at this apparition crawling towards me, I felt a tickling on my cheek as though a fly had lighted there. I tried to brush it away with my hand, but in a moment it returned, and almost immediately came another by my ear. I struck at this, and caught something threadlike. It was drawn swiftly out of my hand. With a frightful qualm, I turned, and I saw that I had grasped the antenna of another monster crab that stood just behind me. Its evil eyes were wriggling on their stalks, its mouth was all alive with appetite, and its vast ungainly claws, smeared with an algal slime, were descending upon me. In a moment my hand was on the lever, and I had placed a month between myself and these monsters. But I was still on the same beach, and I saw them distinctly now as soon as I stopped. Dozens of them seemed to be crawling here and there, in the sombre light, among the foliated sheets of intense green.

"I cannot convey the sense of desolation that hung over the world. The red eastern sky, the northward blackness, the salt Dead Sea, the stony beach crawling with these foul, slow-stirring monsters, the uniform poisonous-looking green of the lichenous plants, the thin air that hurts one's lungs. All contributed to an appalling effect. I moved on a hundred years, and there was the same red sun – a little larger, a little duller – the same dying sea, the same chill air, and the same crowd of earthy crustacea creeping in and out among the green weed and red rocks. And in the westward sky, I saw a curved pale line like a vast new moon.

"So I travelled, stopping ever and again, in great strides of a thousand years or more, drawn on by the mystery of the Earth's fate, watching with a strange fascination the Sun grow larger and duller in the westward sky, and the life of the old earth ebb away. At last, more than thirty million years hence, the huge red-hot dome of the Sun had come to obscure nearly a tenth part of the darkling heavens. Then I stopped once more, for the crawling multitude of crabs had disappeared, and the red beach, save for its livid green mosses and lichens, seemed lifeless. And now it was flecked with white. A bitter cold assailed me. Rare white flakes ever and again came eddying down. To the north eastward, the glare of snow lay under the starlight of the sable sky and I could see an undulating crest of hillocks pinkish white. There were fringes of ice along the sea margin, with drifting masses further out; but the main expanse of that salt ocean, all bloody under the eternal sunset, was still unfrozen.

"I looked about me to see if any traces of animal life remained. A certain indefinable apprehension still kept me in the saddle of the machine. But I saw nothing moving, in earth or sky or sea. The green slime on the rocks alone testified that life was not extinct. A shallow sandbank had appeared in the sea and the water had receded from the beach. I fancied I saw some black object flopping about upon this bank, but it became motionless as I looked at it, and I judged that my eye had been deceived, and that the black object was merely a rock. The stars in the sky were intensely bright and seemed to me to twinkle very little.

"Suddenly I noticed that the circular westward outline of the Sun had changed; that a concavity, a bay, had appeared in the curve. I saw this grow larger. For a minute perhaps I stared aghast at this blackness that was creeping over the day, and then I realized that an eclipse was beginning. Either the Moon or the planet Mercury was passing across the sun's disk. Naturally, at first I took it to be the moon, but there is much to incline me to believe that what I really saw was the transit of an inner planet passing very near to the earth.

"The darkness grew apace; a cold wind began to blow in freshening gusts from the east, and the showering white flakes in the air increased in number. From the edge of the sea came a ripple and whisper. Beyond these lifeless sounds the world was silent. Silent? It would be hard to convey the stillness of it. All the sounds of man, the bleating of sheep, the cries of birds, the hum of insects, the stir that makes the background of our lives – all that was over. As the darkness thickened, the eddying flakes grew more abundant, dancing before my eyes; and the cold of the air more intense. At last, one by one, swiftly, one after the other, the white peaks of the distant hills vanished into blackness. The breeze rose to a moaning wind. I saw the black central shadow of the eclipse sweeping towards me. In another moment the pale stars alone were visible. All else was rayless obscurity. The sky was absolutely black.

"A horror of this great darkness came on me. The cold, that smote to my marrow, and the pain I felt in breathing, overcame

me. I shivered, and a deadly nausea seized me. Then, like a red-
hot bow in the sky, appeared the edge of the sun. I got off the
machine to recover myself. I felt giddy and incapable of facing
the return journey. As I stood sick and confused I saw again the
moving thing upon the shoal – there was no mistake now that it
was a moving thing – against the red water of the sea. It was a
round thing, the size of a football perhaps, or, it may be, bigger,
and tentacles trailed down from it; it seemed black against the
weltering blood-red water, and it was hopping fitfully about.
Then I felt I was fainting. But a terrible dread of lying helpless in
that remote and awful twilight sustained me while I clambered
upon the saddle.

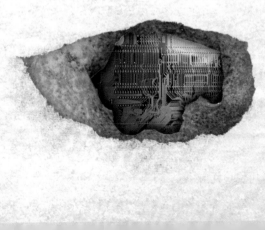

THE MIND OF THE SCIENTIST

THE SHADOW AND THE FLASH

1903

JACK LONDON

WHEN I LOOK BACK, I realize what a peculiar friendship it was. First, there was Lloyd Inwood, tall, slender, and finely knit, nervous and dark. And then Paul Tichlorne, tall, slender, and finely knit, nervous and blond. Each was the replica of the other in everything except colour. Lloyd's eyes were black; Paul's were blue. Under the stress of excitement, the blood coursed olive in the face of Lloyd, crimson in the face of Paul. But outside this matter of colouring they were as like as two peas in a pod. Both were highly strung, prone to excessive tension and endurance, and they lived at concert pitch.

But there was a trio involved in this remarkable friendship, and the third was short, and fat, and chunky, and lazy, and, loath to say, it was I. Paul and Lloyd seemed born to rivalry with each other, and I to be the peacemaker between them. We grew up together, the three of us, and very often have I received the angry blows each intended for the other. They were always competing, striving to outdo each other, and when entered upon some such struggle there was no limit either to their endeavours or passions.

This intense spirit of rivalry obtained in their studies and their games. I remember an incident that occurred at the swimming hole – an incident tragically significant of the life-struggle between them. The boys had a game of diving to the bottom of a ten-foot pool and holding on by submerged roots to see who could stay under the longest. Paul and Lloyd allowed themselves to be bantered into making the descent together. When I saw their faces, set and determined, disappear in the water as they sank swiftly down, I felt a foreboding of something dreadful. The moments sped, the ripples died away, the surface of the pool grew placid and untroubled, and neither black nor golden head broke surface in quest of air. We above grew anxious. The record of the longest-winded boy had been exceeded, and still there was no sign of them. Air bubbles trickled slowly upwards, showing that the breath had been expelled from their lungs, and after that the bubbles ceased to trickle upwards. Each second became interminable, and, unable longer to endure the suspense any longer, I plunged headfirst into the water.

I found them down at the bottom, clutching tight to the roots, their heads not a foot apart, their eyes wide open, each glaring fixedly at the other. They were suffering frightful

torment, writhing and twisting in the pangs of voluntary suffocation; for neither would let go and acknowledge himself beaten. I tried to break Paul's hold on the root, but he resisted me fiercely. Then I lost my breath and came to the surface, badly scared. I quickly explained the situation, and half a dozen of us went down and by main strength tore them loose. By the time we got them out, both were unconscious, and it was only after much barrel-rolling and rubbing and pounding that they finally came to their senses. They would have drowned there, had no one rescued them.

When Paul Tichlorne entered college, he let it be generally understood that he was going in for the social sciences. Lloyd Inwood, entering at the same time, elected to take the same course. But Paul had had it secretly in mind all the time to study the natural sciences, specialising on chemistry, and at the last moment he switched over. Though Lloyd had already arranged his year's work and attended the first lectures, he at once followed Paul's lead and went in for the natural sciences and especially for chemistry. Their rivalry soon became a noted thing throughout the university. Each was a spur to the other, and they went into chemistry deeper than students ever had before – so deep, in fact, that they could have stumped any chemistry professor in the institution, save 'old' Moss, head of the department, and even him they puzzled and edified more than once. Lloyd's discovery of the 'death bacillus' of the sea toad, and his experiments on it with potassium cyanide, sent his name and that of his university ringing round the world; nor was Paul a whit behind when he succeeded in producing laboratory colloids exhibiting amoeba-like activities, and when he cast new light upon the processes of fertilization through his startling experiments with simple sodium chlorides and magnesium solutions on low forms of marine life.

It was in their undergraduate days, however, in the midst of their profoundest plunges into the mysteries of organic chemistry, that Doris Van Benschoten entered into their lives. Lloyd met her first, but within twenty-four hours Paul saw to it that he also made her acquaintance. Of course, they fell in love with her, and she became the only thing in life worth living for. They wooed her with equal ardour and fire, and so intense became their struggle for her that half the student-body took to wagering wildly on the result. Even 'old' Moss, one day, after an astounding demonstration in his private laboratory by Paul, was guilty to the extent of a month's salary of backing him to become the bridegroom of Doris Van Benschoten.

In the end she solved the problem in her own way, to everybody's satisfaction except Paul's and Lloyd's. Getting them together, she said that she really could not choose between them because she loved them both equally well; and that, unfortunately, since polyandry was not permitted in the United States she would be compelled to forego the honour and happiness of marrying either of them. Each blamed the other for this lamentable outcome, and the bitterness between them grew more bitter.

But things came to a head soon enough. It was at my home, after they had taken their degrees and dropped out of the world's sight, that the beginning of the end came to pass. Both were men of means, with little inclination and no necessity for professional life. My friendship and their mutual animosity were the two things that linked them in any way together. While they were very often at my place, they made it a fastidious point to avoid each other on such visits, though it was inevitable, under the circumstances, that they should come upon each other occasionally.

On the day I have in recollection, Paul Tichlorne had been mooning all morning in my study over a current scientific review. This left me free to my own affairs, and I was out among my roses when Lloyd Inwood arrived. Clipping and pruning and tacking the climbers on the porch, with my mouth full of nails, and Lloyd following me about and lending a hand now and again, we fell to discussing the mythical race of invisible people, that strange and vagrant people the traditions of which have come down to us. Lloyd warmed to the talk in his nervous, jerky fashion, and was soon interrogating the physical properties and possibilities of invisibility. A perfectly black object, he contended, would elude and defy the acutest vision.

"Colour is a sensation," he was saying. "It has no objective reality. Without light, we can see neither colours nor objects themselves. All objects are black in the dark, and in the dark it is impossible to see them. If no light strikes upon them, then no light is flung back from them to the eye, and so we have no vision-evidence of their being."

"But we see black objects in daylight," I objected.

"Very true," he went on warmly. "And that is because they are not perfectly black. Were they perfectly black, absolutely black, as it were, we could not see them — ay, not in the blaze of a thousand suns could we see them! And so I say, with the right pigments, properly compounded, an absolutely black paint could be produced which would render invisible whatever it was applied to."

"It would be a remarkable discovery," I said non-committally, for the whole thing seemed too fantastic for anything but speculative purposes.

"Remarkable!" Lloyd slapped me on the shoulder. "I should say so. Why, old chap, to coat myself with such a paint would be to put the world at my feet. The secrets of kings would be mine, the machinations of diplomats and politicians, the play of stock gamblers, the plans of trusts and corporations. I could keep my finger on the inner pulse of things and become the greatest power in the world. And I..." He broke off shortly, then added, "Well, I have begun my experiments, and I don't mind telling you that I'm right in line for it."

A laugh from the doorway startled us. Paul Tichlorne was standing there, a smile of mockery on his lips.

"You forget, my dear Lloyd," he said.

"Forget what?"

"You forget," Paul went on – "ah, you forget the shadow."

I saw Lloyd's face drop, but he answered sneeringly, "I can carry a sunshade, you know." Then he turned suddenly and fiercely upon him. "Look here, Paul, you'll keep out of this if you know what's good for you."

A rupture seemed imminent, but Paul laughed good-naturedly. "I wouldn't lay my fingers on your dirty pigments. Succeed beyond your most sanguine expectations, yet you will always fetch up against the shadow. You can't get away from it. Now I shall go on the very opposite tack. In the very nature of my proposition the shadow will be eliminated..."

"Transparency!" cried Lloyd. "But it can't be achieved."

"Oh, no; of course not." And Paul shrugged his shoulders and strolled off down the briar-rose path.

This was the beginning of it. Both men attacked the problem with all the tremendous energy for which they were noted, and with a bitterness that made me tremble for the success of either. Each trusted me to the utmost, and in the long weeks of experimentation that followed I was made a party to both sides, listening to their theories and witnessing their demonstrations. Never, by word or sign, did I convey to either the slightest hint of the other's progress, and they respected me for the seal I put upon my lips.

I visited Lloyd's laboratory a number of times, and found him always deep in his search after the absolute black. His experiments covered all sorts of pigments, such as lamp-blacks, tars, carbonised vegetable matters, soots of oils and fats, and the various carbonized animal substances.

"White light is composed of the seven primary colours," he argued to me. "But it is itself, of itself, invisible. Only by being reflected from objects do it and the objects become visible. But only that portion of it that is reflected becomes visible. For instance, here is a blue tobacco box. The white light strikes against it, and, with one exception, all its component colours – violet, indigo, green, yellow, orange, and red – are absorbed. The one exception is blue. It is not absorbed, but reflected. Therefore the tobacco box gives us a sensation of blueness. We do not see the other colours because they are absorbed. We see only the blue. For the same reason grass is green. The green waves of white light are thrown upon our eyes."

"When we paint our houses, we do not apply colour to them," he said at another time. "What we do is to apply certain substances that have the property of absorbing from white light all the colours except those that we would have our houses appear. When a substance reflects all the colours to the eye, it seems to us white. When it absorbs all the colours, it is black. But, as I said before, we have as yet no perfect black. All the

colours are not absorbed. The perfect black, guarding against highlights, will be utterly and absolutely invisible. Look at that, for example."

He pointed to the palette lying on his work table. Different shades of black pigments were brushed on it. One, in particular, I could hardly see. It gave my eyes a blurring sensation, and I rubbed them and looked again.

"That," he said impressively, "is the blackest black you or any mortal man ever looked upon. But just you wait, and I'll have a

278

black so black that no mortal man will be able to look upon it – and see it!"

On the other hand, I used to find Paul Tichlorne plunged as deeply into the study of light polarization, diffraction, and interference, single and double refraction, and all manner of strange organic compounds.

"Transparency: a state or quality of body which permits all rays of light to pass through," he defined for me. "That is what I am seeking. Lloyd blunders up against the shadow with his perfect opaqueness. But I escape it. A transparent body casts no shadow; neither does it reflect light waves – that is, the perfectly transparent does not. So, avoiding highlights, not only will such a body cast no shadow, but, since it reflects no light, it will also be invisible."

We were standing by the window at another time. Paul was engaged in polishing a number of lenses, which were ranged along the sill. Suddenly, after a pause in the conversation, he said, "Oh! I've dropped a lens. Stick your head out, old man, and see where it went to."

I started to thrust out my head, but a sharp blow on the forehead caused me to recoil. I rubbed my bruised brow and gazed with reproachful inquiry at Paul, who was laughing in gleeful, boyish fashion.

"Well?" he said.

"Well?" I echoed.

"Why don't you investigate?" he demanded. And investigate I did. Before thrusting out my head, my senses, automatically active, had told me there was nothing there, that nothing intervened between me and out-of-doors, that the aperture of the window opening was utterly empty. I stretched forth my hand and felt a hard object, smooth and cool and flat, which my touch, out of its experience, told me to be glass. I looked again, but could see positively nothing.

"White quartzose sand," Paul rattled off, "sodic carbonate, slaked lime, cutlet, manganese peroxide – there you have it, the finest French plate glass, made by the great St Gobain Company, who made the finest plate glass in the world, and this is the finest piece they ever made. It cost a king's ransom. But look at it! You can't see it. You don't know it's there till you run your head against it.

"Eh, old boy! That's merely an object lesson – certain elements, in themselves opaque, yet so compounded as to give a resultant body which is transparent. But that is a matter of inorganic chemistry, you say. Very true. But I dare to assert, standing here on my two feet, that in the organic I can duplicate whatever occurs in the inorganic.

"Here!" He held a test tube between me and the light, and I noted the cloudy or muddy liquid it contained. He emptied the contents of another test tube into it, and almost instantly it became clear and sparkling.

"Or here!" With quick, nervous movements among his array of test-tubes, he turned a white solution to a wine colour, and a light yellow solution to a dark brown. He dropped a piece of litmus paper into an acid, when it changed instantly to red, and on floating it in an alkali it turned as quickly to blue.

"The litmus paper is still the litmus paper," he enunciated in the formal manner of the lecturer. "I have not changed it into something else. Then what did I do? I merely changed the arrangement of its molecules. Where, at first, it absorbed all colours from the light but red, its molecular structure was so changed that it absorbed red and all colours except blue. And so it goes, *ad infinitum*. Now, what I purpose to do is this." He paused for a space. "I purpose to seek – ay, and to find – the proper reagents, which, acting upon the living organism, will bring about molecular changes analogous to those you have just witnessed. But these reagents, which I shall find, and for that matter, upon which I already have my hands, will not turn the living body to blue or red or black, but they will turn it to transparency. All light will pass through it. It will be invisible. It will cast no shadow."

A few weeks later I went hunting with Paul. He had been promising me for some time that I should have the pleasure of shooting with a wonderful dog – the most wonderful dog, in fact, that ever man shot with, so he told, and continued to tell until my curiosity was aroused. But on the morning in question I was disappointed, for there was no dog in evidence.

"Don't see him about," Paul remarked unconcernedly, and we set off across the fields.

I could not imagine, at the time, what was ailing me, but I had a feeling of some impending and deadly illness. My nerves were all awry, and, from the astounding tricks they played me, my senses seemed to have run riot. Strange sounds disturbed me. At times I heard the swish-swish of grass being shoved aside, and once the patter of feet across a patch of stony ground.

"Did you hear anything, Paul?" I asked once.

But he shook his head, and thrust his feet steadily forward.

While climbing a fence, I heard the low, eager whine of a

dog, apparently from within a couple of feet of me; but on looking about me I saw nothing.

I dropped to the ground, limp and trembling.

"Paul," I said, "we had better return to the house. I am afraid I am going to be sick."

"Nonsense, old man," he answered. "The sunshine has gone to your head like wine. You'll be all right."

But, passing along a narrow path through a clump of cottonwoods, some object brushed against my legs and I stumbled and nearly fell. I looked with sudden anxiety at Paul.

"What's the matter?" he asked. "Tripping over your own feet?"

I kept my tongue between my teeth and plodded on, though

extremely perplexed and thoroughly satisfied that some acute and mysterious malady had attacked my nerves. So far my eyes had escaped; but, when we got to the open fields again, even my vision went back on me. Strange flashes of varicoloured, rainbow light began to appear and disappear on the path in front of me. Still, I managed to hold myself together, until the varicoloured lights persisted for a space of fully twenty seconds, dancing and flashing in continuous play. At that point I sat down, feeling weak and shaky.

"It's all up with me," I gasped, covering my eyes with my hands. "It has attacked my eyes. Paul, take me home."

But Paul laughed long and loud. "What did I tell you? The

most wonderful dog, eh? Well, what do you think?"

He turned partly from me and began to whistle. I heard the patter of feet, the panting of a heated animal, and the unmistakable yelp of a dog. Then Paul stooped down and apparently fondled the empty air.

"Here! Give me your fist."

And he rubbed my hand over the cold nose and jowls of a dog. A dog it certainly was, with the shape and the smooth, short coat of a pointer.

Suffice to say, I speedily recovered my spirits and control. Paul put a collar around the animal's neck and tied his handkerchief to its tail. And then was vouchsafed us the remarkable sight of an empty collar and a waving handkerchief cavorting over the fields. It was something to see that collar and handkerchief pin a bevy of quail in a clump of locusts and remain rigid and immovable till we had flushed the birds.

Now and again the dog emitted the varicoloured light flashes I have mentioned. The one thing, Paul explained, which he had not anticipated and which he doubted could be overcome.

"They are produced by refraction of light from mineral and ice crystals, from mist, rain, spray, and no end of things; and I am afraid they are the penalty I must pay for transparency. I escaped Lloyd's shadow only to fetch up against the rainbow flash."

A couple of days after this, at the entrance to Paul's laboratory, I encountered a terrible stench. So overpowering was it that it was easy to discover the source – a mass of putrescent matter on the doorstep which resembled a dog.

Paul was startled when he investigated my find. It was his

invisible dog, or rather, what had been his invisible dog, for it was now plainly visible. It had been playing about but a few minutes before in all health and strength. Closer examination revealed that the skull had been crushed by some heavy blow. While it was strange that the animal should have been killed, the inexplicable thing was that it should so quickly decay.

"The reagents I injected into its system were harmless," Paul explained. "Yet they were powerful, and it appears that when death comes they force practically instantaneous disintegration. Remarkable! Most remarkable! Well, the only thing is not to die. They do not harm so long as one lives. But I do wonder who smashed in that dog's head."

Light, however, was thrown upon this when a frightened housemaid brought the news that Gaffer Bedshaw had that very morning, not more than an hour back, gone violently insane, and was strapped down at home, in the huntsman's lodge, where he raved of a battle with a ferocious and gigantic beast that he had encountered in the Tichlorne pasture.

Nor, while Paul Tichlorne was thus successfully mastering the problem of invisibility, was Lloyd Inwood a whit behind. I went over in answer to a message of his to come and see how he was getting on. Now his laboratory occupied an isolated situation in the midst of his vast grounds. It was built in a pleasant little glade, surrounded on all sides by a dense forest growth, and was to be gained by way of a winding and erratic path. But I have travelled that path so often as to know every foot of it, and conceive my surprise when I came upon the glade and found no laboratory. The quaint shed structure with its red sandstone chimney was not. Nor did it look as if it ever had been. There were no signs of ruin, no debris, nothing.

I started to walk across what had once been its site. "This," I said to myself, "should be where the step went up to the door." Barely were the words out of my mouth when I stubbed my toe on some obstacle, pitched forward, and butted my head into something that felt very much like a door. I reached out my hand. It *was* a door. I found the knob and turned it. And at once, as the door swung inward on its hinges, the whole interior of the laboratory impinged upon my vision. Greeting Lloyd, I closed the door and backed up the path a few paces. I could see nothing of the building. Returning and opening the door, at once all the furniture and every detail of the interior were visible. It was indeed startling, the sudden transition from void to light and form and colour.

"What do you think of it, eh?" Lloyd asked, wringing my hand. "I slapped a couple of coats of absolute black on the outside yesterday afternoon to see how it worked. How's your head? you bumped it pretty solidly, I imagine."

"Never mind that," he interrupted my congratulations. "I've something better for you to do."

While he talked he began to strip, and when he stood naked before me he thrust a pot and brush into my hand and said, "Here, give me a coat of this."

It was an oily, shellac-like stuff, which spread quickly and easily over the skin and dried immediately.

"Merely preliminary and precautionary," he explained when I had finished; "but now for the real stuff."

I picked up another pot he indicated, and glanced inside, but could see nothing.

"It's empty," I said.

"Stick your finger in it."

I obeyed, and was aware of a sensation of cool moistness. On withdrawing my hand I glanced at the forefinger, the one I had immersed, but it had disappeared. I moved and knew from the alternate tension and relaxation of the muscles that I moved it, but it defied my sense of sight. To all appearances I had been shorn of a finger; nor could I get any visual impression of it till I extended it under the skylight and saw its shadow plainly blotted on the floor.

Lloyd chuckled. "Now spread it on, and keep your eyes open."

I dipped the brush into the seemingly empty pot, and gave him a long stroke across his chest. With the passage of the brush the living flesh disappeared from beneath. I covered his right leg, and he was a one-legged man defying all laws of gravitation. And so, stroke by stroke, I painted Lloyd Inwood into nothingness. It was a creepy experience, and I was glad when naught remained in sight but his burning black eyes, poised apparently unsupported in mid-air.

"I have a refined a harmless solution for them," he said. "A fine spray with an air-brush, and presto! I am not."

This deftly accomplished, he said, "Now I shall move about, and do tell me what sensations you experience."

"In the first place, I cannot see you," I said, and I heard him laugh from the midst of the emptiness. "Of course," I continued, "you cannot escape your shadow, but that was to be expected. When you pass between my eye and an object, the object disappears, but so unusual and incomprehensible is its disappearance that it seems to me as though my eyes had blurred. When you move rapidly, I experience a bewildering succession of blurs. The blurring sensation makes my eyes ache and my brain tired."

"Have you any other warnings of my presence?" he asked.

"No, and yes," I answered. "When you are near me I have

feelings similar to those produced by dank warehouses, gloomy crypts, and deep mines. And as sailors feel the loom of the land on dark nights, so I think I feel the loom of your body. But it is all very vague and intangible."

Long we talked that last morning in his laboratory; and when I turned to go, he put his unseen hand in mine with nervous grip, and said, "Now I shall conquer the world!" And I could not dare to tell him of Paul Tichlorne's equal success.

At home I found a note from Paul, asking me to come up immediately, and it was high noon when I came. Paul called me from the tennis court, and I dismounted and went over. But the court was empty. As I stood there, gaping open-mouthed, a tennis ball struck me on the arm, and as I turned about, another whizzed past my ear. For aught I could see of my assailant, they came whirling at me from out of space, and right well was I peppered with them. But when the balls already flung at me began to come back for a second whack, I realized the situation. Seizing a racquet and keeping my eyes open, I quickly saw a rainbow flash appearing and disappearing and darting over the ground. I took out after it, and when I laid the racquet upon it for a half-dozen stout blows, Paul's voice rang out:

"Enough! Enough! Oh! Ouch! Stop! You're landing on my naked skin, you know! Ow! O-w-w! I'll be good! I'll be good! I only wanted you to see my metamorphosis," he said ruefully, and I imagined he was rubbing his hurts.

A few minutes later we were playing tennis – a handicap on my part, for I could have no knowledge of his position save when all the angles between himself, the sun, and me, were in proper conjunction. Then he flashed, and only then. But the flashes were more brilliant than the rainbow – purest blue, most delicate violet, brightest yellow, and all the intermediary shades, with the brilliance of the diamond, dazzling, blinding, iridescent.

But in the midst of our play I felt a sudden cold chill,

reminding me of deep mines and gloomy crypts, such a chill as I had experienced that very morning. The next moment, close to the net, I saw a ball rebound in mid-air and empty space, and at the same instant, a score of feet away, Paul Tichlorne emitted a rainbow flash. It could not be he from whom the ball had rebounded, and with sickening dread I realized that Lloyd Inwood had come upon the scene. To make sure, I looked for his shadow, and there it was, a shapeless blotch the girth of his body, (the sun was overhead), moving along the ground. I remembered his threat, and felt sure that all the long years of rivalry were about to culminate in uncanny battle.

I cried a warning to Paul, and heard a snarl as of a wild beast, and an answering snarl. I saw the dark blotch move swiftly across the court, and a brilliant burst of varicoloured light moving with equal swiftness to meet it; and then shadow and flash came together and there was the sound of unseen blows. The net went down before my frightened eyes. I sprang toward the fighters, crying:

"For God's sake!"

But their locked bodies smote against my knees, and I was overthrown.

"You keep out of this, old man!" I heard the voice of Lloyd Inwood from out of the emptiness. And then Paul's voice crying, "Yes, we've had enough of peacemaking!"

From the sound of their voices I realized that they had separated. I could not locate Paul, and so approached the shadow that represented Lloyd. But from the other side came a stunning blow on the point of my jaw, and I heard Paul scream angrily, "Now will you keep away?"

Then they came together again, the impact of their blows, their groans and gasps, and the swift flashings and shadow-movings telling plainly of the deadliness of the struggle.

I shouted for help, and Gaffer Bedshaw came running into the court. I could see, as he approached, that he was looking at me strangely, but he collided with the combatants and was hurled headlong to the ground. With despairing shriek and a cry of, "Oh

Lord, I've got 'em!" he sprang to his feet and tore madly out of the court.

I could do nothing, so I sat up, fascinated and powerless, and watched the struggle. The noonday sun beat down with dazzling brightness on the naked tennis court. And it was naked. All I could see was the blotch of shadow and the rainbow flashes, the dust rising from the invisible feet, the earth tearing up from beneath the straining foot-grips, and the wire screen bulge once or twice as their bodies hurled against it. That was all, and after a time even that ceased. There were no more flashes, and the shadow had become long and stationary; and I remembered their set boyish faces when they clung to the roots in the deep coolness of the pool.

They found me an hour afterward. Some inkling of what had happened got to the servants and they quitted the Tichlorne service in a body. Gaffer Bedshaw never recovered from the second shock he received, and is confined in a madhouse, hopelessly incurable. The secrets of their marvellous discoveries died with Paul and Lloyd, both laboratories being destroyed by grief-stricken relatives. As for myself, I no longer care for chemical research, and science is a tabooed topic in my household. I have returned to my roses. Nature's colours are good enough for me.

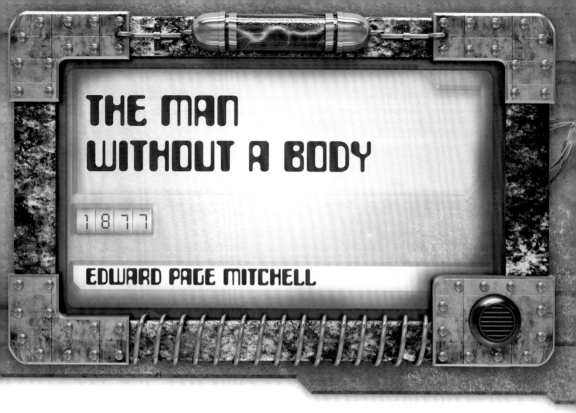

THE MAN WITHOUT A BODY

1877

EDWARD PAGE MITCHELL

On a shelf in the old Arsenal Museum, in the Central Park, in the midst of stuffed hummingbirds, ermines, silver foxes, and bright-coloured parakeets, there is a ghastly row of human heads. I pass by the mummied Peruvian, the Maori chief, and the Flathead Indian to speak of a Caucasian head which has had a fascinating interest to me ever since it was added to the grim collection a little more than a year ago.

I was struck with the Head when I first saw it. The pensive intelligence of the features won me. The face is remarkable, although the nose is gone, and the nasal fossae are somewhat the worse for wear. The eyes are likewise wanting, but the empty orbs have an expression of their own. The parchmenty skin is so shrivelled that the teeth show to their roots in the jaws. The

294

mouth has been much affected by the ravages of decay, but what mouth there is displays character. The features of the Head are of the Teutonic cast, and the skull is the skull of a philosopher. What particularly attracted my attention, however, was the vague resemblance which this dilapidated countenance bore to some face which had at some time been familiar to me – some face which lingered in my memory, but which I could not place.

After all, I was not greatly surprised, when I had known the Head for nearly a year, to see it acknowledge our acquaintance and express its appreciation of friendly interest on my part by deliberately winking at me as I stood before it.

This was on a Trustees' Day, and I was the only visitor in the hall. The faithful attendant had gone to enjoy a can of beer with his friend, the superintendent of the monkeys.

The Head winked a second time, and even more cordially than before. I gazed upon its efforts with the critical delight of an anatomist. I saw the masseter muscle flex beneath the leathery skin. I saw the play of the glutinators, and the beautiful lateral movement of the internal playtsyma. I knew the Head was trying to speak to me. I noted the convulsive twitchings of the risorius and the zygomatie major, and knew that it was endeavouring to smile.

'Here,' I thought, 'is either a case of vitality long after decapitation, or, an instance of reflex action where there is no diastaltic or excitor-motory system. In either case the phenomenon is unprecedented, and should be carefully observed. Besides, the Head is evidently well disposed toward me.' I found a key on my bunch which opened the glass door.

"Thanks," said the Head. "A breath of fresh air is quite a treat."

"How do you feel?" I asked politely. "How does it seem without a body?"

The Head shook itself sadly and sighed. "I would give," it said, speaking through its ruined nose, and for obvious reasons using chest tones sparingly, "I would give both ears for a single leg. I cannot walk. I cannot even hop or waddle. I would fain travel, roam, promenade, circulate in the busy paths of men, but I am chained to this accursed shelf. I am no better off than these barbarian heads – I, a man of science! I am compelled to sit here on my neck and see sandpipers and storks all around me, with legs and to spare. Look at that infernal little Oedieneninus longpipes over there. Look at that miserable grey-headed porphyric. They have no brains, no ambition, no yearnings. Yet they have legs, legs, legs, in profusion." He cast an envious glance across the alcove at the tantalizing limbs of the birds in question.

I did not exactly know how to console him in so delicate a manner, but ventured to hint that perhaps his condition had its compensations in immunity from corns and the gout.

"And as to arms," he went on, "there's another misfortune for you! I am unable to brush away the flies that get in here – Lord knows how – in the summertime. I cannot reach over and cuff that confounded Chinook mummy that sits there grinning at me like a jack-in-the-box. I cannot scratch my head or even blow my nose (his nose!) decently when I get cold in this thundering draft. As to eating and drinking, I don't care. My soul is wrapped up in science. Science is my bride, my divinity. I worship her footsteps in the past and hail the prophecy of her future progress. I —"

I had heard these sentiments before. In a flash I had accounted for the familiar look which had haunted me ever since I first saw the Head. "Pardon me," I said, "you are the celebrated Professor Dummkopf?"

"That is, or was, my name," he replied, with dignity.

"And you formerly lived in Boston, where you carried on scientific experiments of startling originality. It was you who first discovered how to photograph smell, how to bottle music, how to freeze the aurora borealis. It was you who first applied spectrW analysis to Mind."

"Those were some of my minor achievements," said the Head,

sadly nodding itself – "small when compared with my final invention, the grand discovery which was at the same time my greatest triumph and my ruin. I lost my Body in an experiment."

"How was that?" I asked. "I had not heard."

"No," said the Head. "I being alone and friendless, my disappearance was hardly noticed. I will tell you."

There was a sound upon the stairway. "Hush!" cried the Head. "Here comes somebody. We must not be discovered. You must dissemble."

I hastily closed the door of the glass case, locking it just in time to evade the vigilance of the returning keeper, and dissembled by pretending to examine, with great interest, a nearby exhibit.

On the next Trustees' Day I revisited the museum and gave the keeper of the Head a dollar on the pretence of purchasing information in regard to the curiosities in his charge. He made the circuit of the hall with me, talking volubly all the while.

"That there," he said, as we stood before the Head, "is a relic of morality presented to the museum fifteen months ago. The head of a notorious murderer guillotined at Paris in the last century, sir."

I fancied that I saw a slight twitching about the corners of Professor Dummkopf's mouth and an almost imperceptible depression of what was once his left eyelid, but he kept his face remarkably well under the circumstances. I dismissed my guide with many thanks for his intelligent services, and, as I had anticipated, he departed forthwith to invest his easily earned dollar in beer, leaving me to pursue my conversation with the Head.

"Think of putting a wooden-headed idiot like that," said the professor, after I had opened his glass prison, "in charge of a portion, however small, of a man of science – of the inventor of the Telepomp! Paris! Murderer! Last century, indeed!" and the Head shook with laughter until I feared that it would tumble off the shelf.

"You spoke of your invention, the Telepomp," I suggested.

"Ah, yes," said the Head, simultaneously recovering its gravity and its centre of gravity; "I promised to tell you how I happen to be a Man without a Body. You see that some three or four years ago I discovered the principle of the transmission of sound by electricity. My telephone, as I called it, would have been an invention of great practical utility if I had been spared to introduce it to the public. But, alas –"

"Excuse the interruption," I said, "but I must inform you that somebody else has recently accomplished the same thing. The telephone is a realized fact."

"Have they gone any further?" he eagerly asked. "Have they discovered the great secret of the transmission of atoms? In other words, have they accomplished the Telepomp?"

"I have heard nothing of the kind," I hastened to assure him, "but what do you mean?"

"Listen," he said. "In the course of my experiments with the telephone I became convinced that the same principle was capable of indefinite expansion. Matter is made up of molecules, and molecules, in their turn, are made up of atoms. The atom, you know, is the unit of being. The molecules differ according to the number and the arrangement of their constituent atoms. Chemical changes are effected by the dissolution of the atoms in the molecules and their rearrangements into molecules of another kind. This dissolution may be accomplished by chemical affinity or by a sufficiently strong electric current. Do you understand me?"

"Perfectly."

"Well, then, following out this line of thought, I conceived a great idea. There was no reason why matter could not be telegraphed, or, to be etymologically accurate, 'telepomped.' It was only necessary to effect at one end of the line the disintegration of the molecules into atoms and to convey the vibrations of the chemical dissolution by electricity to the other pole, where a corresponding reconstruction could be effected from other atoms. As all atoms are alike, their arrangement into molecules of the same order, and the arrangement of those molecules into an organization similar to the original organization, would be practically a reproduction of the original. It would be a materialization – not in the sense of the spiritualists' cant, but in all the truth and logic of stern science. Do you still follow me?"

"It is a little misty," I said, "but I think I get the point."

"A candle flame is the same candle flame although the burning gas is continually changing. A wave on the surface of water is the same wave, although the water composing it is shifting as it moves. A man is the same man although there is not an atom in his body which was there five years before. It is the form, the shape, the idea, that is essential. The vibrations that give individuality to matter may be transmitted to a distance by wire just as readily as the vibrations that give individuality to sound. So I constructed an instrument by which I could pull down matter, so to speak, at the anode and build it up again on the same plan at the cathode. This was my Telepomp."

"But in practice – how did the Telepomp work?"

"To perfection! In my rooms on Joy Street, in Boston, I had about five miles of wire. I had no difficulty in sending simple compounds, such as quartz, starch, and water, from one room to another over this five-mile coil. I shall never forget the joy with which I disintegrated a three-cent postage stamp in one room and found it immediately reproduced at the receiving instrument in another. This success with inorganic matter emboldened me to attempt the same thing with a living organism. I caught a cat and I submitted him to a terrible current from my two-hundred-cup battery. The cat disappeared in a twinkling. I hastened to the next room and, to my immense satisfaction, found him there, alive and purring, although somewhat astonished. It worked like a charm."

"This is certainly very remarkable."

"Isn't it? After my experiment with the cat, a gigantic idea took possession of me. If I could send a feline being, why not send a human being? If I could transmit a cat five miles by wire in an instant by electricity, why not transmit a man to London by Atlantic cable and with equal dispatch? I resolved to strengthen my already powerful battery and try the experiment. Like a thorough votary of science, I resolved to try the experiment on myself.

"I do not like to dwell upon this chapter of my experience," continued the Head, winking at a tear which had trickled down onto his cheek and which I gently wiped away for him with my own pocket handkerchief.

"Suffice it that I trebled the cups in my battery, stretched my wire over housetops to my lodgings in Phillips Street, made everything ready, and with a solemn calmness born of my confidence in the theory, placed myself in the receiving instrument of the Telepomp at my Joy Street office. I was as sure that when I made the connection with the battery I would find myself in my rooms in Phillips Street as I was sure of my existence. Then I touched the key that turned on the electricity."

For some moments my friend was unable to speak. At last, with an effort, he resumed his narrative.

"I began to disintegrate at my feet and slowly disappeared under my own eyes. My legs melted away, and then my trunk and arms. That something was wrong, I knew from the exceeding slowness of my dissolution, but I was helpless. Then my head went and I lost all consciousness. According to my theory, my head, having been the last to disappear, should have been the first to materialize at the other end of the wire. The theory was confirmed in fact. I recovered consciousness. I opened my eyes in my Phillips Street apartments. My chin was materializing, and with great satisfaction I saw my neck slowly taking shape. Suddenly, and about at the third cervical vertebra, the process stopped. In a flash I knew the reason. I had forgotten to replenish the cups of my battery with fresh sulphuric acid, and there was not electricity enough to materialize the rest of me. I was a Head, but my body was Lord knows where."

I did not attempt to offer consolation. Words would have been mockery in the presence of Professor Dummkopf's grief. "What matters it about the rest?" he sadly continued.

"The house in Phillips Street was full of medical students. I suppose that some of them found my head, and knowing nothing of me or of the Telepomp, appropriated it for purposes of anatomical study. I suppose that they attempted to preserve it by means of some arsenical preparation. How badly the work was done is shown by my defective nose. I suppose that I drifted from medical student to medical student and from anatomical cabinet to anatomical cabinet until some would-be humourist presented me to this collection as a French murderer of the last century. For some months I knew nothing, and when I recovered consciousness I found myself here.

"Such," added the Head, with a dry, harsh laugh, "is the irony of fate!"

"Is there nothing I can do for you?" I asked, after a pause.

"Thank you," the Head replied; "I am tolerably cheerful and resigned. I have lost pretty much all interest in experimental science. I sit here day after day and watch the objects of zoological, ichthyological, ethnological, and conchological interest with which this admirable museum abounds. I don't know of anything you can do for me.

"Stay," he added, as his gaze fell once more upon the exasperating legs of the Oedienenius longpipes opposite him. "If there is anything I do feel the need of, it is outdoor exercise. Couldn't you manage in some way to take me out for a walk?"

I confess that I was somewhat staggered by this request, but promised to do what I could. After some deliberation, I formed a plan, which was carried out in the following manner:

I returned to the museum that afternoon just before the closing hour, and hid myself behind the mammoth sea cow, or *Manatus americanus*. The attendant, after a cursory glance through the hall, locked up the building and departed. Then I came boldly forth and removed my friend from his shelf. With a piece of stout twine, I lashed his one or two vertebrae to the headless vertebrae of a moa. This gigantic and extinct bird of New Zealand is heavy-legged, full-breasted, tall as a man, and has huge, sprawling feet. My friend, thus provided with legs and arms, manifested extraordinary glee. He walked about, stamped his big feet, swung his wings, and occasionally broke forth into a hilarious shuffle. I despoiled the African lion of his glass eyes, and inserted them in the empty orbits of the Head. I gave Professor Dummkopf a Fiji war lance for a walking stick, covered him with a Sioux blanket, and then we issued forth from the old arsenal into the fresh night air and the moonlight, and wandered arm in arm along the shores of the quiet lake and through the mazy paths of the Ramble.

THE NEW SUN

J S FLETCHER

FROM THE TIME that he had taken up the study of astronomy, and had built himself a small but well-equipped observatory as an adjunct to his house, which stood on one of the highest slopes of Leith Hill, Mequillen had formed the habit of rising from his bed every two or three hours of a cloudy night to see if the sky had cleared. To some men such a habit would have been highly inconvenient, for many obvious reasons. But Mequillen was in a lucky position. He was unmarried; he possessed much more than ample means; he had therefore no business or profession to attend to, and accordingly no train to catch in the morning in order to keep office hours. He could sleep at any time of the day he chose; and if he did jump out of bed at two o'clock in the morning, to find that the sky was still cloudy, he could jump back and go to sleep again on the instant.

On a certain night in February, Mequillen, who had gone to bed at ten o'clock, suddenly awoke, switched on the electric light at the side of his bed, and, seeing that it was then ten minutes past twelve, sprang out, shuffled himself into his thickly padded dressing gown, and hurried up the winding stair which led to the observatory. One glance into the night showed him a perfectly clear sky. From the vast dome of heaven, wondrously blue, the stars shone out like points of fire. And Mequillen, with a sigh of satisfaction, began his work at the telescope, comparing the sky, field by field, with his star chart, on the chance of

finding new variable stars. After his usual fashion, he was immediately absorbed, and the sky remaining clear, he went on working, unconscious of time, until a deep-toned clock in the room beneath struck the hour of three. Then Mequillen started, and realized that he had been so absorbed that he had not noticed the striking of one or two, and he leaned back from the telescope in a suddenly assumed attitude of relaxation, stretching his arms, and casting up his eyes to the still, clear vault above him. The next instant he became rigid; the next he began to tremble with excitement; the next he could have shouted for joy. For there, in the constellation which astronomers have named Andromeda, Mequillen detected a new star!

He knew as he gazed and gazed, intoxicated with the delight and wonder of his discovery, that the burning and glittering object at which he was looking had never shown its light to man before. There was no need to turn to his star charts. Mequillen, being a rich man, was always equipped with the latest information from all the great observatories of the world. That star, burning with such magnificence, was on no chart.

Nay, he himself had taken a photograph of that particular field in the heavens only twenty-four hours previously, wherein were stars to the twelfth magnitude; but the star at which he gazed was not amongst them.

It had suddenly blazed up and as he watched he saw it visibly, plainly, increase in brightness and magnitude.

"A new star!" he murmured mechanically. "A new star! I wonder who else has seen it?"

Mequillen continued to watch until, as the February dawn drew near, the clouds spread great curtains between him and the heavens, and sky and stars were blotted out. Then he went to his bed, and, in spite of his excitement, he slept soundly until ten o'clock in the morning.

When Mequillen woke and looked out across the Surrey hills and vales, the entire landscape was being rapidly blotted out by a curious mist, or fog, which seemed to come from nowhere. A vast, mighty blanket of yellow seemed to be dropped between him and everything as he looked. At one moment he saw the summit of a hill many miles away; the next he could not even see his own garden beneath his windows. And when he went downstairs, half an hour later, the fog had become of the colour of grey ash, and the house was full of it, and the electric light was turned on everywhere, and to little effect.

Mequillen's sister, Adela, who kept house for him – with the assistance of a housekeeper – came to him in his study, looking scared.

"Dan," she said, "isn't there something strange about this fog? It's – it's getting worse."

Mequillen laid down a bundle of letters which he had just taken up, and walked out to the front door and into the garden. He looked all around him, and he sniffed.

"Hmm! It certainly does seem odd, Addie," he said. "We've certainly never had a fog like this in these parts since we knew them."

The girl sniffed too.

"Dan," she said, "it's like as if it were the very finest dust. And – look there!"

She had been wiping her hand with a tiny wisp of a handkerchief as she spoke, and now she held the handkerchief out to Mequillen.

"Look!" she repeated.

Mequillen looked down, and saw a curious stain – a species of smudge or smear of a faint grey colour. Without making any remark he ran the tip of his finger along the nearest object. The same smudge or smear appeared on his finger.

"It's on everything," whispered the girl. "See, it's on my cheek! It is some sort of dust, Dan. What's the matter?"

But Mequillen made no answer. He asked for breakfast, and they went in together. By that time the interior of the house was as full of the fog as the exterior was hidden by it, and everything that they touched–plate, china, linen – gave off the grey smear. And by noon everything was wrapped in an ashen-grey atmosphere, and the electrical lights had no power beyond a very limited compass.

"This is vexatious," said Mequillen. "I was going to have the motor out and take you across to Greenwich. I wanted to make an inquiry at the Observatory. Do you know, Addie, I found a new star last night!"

"A new star!" she said wonderingly. "But you won't go, Dan?"

"Won't go?" he said, laughing. "I should like to see anybody go anywhere in this, though it may be only local. Ah! I'll ring Dick Cockerlyne up, and ask him what the weather's like in town. And then I'll ring up the Observatory."

He went off to the small room in which the telephone was placed. His sister followed him, and as they passed close beneath the cluster of lights in the hall Mequillen saw that the girl's face was drawn and pallid. He stopped sharply.

"Why, Addie," he said; "frightened?"

She laid her hand on his arm, and he felt it trembling.

"Dan," she whispered. "I'm – I'm horribly frightened! What – what is this? You know, there's never been anything like this before – in our time. What's happened?"

Mequillen laughed, and patted the hand that lay on his arm.

"Come, come, Addie!" he said soothingly. "This isn't like you. I think this fog is uncommon, and I can't account for it, but I've no doubt it can be accounted for. Now, let me ring up Cockerlyne. I've a notion we shall hear they've got a bright morning there in London."

The girl shook her head, made as if she would follow him to the telephone, and then suddenly turned away.

Nearly an hour later Mequillen came out of the little room,

and called his sister into the study. He closed the door, and beckoned her into the arc of the electric light.

"This is queer!" he said, in a whisper. "I've been talking to Cockerlyne and to the Observatory. Dick says this fog struck London at ten o'clock. It's just there as it is here, and everything's at a standstill. Dick hasn't the remotest notion how he's going to get away from the city. But – that's nothing. Addie, it's all over Europe."

The girl made a little inarticulate sound of horror in her throat, and her face whitened.

"All over Europe, so they say at Greenwich," continued Mequillen. "From Lisbon to Moscow, and from Inverness to Constantinople! Land and sea – it's everywhere. It – well, it's something unexplainable. Such a thing has never been known before. But it's no use getting frightened, Addie; you must be brave. It's no doubt some natural phenomena that will be accounted for. And – phew, how very hot this room is!"

The girl went close to her brother, and laid her hand on his arm.

"Dan," she said, "it isn't the room. See, the fire's very low, and the ventilating fan's working. It's the same everywhere. Come into the garden."

Mequilleri followed her out of the house. For several days the weather had been unusually cold for the time of year. Released now from the preoccupation of the last few hours, he suddenly realized that the day was as hot as a July day should be under normal conditions. He turned to an outdoor thermometer.

"Why – why," he exclaimed, "it's over seventy now! Seventy in February! Addie, something's happened to this old world of ours. That's certain. Look there!"

As they watched the mercury rose one, two, three figures. The brother and sister stared at each other. And Mequillen suddenly dropped his hand with a gesture of helplessness.

"Well," he said, "all we can do is wait. I don't understand it."

They went back into the house together, and into Mequillen's study, only to stand and stare at each other in silence. Then Addie made a sudden effort at conversation.

"Tell me about the new star, Dan," she said.

Mequillen started.

"The new star!" he exclaimed. "The new star! My God, I wonder if that has anything to do with this? If…"

The housekeeper, white and scared, came noiselessly into the circle of electric light within which the brother and sister were standing.

"You are wanted at the telephone, sir," she said.

Mequillen went off. In a few minutes he came back, shaking his head.

"That was the Observatory," he said quietly. "This fog, or whatever it is, is all over the world – over South Africa, North and South America, India, Australia, anyway. And the heat's increasing."

"And – the reason?" whispered Addie.

Mequillen sat down, and dropped his head in his hands.

"There's no man can tell the reason," he answered. "He can't even make a guess at it. Something's happened, that's all. We must wait – wait."

Mequillen went outside again, and looked at the thermometer hanging on the wall.

"My God," he said, "eighty already! What can it mean?"

And then, standing there in the strange all-wrapping fog in his quiet garden on the slope of the peaceful Surrey hills, Mequillen's thoughts turned to the great city lying only a few miles away. What was happening in London? He saw, with small exercise of imagination, the congested traffic, the discomfort, the inconvenience, the upsetting of all arrangement and order in an ordinary fog. What, then, must be the effect of this extraordinary one? For Mequillen was sufficiently versed in science to know that the world had never – never, at any rate, since historical records of it began – known such a day as this. And supposing it lasted, supposing…

And then he interrupted his train of thought to glance once more at the thermometer.

"Yes, yes!" he, muttered to himself. "Yes, but supposing the heat goes on increasing, increasing as it's increased during the last few hours? My God, it's awful to contemplate!"

The house was very quiet. Mequillen and his sister made some attempt to eat lunch but the attempt was a farce, and presently they found themselves pacing up and down, from room to room, from house to garden, waiting for they knew not what. There was no change in the atmosphere, so far as the fog was concerned, but the thermometer rose steadily, until at six o'clock at night it was at ninety, and they were feeling as if they must soon gasp for breath. And, unknown to Addie, Mequillen went to the telephone, and eventually got into communication with Dick Cockerlyne, who was still at his city office.

"Dick!" he said as steadily as he could. "Are you still there?"

"I am," came back the answer, in tones that Mequillen could

scarcely recognize. "How is it with you there?"

One word came along. Mequillen felt it to be the only word that could come.

"Hell!"

Mequillen shivered, and again spoke.

"Dick, what is happening? What…"

And then he was sharply rung off. From that moment he had no further communication with the outer world. Once – twice – thrice he tried the telephone again before midnight; no response was given. And all around the house a silence reigned which was like the silence of a deserted ocean. Nothing but the fog was there – not a voice, even of fear or terror, came up from the valley. And the heat went on steadily increasing.

There was no sleep for Mequillen or his sister or the housekeeper that night. They had all changed into the lightest summer garments they could find, by the middle of the night the two women were lying prostrate with exhaustion, and the thermometer was a long way over one hundred degrees. Mequillen did all that knowledge could suggest to him to obtain relief and coolness for them, but there was no air – the atmosphere was still, lifeless, leaden. And when the morning came the all-enveloping fog was still there, and the heat was still increasing.

How they got through that second day Mequillen never knew. He had visions of what might be going on in places where the water supply was bad. He, fortunately, was in command of a splendid and probably inexhaustible supply; he had, too, a well-stocked larder and a well-provided cellar of good wine. Addie's wiriness and excellent physique kept her going. But as it grew to the second midnight they were all gasping for breath, and Mequillen, making brave efforts to keep the women alive, knew that before many hours were over all would be over with them too. And then, as he lay stretched out in a lounging chair, anxiously watching his sister who lay on a sofa close by, the door was pushed open, and Dick Cockerlyne, reeling like a drunken man, staggered in, and dropped headlong at Mequillen's side.

Mequillen summoned up what strength remained in him, and set himself with clenched teeth and fierce resolution to bring Cockerlyne round. Cockerlyne was a big man, a fellow of brawn and muscle, that in ordinary times would have thought nothing of walking fifty miles on end, if need arose; now, looking at his great limbs, scarcely hidden by the thin silk shirt and flannel trousers which clothed them, Mequillen saw that he was wasted as if he had undergone starvation. His face had aged by ten years, and there was a look of horror in its lines and in his half-open eyes which told of human fear and terror. And once more Mequillen wondered what was going on in London.

As he poured liquid down the fallen man's throat, Mequillen glanced at his sister. She had paid no attention whatever to Cockerlyne's entrance; she lay motionless, her hands clasped across her bosom, slowly and regularly gasping for breath. But Mequillen knew what would rouse her, for she and Cockerlyne had been engaged for the past six months, and were about to be married, and one great source of her anxiety during the past two days had been in her fears for his safety. And as he saw Cockerlyne returning to consciousness, he turned to her.

"Addie!" he whispered. "Here is Dick!"

The girl slowly opened her eyes and turned her head, and a

faint flush came into her white cheeks. Mequillen reached across, and handed her a glass out of which he had been giving her liquid food at intervals during the past hour.

"Drink that, and then get up and help me with him," he said.

Cockerlyne opened his eyes to the full at last, and saw the brother and sister, and he struggled up from the floor.

"I got through, anyway," he said. "I thought that if we – are all going to – to die, eh? – I'd see Addie first. I – have I been fainting, Dan?"

"Lie down again, Addie, this instant!" commanded Mequillen sharply. "Now then, Dick, drink the rest of that, and then you shall have some of this concentrated meat extract. No nonsense, now. What we've all got to do is to keep up strength till this – passes. I'm off to our housekeeper. I forbid you two to move or to speak until I come back."

When he returned Mequillen found his sister staring at Cockerlyne, and Cockerlyne staring at her, as if they were looking their last at each other.

"Come, come!" he said, with the best imitation of a laugh that he could raise. "We're not at that stage yet. Now, then, obey your doctor."

And he fed them both as if they were children, and presently had the gratification of seeing the colour come back to Cockerlyne's face, and a new light into his eyes. The big man suddenly rose, and shook his limbs, and smiled grimly. There were sandwiches on the table, and he reached over and took one in each hand, and began to eat voraciously.

"Chuck the nursing, Dan," he growled. "I'm all right. I said I'd get it done, and I've done it. I'm here!"

Mequillen saw with thankfulness that Cockerlyne was going to be something to stand by. He nodded with assumed coolness.

"All right, old chap," he said. "And – how did you get here?"

Cockerlyne moistened his tongue.

"Fought through it," he said grimly. "I've been thirty hours at it – thirty hours!"

"Yes?" said Mequillen.

"You know," continued Cockerlyne, "you know when you telephoned to me at six last night? After that I think I went mad for a while. Then I got out of the office, and somehow got to the Bank station of the South London – the Tube trains ran now and

then. I don't know how I did it, but I travelled that way as far as the train ran – Clapham, or somewhere. And then – well, I just made along this way. Of course, I knew every bit of the road. It was like sleepwalking."

Mequillen nodded, and, picking up a fan, resumed his occupation of trying to agitate the air about his sister's face.

"Well, you're here, Dick," he said. "But – London?"

Cockerlyne shivered.

"London is – oh, I don't know what London is!" he answered. "I think half the people are dead, and the other half mad. Once or twice I went out into the streets. One man you met was on his knees, praying aloud; the next was – oh, I don't know! It seemed that hell was let loose; and yet the churches were crammed to the doors. And people were fighting for the liquor in the dram shops and the public houses. I – I don't seem to remember much; perhaps I'm mad myself now. How long will it be, Dan?"

"How long will what be?" asked Mequillen.

"The – the end? I expect this is the end, isn't it?" said Cockerlyne. "What else can it be?"

"Don't talk rot!" said Mequillen sharply. "I thought you'd come round again. Here, pour some of the stuff out of that bottle into that glass, and carry it to the housekeeper in the next room. Pull yourself together, man!"

"Sorry," said Cockerlyne, and rose to carry out Mequillen's commands. "I – I'm light-headed, perhaps. Don't ask me any more about what I saw. It sends me off."

He went away to the housekeeper, and Mequillen heard him speaking to her in the dry, croaking tones in which they all spoke. And presently Cockerlyne came hurriedly back, and, standing at the open door, beckoned to him with a shaking hand. Mequillen rose, and shambled across to him.

"Come out to the garden!" whispered Cockerlyne, and led the way to the front door. "Listen!" he said. "I caught the sound in there! Listen!"

Mequillen grasped one of the pillars of the porch and strained his ears. And somewhere, so far off that it might have been thousands of miles away, he heard what he knew to be the coming of a mighty wind, and instinctively he tightened his grip on the pillar.

"It's a cyclone coming, Cockerlyne!" he shouted, though all around them was still and quiet. "It'll sweep all before it – house, everything! Quick – the two women!"

But before either man could turn to the open door the great fog was swept away before their eyes as if it had been literally snatched from them by some gigantic hand from heaven, and where it had been was a burning and a dazzling light of such power that in an instant they were grovelling on the ground before it with their eyes pressed instinctively into the crooks of their quivering elbows.

Of the two men, Mequillen was the first to comprehend what had happened, and with his comprehension came coolness and resource. Never had he thought so quickly in his life.

"Dick," he whispered, "keep your eyes shut tightly, and turn and creep back into the hall. I'm doing the same thing. You know the little room on the left? Don't open your eyes until you get in there. Now, then," he continued, with a gasp, as the two men reached the room and stood upright, "you can open them here, for the shutters are up. Ah! And yet, you see, although this room should be quite dark, it's almost as light as a normal winter morning."

Cockerlyne stared stupidly about him. "For God's sake, Dan, what's happened?" he exclaimed.

Mequillen was fumbling in a drawer. He brought out two silk mufflers, and passed one to his friend.

"I have a very good idea as to what's happened," he answered gravely. "And I'll tell you in a few minutes. But first muffle your eyes — there, you'll see through two thicknesses of the silk. Now for the women. Fortunately, the curtains are closely drawn in both rooms, or I should have feared for their eyesight in that sudden rush of light — light, Dick, such as this globe has never seen before! Dick, we've got to blindfold them, and then get them into the darkest place in this house. There's an underground room — not a cellar — which I've sometimes used for experiments. We must get them downstairs."

It was easy to see, in spite of the mufflers, that the light in the hall was blinding, and in the curtained study as bright as on an open sea on a cloudless day in summer. And Addie was lying on her sofa with her arms crossed over her forehead and eyes, obviously surprised and distressed by the sudden glare.

"Don't move your arms!" exclaimed Mequillen sharply. "Keep your eyes shut as tight as you can."

"What is it?" she asked. "Has the fog gone, and the sun come?"

"The fog has gone, and a sun has come," replied Mequillen. "And its light is unbearable — just yet. Now, Addie, I am going to blindfold you and take you and Mrs Jepson down to the underground room. We shall all have to get used to the light by degrees, do just what I tell you, and Dick and I will make you comfortable."

But when the two women were safely disposed of in a room into which scarcely any light ever penetrated in an ordinary way, but which was then as light as noontide, Mequillen drew Cockerlyne into the study, and, groping his way to the windows, closed the shutters and drew the curtains over them.

"Now you can take off your muffler," he said quietly. "There, you see it's light enough even now, to read print and to see the time. And – you perceive the time? Half-past twelve, midnight!"

Cockerlyne's face blanched. He swallowed something, and straightened himself.

"What is this, Mequillen?" he asked quietly. "Do you know?" Mequillen shook his head.

"Not with certainty," he answered. "But I think I know. Forty-eight hours ago I discovered a new star, which increased in magnitude at a surprising rate even while I watched it. Now I think that it is a new sun."

"A – new – sun!" exclaimed Cockerlyne. "Impossible!"

"Call it what you will," said Mequillen. "It is, I am certain, at any rate, a vast heavenly body of fire, which was travelling towards this part of space at an inconceivable rate when I first saw it, and is probably at this moment nearer to us than our sun is. Do you feel that the heat is increasing?"

"Yes," replied Cockerlyne; "but it is different in character."

"It is different in character because the wrapping of infinitely fine dust which has been round us has been drawn away," said Mequillen. "But it will increase in intensity."

Cockerlyne gripped the table.

"And?" he whispered.

"In an hour or two we shall be shrivelled up, consumed, like shreds of wool thrown into a furnace!" answered Mequillen. Cockerlyne straightened himself.

"All right, Dan," he said quietly. "I'm glad I came here. What's to be done now?"

Mequillen had turned to a nest of drawers in one of the recesses of his study. He brought out some spectacles fitted with lenses of very dark glass, and handed one to Cockerlyne.

"We will make an attempt to see this new sun," he said. "Put these spectacles on, and for the present fold that muffler about your eyes again once. You'll see through both muffler and spectacles. And now come up to the observatory."

In the observatory, Cockerlyne understood little or nothing of the preparations which Mequillen made. Conscious only of the terrible heat, he stood waiting and thinking of the fate which was about to befall them; and suddenly a terrible impatience seized upon him. If there was but an hour or so to live, his place was with the woman he loved.

"Look here, Dan!" he exclaimed. "I'm going down! If the end's coming, then…"

But Mequillen laid a hand on his arm and drew him forward, at the same tune removing the muffler from his head. "We will go down soon, Cockerlyne," he said. "We must, for we shall have to tell them. But first – look! You can look with safety now."

And then Cockerlyne, following his friend's instructions, looked, and saw widespread above him the dome of the heavens. But never had he so seen it in all his life. From north to south, from east to west, it glowed with the radiance of shining brass;

and in the northeast hung a great globe of fiery red, vaster in dimension than the sun which the world had known till then, and, even when seen through the protections which Mequillen had prepared, sparkling and glittering with darting and leaping flame.

"My God!" said Cockerlyne, in a hushed voice. "My God! Dan, is that – It?"

"That is It," answered Mequillen quietly. "It is now nearly twice the magnitude of our sun, and it is coming nearer. This is no time to make calculations, or even speculations; but I believe it is, at any rate, as near to us as our sun is. Come away, Cockerlyne; I want to look out on the world. Hold my hand and follow me."

And he dragged Cockerlyne away through a trapdoor and into a dark passage, and then into a darker room.

"Keep your hands over your spectacles for a while, and get accustomed to the light by degrees," he said. "I am going to open an observation shutter here, through which we can see a vast stretch of country to the north. It will be a surprise to me if much of it is not already in flames. Now, if you are ready."

Cockerlyne covered his eyes as he heard the click of the observation shutter. Even then, and through the thick black glasses which he was wearing, he felt the extraordinary glare of the light which entered. Presently Mequillen touched his arm.

"You can look now," he said. "See. it's just as I thought! The land's on fire!"

Cockerlyne looked out upon the great sweep of hill and valley, wood and common which stretches across the fairest part of Surrey from the heights above Shere and Albury to those beyond Reigate. He saw the little villages, with their spires and towers and red roofs and tall grey gables; he saw the isolated farms, the stretches of wood, the hillside coppices, the patches of heath and the expanses of green which indicated land untouched by spade or plough.

It was a scene with which he had been familiar from boyhood. Of late he had explored every nook and corner of it with Addie Mequillen, and at all times of the year it had seemed beautiful to him. But under the glare and brilliance of this extraordinary light everything seemed changed. All over that vast prospect great pillars of smoke and flame were rising to the sky. From the valley beneath them came the shrieks and cries of men and women, and as the two men watched they saw the evergreens in Mequillen's garden suddenly turn to the whiteness of paper, and shrivel and disappear in fine ashes.

"Look there!" whispered Mequillen, pointing a shaking finger. "There – Dorking's on fire! And yonder, Reigate, too!"

Cockerlyne tried to speak, but his tongue rattled in his mouth like a dry pea, in a drier pod. He touched Mequillen's arm and pointed downward, and Mequillen nodded.

"Yes," he said. "We had better go down to them; they've got to know."

He took Cockerlyne by the hand and led him back to the observatory, which, in spite of the fact that all its shutters were drawn, was full of light. And as they stepped into it a spark of white flame suddenly appeared in the woodwork, and ran like lightning round the rim of the dome.

"On fire!" said Mequillen quietly. "It's no good, Cockerlyne; we can't do anything. The end's come! We – oh, my God, what's this? What is this? Cockerlyne – Cockerlyne, where are you?"

For just as suddenly as they had seen the greyness of the great fog snatched away from the earth, so now they saw the extraordinary light which had succeeded it snatched away. It was gone in the flash of an eye, with the speed of lightning, and as it went they felt the earth move and shudder, and all around them fell a blackness such as they had never known. And as the two men gripped each other in their terror there suddenly burst upon the dome of the observatory a storm of what seemed to be bullets – fierce, insistent, incessant. The serpent-like trail of fire in the woodwork quivered once and died out. And Mequillen, trembling in every limb, released his hold on Cockerlyne, and staggered against the nearest wall.

"Rain!" he said. "Rain!"

In the darkness, Mequillen heard Cockerlyne first stumble about, and then fall heavily. Then he knew that Cockerlyne had fainted, and he made his way to a switch and turned on the ° electric light, and got water to bring him round. But when he came round, Cockerlyne for some minutes croaked and gabbled incessantly, and it was not until Mequillen had hurried down to the dining room for brandy for him that he regained his senses and was able to sit up, gasping and staring about him. He pointed a shaking finger to the aperture in the dome, through which the rain was pouring, unheeded by Mequillen, in a ceaseless cascade.

"Where is – It?" he gasped. "What – what's come of It?"

Mequillen shook him to his feet, and made him swallow more brandy.

"Pull yourself together, Cockerlyne!" he said. "This is no time to talk science; this is a time to act. Come down, man; we must see to the women! We've just escaped from fire; now we're likely to meet our deaths by water. Listen to that rain, Here, help me to close that shutter. Now, downstairs! It's lucky we're on a hillside! But the people in the valleys! Come on!"

And, leaving Cockerlyne to follow him, Mequillen ran down through the house, to find his sister and the housekeeper in the hall. As he saw them, he knew that they had realized what he now had time to realize – that the terrible heat was dying away, and that it was becoming easier and easier to breathe. As he passed it he glanced at a hanging thermometer, and saw the mercury falling in a steady, swift descent.

Mequillen caught his sister in his arms and pressed her to him. She looked anxiously into his face.

"Dick?" she said.

"He's safe – he's coming," said Mequillen.

Addie suddenly collapsed, and hid her face in her hands. The housekeeper was already in a heap in the nearest chair, sobbing and moaning. And as Cockerlyne came slowly down the stairs, Mequillen saw that, strong man as he was, his nerves had been shaken so much that he was trembling like a leaf. Once more Mequillen had to summon all his energies together in the task of bringing his companions round, and as he moved about from one to the other his quick ear heard the never-ceasing rattle of the rain, which was heavier than any tropical rain that ever fell. And presently he caught the sound of newly forming cascades and waterfalls, cutting new ways from the hilltops to the level lands of the valleys. Now the normal coolness of middle winter was coming back. The women picked up the wraps they had thrown aside; the men hurried into greatcoats. And as the February dawn came grey and slow across the hills, Mequillen and Cockerlyne went up to the observatory, and into the little look-out turret from which they had seen the spirals of smoke and flame rising from the land only a few hours before.

The rain was still falling, but with no more violence than that of a tropical rainstorm. But the air was throbbing, pulsating, humming with the noise of falling waters. A hundred yards away from the house a churning and seething mass of yellow foam was tearing a path, wide and deep, through a copse of young pine; down in the valley immediately beneath them lay a newly formed lake. In the valleys on every side, as far as the eye could reach, lay patches of silvery hue, which they knew to be great sheets of water; and now the air was cool, and the hitherto tortured lungs could breathe it in comfort.

"Mequillen," said Cockerlyne, after a long silence, "what happened?" But Mequillen shook his head.

"I am as a child standing at the edge of a great ocean," he answered. "I cannot say definitely. I think that the great star which we saw, rushing upon us, was suddenly arrested, split into fragments, when that darkness fell, and that we were saved. Once more, Cockerlyne, the old world, a speck in space, will move on. For look there!"

And Cockerlyne turned as Mequillen pointed, and saw, slowly rising over the Surrey hills, the kindly sun of a grey February morning.

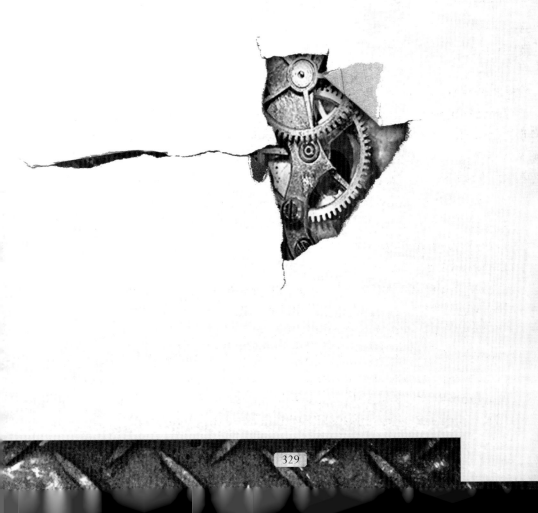

LONDON TIMES 1904

1898

MARK TWAIN

Chicago, April 1, 1904

I **RESUME** by cable telephone where I left off yesterday. For many hours, now, this vast city – along with the rest of the globe, of course – has talked of nothing but the extraordinary episode mentioned in my last report. In accord with your instructions, I will now trace the romance from its beginnings down to the culmination of yesterday. By odd chance, I was a personal actor in part of this drama myself. The opening scene plays in Vienna. Date, 1:00 a.m., March 31, 1898. I had spent the evening at a social entertainment. About midnight, I went away, in company with the attaches of the British, Italian, and American embassies, to finish with a late smoke. This function had been appointed to take place in the house of Lieutenant

Hillyer, the third attache mentioned above. When we arrived there we found several visitors in the room: young Szczepanik (pronounced, approximately, *Zepan*nik); Mr K, his financial backer; Mr W, the latter's secretary; and Lieutenant Clayton of the United States army. War was at that time threatening between Spain and our country, and Lieutenant Clayton had been sent to Europe on military business. I was well acquainted with young Szczepanik and his two friends, and I knew Mr Clayton slightly. I had met him at West Point years before, when he was a cadet. He had the reputation of being an able officer, and also of being quick-tempered and plain-spoken.

This smoking party had been gathered together partly for business: to consider the availability of the telelectroscope for military service. It sounds odd enough now, but at that time the invention was not taken seriously by anyone except its inventor. Even his financial supporter regarded it merely as a curious and interesting toy. Indeed, he was so convinced of this that he had actually postponed its use by the general world to the end of the dying century by granting a two years' exclusive lease of it to a syndicate whose intent was to exploit it at the Paris World's Fair.

When we entered the smoking room we found Lieutenant Clayton and Szczepanik engaged in a warm talk over the telelectroscope in the German tongue. Clayton was saying:

"Well, you know *my* opinion of it, anyway!" And he brought his fist down with emphasis upon the table.

"And I do not value it," retorted the young inventor, with provokingly calm tone and manner. Clayton turned to Mr K, and said:

"I cannot see why you are wasting money on this toy. The day

will never come when it will do a farthing's worth of real service for any human being."

"That may be; yes, that may be; still, I have put the money in it, and am content. I think, myself, that it is only a toy, but Szczepanik claims more for it, and I know him well enough to believe that he can see farther than I – either with his telelectroscope or without it."

The soft answer did not cool Clayton down; it seemed only to irritate him more; and he repeated and emphasized his conviction that the invention would never do any man a farthing's worth of *real* service. He even made it a 'brass' farthing, this time. Then he laid an English farthing on the table, and added: "Take that, Mr K, and put it away; and if ever the telelectroscope does any man an actual service – mind, a real service – please mail it to me as a reminder, and I will take back what I have been saying. Will you?"

"I will." And Mr K. put the coin in his pocket.

Mr Clayton now turned toward Szczepanik, and began a taunt – a taunt which did not reach a finish; Szczepanik interrupted it with a hardy retort, and followed this with a blow. There was a brisk fight for a moment; then the attaches separated the men.

The scene now changes to Chicago. Time, the autumn of 1901. As soon as the Paris contract released the telelectroscope, it was delivered to public use, and was soon connected with the telephonic systems of the whole world. The improved 'limitless-distance' telephone was presently introduced, and the daily doings of the globe made visible to everybody, and audibly discussable, too, by witnesses separated by any number of leagues.

By and by Szczepanik arrived in Chicago, and, unfortunately, Clayton (now captain) happened to be transferred there as well at about the same time. The two men resumed the quarrel of 1898. On three different occasions they quarrelled, and were separated by witnesses. Then came an interval of two months, during which Szczepanik was not seen by any of his friends, and it was at first supposed that he had gone off on a sightseeing tour and would soon be heard from. But no word came came from him. Then it was supposed that he had returned to Europe. Still, time drifted on, and he was not heard from. Nobody was troubled, for he was like most inventors and other kinds of poets, and went and came capriciously, and often without notice.

Now comes the tragedy. On the 29th of December, in a dark and unused compartment of the cellar under Captain Clayton's house, a corpse was discovered by one of Clayton's maidservants. Though unrecognizable due to its violent demise and subsequent deterioration, the body's height and build matched that of Szczepanik.

Clayton was arrested, indicted, and brought to trial, charged with Szczepanik's murder. The evidence against him was damning. Clayton admitted this himself. He said that a reasonable man could not examine this testimony with a dispassionate mind and not be convinced by it; yet the man would be in error, nevertheless. Clayton swore that he did not commit the murder, and that he had nothing to do with it. His feeble and far-fetched explanation – that an unknown murderer must have somehow sneaked the body of his equally unknown victim into the vacant house before Clayton purchased it – fell on deaf ears.

As your readers will remember, he was condemned to death. He had numerous and powerful friends, and they worked hard to save him, for none of them doubted the truth of his assertion. I did what little I could to help, for I had long since become a close friend of his, and thought it was not in his character to back an enemy into a corner and assassinate him. During 1902 and 1903 he was several times reprieved by the governor; he was reprieved once more in the beginning of the present year, and the execution day postponed to March 31.

The governor's situation has been embarrassing, from the day of the condemnation, because of the fact that Clayton's wife is the governor's niece. The marriage took place in 1899, when Clayton was 34 and the girl 23, and has been a happy one. There is one child, a little girl three years old. Pity for the poor mother and child kept the mouths of grumblers closed at first; but this could not last forever – for in America politics has a hand in everything – and by and by the governor's political opponents began to call attention to his delay in allowing the law to take its course. These hints have grown more and more frequent, and more and more pronounced. Naturally his own party grew nervous. Its leaders began to visit Springfield and hold long private conferences with him. He was now between two fires. On the one hand, his niece was imploring him to pardon her husband; on the other were the leaders, insisting that he stand to his plain duty as chief magistrate of the State, and place no further bar to Clayton's execution. Duty won in the struggle, and the governor gave his word that he would not again respite the condemned man.

This was two weeks ago. Mrs Clayton now said: "Now that you have given your word, my last hope is gone, for I know you will never go back on it. But you have done your best for John, and I have no reproaches for you. You love him, and you love me, and we both know that if you could honourably save him, you would. I will go to him now, and be what help I can, and get what comfort I may out of the few days left to us before the night comes which will have no end for me in life. You will be with me that day? You will not let me bear it alone?"

"I will take you to him myself, poor child, and be near you to the last."

By the governor's command, Clayton was now allowed every indulgence he might ask for which could interest his mind and soften the hardships of his imprisonment. His wife and child spent the days with him; I was his companion by night. He was removed from the narrow cell which he had occupied during such a dreary stretch of time, and given the chief warden's roomy and comfortable quarters. His mind was always busy with the catastrophe of his life, and with the slaughtered inventor, and he now took the fancy that he would like to have the telelectroscope and divert his mind with it. He had his wish. The connection was made with the international telephone station, and day by day, and night by night, he called up one corner of the globe after another, and looked upon its life, and studied its strange sights, and spoke with its people, and realized that by grace of this marvellous instrument he was almost as free as the birds of the air, although a prisoner under lock and bars. He seldom spoke to me, and I never interrupted him when he was absorbed in his amusement. I sat in his parlour and read and smoked, and the nights were very quiet and reposefully sociable, and I found them pleasant. Now and then I would hear him say, 'Give me Yedo'; next, 'Give me Hong Kong'; next, 'Give me Melbourne'. And I smoked on, and read in comfort, while he wandered about the remote underworld, where the sun was shining in the sky, and the people were at their daily work. Sometimes the talk that came from those far regions through the microphone attachment interested me, and I listened.

Yesterday – I keep calling it yesterday, which is quite natural, for certain reasons – the instrument remained unused, and that, also, was natural, for it was the eve of the execution day. It was spent in tears and lamentations and farewells. The governor and the wife and child remained until a quarter past eleven at night, and the scenes I witnessed were pitiful to see. The execution was to take place at four in the morning. A little after eleven, a sound of hammering began, and there was a glare of light outside, and

the child cried out, "What is that, papa?" and ran to the window before she could be stopped, and clapped her small hands, and said: "Oh, come and see, mama – such a pretty thing they are making!" The mother knew – and fainted. It was the gallows!

She was carried away to her lodging, poor woman, and Clayton and I were alone – alone, and thinking, brooding, dreaming. We might have been statues, we sat so motionless and still. It was a wild night, for winter was come again for a moment, after the habit of this region in early spring. The sky was starless and black, and a strong wind was blowing from the lake. The silence in the room was so deep that all outside sounds seemed exaggerated by contrast with it. These sounds were fitting ones; they harmonized with the situation and the conditions: the boom and thunder of sudden storm gusts among the roofs and chimneys, then the dying down into moanings and wailings about the eaves and angles; now and then a gnashing and lashing rush of sleet along the windowpanes; and always the muffled and uncanny hammering of the gallows-builders in the courtyard. After an age of this, another sound – far off, and coming smothered and faint through the riot of the tempest – a bell tolling twelve! Another age, and it tolled again. By and by, again. A dreary, long interval after this, then the spectral sound floated to us once more – one, two, three; and this time we caught our breath: 60 minutes of life left!

Clayton rose, and stood by the window, and looked up into the black sky, and listened to the thrashing sleet and the piping wind; then he said: "That a dying man's last of earth should be – this!" After a little he said: "I must see the sun again – the sun!" and the next moment he was feverishly calling: "China! Give me China – Peking!"

I was strangely stirred, and said to myself: "To think that it is a mere human being who does this unimaginable miracle – turns winter into summer, night into day, storm into calm, gives the

338

freedom of the great globe to a prisoner in his cell, and the sun in his naked splendour to a man dying in Egyptian darkness!"

I was listening.

"What light! What brilliancy! What radiance! This is Peking?"

"Yes."

"The time?"

"Mid afternoon."

"What is the great crowd for, and in such gorgeous costumes? What masses and masses of rich colour and barbaric magnificence! And how they flash and glow and burn in the flooding sunlight! What is the occasion of it all?"

"The coronation of our new emperor."

"But I thought that was to take place yesterday."

"This *is* yesterday – to you."

"Certainly it is. But my mind is confused, these days; there are reasons for it… Is this the beginning of the procession?"

"Oh, no; it began to move an hour ago."

"Is there much more of it still to come?"

"Two hours. Why do you sigh?"

"Because I should like to see it all."

"And why can't you?"

"I have to go – presently."

"You have an engagement?"

After a pause, softly: "Yes." After another pause: "Who are these in the splendid pavilion?"

"The imperial family, and visiting royalties from here and there and yonder about Earth."

"And who are those in the adjoining pavilions to the right and left?"

"Ambassadors and their families and suites to the right; unofficial foreigners to the left."

"If you will be so good, I..."

Boom! That distant bell again, tolling the half hour faintly through the tempest of wind and sleet. The door opened, and

the governor and the mother and child entered – the woman in widow's weeds! She fell upon her husband's breast in a passion of sobs, and I – I could not stay; I could not bear it. I went into the bedchamber, and closed the door. I sat there waiting – waiting – waiting, and listening to the rattling sashes and the blustering of the storm. After what seemed to be a long, long time, I heard a rustle and movement in the parlour, and knew that the clergyman and the sheriff and the guard were come. There was some low-voiced talking; then a hush; then a prayer, with a sound of sobbing; presently, footfalls – the departure for the gallows; then the child's happy voice: "Don't cry *now*, mama, when we've got papa again, and taking him home."

The door closed; they were gone. I felt ashamed of myself. I was the only friend of the dying man that had no spirit, no courage. I stepped into the room, and said I would be a man and would follow. But we are made as we are made, and we cannot help it. I did not go.

I fidgeted about the room nervously, and presently went to the window, and softly raised it – drawn by that dread fascination which the terrible and the awful exert – and looked down upon the courtyard. By the garish light of the electric lamps I saw the little group of privileged witnesses, the wife crying on her uncle's breast, the condemned man standing on the scaffold with the halter around his neck, his arms strapped to his body, the black cap on his head, the sheriff at his side with his hand on the drop, the clergyman in front of him with bare head and his book in his hand.

"I am the resurrection and the life..."

I turned away. I could not listen; I could not look. I did not know whither to go or what to do. Mechanically, and without knowing it, I put my eye to that strange instrument, and there was Peking and the procession! The next moment I was leaning out the window, gasping, suffocating, trying to speak, but dumb from the very imminence of the necessity of speaking. The preacher could speak, but I, who had such need of words…

"And may God have mercy upon your soul. Amen."

The sheriff drew down the black cap, and laid his hand upon the lever. I got my voice.

"Stop, for God's sake! The man is innocent. Come here and see Szczepanik face to face!"

Hardly three minutes later the governor had my place at the window, and was saying: "Strike off his bonds and set him free!"

Three minutes later all were in the parlour again. The reader will imagine the scene; I have no need to describe it. It was a sort of mad orgy of joy.

A messenger carried word to Szczepanik in the pavilion, and one could see the distressed amazement dawn in his face as he listened to the tale. Then he came to his end of the line, and talked with Clayton and the governor and the others; and the wife poured out her gratitude for saving her husband's life, and in her thankfulness she kissed him at 12,000 miles' range.

The telelectroscopes of the globe were put to service now, and for many hours the kings and queens of many realms (with here and there a reporter) talked with Szczepanik, and praised him; and the few scientific societies which had not already made him an honourary member conferred that grace upon him.

How had he come to disappear from among us? It was easily explained. He had not grown used to being world-famous, and

had been forced to break away from the lionizing that was robbing him of all privacy and repose. So he grew a beard, put on coloured glasses, disguised himself a little in other ways, then took a fictitious name, and went off to wander about the world in peace.

As for the corpse, Clayton's 'feeble' and 'far-fetched' explanation must in fact have been correct. The body's resemblance to Szczepanik and discovery after the inventor's disappearance were nothing more than extremely unlucky coincidences.

Such is the tale of the drama which began with an inconsequential quarrel in Vienna in the spring of 1898, and came near ending as a tragedy in the spring of 1904.

Chicago, April 5, 1904

Today, by a clipper of the Electric Line, and the latter's Electric Railway connections, arrived an envelope from Vienna, for Captain Clayton, containing an English farthing. The receiver of it was a good deal moved. He called up Vienna, and stood face to face with Mr K, and said:

"I do not need to say anything; you can see it all in my face. My wife has the farthing. She will keep it always."

A TALE OF NEGATIVE GRAVITY

1884

FRANK R STOCKTON

MY WIFE AND I were staying at a small town in northern Italy; and on a certain pleasant afternoon in spring we had taken a walk of six or seven miles to see the sun set behind some low mountains to the west of the town. Nearing the mountain, to a low spur of which we intended to ascend, we easily scaled a wall about four feet high, and found ourselves upon pasture land, which led, sometimes by gradual ascents, and sometimes by bits of rough climbing, to the spot we wished to reach. We were afraid we were a little late, and therefore hurried on, running up the grassy hills, and bounding briskly over the rough and rocky places. I carried a knapsack strapped firmly to my shoulders, and under my wife's arm was a large, soft basket of a kind much used by tourists. This was the way she always carried it. The basket contained two bottles of wine, one sweet for my wife, and another a little acid for myself. Sweet wines give me a headache.

When we reached the grassy bluff, well known thereabouts to lovers of sunset views, I stepped immediately to the edge to gaze upon the scene, but my wife sat down to take a sip of wine, for she was very thirsty; and then, leaving her basket, she came to my side. The scene was indeed one of great beauty. Beneath us stretched a wide valley of many shades of green, with a little river running through it, and red-tiled houses here and there. Beyond rose a range of mountains, pink, pale green, and purple where their tips caught the reflection of the setting sun, and of a rich gray-green in shadows. Beyond all was the blue Italian sky, illuminated by an especially fine sunset.

My wife and I are Americans, and at the time of this story were middle-aged people and very fond of seeing in each other's company whatever there was of interest or beauty around us. We had a son about twenty-two years old, of whom we were also very fond; but he was not with us, being at that time a student in Germany. Although we had good health, we were not very robust people, and, under ordinary circumstances, not much given to long country tramps. I was of medium size, without much muscular development, while my wife was quite stout, and growing stouter.

The reader may, perhaps, be somewhat surprised that a middle-aged couple, not very strong, or very good walkers, the lady loaded with a basket containing two bottles of wine and a metal drinking cup, and the gentleman carrying a heavy knapsack, filled with all sorts of odds and ends, strapped to his shoulders, should set off on a seven-mile walk, jump over a wall, run up a hillside, and yet feel in very good trim to enjoy a sunset view. This peculiar state of things I will proceed to explain.

I had been a professional man, but some years before had retired upon a very comfortable income. I had always been very fond of scientific pursuits, and now made these the occupation and pleasure of much of my leisure time. Our home was in a small town; and in a corner of my grounds I built a laboratory, where I carried on my work and my experiments. I had long been anxious to discover the means not only of producing, but of retaining and controlling, a natural force, really the same as centrifugal force, but which I called negative gravity. This name I adopted because it indicated better than any other the action of the force in question, as I produced it. Positive gravity attracts everything toward the centre of the earth. Negative gravity, therefore, would be that power which repels everything from the centre of the earth, just as the negative pole of a magnet repels the needle, while the positive pole attracts it. My object was, in fact, to store centrifugal force and to render it constant, controllable, and available for use. The advantages of such a discovery could scarcely be described. In a word, it would lighten the burdens of the world.

I will not touch upon the labours and disappointments of several years. It is enough to say that at last I discovered a method of producing, storing, and controlling negative gravity.

The mechanism of my invention was rather complicated, but the method of operating it was very simple. A strong metallic case, about eight inches long, and half as wide, contained the machinery for producing the force; and this was put into action

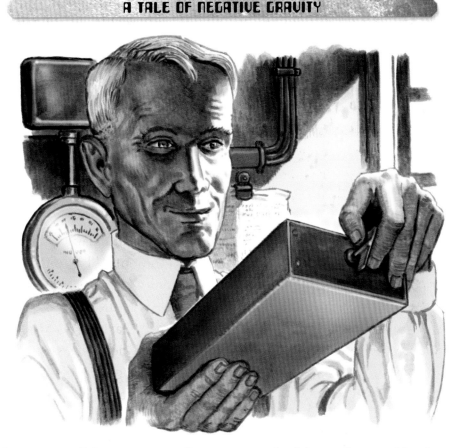

by means of the pressure of a screw worked from the outside. As soon as this pressure was produced, negative gravity began to be evolved and stored, and the greater the pressure the greater the force. As the screw was moved outward, and the pressure diminished, the force decreased, and when the screw was withdrawn to its fullest extent, the action of negative gravity entirely ceased. Thus this force could be produced or dissipated at will to such degrees as might be desired, and its action, so long as the requisite pressure was maintained, was constant.

When this little apparatus worked to my satisfaction I called my wife into my laboratory and explained to her my invention and its value – the construction of the machine, and the wonderful uses to which this invention could be applied. I told her that it could diminish, or entirely dissipate, the weight of objects of any kind. A heavily loaded wagon, with two of these instruments fastened to its sides, and each screwed to a proper force, would be so lifted and supported that it would press upon the ground as lightly as an empty cart, and a small horse could draw it with ease. A car, with a number of these machines, could be made to rise in the air like a balloon. Everything, in fact, that was heavy could be made light; and as a great part of labour, all over the world, is caused by the attraction of gravitation, so this repellent force, wherever applied, would make weight less and work easier. I told her of many, many ways in which the invention might be used, and would have told her of many more if she had not suddenly burst into tears.

"The world has gained something wonderful," she exclaimed, between her sobs, "but I have lost a husband!"

"What do you mean by that?" I asked, in surprise.

"You will never be your own master again. It will succeed, I am sure, and you may make a great deal of money, but we don't need money. What we need is the happiness which we have always had until now. Now there will be companies, and patents, and lawsuits, and experiments, and people calling you a humbug, and other people saying they discovered it long ago, and all sorts of persons coming to see you. No amount of money could repay us for the happiness we have lost."

These words from my wife struck me with much force. Before I had called her my mind had begun to be filled and perplexed with ideas of what I ought to do now that the great invention was perfected. A turmoil of this sort did not suit my age or disposition. I could not but agree with my wife that the joys of a quiet and contented life were about to be broken into.

"Now listen," said my wife, eagerly; "don't you think it would be best to do this: use the thing as much as you please for your own amusement and satisfaction, but let the world wait? It has waited a long time, and let it wait a little longer. When we are dead let Herbert have the invention. He will then be old enough to judge for himself whether it will be better to take advantage of it for his own profit, or simply to give it to the public for nothing."

I took my wife's advice. I wrote a careful and complete account of the invention, and, sealing it up, I gave it to my lawyers to be handed to my son after my death. Then I determined to get all the good and fun out of the thing that was possible without telling anyone anything about it.

The first thing I did was to buy a strong leather knapsack, and inside of this I fastened my little machine, with a screw so arranged that it could be worked from the outside. Strapping this firmly to my shoulders, my wife gently turned the screw at the back until the upward tendency of the knapsack began to lift and sustain me. When I felt myself so gently supported and upheld that I seemed to weigh about thirty or forty pounds, I would set out for a walk. The knapsack did not raise me from the ground, but it gave me a very buoyant step. It was no labour at all to walk; it was a delight, an ecstasy in fact. With the strength of a man and the weight of a child, I strode easily along. The first day I walked half a dozen miles at a very brisk pace, and came back without feeling in the least degree tired. These walks now became one of the greatest joys of my life. When nobody was looking, I would bound over a fence, sometimes just touching it with one hand, and sometimes not touching it at all. I delighted in rough places. I sprang over streams. I jumped and I ran. I felt like Mercury himself.

Some repairs were needed to the foundation walls of my barn, and a two-horse wagon, loaded with building stone, had been brought into my yard and left there. In the evening, when the men had gone away, I took two machines and fastened them, with strong chains, one on each side of the loaded wagon. Then, gradually turning the screws, the wagon was so lifted that its weight became very greatly diminished. We had an old donkey which was occasionally used with a small cart to bring packages from the station. I went into the barn and put the harness on the little fellow, and, bringing him out to the wagon, I attached him to it. When all was ready I set him off; and, to my great delight, he moved off with the two-horse load of stone as easily as if he were drawing his own cart. I led him out into the public road, along which he proceeded without difficulty. He was an opinionated little beast, and sometimes stopped, not liking the peculiar manner in which he was harnessed; but a touch of the switch made him move on, and I soon turned him and brought the wagon back into the yard.

Our trip to Europe was made a few months after this, and was mainly on our son Herbert's account. He, poor fellow, was in great trouble, and so, therefore, were we. He had become engaged, with our full consent, to Janet Gilbert, a young lady in our town, the daughter of a gentleman whom we esteemed very highly. Herbert was young to be engaged to be married, but as we felt that he would never find a girl to make him so good a wife, we were entirely satisfied, especially as it was agreed on all hands that the marriage was not to take place for some time. But suddenly, without any reason that seemed to us justifiable, Mr Gilbert, the only surviving parent of Janet, broke off the match; and he and his daughter soon after left the town for a trip to the West.

This blow nearly broke poor Herbert's heart. He gave up his professional studies and came home to us, and for a time we thought he would be seriously ill. Then we took him to Europe, and after a Continental tour of a month or two we left him, at his own request, in Goettingen, where he thought it would do him good to go to work again. Then we went down to the little town in Italy where my story first finds us.

I had brought with me both my little machines. One was still in my knapsack, and the other I had fastened to the inside of an enormous family trunk. As one is obliged to pay for nearly every pound of his baggage on the Continent, this saved me a great deal of money. Everything heavy was packed into this great trunk – books, papers, the bronze, iron, and marble relics we had picked up, and all the articles that usually weigh down a tourist's baggage. I screwed up the negative gravity apparatus until the trunk could be handled with ease by an ordinary porter. I could have made it weigh nothing at all, but this, of course, I did not wish to do.

Desirous that my wife should have the advantage of negative gravity while taking our walks, I had removed the machine from the trunk and fastened it inside of the basket, which she could carry under her arm. This assisted her wonderfully.

There were English-speaking people stopping at the hotel

where we were, but none of them offered to accompany us on our rambles, for which we were very glad. There was one man there, however, who was a great walker. He was an Englishman, a member of an Alpine Club. One evening this gentleman was talking to me and some others about the ascent of the Matterhorn, and I took occasion to deliver in pretty strong language my opinion upon such exploits. I declared them to be useless, foolhardy, and, if the climber had anyone who loved him, wicked.

"Even if the weather should permit a view," I said, "what is that compared to the terrible risk to life? Under certain circumstances," I added (thinking of a kind of waistcoat I had some idea of making, which, set about with little negative-gravity machines, all connected with a conveniently handled screw, would enable the wearer at times to dispense with his weight altogether), "such ascents might be divested of danger, and be quite admissible; but ordinarily they should be frowned upon by the intelligent public."

The Alpine Club man looked at me, especially regarding my somewhat slight figure and thinnish legs.

"It's all very well for you to talk that way," he said, "because it is easy to see that you are not up to that sort of thing."

"In conversations of this kind," I replied, "I never make personal allusions; but since you have chosen to do so, I feel inclined to invite you to walk with me tomorrow to the top of the mountain to the north of this town."

The next afternoon, about two o'clock, the Alpine Club man and myself set out for the mountain.

"What have you got in your knapsack?" he said.

"A hammer to use if I come across geological specimens, a field glass, a flask of wine, and some other things."

"I wouldn't carry any weight, if I were you," he said.

"Oh, I don't mind it," I answered, and off we started.

The mountain to which we were bound was about two miles from the town. Its nearest side was steep, and in places almost precipitous, but it sloped away more gradually toward the north, and up that side a road led by devious windings to a village near the summit. It was not a very high mountain, but it would do for an afternoon's climb.

"I suppose you want to go up by the road," said my companion.

"Oh no," I answered, "we won't go so far around as that. There is a path up this side, along which I have seen men driving their goats. I prefer to take that."

"Alright, if you say so," he answered, with a smile; "but you'll find it pretty tough."

After a time he remarked:

"I wouldn't walk so fast, if I were you."

"Oh, I like to walk along briskly," I said. And briskly on we continued.

My wife had screwed up the machine in the knapsack even more than usual, and walking seemed scarcely any effort at all. My companion had taken the lead, so as to show me how to climb. However, making a detour over some rocks, I quickly passed him and went ahead. After that it was all but impossible for him to keep up with me.

I ran up steep places, I cut off the windings of the path by lightly clambering over rocks, and even when I followed the

beaten track my step was as rapid as if I had been walking on level ground.

Twenty minutes after I arrived at the summit my companion joined me, puffing, and wiping his red face with his handkerchief.

"Confound it!" he cried, "I never came up a mountain so fast in my life."

I found the descent of the mountain much more pleasant than the ascent. It was positively exhilarating. I jumped from rocks and bluffs eight and ten feet in height, and touched the ground as gently as if I had stepped down but two feet. I was careful to avoid dangerous places, but the runs and jumps I made were such as no man had ever made before upon that mountainside. Once only I heard my companion's voice.

"You'll break your damned neck!" he yelled.

"Never fear!" I called back, and soon left him far above.

When I reached the bottom I would have waited for him, but my activity had warmed me up, and as a cool evening breeze was beginning to blow I thought it better not to stop and take cold. Half an hour after my arrival at the hotel I came down to the court, cool, fresh, and dressed for dinner, and just in time to meet the Alpine man as he entered, hot, dusty, and growling.

"Excuse me for not waiting for you," I said.

There was no doubt that what I had done tickled my vanity.

"I think now," I said, when I related the matter to my wife, "that he will scarcely say that I am not up to that sort of thing."

And now, after this long digression, we will return to ourselves, standing on the little bluff and gazing out upon the sunset view. When the sky began to fade a little we turned from it and prepared to go back to the town.

"Where is the basket?" I said.

"I left it right here," answered my wife. "I unscrewed the machine and it lay perfectly flat."

"Did you afterward take out the bottles?" I asked, seeing them lying on the grass.

"Yes, I believe I did. I had to take out yours in order to get at mine."

"Then," said I, after looking all about the grassy patch on which we stood, "I am afraid you did not entirely unscrew the instrument, and that when the weight of the bottles was removed the basket gently rose into the air."

"It may be so," she said, lugubriously.

"I believe that is just what has happened," I said. "Look up there! I vow that is our basket!"

I pulled out my field glass and directed it at a little speck high above our heads. It was the basket floating high in the air. I gave the glass to my wife to look, but she did not want to use it.

"What shall I do?" she cried. "I can't walk home without that basket. It's perfectly dreadful!" And she looked as if she was going to cry.

"Do not distress yourself," I said. "We shall get home very well. You shall put your hand on my shoulder, while I put my arm around you. Then you can screw up my machine a good deal higher, and it will support us both. In this way I am sure that we shall get on very well."

We carried out this plan, and managed to walk on with moderate comfort. The road for the most part declined gently toward the town, and with moderate ease we made our way along it. But we walked much more slowly than we had done before, and it was quite dark when we reached our hotel. A travelling carriage was standing before the entrance, and against the light. It was necessary to pass around it, and my wife went first. I attempted to follow her, but, strange to say, there was nothing under my feet. I stepped vigorously, but only wagged my legs in the air. To my horror I found that I was rising in the air! I soon saw, by the light below me, that I was some fifteen feet from the ground. The carriage drove away, and in the darkness I was not noticed. Of course I knew what had happened. The instrument in my knapsack had been screwed up to such an intensity, in order to support both myself and my wife, that when her weight was removed the force of the negative gravity was sufficient to raise me from the ground. But I was glad to find that when I had risen to the height I have mentioned I did not go up any higher, but hung in the air, about on a level with the second tier of windows of the hotel.

I now began to try to reach the screw in my knapsack in order to reduce the force of the negative gravity; but, do what I would, I could not get my hand to it. The machine in the knapsack had been placed so as to support me in a well-balanced and comfortable way; and in doing this it had been impossible to set the screw so that I could reach it. But in a temporary arrangement of the kind this had not been considered necessary, as my wife always turned the screw for me until sufficient lifting power had been attained. When I found that I could not turn the screw I began to be much alarmed. I did not dare to call for assistance, for if any of the simple-minded inhabitants of the town had discovered me floating in the air they would have taken me for a demon, and would probably have shot at me. A moderate breeze was blowing, and it wafted me gently down the street. If it had blown me against a tree I would have seized it, and have endeavoured, so to speak, to climb down it; but there were no trees. On many accounts I was glad that the night was so dark, for, much as I desired to get down, I wanted no one to see me in my strange position, which, to anyone but myself and wife, would be utterly unaccountable. If I could rise as high as the roofs I might get on one of them, and, tearing off an armful of tiles, so load myself that I would be heavy enough to descend. But I did not rise to the eaves of any of the houses. What was to be done? Should I call out? In that case, if I were not shot or stoned, my strange predicament, and the secret of my invention, would be exposed to the world. If I did not do this, I must either let myself drop and be killed or mangled, or hang there and die.

Such thoughts were not reassuring, and I determined that if I could find no means of getting down without assistance, I would call out and run all risks; but so long as I could endure the tension of the straps I would hold out, and hope for a tree or a pole. Perhaps it might rain, and my wet clothes would then become so heavy that I would descend as low as the top of a lamp post.

As this thought was passing through my mind I saw a spark of light upon the street approaching me. I rightly imagined that it came from a tobacco pipe, and presently I heard a voice. It was that of the Alpine Club man. Of all people in the world I did not want him to discover me, and I hung as motionless as possible. He was speaking to another person who was walking with him.

"He is crazy beyond a doubt," said the Alpine man. "Nobody but a maniac could have gone up and down that mountain as he did! He hasn't any muscles, and one need only look at him to know that he couldn't do any climbing in a natural way. It is only the excitement of insanity that gives him strength."

The two now stopped almost under me, and then the other person spoke.

"I am afraid what you say is too true," he remarked. "Indeed, I have known it for some time."

At these words my breath almost stopped. It was the voice of Mr Gilbert, my townsman, and the father of Janet. It must have been he who had arrived in the travelling-carriage. Proper or improper, I listened with all my ears.

"It is a very sad case," Mr Gilbert continued. "My daughter was engaged to marry his son, but I broke off the match. I could not have her marry the son of a lunatic, and there could be no doubt of his condition. I myself saw a most heartrending instance of how a kindly man's nature can be changed by the derangement of his intellect. I was at some distance from his house, but I plainly saw him harness a little donkey which he owns to a large two-horse wagon loaded with stone, and beat and lash the poor little beast until it drew the heavy load some distance along the public road. I would have remonstrated with him on this horrible cruelty, but he had the wagon back in his yard before I could reach him.

"There can be no doubt of his insanity," said the Alpine Club man, "and he oughtn't to be allowed to travel about in this way."

"I am sorry he is here," said Mr Gilbert, "for it would be very painful to meet him. My daughter and I will retire very soon, and go away as early tomorrow morning as possible, so as to avoid seeing him."

And then they walked back to the hotel.

For a few moments I hung, utterly forgetful of my condition, and absorbed in the consideration of these revelations. One idea filled my mind. Everything must be explained to Mr Gilbert, even if it should be necessary to have him called to me, and for me to speak to him from the upper air.

Just then I saw something white approaching me along the road. My eyes had become accustomed to the darkness, and I perceived that it was an upturned face. I recognized the hurried gait, the form; it was my wife. As she came near me, I called her name, and in the same breath entreated her not to scream. "You must help me to get down," I said, "without anybody seeing us."

"What shall I do?" she whispered.

"Try to catch hold of this string."

Taking a piece of twine from my pocket, I lowered one end to her. But it was too short; she could not reach it. I then tied my handkerchief to it, but still it was not long enough.

"I can get more string, or handkerchiefs," she whispered, hurriedly.

"No," I said; "you could not get them up to me. But, leaning against the hotel wall, on this side, in the corner, just inside of the garden gate, are some fishing poles. I have seen them there every day. You can easily find them in the dark."

The hotel was not far away, and in a few minutes my wife returned with a fishing pole. She stood on tiptoe, and reached it high in air; but all she could do was to strike my feet and legs with it. My most frantic exertions did not enable me to get my hands low enough to touch it.

"Wait a minute," she said; and the rod was withdrawn.

I knew what she was doing. There was a hook and line attached to the pole, and with womanly dexterity she was fastening the hook to the extreme end of the rod. Soon she reached up, and gently struck at my legs. After a few attempts the hook caught in my trousers, a little below my right knee. Then there was a slight pull, a long scratch down my leg, and the hook was stopped by the top of my boot. Then came a steady downward pull, and I felt myself descending. Gently and firmly the rod was drawn down; carefully the lower end was kept free from the ground; and in a few moments my ankle was seized with a vigorous grasp. Then some one seemed to climb up me, my feet touched the ground, an arm was thrown around my neck, the hand of another arm was busy at the back of my knapsack, and I soon stood firmly in the road, entirely divested of negative gravity.

"Oh that I should have forgotten," sobbed my wife, "and that I should have dropped your arms and let you go up into the air! I knew that you had wax matches in your pocket, and hoped that you would keep on striking them, so that you would be seen."

"But I did not wish to be seen," I said, as we hurried to the hotel; "and I can never be sufficiently thankful that it was you who found me and brought me down. Do you know that it is Mr Gilbert and his daughter who have just arrived? I must see him instantly. I will explain it all to you when I come upstairs."

I took off my knapsack and gave it to my wife, who carried it to our room, while I went to look for Mr Gilbert. Fortunately I found him just as he was about to go up to his chamber. He took my offered hand, but looked at me sadly and gravely.

"Mr Gilbert," I said, "I must speak to you in private. Let us step into this room."

"My friend," said Mr Gilbert, "it will be much better to avoid discussing this subject. It is very painful to both of us, and no good can come from talking of it."

"You cannot now comprehend what it is I want to say to you," I replied. "Come in here, and in a few minutes you will be very glad that you listened to me."

My manner was so earnest and impressive that Mr Gilbert was constrained to follow me, and we went into a small room and closed the door. I gave him the whole history of my invention, and explained the reason of the actions that had appeared to him those of a lunatic. I said nothing about the little incident of that evening. That was a mere accident, and I did not care now to speak of it.

Mr Gilbert listened to me very attentively.

"Your wife is here?" he asked, when I had finished.

"Yes," I said; "and she will corroborate my story in every item, and no one could ever suspect her of being crazy. I will go and bring her to you."

In a few minutes my wife was in the room, had shaken hands with Mr Gilbert, and had been told of my suspected madness. She turned pale, but smiled.

"He did act like a crazy man," she said, "but I never supposed that anybody would think him one."

"And now, my dear," said I, "perhaps you will tell Mr Gilbert how I did all this."

And then she told him the story that I had told.

Mr Gilbert looked from the one to the other of us with a troubled air.

"Of course I do not doubt either of you, or rather I do not doubt that you believe what you say. All would be right if I could bring myself to credit that such a force as that you speak of can possibly exist."

"That is a matter," said I, "which I can easily prove to you by actual demonstration. If you can wait a short time, until my wife and I have had something to eat – for I am nearly famished, and I am sure she must be – I will set your mind at rest upon that point."

"I will wait here," said Mr Gilbert, "and smoke a cigar. Don't hurry yourselves. I shall be glad to have some time to think about what you have told me."

When we had finished the dinner, which had been set aside for us, I went upstairs and got my knapsack, and we both joined Mr Gilbert in the smoking-room. I showed him the little machine, and explained, very briefly, the principle of its construction.

"If you will come with me," said I to Mr Gilbert, "I will show you how this thing works."

"That is just what I want to see," he answered.

"I will go with you," said my wife, throwing a shawl over her head. And we started up the street.

When we were outside the little town I found the starlight was quite sufficient for my purpose. The white roadway, the low walls, and objects about us, could easily be distinguished.

"Now," said I to Mr Gilbert, "I want to put this knapsack on you, and let you see how it feels, and how it will help you to walk." To this he assented with some eagerness, and I strapped it firmly on him. "I will now turn this screw," said I, "until you shall become lighter and lighter."

"Be very careful not to turn it too much," said my wife, earnestly.

"Oh, you may depend on me for that," said I, turning the screw very gradually.

Mr Gilbert was a stout man, and I was obliged to give the screw a good many turns.

"There seems to be considerable hoist in it," he said, directly. And then I put my arms around him, and found that I could raise him from the ground.

"Are you lifting me?" he exclaimed, in surprise.

"Yes; I did it with ease," I answered.

"Upon – my – word!" exclaimed Mr Gilbert.

I then gave the screw a half-turn more, and told him to walk and run. He started off, at first slowly, then he made long strides, then he began to run, and then to skip and jump. It had been years since Mr Gilbert had skipped and jumped. No one was in sight, and he was free to gambol as much as he pleased. "Could you give it another turn?" said he, bounding up to me. "I want to try that wall." I put on a little more negative gravity, and he vaulted over a five-foot wall with great ease. In an instant he had leaped back into the road, and in two bounds was at my side. "I came down as light as a cat," he said. "There was never anything like it." And away he went up the road, taking steps at least eight feet long, leaving my wife and me laughing. In a few minutes he was with us again. "Take it off," he said. "If I wear it any longer I shall want one myself, and then I shall be taken for a crazy man, and perhaps clapped into an asylum."

"Now," said I, as I turned back the screw before unstrapping the knapsack, "do you understand how I took long walks, and leaped and jumped; how I ran uphill and downhill, and how the little donkey drew the loaded wagon?"

"I understand it all," cried he. "I take back all I ever said or thought about you, my friend."

"And Herbert may marry Janet?" cried my wife.

"*May* marry her!" cried Mr Gilbert. "Indeed, he *shall* marry her, if I have anything to say about it! My poor girl has been drooping ever since I told her it could not be."

My wife rushed at him, but whether she embraced him or

only shook his hands I cannot say; for I had the knapsack in one hand and was rubbing my eyes with the other.

"But, my dear fellow," said Mr Gilbert, directly, "if you still consider it to your interest to keep your invention a secret, I wish you had never made it. No one having a machine like that can help using it, and it is often quite as bad to be considered a maniac as to be one."

"My friend," I cried, with some excitement, "I have made up my mind on this subject. The little machine in this knapsack, which is the only one I now possess, has been a great pleasure to me. But I now know it has also been of the greatest injury indirectly to me and mine, not to mention some direct inconvenience and danger, which I will speak of another time. The secret lies with us, and we will keep it. But the invention itself is too full of temptation and danger for any of us."

As I said this I held the knapsack with one hand while I quickly turned the screw with the other. In a few moments it was high above my head, while I with difficulty held it down by the straps.

"Look!" I cried. And then I released my hold, and the knapsack shot into the air and disappeared into the upper gloom.

I was about to make a remark, but had no chance, for my wife threw herself upon my bosom, sobbing with joy.

"Oh, I am so glad – so glad!" she said. "And you will never make another?"

"Never another!" I answered.

"And now let us hurry in and see Janet," said my wife.

"You don't know how heavy and clumsy I feel," said Mr Gilbert, striving to keep up with us as we walked back. "If I had worn that thing much longer, I should never have been willing to take it off!"

Janet had retired, but my wife went up to her room.

"I think she has felt it as much as our boy," she said, when she rejoined me. "But I tell you, my dear, I left a very happy girl in that little bedchamber over the garden."

And there were three very happy elderly people talking together until quite late that evening. "I shall write to Herbert tonight," I said, when we separated, "and tell him to meet us all in Geneva. It will do the young man no harm if we interrupt his studies just now."

"Let me add a postscript to the letter," said Mr Gilbert, "and I am sure it will require no knapsack with a screw in the back to bring him quickly to us."

And it did not.

What became of the basket and the knapsack, or whether they ever met in upper air, I do not know. If they but float away and stay away from ken of mortal man, I shall be satisfied.

And whether or not the world will ever know more of the power of negative gravity depends entirely upon the disposition of my son Herbert, when – after a good many years, I hope – he shall open the packet my lawyers have in keeping.

Note: It would be quite useless for any one to interview my wife on this subject, for she has entirely forgotten how my machine was made. And as for Mr Gilbert, he never knew.

THE OTHER

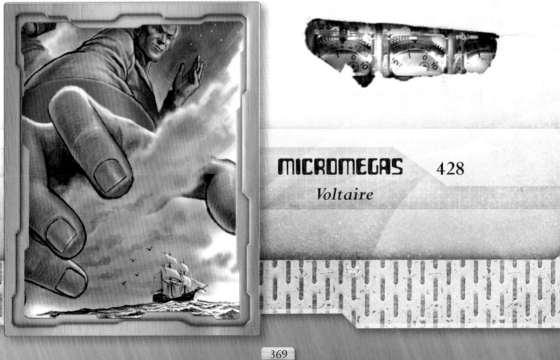

THE CYLINDER OPENS

1898 FROM **THE WAR OF THE WORLDS**

H G WELLS

WHEN I RETURNED to the common the sun was setting. Scattered groups were hurrying from the direction of Woking, and one or two persons were returning. The crowd about the pit had increased, and stood out black against the lemon yellow of the sky – a couple of hundred people, perhaps. There were raised voices, and some sort of struggle appeared to be going on about the pit. Strange imaginings passed through my mind. As I drew nearer I heard Stent's voice:

"Keep back! Keep back!"

A boy came running towards me.

"It's a-movin'," he said to me as he passed; "a-screwin' and a-screwin' out. I don't like it. I'm a-goin' 'ome, I am."

I went on to the crowd. There were really, I should think,

two or three hundred people elbowing and jostling one another, the one or two ladies there being by no means the least active.

"He's fallen in the pit!" cried someone.

"Keep back!" said several.

The crowd swayed a little, and I elbowed my way through. Everyone seemed greatly excited. I heard a peculiar humming sound from the pit.

"I say!" said Ogilvy; "help keep these idiots back. We don't know what's in the confounded thing, you know!"

I saw a young man, a shop assistant in Woking I believe he was, standing on the cylinder and trying to scramble out of the hole again. The crowd had pushed him in.

The end of the cylinder was being screwed out from within. Nearly two feet of shining screw projected. Somebody blundered against me, and I narrowly missed being pitched onto the top of the screw. I turned, and as I did so the screw must have come out, for the lid of the cylinder fell upon the gravel with a ringing concussion. I stuck my elbow into the person behind me, and turned my head towards the Thing again. For a moment that circular cavity seemed perfectly black. I had the sunset in my eyes.

I think everyone expected to see a man emerge – possibly something a little unlike us terrestrial men, but in all essentials a man. I know I did. But, looking, I presently saw something stirring within the shadow: greyish billowy movements, one above another, and then two luminous discs – like eyes. Then something resembling a little grey snake, about the thickness of a walking stick, coiled up out of the writhing middle, and wriggled in the air towards me – and then another.

A sudden chill came over me. There was a loud shriek from a woman behind. I half turned, keeping my eyes fixed upon the cylinder still, from which other tentacles were now projecting, and began pushing my way back from the edge of the pit. I saw astonishment giving place to horror on the faces of the people about me. I heard inarticulate exclamations on all sides. There was a general movement backwards. I saw the shopman struggling still on the edge of the pit. I found myself alone, and saw the people on the other side of the pit running off, Stent among them. I looked again at the cylinder, and ungovernable terror gripped me. I stood petrified and staring.

A big, greyish, rounded bulk, the size, perhaps, of a bear, was rising slowly and painfully out of the cylinder. As it bulged up and caught the light, it glistened like wet leather.

Two large dark-coloured eyes were regarding me steadfastly. The mass that framed them, the head of the thing, was rounded, and had, one might say, a face. There was a mouth under the eyes, the lipless brim of which quivered and panted, and dropped saliva. The whole creature heaved and pulsated convulsively.

Those who have never seen a living Martian can scarcely imagine the strange horror of its appearance. The peculiar V-shaped mouth with its pointed upper lip, the absence of brow ridges, the absence of a chin beneath the wedgelike lower lip, the incessant quivering of this mouth, the Gorgon groups of tentacles, the tumultuous breathing of the lungs in a strange atmosphere, the evident heaviness and painfulness of movement due to the greater gravitational energy of the earth – above all, the extraordinary intensity of the immense eyes – were at once

vital, intense, inhuman, crippled and monstrous. There was something fungoid in the oily brown skin, something in the clumsy deliberation of the tedious movements unspeakably nasty. Even at this first encounter, this first glimpse, I was overcome with disgust and dread.

Suddenly the monster vanished. It had toppled over the brim of the cylinder and fallen into the pit, with a thud like the fall of a great mass of leather. I heard it give a peculiar thick cry, and forthwith another of these creatures appeared darkly in the deep shadow of the aperture.

I turned and, running madly, made for the first group of

trees, perhaps a hundred yards away; but I ran slantingly and stumbling, for I could not avert my face from these things.

There, among some young pine trees and furze bushes, I stopped, panting, and waited for further developments. The common round the sand pits was dotted with people, standing like myself in a half-fascinated terror, staring at these creatures, or rather at the heaped gravel at the edge of the pit in which they lay. And then, with a renewed horror, I saw a round, black object bobbing up and down on the edge of the pit. It was the head of the shopman who had fallen in, but showing as a little black object against the hot western sun. Now he got his shoulder and knee up, and again he seemed to slip back until only his head was visible. Suddenly he vanished, and I could have fancied a faint shriek had reached me. I had a momentary impulse to go back and help him that my fears overruled.

Everything was then quite invisible, hidden by the deep pit and the heap of sand that the fall of the cylinder had made. Anyone coming along the road from Chobham or Woking would have been amazed at the sight – a dwindling multitude of perhaps a hundred people or more standing in a great irregular circle, in ditches, behind bushes, behind gates and hedges, saying little to one another and that in short, excited shouts, and staring, staring hard at a few heaps of sand. The barrow of ginger beer stood, a queer derelict, black against the burning sky, and in the sand pits was a row of deserted vehicles with their horses feeding out of nosebags or pawing the ground.

THE HEAT-RAY

After the glimpse I had had of the Martians emerging from the cylinder in which they had come to the earth from their planet, a kind of fascination paralyzed my actions. I remained standing knee-deep in the heather, staring at the mound that hid them. I was a battleground of fear and curiosity.

I did not dare to go back towards the pit, but I felt a passionate longing to peer into it. I began walking, therefore, in a big curve, seeking some point of vantage and continually looking at the sand heaps that hid these new-comers to our earth. Once a leash of thin black whips, like the arms of an octopus, flashed across the sunset and was immediately withdrawn, and afterwards a thin rod rose up, joint by joint, bearing at its apex a circular disc that spun with a wobbling motion. What could be going on there?

Most of the spectators had gathered in one or two groups — one a little crowd towards Woking, the other a knot of people in the direction of Chobham. Evidently they shared my mental conflict. There were few near me. One man I approached — he was, I perceived, a neighbour of mine, though I did not know his name — and accosted. But it was scarcely a time for articulate conversation.

"What ugly *brutes*!" he said. "Good God! What ugly brutes!" He repeated this over and over again.

"Did you see a man in the pit?" I said; but he made no answer to that. We became silent, and stood watching for a time side by side, deriving, I fancy, a certain comfort in one another's company. Then I shifted my position to a little knoll that gave me the advantage of a yard or more of elevation and when I looked for him presently he was walking towards Woking.

The sunset faded to twilight before anything further happened. The crowd far away on the left, towards Woking, seemed to grow, and I heard now a faint murmur from it. The little knot of people towards Chobham dispersed. There was scarcely an intimation of movement from the pit.

It was this, as much as anything, that gave people courage, and I suppose the new arrivals from Woking also helped to restore confidence. At any rate, as the dusk came on a slow, intermittent movement upon the sand pits began, a movement that seemed to gather force as the stillness of the evening about the cylinder remained unbroken. Vertical black figures in twos and threes would advance, stop, watch, and advance again, spreading out as they did so in a thin irregular crescent that promised to enclose the pit in its attenuated horns. I, too, on my side began to move towards the pit.

Then I saw some cabmen and others had walked boldly into the sand pits, and heard the clatter of hoofs and the grind of wheels. I saw a lad trundling off the barrow of apples. And then, within thirty yards of the pit, advancing from the direction of Horsell, I noted a little black knot of men, the foremost of whom was waving a white flag.

This was the Deputation. There had been a hasty consultation, and since the Martians were evidently, in spite of their repulsive forms, intelligent creatures, it had been resolved to show them, by approaching them with signals, that we too were intelligent.

Flutter, flutter, went the flag, first to the right, then to the left. It was too far for me to recognize anyone there, but afterwards I learned that Ogilvy, Stent, and Henderson were with others in this attempt at communication. This little group had in its advance dragged inward, so to speak, the circumference of the now almost complete circle of people, and a number of dim black figures followed it at discreet distances.

Suddenly there was a flash of light, and a quantity of luminous greenish smoke came out of the pit in three distinct puffs, which drove up, one after the other, straight into the still air.

This smoke (or flame, perhaps, would be the better word for it) was so bright that the deep blue sky overhead and the hazy

stretches of brown common towards Chertsey, set with black pine trees, seemed to darken abruptly as these puffs arose, and to remain the darker after their dispersal. At the same time a faint hissing sound became audible.

Beyond the pit stood the little wedge of people with the white flag at its apex, arrested by these phenomena, a little knot of small vertical black shapes upon the black ground. As the green smoke arose, their faces flashed out pallid green, and faded again as it vanished. Then slowly the hissing passed into a humming, into a long, loud, droning noise. Slowly a humped shape rose out of the pit, and the ghost of a beam of light seemed to flicker out from it.

Forthwith flashes of actual flame, a bright glare leaping from one to another, sprang from the scattered group of men. It was as if some invisible jet impinged upon them and flashed into white flame. It was as if each man were suddenly and momentarily turned to fire.

Then, by the light of their own destruction, I saw them staggering and falling, and their supporters turning to run.

I stood staring, not as yet realizing that this was death leaping from man to man in that little distant crowd. All I felt was that it was something very strange. An almost noiseless and blinding flash of light, and a man fell headlong and lay still; and as the unseen shaft of heat passed over them, pine trees burst into fire, and every dry furze bush became with one dull thud a mass of flames. And far away towards Knaphill I saw the flashes of trees and hedges and wooden buildings suddenly set alight.

It was sweeping round swiftly and steadily, this flaming death, this invisible, inevitable sword of heat. I perceived it coming towards me by the flashing bushes it touched, and was too astounded and stupefied to stir. I heard the crackle of fire in the sand pits and the sudden squeal of a horse that was as suddenly stilled. Then it was as if an invisible yet intensely heated finger were drawn through the heather between me and the Martians, and all along a curving line beyond the sand pits the dark ground smoked and crackled. Something fell with a crash far away to the left where the road from Woking station opens out on the common. The hissing and humming ceased, and the black, dome-like object sank slowly out of sight into the pit.

All this had happened with such swiftness that I had stood motionless, dumbfounded and dazzled by the flashes of light. Had that death swept through a full circle, it must inevitably have slain me in my surprise. But it passed and spared me, and left the night about me suddenly dark and unfamiliar.

The undulating common seemed now dark almost to blackness, except where its roadways lay grey and pale under the deep blue sky of the early night. It was dark, and suddenly void of men. Overhead the stars were mustering, and in the west the sky was still a pale, bright, almost greenish blue. The tops of the pine trees and the roofs of Horsell came out sharp and black against the western afterglow. The Martians and their appliances were altogether invisible, save for that thin mast upon which their restless mirror wobbled. Patches of bush and isolated trees here and there smoked and glowed still, and the houses towards Woking station were sending up spires of flame into the stillness of the evening air.

Nothing was changed save for that and a terrible astonishment. The little group of black specks with the flag of white had been swept out of existence, and the stillness of the evening, so it seemed to me, had scarcely been broken.

It came to me that I was upon this dark common, helpless, unprotected, and alone. Suddenly, like a thing falling upon me from without, came – fear.

With an effort I turned and began a stumbling run through the heather.

The fear I felt was no rational fear, but a panic terror not only of the Martians, but of the dusk and stillness all about me. Such an extraordinary effect in unmanning me it had that I ran weeping silently as a child might do. Once I had turned, I did not dare to look back.

I remember I felt an extraordinary persuasion that I was being played with, that presently, when I was upon the very verge of safety, this mysterious death – as swift as the passage of light – would leap after me from the pit about the cylinder and strike me down.

THE HEAT-RAY IN THE CHOBHAM ROAD

Stent and Ogilvy, anticipating some possibilities of a collision, had telegraphed from Horsell to the barracks as soon as the Martians emerged, for the help of a company of soldiers to protect these strange creatures from violence. After that they returned to lead that ill-fated advance. The description of their death, as it was seen by the crowd, tallies very closely with my own impressions: the three puffs of green smoke, the deep humming note, and the flashes of flame.

But that crowd of people had a far narrower escape than mine. Only the fact that a hummock of heathery sand intercepted the lower part of the Heat-Ray saved them. Had the elevation of the parabolic mirror been a few yards higher, none could have lived to tell the tale. They saw the flashes and the men falling and an invisible hand, as it were, lit the bushes as it hurried towards them through the twilight. Then, with a whistling note that rose above the droning of the pit, the beam swung close over their heads, lighting the tops of the beech trees that line the road, and splitting the bricks, smashing the windows, firing the window frames, and bringing down in crumbling ruin a portion of the gable of the house nearest the corner.

In the sudden thud, hiss, and glare of the igniting trees, the panic-stricken crowd seems to have swayed hesitatingly for some moments. Sparks and burning twigs began to fall into the road, and single leaves like puffs of flame. Hats and dresses caught fire. Then came a crying from the common. There were shrieks and shouts, and suddenly a mounted policeman came galloping through the confusion with his hands clasped over his head, screaming.

"They're coming!" a woman shrieked, and incontinently everyone was turning and pushing at those behind, in order to clear their way to Woking again. They must have bolted as blindly as a flock of sheep. Where the road grows narrow and black between the high banks the crowd jammed, and a desperate struggle occurred. All that crowd did not escape; three persons at least, two women and a little boy, were crushed and trampled there, and left to die amid the terror and the darkness.

THE HORROR OF THE HEIGHTS

1913

ARTHUR CONAN DOYLE

THE IDEA that the extraordinary narrative which has been called the Joyce-Armstrong Fragment is an elaborate practical joke evolved by some unknown person, cursed by a perverted and sinister sense of humour, has now been abandoned by all who have examined the matter. Though the assertions contained in it are amazing and even monstrous, it is none the less forcing itself upon the general intelligence that they are true, and that we must readjust our ideas to the new situation. This world of ours appears to be separated by a slight and precarious margin of safety from a most singular and unexpected danger. I will endeavour in this narrative, which reproduces the original document in its necessarily somewhat fragmentary form, to lay before the reader the whole of the facts up to date, prefacing my statement by saying that, if there be any who doubt the narrative of Joyce-Armstrong, there can be no question at all as to the facts concerning Lieutenant Myrtle, R. N., and Mr Hay Connor, who undoubtedly met their end in the manner described.

The Joyce-Armstrong Fragment was found in the field which is called Lower Haycock, lying one mile to the westward of the village of Withyham, upon the Kent and Sussex border. It was on the 15th of September last year that an agricultural labourer, James Flynn, in the employment of Mathew Dodd, farmer, of the Chauntry Farm, Withyham, perceived a briar pipe lying near the footpath which skirts the hedge in Lower Haycock. A few paces farther on he picked up a pair of broken binocular glasses. Finally, among some nettles in the ditch, he caught sight of a flat, canvas-backed book, which proved to be a notebook with detachable leaves, some of which had come loose and were fluttering along the base of the hedge. These he collected, but some, including the first, were never recovered, and leave a deplorable hiatus in this all-important statement. The notebook was taken by the labourer to his master, who in turn showed it to Dr J. H. Atherton, of Hartfield. This gentleman at once recognized the need for an expert examination, and the manuscript was forwarded to the Aero Club in London, where it now lies.

The first two pages of the manuscript are missing. There is also one torn away at the end of the narrative, though none of these affect the general story. It is conjectured that the missing opening is concerned with the record of Mr Joyce-Armstrong's qualifications as an aeronaut, which can be gathered from other

sources and are admitted to be unsurpassed among the air-pilots of England. For many years he has been looked upon as among the most daring and the most intellectual of flying men, a combination which has enabled him to both invent and test several new devices, including the common gyroscopic attachment which is known by his name. The main body of the manuscript is written neatly in ink, but the last few lines are in pencil and are so ragged as to be hardly legible – exactly, in fact, as they might be expected to appear if they were scribbled off hurriedly from the seat of a moving aeroplane. There are, it may be added, several stains, both on the last page and on the outside cover which have been pronounced by the Home Office experts to be blood – probably human and certainly mammalian.

And now a word as to the personality of the author of this epoch-making statement. Joyce-Armstrong, according to the few friends who really knew something of the man, was a poet and a dreamer, as well as a mechanic and an inventor. He was a man of considerable wealth, much of which he had spent in the pursuit of his aeronautical hobby. He had four private aeroplanes in his hangars near Devizes, and is said to have made no fewer than one hundred and seventy ascents in the course of last year. He was a retiring man with dark moods, in which he would avoid the society of his fellows. Captain Dangerfield, who knew him better than anyone, says that there were times when his eccentricity threatened to develop into something more serious. His habit of carrying a shotgun with him in his aeroplane was one manifestation of it.

Another was the morbid effect which the fall of Lieutenant Myrtle had upon his mind. Myrtle, who was attempting the height record, fell from an altitude of something over thirty thousand feet. Horrible to narrate, his head was entirely obliterated, though his body and limbs preserved their configuration. At every gathering of airmen, Joyce-Armstrong, according to Dangerfield, would ask, with an enigmatic smile: "And where, pray, is Myrtle's head?"

It is worth remarking that after his own complete disappearance it was found that his private affairs were arranged with a precision which may show that he had a strong premonition of disaster. With these essential explanations I will now give the narrative exactly as it stands, beginning at page three of the blood-soaked notebook:

"Nevertheless, when I dined at Rheims with Coselli and Gustav Raymond I found that neither of them was aware of any particular danger in the higher layers of the atmosphere. I did not actually say what was in my thoughts, but I got so near to it that if they had any corresponding idea they could not have failed to express it. But then they are two empty, vainglorious fellows with no thought beyond seeing their silly names in the newspaper. It is interesting to note that neither of them had ever been much beyond the twenty-thousand-foot level.

Of course, men have been higher than this both in balloons and in the ascent of mountains. It must be well above that point that the aeroplane enters the danger zone – always presuming that my premonitions are correct.

"Aeroplaning has been with us now for more than twenty years, and one might well ask: Why should this peril be only revealing itself in our day? The answer is obvious. In the old days of weak engines, when a hundred horse-power Gnome or Green was considered ample for every need, the flights were very restricted. Now that three hundred horse-power is the rule rather than the exception, visits to the upper layers have become easier and more common. Some of us can remember how, in our youth, Garros made a world-wide reputation by attaining nineteen thousand feet, and it was considered a remarkable achievement to fly over the Alps. Our standard now has been immeasurably raised, and there are twenty high flights for one in former years. Many of them have been undertaken with impunity. The thirty-thousand-foot level has been reached time after time with no discomfort beyond cold and asthma. What does this prove? A visitor might descend upon this planet a thousand times and never see a tiger. Yet tigers exist, and if he chanced to come down into a jungle he might be devoured. There are jungles of the upper air, and there are worse things than tigers which inhabit them. I believe in time they will map these jungles accurately out. Even at the present moment I could name two of them. One of them lies over the Pau-Biarritz district of France. Another is just over my head as I write here in my house in Wiltshire. I rather think there is a third in the Homburg-Wiesbaden district.

"It was the disappearance of the airmen that first set me thinking. Of course, everyone said that they had fallen into the sea, but that did not satisfy me at all. First, there was Verrier in France; his machine was found near Bayonne, but they never got his body. There was the case of Baxter also, who vanished, though his engine and some of the iron fixings were found in a wood in Leicestershire. In that case, Dr Middleton, of Amesbury, who was watching the flight with a telescope, declares that just before the clouds obscured the view he saw the machine, which was at an enormous height, suddenly rise perpendicularly upwards in a succession of jerks in a manner that he would have thought to be impossible. That was the last seen of Baxter. There was a correspondence in the papers, but it never led to anything. There were several other similar cases, and then there was the death of Hay Connor. What a cackle there was about an unsolved mystery of the air, and what columns in the halfpenny papers, and yet how little was ever done to get to the bottom of the business! He came down in a tremendous volplane from an unknown height. He never got off his machine and died in his pilot's seat. Died of what? 'Heart disease,' said the doctors. Rubbish! Hay Connor's heart was as sound as mine is. What did Venables say? Venables was the only man who was at his side when he died. He said that he was shivering and looked like a man who had been badly scared. 'Died of fright,' said Venables, but could not imagine what he was frightened about. Only said one word to Venables, which sounded like 'monstrous'. They could make nothing of that at the inquest. But I could make something of it. Monsters! That was the last word of poor Harry Hay Connor. And he *did* die of fright, just as Venables thought.

"And then there was Myrtle's head. Do you really believe – does anybody really believe – that a man's head could be driven clean into his body by the force of a fall? Well, perhaps it may be possible, but I, for one, have never believed that it was so with Myrtle. And the grease upon his clothes – 'all slimy with grease,' said somebody at the inquest. Queer that nobody got thinking after that! I did – but, then, I had been thinking for a good long time. I've made three ascents but I've never been high enough. Now, with this new, light Paul Veroner machine and its one hundred and seventy-five Robur, I should easily touch the thirty thousand tomorrow. I'll have a shot at the record. Maybe I shall have a shot at something else as well. Of course, it's dangerous.

If a fellow wants to avoid danger he had best keep out of flying altogether and subside finally into flannel slippers and a dressing gown. But I'll visit the air-jungle tomorrow – and if there's anything there I shall know it. If I return, I'll find myself a bit of a celebrity. If I don't this notebook may explain what I am trying to do, and how I lost my life in doing it. But no drivel about accidents or mysteries, if *you* please.

"I chose my Paul Veroner monoplane for the job. There's nothing like a monoplane when real work is to be done. I took a shotgun with me and a dozen cartridges filled with buckshot. You should have seen the face of Perkins, my old mechanic, when I directed him to put them in. I was dressed like an Arctic explorer, with two jerseys under my overalls, thick socks inside my padded boots, a storm-cap with flaps, and my goggles. It was stifling outside the hangars, but I was going for the summit of the Himalayas, and had to dress for the part. Perkins knew there was something on and implored me to take him with me. Perhaps I should if I were using the biplane, but a monoplane is a one-man show – if you want to get the last foot of life out of it. Of course, I took an oxygen bag; the man who goes for the altitude record without one will either be frozen or smothered – or both.

"I had a good look at the planes, the rudder-bar, and the elevating lever before I got in. Everything was in order so far as I could see. Then I switched on my engine and found that she was running sweetly. When they let her go she rose almost at once upon the lowest speed. I circled my home field once or twice just to warm her up, and then with a wave to Perkins and the others, I put her on her highest. She skimmed like a swallow down wind for eight or ten miles until I turned her nose up a little and she began to climb in a great spiral for the cloud-bank above me. It's all-important to rise slowly and adapt yourself to the pressure as you go.

"It was a close, warm day for an English September, and there was the hush and heaviness of impending rain. Now and then there came sudden puffs of wind from the southwest – one of them so gusty and unexpected that it caught me napping and turned me half-round for an instant. I remember the time when gusts and whirls and air-pockets used to be things of danger – before we learned to put an overmastering power into our engines. Just as I reached the cloud-banks, with the altimeter marking three thousand, down came the rain. My word, how it poured! It drummed upon my wings and lashed against my face, blurring my glasses so that I could hardly see. I got down on to a low speed, for it was painful to travel against it. As I got higher it became hail, and I had to turn tail to it. One of my cylinders was out of action – a dirty plug, I should imagine, but still I was rising steadily with plenty of power. After a bit the trouble passed, whatever it was, and I heard the full, deep-throated purr – the ten singing as one.

"About nine-thirty I was nearing the clouds. Down below me, all blurred and shadowed with rain, lay the vast expanse of Salisbury Plain. Half a dozen flying machines were at the thousand-foot level, looking like little black swallows against the green background. I dare say they were wondering what I was doing up in cloud-land. Suddenly a grey curtain drew across beneath me and the wet folds of vapours were swirling round my face. It was clammily cold and miserable. But I was above the

hailstorm, and that was something gained. The cloud was as dark and thick as a London fog. In my anxiety to get clear, I cocked her nose up until the automatic alarm-bell rang, and I actually began to slide backwards. My sopped and dripping wings had made me heavier than I thought, but presently I was in lighter cloud, and soon had cleared the first layer. There was a second – opal-coloured and fleecy – at a great height above my head, a white, unbroken ceiling above, and a dark, unbroken floor below, with the monoplane labouring upwards upon a vast spiral between them. It is deadly lonely in these cloud-spaces. Once a great flight of some small water-birds went past me, flying very fast to the westwards. The quick whir of their wings and their musical cry were cheery to my ear. I fancy that they were teal, but I am a wretched zoologist. Now that we humans have become birds we must really learn to know our brethren by sight.

"The wind down beneath me whirled and swayed the broad cloud-plain. Once a great eddy formed in it, a whirlpool of vapour, and through it, as down a funnel, I caught sight of the distant world. A large white biplane was passing at a vast depth beneath me. I fancy it was the morning mail service between Bristol and London. Then the drift swirled inwards again and the great solitude was unbroken.

"Just after ten I touched the lower edge of the upper cloud-stratum. It consisted of fine vapour drifting swiftly from the westwards. The wind had been steadily rising all this time and it was now blowing a sharp breeze – twenty-eight an hour by my gauge. Already it was very cold, though my altimeter only marked nine thousand. The engines were working beautifully, and we went droning steadily upwards. The cloud-bank was thicker than I had expected, but at last it thinned out into a golden mist before me, and then in an instant I had shot out from it, and there was an unclouded sky and a brilliant sun above my head – all blue and gold above, all shining silver below, one vast, glimmering plain as far as my eyes could reach. It was a quarter past ten o'clock, and the barograph needle pointed to twelve thousand eight hundred. Up I went and up, my ears concentrated upon the deep purring of my motor, my eyes busy always with the watch, the revolution indicator, the petrol lever, and the oil pump. No wonder aviators are said to be a fearless race. With so many things to think of there is no time to trouble about oneself. About this time I noted how unreliable is the compass when above a certain height from earth. At fifteen thousand feet mine was pointing east and a point south. The sun and the wind gave me my true bearings.

"I had hoped to reach an eternal stillness in these high altitudes, but with every thousand feet of ascent the gale grew stronger. My machine groaned and trembled in every joint and rivet as she faced it, and swept away like a sheet of paper when I banked her on the turn, skimming down wind at a greater pace, perhaps, than ever mortal man has moved. Yet I had always to turn again and tack up in the wind's eye, for it was not merely a height record that I was after. By all my calculations it was above little Wiltshire that my air-jungle lay, and all my labour might be lost if I struck the outer layers at some farther point.

"When I reached the nineteen-thousand-foot level, which was about midday, the wind was so severe that I looked with some anxiety to the stays of my wings, expecting momentarily to see them snap or slacken. I even cast loose the parachute behind me, and fastened its hook into the ring of my belt, so as to be ready for the worst. Now was the time when a bit of scamped work by the mechanic is paid for by the life of the aeronaut. But she held together bravely. Every cord and strut was humming and vibrating like so many harp strings, but it was glorious to see how, for all the beating and the buffeting, she was still the conqueror of Nature and the mistress of the sky.

"These were the thoughts in my head as I climbed that monstrous, inclined plane with the wind sometimes beating in my face and sometimes whistling behind my ears, while the cloud-land beneath me fell away to such a distance that the folds and hummocks of silver had all smoothed out into one flat, shining plain. But suddenly I had a horrible and unprecedented experience. That huge, sweeping river of wind of which I have spoken had, as it appears, whirlpools within it which were as monstrous as itself.

Without a moment's warning I was dragged suddenly into the heart of one. I spun round for a minute or two with such velocity that I almost lost my senses, and then fell suddenly, left wing foremost, down the vacuum funnel in the centre. I dropped like a stone, and lost nearly a thousand feet. It was only my belt that kept me in my seat, and the shock and breathlessness left me hanging half-insensible over the side of the fuselage. But I am always capable of a supreme effort — it is my one great merit as an aviator. I was conscious that the descent was slower. The whirlpool was a cone rather than a funnel, and I had come to the apex. With a terrific wrench, throwing my weight all to one side, I brought her head away from the wind. In an instant I had shot out of the eddies and was skimming down the sky. Then, shaken but victorious, I turned her nose upward and began once more my steady grind on the upward spiral. I took a large sweep to avoid the danger-spot of the whirlpool, and soon I was safely above it.

"Just after one o'clock I was twenty-one thousand feet above the sea level. To my great joy I had topped the gale, and with every hundred feet of ascent the air grew stiller. On the other hand, it was very cold, and I was conscious of that peculiar nausea which goes with rarefaction of the air. For the first time I unscrewed the mouth of my oxygen bag and took an occasional whiff of the glorious gas. I could feel it running like a cordial through my veins, and I was exhilarated almost to the point of drunkenness. I shouted and sang as I soared upwards into the cold, still outer world.

"It was bitterly cold, however, and my thermometer was at zero, Fahrenheit. At one-thirty I was nearly seven miles above

the surface of the earth, and still ascending steadily. I found, however, that the rarefied air was giving markedly less support to my planes, and that my angle of ascent had to be considerably lowered in consequence. It was already clear that even with my light weight and strong engine-power there was a point in front of me where I should be held. To make matters worse, one of my sparking-plugs was in trouble again and there was intermittent misfiring in the engine. My heart was heavy with the fear of failure.

"It was about that time that I had a most extraordinary experience. Something whizzed past me in a trail of smoke and exploded with a loud, hissing sound, sending forth a cloud of steam. For the instant I could not imagine what had happened. Then I remembered that the earth is forever being bombarded by meteor stones, and would be hardly inhabitable were they not in nearly every case turned to vapour in the outer layers of the atmosphere. Here is a new danger for the high-altitude man, for two others passed me when I was nearing the forty-thousand-foot mark. I cannot doubt that at the edge of the earth's envelope the risk would be a very real one.

"My barograph needle marked forty-one thousand three hundred when I became aware that I could go no farther. Physically, the strain was not as yet greater than I could bear but my machine had reached its limit. The air gave no firm support to the wings, and the least tilt developed into side-slip, while she seemed sluggish on her controls. Possibly, had the engine been at its best, another thousand feet might have been within our capacity, but it was still misfiring, and two out of the ten cylinders appeared to be out of action. If I had not already reached the zone for which I was searching then I should never see it upon this journey. But was it not possible that I had attained it? Soaring in circles like a monstrous hawk upon the forty-thousand-foot level I let the monoplane guide herself, and made a careful observation of my surroundings. The heavens were perfectly clear; there was no indication of those dangers which I had imagined.

"I have said that I was soaring in circles. It struck me

suddenly that I would do well to take a wider sweep and open up a new airtract. If the hunter entered an earth-jungle he would drive through it if he wished to find his game. My reasoning had led me to believe that the air-jungle which I had imagined lay somewhere over Wiltshire. This should be to the south and west of me. I took my bearings from the sun, for the compass was hopeless and no trace of earth was to be seen – nothing but the distant, silver cloud-plain. However, I got my direction as best I might and kept her head straight to the mark. I reckoned that my petrol supply would not last for more than another hour or so, but I could afford to use it to the last drop, since a single magnificent volplane could at any time take me to the earth.

"Suddenly I was aware of something new. The air in front of me had lost its crystal clearness. It was full of long, ragged wisps of something which I can only compare to very fine cigarette smoke. It hung about in wreaths and coils, turning and twisting slowly in the sunlight. As the monoplane shot through it, I was aware of a faint taste of oil upon my lips, and there was a greasy scum upon the woodwork of the machine. Some infinitely fine organic matter appeared to be suspended in the atmosphere. There was no life there. But might it not be the remains of life? Above all, might it not be the food of life, of monstrous life, even as the humble grease of the ocean is the food for the mighty whale? The thought was in my mind when my eyes looked upwards and I saw the most wonderful vision that ever man has seen. Can I hope to convey it to you even as I saw it myself last Thursday?

"Conceive a jellyfish such as sails in our summer seas, bell-shaped and of enormous size – far larger, I should judge,

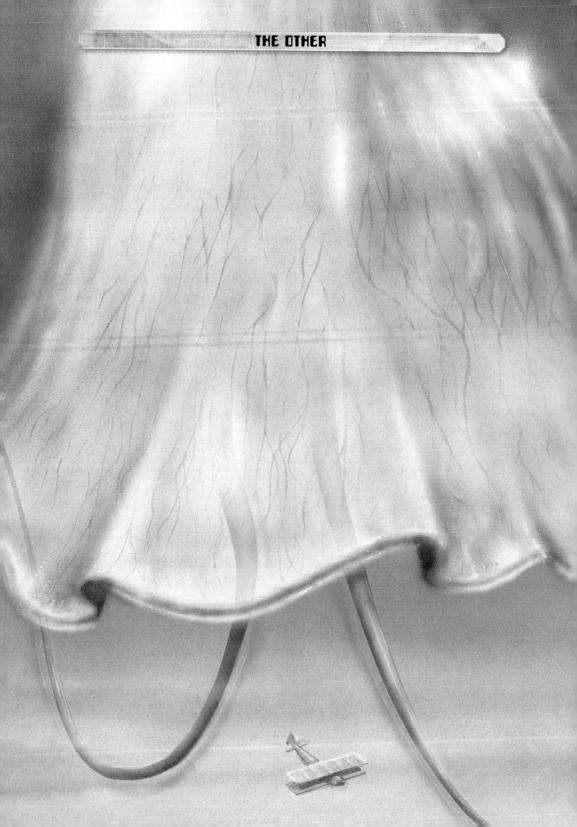

than the dome of St. Paul's. It was of a light pink colour veined with a delicate green, but the whole huge fabric so tenuous that it was but a fairy outline against the dark blue sky. It pulsated with a delicate and regular rhythm. From it there depended two long, drooping, green tentacles, which swayed slowly backwards and forwards. This gorgeous vision passed gently with noiseless dignity over my head, as light and fragile as a soap bubble, and drifted upon its stately way.

"I had half-turned my monoplane, that I might look after this beautiful creature, when, in a moment, I found myself amidst a perfect fleet of them, of all sizes, but none so large as the first. Some were quite small, but the majority about as big as an average balloon, and with much the same curvature at the top. There was in them a delicacy of texture and colouring which reminded me of the finest Venetian glass. Pale shades of pink and green were the prevailing tints, but all had a lovely iridescence where the sun shimmered through their dainty forms. Some hundreds of them drifted past me, a wonderful fairy squadron of strange unknown galleons of the sky – creatures whose forms and substance were so attuned to these pure heights that one could not conceive anything so delicate within actual sight or sound of earth.

"But soon my attention was drawn to a new phenomenon – the serpents of the outer air. These were long, thin, fantastic coils of vapour-like material, which turned and twisted with great speed, flying round and round at such a pace that the eyes could hardly follow them. Some of these ghost-like creatures were twenty or thirty feet long, but it was difficult to tell their girth, for their outline was so hazy that it seemed to fade away

into the air around them. These air-snakes were of a very light grey or smoke colour, with some darker lines within, which gave the impression of a definite organism. One of them whisked past my very face, and I was conscious of a cold, clammy contact, but their composition was so unsubstantial that I could not connect them with any thought of physical danger, any more than the beautiful bell-like creatures which had preceded them. There was no more solidity in their frames than in the floating spume from a broken wave.

"But a more terrible experience was in store for me. Floating downwards from a great height there came a purplish patch of vapour, small as I saw it first, but rapidly enlarging as it approached me, until it appeared to be hundreds of square feet in size. Though fashioned of some transparent, jelly-like substance, it was none the less of much more definite outline and solid consistence than anything which I had seen before. There were more traces, too, of a physical organization, especially two vast, shadowy, circular plates upon either side, which may have been eyes, and a perfectly solid white projection between them which was as curved and cruel as the beak of a vulture.

"The whole aspect of this monster was formidable and threatening, and it kept changing its colour from a very light mauve to a dark, angry purple so thick that it cast a shadow as it drifted between my monoplane and the sun. On the upper curve of its huge body there were three great projections which I can only describe as enormous bubbles, and I was convinced as I looked at them that they were charged with some extremely light gas which served to buoy up the misshapen and semi-solid mass in the rarefied air. The creature moved swiftly along, keeping pace easily with the monoplane, and for twenty miles or more it formed my horrible escort, hovering over me like a bird of prey which is waiting to pounce. Its method of progression – done so swiftly that it was not easy to follow – was to throw out a long, glutinous streamer in front of it, which in turn seemed to draw forward the rest of the writhing body. So elastic and gelatinous was it that never for two successive minutes was it the same shape, and yet each change made it more threatening and loathsome than the last.

"I knew that it meant mischief. Every purple flush of its hideous body told me so. The vague, goggling eyes which were turned always upon me were cold and merciless. I dipped the nose of my monoplane downwards to escape it. As I did so, as quick as a flash there shot out a long tentacle from this mass of floating blubber, and it fell as light and sinuous as a whiplash across the front of my machine. There was a loud hiss as it lay for a moment across the hot engine, and it whisked itself into the air again, while the huge, flat body drew itself together as if in sudden pain. I dipped to a vol-pique, but again a tentacle fell over the monoplane and was shorn off by the propeller as easily as it might have cut through a smoke wreath. A long, gliding, sticky, serpent-like coil came from behind and caught me round the waist, dragging me out of the fuselage. I tore at it, my fingers sinking into the smooth, glue-like surface, and for an instant I disengaged myself, but only to be caught round the boot by another coil, which gave me a jerk that tilted me almost on to my back.

"As I fell over I blazed off both barrels of my gun, though, indeed, it was like attacking an elephant with a pea-shooter to imagine that any human weapon could cripple that mighty bulk. And yet I aimed better than I knew, for, with a loud report, one of the great blisters upon the creature's back exploded with the puncture of the buck-shot. It was very clear that my conjecture was right, and that these vast, clear bladders were distended with some lifting gas, for in an instant the huge, cloud-like body turned sideways, writhing desperately to find its balance, while the white beak snapped and gaped in horrible fury. But already I had shot away on the steepest glide that I dared to attempt, my engine still full on, the flying propeller and the force of gravity shooting me downwards like an aerolite. Far behind me I saw a dull, purplish smudge growing swiftly smaller and merging into the blue sky behind it. I was safe out of the deadly jungle of the outer air.

"Once out of danger I throttled my engine, for nothing tears a machine to pieces quicker than running on full power from a height. It was a glorious, spiral volplane from nearly eight miles of altitude – first, to the level of the silver cloud-bank, then to that of the stormcloud beneath it, and finally, in beating rain, to the surface of the earth. I saw the Bristol Channel beneath me as I broke from the clouds, but, having still some petrol in my tank, I got twenty miles inland before I found myself stranded in a field half a mile from the village of Ashcombe. There I got three tins of petrol from a passing motor car, and at ten minutes past six that evening I alighted gently in my own home meadow at Devizes, after such a journey as no mortal upon earth has ever yet taken and lived to tell the tale. I have seen the beauty and I have seen the horror of the heights – and greater beauty or greater horror than that is not within the knowledge of man.

"And now it is my plan to go once again before I give my results to the world. My reason for this is that I must surely have something to show by way of proof before I lay such a tale before my fellow men. It is true that others will soon follow and will confirm what I have said, and yet I should wish to carry conviction from the first. Those lovely iridescent bubbles of the air should not be hard to capture. They drift slowly upon their way, and the swift monoplane could intercept their leisurely course. It is likely enough that they would dissolve in the heavier layers of the atmosphere, and that some small heap of amorphous jelly might be all that I should bring to earth with me. And yet something there would surely be by which I could substantiate my story. Yes, I will go, even if I run a risk by doing so. These purple horrors would not seem to be numerous. It is probable that I shall not see one. If I do I shall dive at once. At the worst there is always the shotgun and my knowledge of…"

Here a page of the manuscript is unfortunately missing. On the next page is written, in large, straggling writing:

"Forty-three thousand feet. I shall never see earth again. They are beneath me, three of them. God help me; it is a dreadful death to die!"

Such in its entirety is the Joyce-Armstrong Statement. Of the man nothing has since been seen. Pieces of his shattered monoplane have been picked up in the preserves of Mr Budd-Lushington upon the borders of Kent and Sussex, within a few miles of the spot where the notebook was discovered. If the unfortunate aviator's theory is correct that this air-jungle, as he called it, existed only over the southwest of England, then it would seem that he had fled from it at the full speed of his monoplane, but had been overtaken and devoured by these horrible creatures at some spot in the outer atmosphere above the place where the grim relics were found. The picture of that monoplane skimming down the sky, with the nameless terrors flying as swiftly beneath it and cutting it off always from the earth while they gradually closed in upon their victim, is one upon which a man who valued his sanity would prefer not to dwell. There are many, as I am aware, who still jeer at the facts which I have here set down, but even they must admit that Joyce-Armstrong has disappeared, and I would commend to them his own words: "This notebook may explain what I am trying to do, and how I lost my life in doing it. But no drivel about accidents or mysteries, if *you* please."

THE MONSTER MAKER

1887

W C MORROW

A **YOUNG MAN** of refined appearance, but evidently
suffering great mental distress, presented himself one
morning at the residence of a surgeon of remarkable skill. The
house was large, gloomy, and dark, and had long corridors and
dismal rooms; and it was absurdly large for the small family –
man and wife – that occupied it. He was about sixty-five years of
age and she about forty. He was lean, tall, and bald, with a thin,
smooth-shaven face, and very keen eyes. The man was strong, the
woman weak; he dominated, she suffered.

The young man rapped at the door. No answer. He rapped
again. Still no sign. He examined a slip of paper, glanced at the
number of the house, and then, with the impatience of a child,
he furiously kicked the door. There were signs of numerous

other such kicks. A response came in the shape of a shuffling footstep in the hall, a turning of the rusty key, and a sharp face that peered through a cautious opening in the door.

"Are you the doctor?" asked the young man.

"Yes, yes! Come in," briskly replied the master of the house.

The young man entered. The old surgeon closed the door and carefully locked it. "This way," he said, advancing to a rickety flight of stairs. The young man followed. The surgeon led the way up the stairs, turned into a narrow, musty-smelling corridor at the left, traversed it, rattling the loose boards under his feet, at the farther end opened a door, and beckoned his visitor to enter. The young man found himself in a pleasant room, furnished in antique fashion and with hard simplicity.

"Sit down," said the old man, placing a chair so that its occupant should face a window that looked out upon a dead wall about six feet from the house. He threw open the blind, and a pale light entered. He then seated himself near his visitor and directly facing him, and with a searching look, that had all the power of a microscope, he proceeded to diagnosticate the case.

"Well?" he presently asked. The young man shifted uneasily in his seat.

"I – I have come to see you," he finally stammered, "because I'm in trouble."

"Ah!"

"Yes; you see, I – that is – I have given up."

"Ah!" There was pity added to sympathy in the exclamation.

"That's it. Given up," added the visitor. He took from his pocket a role of banknotes, and with the utmost deliberation he counted them out upon his knee. "Five thousand dollars," he calmly remarked. "That is for you. It's all I have; but I presume that five thousand dollars is a sufficient fee for what I want you to do."

The surgeon's lips curled pityingly. "What do you want me to do?" he carelessly inquired.

The young man rose, looked around with a mysterious air, approached the surgeon, and laid the money across his knee. Then he stopped and whispered two words in the surgeon's ear.

These words produced an electric effect. The old man started violently; then, springing to his feet, he caught his visitor angrily, and transfixed him with a look that was as sharp as a knife. His eyes flashed, and he opened his mouth to give utterance, when he suddenly checked himself. The anger left his face, and only pity remained. He relinquished his grasp, picked up the scattered notes, and, offering them to the visitor, slowly said:

"I do not want your money. You are simply foolish. You think you are in trouble. Well, you do not know what trouble is. Your only trouble is that you have not a trace of manhood in your nature. You should surrender yourself to the authorities, and be sent to a lunatic asylum for proper treatment."

The young man keenly felt the intended insult, and his eyes flashed dangerously.

"You old dog – you insult me thus!" he cried. "Don't want my money, eh? When a man comes to you himself and wants it done, you may fly into a passion and spurn his money; but let an enemy of his come and pay you, and you are only too willing. How many such jobs have you done in this miserable old hole? It is a good thing for you that the police have not run you down, and brought spade and shovel with them. Do you know what is said of you? Do you think you have kept your windows so closely shut that no sound has ever penetrated beyond them? Where do you keep your infernal implements?"

"Sit down," commanded the stern voice of the surgeon.

It was the voice of father to child, of master to slave. The fury left the visitor, who, weak and overcome, fell upon a chair.

Meanwhile, a peculiar light had appeared in the old surgeon's face, the dawn of a strange idea. There was something sinister in it, suggesting the sacrifice of something held sacred. After a struggle, mind had vanquished conscience.

Taking a piece of paper and a pencil, the surgeon carefully wrote answers to questions which he peremptorily addressed to his visitor, such as his name, age, place of residence, occupation, and the like, and the same inquiries concerning his parents, together with other particular matters.

"Does anyone know you came to this house?" he asked.

"No."

"You swear it?"

"Yes."

"But your absence will cause alarm and lead to search."

"I have provided against that."

"How?"

"By depositing a note in the post, as I came along, announcing my intention to drown myself."

"The river will be dragged."

"What then?" asked the young man, shrugging his shoulders with careless indifference. "Rapid undercurrent, you know. A good many are never found."

There was a pause.

"Are you ready?" finally asked the surgeon.

"Perfectly." The answer was cool and determined. The manner of the surgeon, however, showed much perturbation. The pallor that had come into his face at the moment his decision was formed became intense. A nervous tremulousness overcame his frame. Above it shone the light of enthusiasm.

"Have you a choice in the method?" he asked.

"Yes; extreme anaesthesia."

"With what agent?"

"The surest and quickest."

"Do you desire any – any subsequent disposition?"

"No; only nullification; simply a blowing out, as of a candle in the wind; a puff – then darkness, without a trace. A sense of your own safety may suggest the method. I leave it to you."

"No delivery to your friends?"

"None whatever."

Another pause.

"Did you say you are quite ready?" asked the surgeon.

"Quite ready."

"And perfectly willing?"

"Anxious."

"Then wait a moment."

With this request the old surgeon rose to his feet and stretched himself. Then with the stealthiness of a cat he opened the door and peered into the hall, listening intently. There was no sound. He softly closed the door and locked it. Then he closed the window-blinds and locked them. This done, he opened a door leading into an adjoining room, which, though it had no window, was lighted by means of a small skylight. The young man watched closely. A strange change had come over him. While his determination had not lessened, a look of great relief came into his face, displacing the haggard, despairing look of a half-hour before. Melancholic then, he was ecstatic now. The opening of a second door disclosed a curious sight. In the centre of the room, directly under the skylight, was an operating-table, such as is used by demonstrators of anatomy. A glass case against the wall held surgical instruments of every kind. Hanging in another case were human skeletons of various sizes. In sealed jars, arranged on shelves, were monstrosities of diverse kinds preserved in alcohol. There were also, among innumerable other articles scattered about the room, a mannequin, a stuffed cat, a desiccated human heart, plaster casts of various parts of the body, numerous charts, and a large assortment of drugs and chemicals. There was also a lounge, which could be opened to form a couch. The surgeon opened it and moved the operating table aside, giving its place to the lounge.

"Come in," he called to his visitor.

The young man obeyed without the least hesitation.

"Take off your coat."

He complied.

"Lie down on that lounge."

In a moment the young man was stretched at full length, eyeing the surgeon. The latter undoubtedly was suffering under great excitement, but he did not waver; his movements were sure and quick. Selecting a bottle containing a liquid, he carefully measured out a certain quantity. While doing this he asked: "Have you ever had any

irregularity of the heart?"

"No."

The answer was prompt, but it was immediately followed by a quizzical look in the speaker's face.

"I presume," he added, "you mean by your question that it might be dangerous to give me a certain drug. Under the circumstances, however, I fail to see any relevancy in your question."

This took the surgeon aback; but he hastened to explain that he did not wish to inflict unnecessary pain, and hence his question.

He placed the glass on a stand, approached his visitor, and carefully examined his pulse.

"Wonderful!" he exclaimed.

"Why?"

"It is perfectly normal."

"Because I am wholly resigned. Indeed, it has been long since I knew such happiness. It is not active, but infinitely sweet."

"You have no lingering desire to retract?"

"None whatever."

The surgeon went to the stand and returned with the draught.

"Take this," he said kindly. The young man partially raised himself and took the glass in his hand. He did not show the vibration of a single nerve. He drank the liquid, draining the last drop. Then he returned the glass with a smile.

"Thank you," he said; "you are the noblest man that lives. May you always prosper and be happy! You are my benefactor, my liberator. Bless you, bless you! You reach down from your seat with the gods and lift me up into glorious peace and rest."

These words, spoken earnestly, in a musical, low voice, and accompanied with a smile of ineffable tenderness, pierced the old man's heart. A suppressed convulsion swept over him; intense anguish wrung his vitals; perspiration trickled down his face. The young man continued to smile.

"Ah, it does me good!" said he.

The surgeon, with a strong effort to control himself, sat down upon the edge of the lounge and took his visitor's wrist, counting the pulse.

"How long will it take?" the young man asked.

"Ten minutes. Two have passed." The voice was hoarse.

"Ah, only eight minutes more! Delicious, delicious! I feel it coming... What was that? Ah, I understand. Music... beautiful! Coming, coming... is that – that – water? ... Trickling? Dripping? Doctor!"

"Well?"

"Thank you... thank you... noble man... my saviour... my bene... bene... factor... trickling... trickling... dripping, dripping... doctor!"

"Well?"

"Doctor!"

"Past hearing," muttered the surgeon.

"Doctor!"

"And blind."

Response was made by a firm grasp of the hand.

"Doctor!"

"And numb."

"Doctor!"

The old man watched and waited.

"Dripping... dripping."

The last drop had run. There was a sigh, and nothing more.

The surgeon laid down the hand.

"The first step," he groaned, rising to his feet; then his whole frame dilated. "The first step is the most difficult, yet the simplest. A providential delivery into my hands of that for which I have hungered for forty years. No withdrawal now! It is possible, because scientific but perilous. If I succeed — if? I shall succeed. I will succeed... and after success — what? Yes, what? Publish the plan and the result? The gallows... So long as it shall exist... and I exist, the gallows. That much... But how to account for its presence? Ah, that pinches hard! I must trust to the future."

He tore himself from the reverie and started.

"I wonder if she heard or saw anything."

With that reflection he cast a glance upon the form on the lounge, and then left the room, locked the door, locked also the door of the outer room, walked down two or three corridors, penetrated to a remote part of the house, and rapped at a door. It was opened by his wife. He, by this time, had regained complete mastery over himself.

"I thought I heard someone in the house just now," he said, "but I can find no one."

"I heard nothing."

He was greatly relieved.

"I did hear someone knock at the door less than an hour ago," she resumed, "and heard you speak, I think. Did he come in?"

"No."

The woman glanced at his feet and seemed perplexed…"
I am almost certain," she said, "that I heard foot-falls in the
house, and yet I see that you are wearing slippers."

"Oh, I had on my shoes then!"

"That explains it," said the woman, satisfied; "I think the
sound you heard must have been caused by rats."

"Ah, that was it!" exclaimed the surgeon. Leaving, he closed
the door, reopened it, and said, "I do not wish to be disturbed
today." He said to himself, as he went down the hall, "All is clear
there."

He returned to the room in which his visitor lay, and made a
careful examination.

"Splendid specimen!" he softly exclaimed; "every organ
sound; every function perfect; fine, large frame; well-shaped
muscles, strong and sinewy; capable of wonderful development
– if given opportunity… I have no doubt it can be done. Already
I have succeeded with a dog – a task less difficult
than this, for in a man the cerebrum overlaps
the cerebellum, which is not the case with a
dog. This gives a wide range for accident,
with but one opportunity in a lifetime!
In the cerebrum, the intellect and the
affections; in the cerebellum, the
senses and the motor forces; in the
medulla oblongata, control of the
diaphragm. In these two latter lie all
the essentials of simple existence. The
cerebrum is merely an adornment; that
is to say, reason and the affections are

almost purely ornamental. I have already proved it. My dog, with its cerebrum removed, was idiotic, but it retained its physical senses to a certain degree."

While thus ruminating he made careful preparations. He moved the couch, replaced the operating table under the skylight, selected a number of surgical instruments, prepared certain drug mixtures, and arranged water, towels, and all the accessories of a tedious surgical operation.

Suddenly he burst into laughter.

"Poor fool!" he exclaimed. "Paid me five thousand dollars to kill him! Didn't have the courage to snuff his own candle! You thought you were dying, poor idiot! Allow me to inform you, sir, that you are as much alive at this moment as ever you were in your life. But it will be all the same to you. You shall never be more conscious than you are now; and for all practical purposes, so far as they concern you, you are dead henceforth, though you shall live. By the way, how should you feel without a head? Ha, ha, ha... but that's a sorry joke."

He lifted the unconscious form from the lounge and laid it upon the operating table.

About three years afterwards the following conversation was held between a captain of police and a detective:

"She may be insane," suggested the captain.

"I think she is."

"And yet you credit her story!"

"I do."

"Singular!"

"Not at all. I myself have learned something."

"What!"

"Much, in one sense; little, in another. You have heard those queer stories of her husband. Well, they are all nonsensical – probably with one exception. He is generally a harmless old fellow, but peculiar. He has performed some wonderful surgical operations. The people in his neighborhood are ignorant, and they fear him and wish to be rid of him; hence they tell a great many lies about him, and they come to believe their own stories. The one important thing that I have learned is that he is almost insanely enthusiastic on the subject of surgery – especially experimental surgery; and with an enthusiast there is hardly such a thing as a scruple. It is this that gives me confidence in the woman's story."

"You say she appeared to be frightened?"

"Doubly so – first, she feared that her husband would learn of her betrayal of him; second, the discovery itself had terrified her."

"But her report of this discovery is very vague," argued the captain. "He conceals everything from her. She is merely guessing."

"In part – yes; in other part – no. She heard the sounds distinctly, though she did not see clearly. Horror closed her eyes. What she thinks she saw is, I admit, preposterous; but she undoubtedly saw something extremely frightful. There are many peculiar little circumstances. He has eaten with her but few times during the last three years, and nearly always carries his food to his private rooms. She says that he either consumes an enormous quantity, throws much away, or is feeding something that eats prodigiously. He explains this to her by saying that he has animals with which he experiments. This is not true. Again, he always keeps the door to these rooms carefully locked; and not only that, but he has had the doors doubled and otherwise strengthened, and has heavily barred a window that looks from one of the rooms upon a dead wall a few feet distant."

"What does it mean?" asked the captain.

"A prison."

"For animals, perhaps."

"Certainly not."

"Why!"

"Because, in the first place, cages would have been better; in the second place, the security that he has provided is infinitely greater than that required for the confinement of ordinary animals."

"All this is easily explained: he has a violent lunatic under treatment."

"I had thought of that, but such is not the fact."

"How do you know?"

"He has always refused to treat cases of lunacy; he confines himself to surgery: the walls are not padded, for the woman has heard sharp blows upon them; he would not be likely to conceal a lunatic's confinement from the woman; the woman has listened at the keyhole and has heard no human voice within: and last, we have heard the woman's vague description of what she saw."

"You have destroyed every possible theory," said the captain, deeply interested, "and have suggested nothing new."

"Unfortunately, I cannot; but the truth may be very simple, after all. The old surgeon is so peculiar that I am prepared to discover something remarkable."

"Have you suspicions?"

"I have."

"Of what?"

"A crime. The woman suspects it."

"And betrays it?"

"Certainly, because it is so terrible that her whole nature demands of her that she hand over the criminal to the law."

"What do you propose to do?" asked the captain.

"Secure evidence. I may need help."

"You shall have all the men you require. Go ahead, but be careful. You are on dangerous ground. "

Two days afterwards the detective again sought the captain. "I have a strange document," he said, exhibiting torn fragments of paper, on which there was writing. "The woman stole it and brought it to me. She snatched a handful out of a book, getting only a part of each of a few leaves."

These fragments, which the men arranged as best they could, were (the detective explained) torn by the surgeon's wife from the first volume of a number of manuscript books which her husband had written on one subject – the very one that was the cause of her excitement. "About the time that he began a certain experiment three years ago," continued the detective, "he removed everything from the suite of two rooms containing his study and his operating room. In one of the bookcases that he removed to a room across the passage was a drawer, which he kept locked, but which he opened from time to time. As is quite common with such pieces of furniture, the lock of the drawer is a very poor one; and so the woman, while making a thorough search yesterday, found a key on her bunch that fitted this lock. She opened the drawer, drew out the bottom book of a pile (so that its mutilation would more likely escape discovery), saw that it might contain a clue, and tore out a handful of the leaves. She had barely replaced the book, locked the drawer, and made her escape when her husband appeared. He hardly ever allows her to be out of his sight when she is in that part of the house."

The fragments read as follows: "It is becoming serious… narrow escape today. By some means, while I was absent, it unscrewed the stopper of the silver feeding-pipe (which I have already herein termed 'the artificial mouth'), and in one of its curious antics, allowed all the chyle to escape from its stomach through the tube. Its hunger then became intense – I may say furious. I placed my hands upon it to push it into a chair, when, feeling my touch, it caught me, clasped me around the neck, and would have crushed me to death instantly had I not slipped from its powerful grasp. Thus I always had to be on my guard. I have provided the screw stopper with a spring catch, and usually docile when not hungry; slow and heavy in its movements, which are, of course, purely unconscious: any apparent excitement in movement being due to local irregularities in the blood supply of the cerebellum, which, if I did not have it enclosed in a silver case that is immovable, I should expose and…"

The captain looked at the detective with a puzzled air.

"I don't understand it all," said he.

"Nor I," agreed the detective. "What do you propose to do?"

"Make a raid."

"Do you want a man?"

"Three. The strongest men in your district."

"Why, the surgeon is old and weak!"

"Nevertheless, I want three strong men; and for that matter, prudence really advises me to take twenty."

At one o'clock the next morning a cautious, scratching sound might have been heard in the ceiling of the surgeon's operating room. Shortly afterwards the skylight sash was carefully raised and laid aside. A man peered into the opening. Nothing could be heard.

"That is singular," thought the detective.

He cautiously lowered himself to the floor by a rope, and then stood for some moments listening intently. There was a dead silence. The room was bare, with the exception of a strong iron staple and ring, screwed to the floor in the centre of the room, with a heavy chain attached. The detective then turned his attention to the outer room; it was perfectly bare. He was deeply perplexed. Returning to the inner room, he called softly to the men to descend. While they were occupied he re-entered the outer room and examined the door. A glance sufficed. It was kept closed by a spring attachment, and was locked with a strong spring-lock that could be drawn from the inside.

"The bird has just flown," mused the detective. "A singular accident! The discovery and proper use of this thumb-bolt might not have happened once in fifty years, if my theory is correct." By this time the men were behind him. He noiselessly drew the spring-bolt, opened the door, and looked out into the hall. He heard a peculiar sound. It was as though a gigantic lobster was floundering and scrambling in some distant part of the old house. Accompanying this sound was a loud, whistling breathing, and frequent rasping gasps.

These sounds were heard by still another person, the surgeon's wife; for they originated near her rooms, which were a considerable distance from her husband's. She had been sleeping lightly, tortured by fear and harassed by frightful dreams.

Startled thus out of fitful slumber by the noise at her door, she sprang from her bed to the floor. The idea of flight – one of the strongest of all instincts – seized upon her, and she ran to the door, beyond all control of reason. She drew the bolt and flung the door wide open, and then fled wildly down the passage, the appalling hissing and rasping gurgle ringing in her ears apparently with a thousandfold intensity. But the passage was in absolute darkness, and she had not taken a half dozen steps when she tripped upon an unseen object on the floor. She fell headlong upon it, encountering in it a large, soft, warm substance that writhed and squirmed, and from which came the sounds that had awakened her. Instantly realizing her situation, she uttered a shriek such as only an unnamable terror can inspire. But hardly had her cry started the echoes in the empty corridor when it was suddenly stifled. Two prodigious arms had closed upon her and crushed the life out of her.

The cry performed the office of directing the detective and his assistants, and it also aroused the old surgeon, who occupied rooms between the officers and the objects of their search. The cry of agony pierced him to the marrow, and a realization of the cause of it burst upon him with frightful force.

"It has come at last!" he gasped, springing from his bed.

Snatching from a table a dimly burning lamp and a long knife which he had kept at hand for three years, he dashed into the corridor. The four officers had already started forward, but when they saw him emerge they halted in silence. In that moment of stillness the surgeon paused to listen. He heard the hissing sound and the clumsy floundering of a bulky, living object in the direction of his wife's apartments. It evidently was advancing towards him. A turn in the corridor shut out the view. He turned up the light, which revealed a ghastly pallor in his face.

"Wife!" he called.

There was no response. He hurriedly advanced, the four men following quietly. He turned the angle of the corridor, and ran so rapidly that by the time the officers had come in sight of him again he was twenty steps away. He ran past a huge, shapeless object, sprawling, crawling, and floundering along, and arrived at the body of his wife.

He gave one horrified glance at her face, and staggered away. Then a fury seized him.

Clutching the knife firmly, and holding the lamp aloft, he sprang toward the object in the corridor. It was then that the officers, still advancing cautiously, saw a little more clearly, though still indistinctly, the object of the surgeon's fury. The hideous sight caused them to pause. They saw what appeared to be a man, yet evidently was not a man; huge, awkward, shapeless; a squirming, lurching, stumbling mass, completely naked. It raised its broad shoulders. It had no head, but instead of it a small metallic ball surmounting its massive neck.

"Devil!" exclaimed the surgeon, raising the knife.

"Hold, there!" commanded a stern voice.

The surgeon quickly raised his eyes and saw the four officers, and for a moment fear paralyzed his arm.

"The police!" he gasped. Then, with a look of redoubled fury, he sent the knife to the hilt into the squirming mass before him. The wounded monster sprang to its feet and wildly threw its arms about, meanwhile emitting fearful sounds from a silver tube through which it breathed. The surgeon aimed another blow, but never gave it. In his blind fury he lost his caution, and was caught in an iron grasp. The struggling threw the lamp some

feet toward the officers, and it fell to the floor, shattered to pieces. Simultaneously with the crash the oil took fire, and the corridor was filled with flame.

The officers could not approach. Before them was the spreading blaze, and secure behind it were two forms struggling in a fearful embrace. They heard cries and gasps, and saw the gleaming of a knife.

The wood in the house was old and dry. It took fire at once, and the flames spread with great rapidity. The four officers turned and fled, barely escaping with their lives. In an hour nothing remained of the mysterious old house and its inmates but a blackened ruin.

MICROMEGAS

1752

VOLTAIRE

On **A PLANET** revolving around the star Sirius there lived a young man of great intelligence, whose acquaintance I had the honour of making during his recent visit to our little anthill. He was called Micromegas, an appropriate name for great people. He had a stature of eight leagues, or 24,000 geometrical paces of five feet each, or 120,000 feet.

We earthmen have an average stature hardly more than five feet – one pace – so Mr Micromegas' world must in turn have a circumference 24,000 times greater than our little Earth. Nothing in nature is simpler, more a matter of course.

Given his Excellency's height, any sculptor or painter would agree his waist should, proportionally, be about 50,000 feet around. His nose being one third the length of his handsome face, and his handsome face being one seventh the height of his handsome body, it follows that the Sirian's nose is some 5,714 feet long.

His mind rivals the most cultivated among us; he knows many things, some of which are his own inventions. He had not yet reached his 250th year, and was studying, as was customary at his age, at the most famous school on the planet. When Micromegas was about 450 years old, and already passing out of childhood, he dissected, with the aid of powerful microscopes, many little insects less than 100 feet in diameter; he wrote an interesting book about them, which got him into trouble.

Those who travel only in coaches will doubtless be astonished at the sort of conveyance adopted up there; for we, on our little mound of mud, can imagine nothing beyond our own experience. Our traveller had such a marvellous acquaintance with the laws of gravitation, and all the forces of attraction and repulsion, and made such good use of his knowledge, that, sometimes by means of a sunbeam, and sometimes with the help of a comet, he went from one world to another as a bird hops from bough to bough. He traversed the Milky Way in a short time; and I am obliged to confess that he never saw, beyond the stars with which it is thickly sown, that beautiful celestial empyrean which the illustrious parson, Derham, boasts of having discovered at the end of his telescope. Not that I would for a moment suggest Mr Derham mistook what he saw; Heaven forbid! But Micromegas was on the spot, he is an accurate observer, and I have no wish to contradict anybody.

Micromegas, after plenty of turns and twists, arrived at the planet Saturn. Accustomed though he was to the sight of

novelties, when he saw the insignificant size of the globe and its
inhabitants, he could not at first refrain from that smile of
superiority which sometimes escapes even the wisest; for in
truth Saturn is scarcely 900 times greater than Earth, and the
citizens of that country are mere dwarfs, only a thousand feet
high, or thereabout. He laughed a little at first at these people.
But, being a sensible fellow, the Sirian was soon convinced that a
thinking being need not be altogether ridiculous because he is
only 6000 feet high. He was soon on familiar terms with the
Saturnians after their astonishment had somewhat subsided. He
formed a close friendship with the secretary of the Academy of
Saturn, a man of great intelligence, who had not indeed invented
anything himself, but excelled at describing the inventions of
others, and who could turn a little verse neatly enough or
perform an elaborate calculation.

One day, after the Sirian had laid down and the secretary had
approached his face to facilitate conversation, Micromegas said,
"I must confess that nature is full of variety."

"Yes," said the Saturnian; "nature is like a flower bed, the
blossoms of which…"

"Oh," said the other, "have done with your flower bed!"

"She is," resumed the secretary, "like an assembly of blondes
and brunettes, whose attire…"

"No, no," said the traveller. "Nature is like nature. Why do
you search for comparisons?"

"To please you," answered the secretary.

"I do not want to be pleased," rejoined the traveller; "I want
to be instructed; begin by telling me how many senses the men
in your world possess."

"We have 72," said the academician; "and we are always complaining that they are so few. Our imagination soars beyond our needs; we find that with our 72 senses, our ring, and our five moons, that our range is too restricted, and, in spite of all our curiosity and the tolerably large number of passions which spring out of our 72 senses, we often feel bored."

"I can well believe it," said Micromegas; "for on our globe, though we have nearly a thousand senses, there lingers even in us a certain vague desire, an unaccountable restlessness, which warns us that we are of little account in the universe, and that there are beings much more perfect than ourselves. I have travelled; I have seen mortals far below us, and others greatly superior; but I have seen none who have more wants than they can satisfy. I shall someday, perhaps, reach the country where there is lack of nothing, but hitherto no one has been able to give me any positive information about it."

"How long do you people live?" asked the Sirian.

"Ah! a very short time," replied the little man of Saturn.

"So too with us," said the Sirian. "We are always complaining of the shortness of life. This must be a universal law of nature."

"Alas!" quoth the Saturnian, "none of us live more than 500 annual revolutions of the Sun." (That amounts to about 15,000 years, according to our manner of counting). "You see how it is our fate to die almost as soon as we are born; our existence is a point, our duration an instant, our globe an atom. Scarcely have we begun to acquire a little information when death arrives before we can put it to use. I myself do not venture to lay any schemes; I feel like a drop of water in a boundless ocean. I am ashamed, especially before you, of the absurd figure

I make in this universe."

Micromegas answered: "I fear to distress you by telling you our lives are 700 times as long as yours; but you know too well that when the time comes to give back one's body to the elements, and reanimate nature under another form – the process called death – it is precisely the same whether we have lived an eternity or only a day. I have been in countries where life is a thousand times longer than with us, and yet have heard murmurs of its brevity even there. But people of good sense exist everywhere, who know how to make the most of what they have, and to thank the Author of nature. What colour is your sun when carefully examined?"

"White deeply tinged with yellow," said the Saturnian; "and when we split up one of its rays, it consists of seven colours."

"Our sun has a reddish light," said the Sirian, "and we have 39 primary colours. There is not a single sun, among all those I have approached, which resembles any other, just as among yourselves there is not a single face which is not different from all the rest."

Meanwhile our two inquirers commenced their travels; they first jumped onto Saturn's ring, which they found pretty flat thence they easily made their way from moon to moon. A comet passed near the last one, so they sprang upon it, along with their instruments. When they had gone about 150,000,000 leagues, they came across the satellites of Jupiter. They landed on Jupiter itself, and remained there a year, during which they learned some very remarkable secrets which would now be appearing in the press, were it not for certain censors who find them too hard to swallow.

Leaving Jupiter, our explorers crossed a space of about 100,000,000 leagues, and, coasting along the planet Mars, which, as is well known, is five times smaller than our own little globe, they saw two moons. These have escaped the observation of our astronomers.

At last they perceived a faint glimmer; it came from our Earth, and they decided to disembark. They passed over the tail of the comet, and with the aid with an aurora borealis close at hand, alighted on Earth by the northern shore of the Baltic Sea, July 5, 1737.

After resting, they consumed for breakfast a couple of mountains. Then wishing to inspect the countryside, they first went from north to south. Each of the Sirian's ordinary steps was about 30,000 feet; the Saturnian dwarf, whose height was only a thousand fathoms, followed panting far behind, for he had to take 20 steps when the other made a single stride. Picture to yourself a tiny little toy spaniel pursuing a captain of the King of Prussia's grenadiers!

The strangers proceeded

quickly, circling the globe in 36 hours; the Sun, indeed, or rather
the Earth, makes the same journey in a day; but it is much easier
to turn on one's axis than to walk on one's feet. Behold our
travellers, then, returned to the same spot from which they had
started, after having set eyes upon that sea, to them almost
imperceptible, called the Mediterranean, and that other little
pond which, under the name of the Great Ocean, surrounds this
molehill. Therein the dwarf had never sunk much above the
knee, while the other had scarcely wetted his ankle. They did all
they could, searching here and there, to ascertain whether Earth
was inhabited. They stooped, lay down, and groped about in all
directions; but their eyes and hands being out of all proportion
to the tiny beings who crawl up and down here, they felt not the
slightest sensation which could lead them to suspect that we and
our fellow creatures have the honour to exist.

The dwarf hastily declared there was not a single creature on
this planet. His first reason was that he had not seen one. But
Micromegas politely explained that that was not a good
argument:

"For," said he, "you, with your little eyes, cannot see certain
stars of the 50th magnitude which I distinctly discern; do you
conclude that those stars have no existence?"

"But," argued the dwarf, "this globe is so ill-constructed, so
irregular, and so ridiculously shaped! All here appears chaotic;
look at these little brooks, not one of which goes in a straight
line, and these ponds, which are neither round, square, oval, nor
of any regular form; and all these little bristles which have
rubbed the skin off my feet!" – he alluded to the trees –
"Observe too the shape of the globe as a whole, how it is flat at

the poles, how it turns around the Sun in a clumsily slanting manner, so that the polar climes are mere wastes. In truth, what chiefly makes me think there is nobody here, is that I cannot suppose any sensible people should wish to occupy such a dwelling."

"Well," said Micromegas, "perhaps the people who inhabit it are not sensible. But there are in fact signs of its not having been made for nothing. Everything here seems irregular, you say; but you judge by the standards of Saturn and Jupiter. Have I not told you that in the course of my travels I have always found variety?"

The Saturnian had answers to these arguments, and the dispute might never have ended, had not he suddenly spied what seemed to him a small tadpole moving half underwater in the Baltic sea. Actually, it was a whale. He caught it cleverly with his little finger, and placing it on his thumbnail, showed it to the Sirian, who burst out laughing a second time at the extreme minuteness of the inhabitants of our system.

The Saturnian, now convinced our world was inhabited, immediately concluded that whales were the only creatures to be found here. Micromegas drew a magnifying glass from his bundle of instruments, examined the creature patiently, and found no evidence that it had a soul lodged in its body. The two travellers then suspected there were no intelligent beings in this habitation of ours, when at last they noticed something as big as a whale, floating on the Baltic Sea.

We know that at that very time, a flock of philosophers was returning from the polar circle, where they had gone to make observations no one had attempted before. The newspapers say their vessel ran aground in the gulf of Bothnia, and that they had great difficulty saving their lives; but we never know in this world the real truth about anything. I will relate honestly what occurred, without adding anything of my own invention – a task which demands no small effort on the part of a historian.

The Saturnian stretched out his hand, seized with great dexterity the ship which carried those gentlemen, and placed it

in the hollow of his hand without squeezing it too much, for fear of crushing it. "Here is an animal quite different from the first," he observed.

The passengers and crew, who thought a tempest had whirled them aloft, and supposed they had struck upon some kind of rock, began to stir; the sailors seized casks of wine, threw them overboard on the Saturnian's hand, then jumped down themselves, while the geometers seized their quadrants, their sectors, and a pair of Lapland girls, and descended on the Saturnian's fingers. They made such a commotion that at last he felt a tickle – a pole with an iron point being driven a foot deep into his forefinger. He surmised that this prick proceeded somehow from the little animal he was holding; but at first he perceived nothing more than minute specks, spilling away from the creature.

It was not until both Sirian and Saturnian examined the specks with microscopes that they realized the amazing truth. What pleasure Micromegas and the dwarf felt in watching the movements of those little machines, in examining their feats, in following their operations! How they shouted with joy!

"I see them!" they exclaimed both at once. "Do you not observe how they are carrying burdens, how they stoop down and rise up?"

As they spoke, their hands trembled with delight at beholding objects so unusual, and with fear lest they lose them.

Micromegas perceived clearly that the atoms were speaking to each other but the dwarf refused to believe that such creatures could have any means of communicating ideas. How could those imperceptible beings have vocal organs, and what could they have to say? To be able to speak, one must think, or at least make some approach to thought; but if those creatures could think, they must have something equivalent of a soul; and to attribute the equivalent of a soul to these little animals seemed absurd.

Using the equipment he had brought with him, he fabricated a pair of monster speaking-trumpets, like huge funnels, the narrow ends of which he and the Saturnian placed in their ears. As the wide part of the trumpets covered the ship and her crew, the faintest voice was conveyed in such a manner that the philosophers high above them clearly heard the buzzing of our insects down below. In a few hours they succeeded in distinguishing the words, and at last in understanding the language. The travellers' astonishment increased every instant. They heard mere mites speaking tolerably good sense; such a freak of nature seemed inexplicable.

You may imagine how impatiently the Sirian and his dwarf longed to converse with the atoms; but the dwarf feared that his voice of thunder, and still more that of Micromegas, might deafen the mites without conveying any meaning. To diminish its strength, they placed in their mouths little toothpicks, the tapering ends of which were brought near the ship. Then the Sirian, holding the dwarf on his knee (who in turn held the vessel with her crew upon his palm), bent his head down and spoke in a low voice, thus at last addressing them:

"Invisible insects, whom the hand of the Creator has been pleased to produce in the abyss of the infinitely little, I thank Him for having deigned to reveal to me secrets which seemed inscrutable. It may be the courtiers of my country would not

condescend to look upon you, but I despise no one, and offer you my protection."

If ever anyone was astonished, it was the people who heard these words, nor could they guess whence they came. The ship's chaplain recited the prayers used in exorcism, the sailors swore, and the philosophers constructed theories; but whatever theories they constructed, they could not divine who was speaking to them. The dwarf of Saturn, who had a softer voice than Micromegas, then told them briefly with what kind of beings they were dealing. He gave an account of their journey from Saturn, and acquainted them with the parts and powers of Mr Micromegas; and, after having commiserated them for being so small, he asked if they had always been in that pitiful condition little better than annihilation, what they found to do on a globe that appeared to belong to whales, if they were happy, if they increased and multiplied, whether they had souls, and a hundred other questions.

A philosopher of the party, bolder than the rest, and shocked that the existence of his soul should be questioned, took observations of the speaker with a quadrant from two different stations, and, at the third, spoke: "Do you then suppose sir, because a thousand fathoms extend between your head and feet, that you are…"

"A thousand fathoms!" cried the dwarf. "Good heavens! How can he know my height? A thousand fathoms! He is not an inch out of his reckoning. What! Has that atom actually measured me? He is a geometer, he knows my size; while I, who can barely see him except through a microscope, am still ignorant of his!"

"Yes, I have taken your measure," said the man of science; "and, based on your relative proportions, I further deduce that your big companion is approximately 120,000 feet tall."

Thereupon Micromegas uttered, "I see more clearly than ever that we should judge nothing by its apparent importance."

The conversation grew more and more interesting, and Micromegas spoke as follows:

"Oh intelligent atoms, you must doubtless taste joys of perfect purity on your globe; for, being encumbered with so little matter, and seeming to be all spirit, you must pass your lives in love and meditation – the true life of spiritual beings. I have nowhere beheld genuine happiness, but here it is to be found, without a doubt."

On hearing these words, all the philosophers shook their heads, and one, more frank than the others, candidly confessed that, with the exception of a small number held in mean estimation among them, all the rest of mankind were a multitude of fools, knaves, and miserable wretches.

"We have more matter than we need," said he, "the cause of much evil, if evil proceeds from matter; and we have too much mind, if evil proceeds from mind. For instance, at this very moment there are 100,000 fools of our species who wear hats, slaying 100,000 fellow creatures who wear turbans, or being massacred by them, and over almost all of Earth such practices have been going on from time immemorial."

"Ah! Wretched creatures!" exclaimed the Sirian with indignation; "Can anyone imagine such frantic ferocity! I should like to take two or three steps, and stamp upon the whole swarm of these ridiculous assassins."

"No need," answered the philosopher; "they are working hard enough to destroy themselves. I assure you, at the end of ten years, not a hundredth part of those wretches will be left; even if they had never drawn the sword, famine, fatigue, or intemperance will sweep them almost all away. Besides, it is not they who deserve punishment, but rather those armchair barbarians, who, from the privacy of their cabinets, and during the process of digestion, command the massacre of a million men, and afterward ordain a solemn thanksgiving to God."

The traveller, moved with compassion for the tiny human race, among whom he found such astonishing contrasts, said to the gentlemen:

"Since you belong to the small number of wise men, and apparently do not kill anyone for money, tell me, pray, how you occupy yourselves."

"We dissect flies," said the same philosopher, "measure

distances, calculate numbers, agree upon two or three points we understand, and dispute two or three thousand points of which we know nothing."

The visitors from Sirius and Saturn immediately desired to question these intelligent atoms about the subjects on which they agreed.

"How far do you reckon it," said the latter, "from the Dog Star to the great star in Gemini?"

They all answered together: "32 degrees and a half."

"How far do you make it from here to the Moon?"

"60 half-diameters of the Earth, in round numbers."

"What is the weight of your air?"

He thought to trick them, but they all answered that air weighs about 900 times less than an equal volume of distilled water, and 19,000 times less than pure gold.

The little dwarf from Saturn, astonished at their replies, was now inclined to take for sorcerers the same people he had disbelieved, just a quarter hour ago, could possess souls.

Then Micromegas said: "Since you know so well what is outside yourselves, doubtless you know still better what is within you. Tell me what is the nature of your soul, and how you form ideas."

The philosophers spoke all at once as before, but this time all their opinons differed.

But unluckily a little animalcule was there in a square cap, who silenced all the other philosophical mites, saying that he knew the whole secret, that it was all to be found in the 'Summa' of St Thomas Aquinas; he scanned the pair of celestial visitors from top to toe, and maintained that they and all their kind, their suns and stars, were made solely for man's benefit.

At this speech our two travellers tumbled over each other, choking with inextinguishable laughter; their shoulders shook, and their bodies heaved up and down, till in those merry convulsions, the ship the Saturnian held on his palm fell into his breeches pocket. These two good people, after a long search, recovered it at last, and duly set to rights all that had been displaced. The Saturnian once more took up the little mites, and Micromegas addressed them again with great kindness, though he was a little disgusted in the bottom of his heart at seeing such infinitely insignificant atoms so puffed up with pride. He promised to give them a rare book of philosophy, written in minute characters, for their special use, telling all that can be known of the ultimate essence of things, and he actually gave them the volume ere his departure. It was carried to Paris and laid before the Academy of Sciences; but when the old secretary came to open it, the pages were blank.

"Ah!" said he. "Just as I expected."

FUTURE IMPERFECT

444

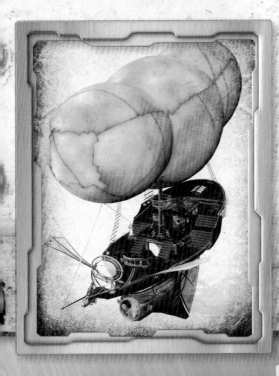

ARMAGEDDON 2419 AD

1928

PHILLIP FRANCES NOWLAN

THERE ARE STILL MANY in the world who are not familiar with my unique experience. I should state therefore, that I, Anthony Rogers, am, so far as I know, the only man alive whose normal span of life has been spread over a period of 573 years. To be precise, I lived the first twenty-nine years of my life between 1898 and 1927; the rest since 2419. The gap between these two, a period of nearly five hundred years, I spent in a state of suspended animation, without any apparent effect on my physical or mental faculties.

When I began my long sleep, man had just begun his real conquest of the air in a sudden series of transoceanic flights in airplanes driven by internal combustion motors. He had barely begun to speculate on the possibilities of harnessing sub-atomic forces, and had made no further practical penetration into the field of ethereal pulsations than the primitive radio and television of that day. The United States of America was the most powerful nation in the world, its political, financial, industrial and scientific influence being supreme.

I awoke to find the America I knew a total wreck – to find Americans a hunted race in their own land, hiding in the dense forests that covered the shattered ruins of their once magnificent cities, desperately preserving, and struggling to develop in their secret retreats, the remnants of their culture and science and their independence.

World domination was in the hands of Mongolians, and the centre of world power lay in inland China, with Americans one of the few races of mankind unsubdued.

They had a magnificently luxurious scheme of civilization within the walls of the fifteen cities of sparkling glass they had flung skyward on the sites of ancient American centres, into the bowels of the earth underneath them, and with relatively small surrounding areas of agriculture.

Complete domination of the air rendered communication between these centres a matter of ease and safety. Occasional destructive raids on the wastelands were considered all that was necessary to keep the 'wild' Americans on the run within the shelter of their forests.

It all resulted from my interest in radioactive gases. During the latter part of 1927 my company, the American Radioactive Gas Corporation, had been keeping me busy investigating reports of unusual phenomena observed in certain abandoned coal mines near the Wyoming Valley in Pennsylvania.

With two assistants and a complete equipment of scientific instruments, I began the exploration of a deserted mine in a mountainous district, where several weeks before, a number of mining engineers had reported traces of carnotite.

On the morning of December 15th, we descended to one of the lowest levels. We noticed too that the rock in the side walls of the shaft was soft, evidently due to the radioactivity, and pieces crumbled underfoot rather easily. We made our way cautiously down the shaft, when suddenly the rotted timbers above us gave way.

I jumped ahead, barely escaping the avalanche of coal and soft rock; my companions, who were several paces behind me, were buried under it, and undoubtedly met instant death.

I was trapped. Return was impossible. With my electric torch I explored the shaft to its end, but could find no other way out. The air became increasingly difficult to breathe, probably from the rapid accumulation of the radioactive gas. In a little while my senses reeled and I lost consciousness.

When I awoke, there was a cool and refreshing circulation of air in the shaft. I had not thought that I had been unconscious more than a few hours, although it seems that the radioactive gas had kept me in a state of suspended animation for something like 500 years. My awakening, I figured out later, had been due to some shifting of the strata which reopened the shaft and cleared the atmosphere in the working. This must have been the case, for I was able to struggle back up the shaft over a pile of debris, and stagger up the long incline to the mouth of the mine, where an entirely different world, overgrown with a vast forest and no visible sign of human habitation, met my eyes.

I shall pass over the days of mental agony that followed in my attempt to grasp the meaning of it all. Had it not been for the necessity of improvising traps and crude clubs with which to slay my food, I believe I should have gone mad.

I shall begin my narrative proper with my first contact with Americans of the year 2419 AD.

My first glimpse of a human being of the 25th century was obtained through a portion of woodland where the trees were thinly scattered, with a dense forest beyond.

I had been wandering along aimlessly, and hopelessly, musing over my strange fate, when I noticed a figure that cautiously backed out of the dense growth across the glade. I was about to call out joyfully, but there was something furtive about the figure that prevented me. The boy's attention (for it seemed to be a lad of fifteen or sixteen) was centred tensely on the heavy growth of the trees from which he had just emerged.

He was clad in rather tight-fitting garments entirely of green, and wore a helmet-like cap of the same colour. High around his waist he wore a broad thick belt, which bulked up in the back across the shoulders into something of the proportions of a knapsack.

As I was taking in these details, there came a vivid flash and heavy detonation, like that of a hand grenade, not far to the left of him. He threw up an arm and staggered a bit in a queer, gliding way; then he recovered himself and slipped cautiously away from the place of the explosion, crouching slightly, and still facing the denser part of the forest. Every few steps he would raise his arm, and point into the forest with something he held in his hand. Wherever he pointed there was a terrible explosion, deeper in among the trees.

After firing several times, he seemed to come to a sudden resolution, and turning in my general direction, leaped – to my amazement sailing through the air between the sparsely scattered trees in such a jump as I had never in my life seen before. That leap must have carried him a full fifty feet, although at the height of his arc, he was not more than ten or twelve feet from the ground.

When he alighted, his foot caught in a projecting root, and he sprawled gently forward. I say 'gently' for he did not crash down as I expected him to do. Due to my surprise, I suppose my brain did not function with its normal quickness, for I gazed at the prone figure for several seconds before I saw the blood that oozed out from under the tight green cap. Regaining my power of action, I dragged him out of sight, back of the big tree. For a few moments I busied myself in an attempt to staunch the flow of blood. The wound was not a deep one. My companion was more dazed than hurt. But what of the pursuers?

I took the weapon from his grasp and examined it hurriedly. It was not unlike the automatic pistol to which I was accustomed, except that it apparently fired with a button instead of a trigger. I inserted several fresh rounds of ammunition into its magazine from my companion's belt as rapidly as I could, for I soon heard near us, the suppressed conversation of his pursuers.

I waited tensely, balancing the gun in my hand, to accustom myself to its weight and probable throw.

Then I saw a movement in the green foliage of a tree not far away, and the head and face of a man appeared. Like my companion, he was clad entirely in green, which made his figure difficult to distinguish. But his face could be seen clearly, and had murder in it.

That decided me, I raised the gun and fired. My aim was bad, for there was no kick in the gun, as I had expected. I hit the trunk of the tree several feet below him. It blew him from his perch like a crumpled bit of paper, and he floated down to the ground, like some limp, dead thing, gently lowered by an invisible hand. The tree, its trunk blown apart by the explosion, crashed down.

There followed another series of explosions around us. These guns we were using made no sound in the firing, and my opponents were evidently as much at sea as to my position as I was to theirs. So I made no attempt to reply to their fire, contenting myself with keeping a sharp lookout in their general direction. And patience had its reward.

Very soon I saw a cautious movement in the top of another tree. Exposing myself as little as possible, I aimed carefully at the tree trunk and fired again. A shriek followed the explosion. I heard the tree crash down, then a groan.

There was silence for a while. Then I heard a faint sound of boughs swishing. I shot three times in its direction, pressing the button as rapidly as I could. Branches crashed down where my shells had exploded, but there was no body.

Now I saw one of them. He was starting one of those amazing leaps from the bough of one tree to another about forty feet away.

I threw up my gun impulsively and fired. By now I had gotten the feel of the weapon, and my aim was good. I hit him. The 'bullet' must have penetrated his body and exploded, for one moment I saw him flying through the air; then the explosion, and he had vanished. He never finished his leap.

How many more of them there were I don't know, but this must have been too much for them. They used a final round of shells on us, all of which exploded harmlessly, and shortly after I heard them swishing and crashing away from us through the tree tops. Not one of them descended to earth.

Now I had time to give some attention to my companion. She was, I found, a girl, and not a boy. Despite her bulky appearance, due to the peculiar belt strapped around her body, she was very slender, and very pretty.

There was a stream not far away, from which I brought water and bathed her face and wound.

Apparently the mystery of these long leaps, the monkey-like ability to jump from bough to bough, and of the bodies that floated gently down instead of falling, lay in the belt. The thing was some sort of anti-gravity belt that almost balanced the weight of the wearer, thereby tremendously multiplying the propulsive power of the leg muscles, and the lifting power of the arms.

When the girl came to, she regarded me as curiously as I did her, and promptly began to quiz me. Her accent puzzled me a lot, but nevertheless we were able to understand each other fairly well, except for certain words and phrases. I explained what had happened while she lay unconscious, and she thanked me simply for saving her life.

"You are a strange exchange," she said, eyeing my clothing quizzically. "Don't you understand what I mean by exchange? I mean – ah – let me see – a stranger, somebody from some other gang. What gang do you belong to?"

"I don't belong to any gang," I explained, "and never did. Does everybody belong to a gang nowadays?"

"Naturally," she said, frowning. "If you don't belong to a gang, where and how do you live? How do you eat? Where do you get your clothing?"

"I've been eating wild game for the past two weeks," I explained, "and this clothing I – er – ah – " I paused, wondering how I could explain that it must be many hundred years old.

In the end I saw I would have to tell my story as well as I could, piecing it together with my assumptions as to what had happened. She listened patiently; incredulously at first, but less so as I went on. When I had finished, she sat thinking for a long time.

"That's hard to believe," she said, "but I believe it." She looked me over with frank interest.

She gave me a brief outline of the system under which her people lived. At least it seemed very peculiar from my 20th century viewpoint.

I learned with amazement that exactly 492 years had passed over my head as I lay unconscious in the mine.

It seemed that another war had followed the First World War, in which nearly all the European nations had banded together to break the financial and industrial power of America. They succeeded in their purpose, though they were beaten, for the war was a terrific one, and left America, like themselves, gasping, bleeding and disorganized, with only the hollow shell of a victory.

This opportunity had been seized by the Russian Soviets, who had made a coalition with the Chinese to sweep over all of Europe and reduce it to a state of chaos.

America, industrially geared to world production and the world trade, collapsed economically, and there ensued desperate attempts at economic reconstruction. But it was impossible to stave off war with the Mongolians, who by now had subjugated the Russians, and were aiming at a world empire.

In about 2109, it seems the conflict was finally precipitated. The Mongolians, with overwhelming fleets of great airships, and

a science that far outstripped that of crippled America, swept in over the Pacific and Atlantic Coasts, and down from Canada, annihilating American aircraft, armies and cities with their terrific disintegrator ray. These rays were projected from a machine not unlike a searchlight in appearance, the reflector of which was a complicated balance of interacting electronic forces. This resulted in a terribly destructive beam. Under its influence, material substance melted into 'nothingness'; i.e. into electronic vibrations. It destroyed all then-known substances, from air to the most dense metals and stone.

They settled down to the establishment of what became known as the Han Dynasty in America, as a sort of province in their World Empire.

Those were terrible days for the Americans. They were hunted like wild beasts. Only those who finally found refuge in mountains, canyons and forests survived. Government was at an end among them. Anarchy prevailed for several generations. Most would have been eager to submit to the Hans, even if it meant slavery. But the Hans did not want them, for they themselves had marvellous machinery and scientific process by which all difficult labour was accomplished.

Ultimately they stopped their active search for, and annihilation of, the widely scattered groups of now savage Americans. So long as Americans remained hidden in their forests, and did not venture near the great cities the Hans had built, little attention was paid to them.

Then began the building of the new American civilization. Families and individuals gathered together in clans or 'gangs' for mutual protection. For nearly a century they lived a nomadic and primitive life, moving from place to place, in desperate fear of the casual and occasional Han air raids, and the terrible disintegrator ray. They lived virtually in the open air, in the forests, in green tents, resorting to camouflage tactics that would conceal their presence from air observers. They dug underground factories and laboratories that they might better be shielded from the electronic detectors of the Hans. They tapped the radio communication lines of the Hans, with crude instruments at first, better ones later on. They bent every effort toward the redevelopment of science. For many generations they laboured as unseen, unknown scholars of the Hans, picking up their knowledge piecemeal.

During the earlier part of this period, there were many deadly wars fought between the various gangs, and occasional courageous but childishly futile attacks upon the Hans, followed by terrible punitive raids.

At the time of my awakening, the gangs were rather loosely organized, but were considering the establishment of a special military force.

Wilma told me she was a member of the Wyoming Gang, which claimed the entire Wyoming Valley as its territory, under the leadership of Boss Hart. Her mother and father were dead, and she was unmarried, so she was not a 'family member'. She lived in a little group of tents known as Camp 17, under a woman Camp Boss, with seven other girls.

For the two-week period which would end the next day, she had been on 'air patrol'. This did not mean, as I first imagined, that she was flying, but rather that she was on the lookout for Han ships over this outlying section of the Wyoming territory, and had spent most of her time perched in the tree tops scanning the skies. Had she seen one she would have fired a 'drop flare' several miles off to one side, which would ignite when it was floating vertically toward the earth, so that the direction or point from which it had been fired might not be guessed by the airship and bring a blasting play of the disintegrator ray in her vicinity. Other members of the air patrol would send up rockets on seeing hers, until finally a scout equipped with an ultrophone, which, unlike the ancient radio, operated on the ultronic ethereal vibrations, would pass the warning simultaneously to the headquarters of the Wyoming Gang and other communities within a radius of several hundred miles.

Wilma cleared up for me the mystery of those flying leaps which she and her assailants had made, and explained the inertron belt balances weight: 'jumpers' were in common use at the time I awoke, though they were costly, for at that time inertron had not been produced in very great quantity.

'Floaters' are a later development of jumpers – rocket motors encased in inertron blocks and strapped to the back in such a way that the wearer floats, when drifting, facing slightly downward. With his motor in operation, he moves like a diver, head foremost, controlling his direction by twisting his body and by movements of his outstretched arms and hands. Ballast weights locked in the front of the belt adjust weight and lift.

"But who were your assailants," I asked, "and why were you attacked?"

Her assailants, she told me, were members of an outlaw gang, referred to as 'Bad Bloods', a group which for several generations had been under the domination of leaders who tried to advance the interests of their clan by tactics which their neighbours had come to regard as unfair, and who in consequence had been virtually boycotted.

"But we must not stay here talking," Wilma concluded. "I have to take you in, and besides I must report this attack right away. But you'll have to have a belt. Mine alone won't help much against our combined weights, and there's little to be gained by jumping heavy. It's almost as bad as walking."

After a little search, we found one of the men I had killed, who had floated down among the trees some distance away and whose belt was not badly damaged.

In going up the side of the mountain, I found that my 20th century muscles did have an advantage, in spite of lack of skill with the belt; and since the slopes were very sharp, and most of our leaps were upward, I could have outdistanced Wilma, but when we crossed the ridge and descended, she outstripped me with her superior technique. Choosing the steepest slopes, she would crouch in the top of a tree, and propel herself outward, literally diving until, with the loss of horizontal momentum, she would assume a more upright position and float downward. In this manner she would sometimes cover as much as a quarter of a mile in a single leap, while I leaped and scrambled clumsily behind, thoroughly enjoying the sensation.

Halfway down the mountain, we saw another green-clad figure leap out above the tree tops toward us. The three of us perched on an outcropping of rock from which a view for many miles around could be had, while Wilma hastily explained her adventure and my presence to her fellow guard, whose name was Alan. I learned later that this was the modern form of Helen.

460

"You want to report by phone then, don't you?" Alan took a compact packet about six inches square from a holster attached to her belt and handed it to Wilma. So far as I could see, it had no special receiver for the ear. Wilma merely threw back a lid, as though she were opening a book, and began to talk. The voice that came back from the machine was as audible as her own.

Wilma was ordered to bring me in at once, and informed that another scout would take her place on the other side of the mountain.

I was received by the assistant Scout Boss, who reported my arrival at once to the historical office, and to officials he called the Psycho Boss and the History Boss, who came in a few minutes later.

For the next two hours, I talked, explained and answered questions. I had to explain, in detail, the manner of my life in the 20th century and my understanding of customs, habits, business, science and the history of that period, and about developments in the centuries that had elapsed. In the end I could see both amazement and belief begin to show in the faces of my inquisitors, and at last the Historical and Psycho Bosses agreed openly that they could find no flaw in my story or reactions, and that my story must be accepted as genuine.

They took me at once to Big Boss Hart. He was a portly man with a 'poker face'. He would probably have been a successful politician even in the 20th century.

They gave him a brief outline of my story and a report of their examination of me. He made no comment other than to nod his acceptance of it; then he turned to me.

"Now that you're here, and can't go back to your own

century, so to speak, what do you want to do? You're welcome to become one of us. Let's see. You and Bill Hearn ought to get along well together. He's Camp Boss of Number 34 when he isn't acting as Raid Boss or Scout Boss. There's a vacancy in his camp."

We all shook hands, for that was one custom that had not died out in five hundred years, and I set out with Hearn.

Bill, like all the others, was clad in green. He was a big man. That is, he was about my own height, five feet eleven. This was considerably above the average now, for the race had lost something in stature, it seemed, through the shifts of five centuries. Most of the women were a bit below five feet, and the men only a trifle above this height.

There was a girl in Wilma's camp named Gerdi Mann, with whom Bill Hearn was desperately in love, and the four of us used to go around a lot together. Gerdi was a distinct type. Whereas Wilma had the usual dark brown hair and hazel eyes that marked nearly every member of the country, Gerdi had red hair, blue eyes and very fair skin. She was a throwback in physical appearance to a certain 20th century type which I have found very rare among modern Americans. The four of us were engaged one day in a discussion of this very point, when I obtained my first experience of a Han air raid.

We were sitting high on the side of a hill overlooking the valley that teemed with human activity, invisible beneath its blanket of foliage.

In the middle of our discussion, we were startled by an alarm rocket that burst high in the air, far to the north, spreading a pall of red smoke that drifted like a cloud. It was followed by others at scattered points in the northern sky.

"A Han raid!" Bill exclaimed in amazement. "The first in seven years!"

"Maybe it's just one of their ships off its course," I ventured.

"No," said Wilma in some agitation. "That would be green rockets. Red means only one thing, Tony. They're sweeping the countryside with their dis beams. Can you see anything, Bill?"

"We had better get under cover," Gerdi said nervously. "The four of us are bunched here in the open. For all we know they may be twelve miles up, out of sight, yet looking at us with a projector."

Bill had been sweeping the horizon hastily with his glass, but apparently saw nothing.

"We had better scatter, at that," he said finally. "It's orders, you know. See!" He pointed to the valley.

Here and there a tiny human figure shot for a moment above the foliage of the tree tops.

"That's bad," Wilma commented, as she counted the jumpers. "No less than fifteen people visible, and all clearly radiating from a central point. Do they want to give away our location?"

The standard orders covering air raids were that the population was to scatter individually. There should be no grouping, or even pairing, in view of the destructiveness of the disintegrator rays. Experience of generations had proved that if this were done, and everybody remained hidden beneath the tree screens, the Hans would have to sweep mile after mile of territory, foot by foot, to catch more than a small percentage of the community.

Gerdi, however, refused to leave Bill, and Wilma developed

an equal stubbornness against quitting my side. I was inexperienced at this sort of thing, she explained, quite ignoring the fact that she was too.

However, since I could not argue her out of it, we leaped together about a quarter of a mile to the right, while Bill and Gerdi disappeared down the hillside among the trees..

No more rockets went up. Except for a few of those waning red clouds, drifting lazily in a blue sky, there was no visible indication of man's past or present existence anywhere in the sky or on the ground.

Then Wilma gripped my arm and pointed. I saw it; away off in the distance; looking like a phantom dirigible in its coat of low-visibility paint.

"Seven thousand feet up," Wilma whispered, crouching close to me. "Watch."

The ship was about the same shape as the great airships of the 20th century that I had seen, but without the suspended control car, engines, propellers; rudders or elevating planes. As it loomed rapidly nearer, I saw that it was wider and somewhat flatter than I had supposed.

Now I could see the repellor rays that held the ship aloft, like searchlight beams faintly visible in the bright daylight (and still faintly visible to the human eye at night). The raider neared with incredible speed.

The ship was operating two disintegrator rays, though only in a casual, intermittent fashion. But whenever they flashed downward with blinding brilliancy, forest, rocks and ground melted instantaneously into nothing where they played upon them.

When later I inspected the scars left by these rays I found them some five feet deep and thirty feet wide.

No systematic use of the rays was made by the ship, however, until it reached a point over the centre of the valley – the centre of the community's activities. There it came to a sudden stop by shooting its repellor beams sharply forward and easing them back gradually to the vertical, holding the ship floating and motionless. Then the work of destruction began systematically.

Back and forth travelled the destroying rays, ploughing

parallel furrows from hillside to hillside. We gasped in dismay, Wilma and I, as time after time we saw it plough through sections where we knew camps or plants were located.

"This is awful," she moaned, a terrified question in her eyes. "How could they know the location so exactly, Tony?"

We did not talk of what might happen if the rays were turned in our direction. We both knew. We would simply disintegrate in a split second into mere scattered electronic vibrations. We knew that many of our companions must have been whisked into absolute non-existence before our eyes in these few moments. The whole thing paralyzed us into mental and physical immobility for I do not know how long.

It couldn't have been long, however, for the rays had not ploughed more than thirty of their twenty-foot furrows or so across the valley, when I regained control of myself, and brought Wilma to herself by shaking her roughly.

"How far will this rocket gun shoot, Wilma?" I demanded, drawing my pistol.

"It depends on your rocket, Tony. It will take even the longest range rocket, but you could shoot more accurately from a longer tube. But why? You couldn't penetrate the shell of that ship with rocket force, even if you could reach it."

I fumbled clumsily with my rocket pouch, for I was excited. I had an idea I wanted to try. With Wilma's help, I selected the longest range explosive rocket in my pouch, and fitted it to my pistol.

"It won't carry seven thousand feet, Tony," Wilma objected. But I took aim carefully. It was another thought that I had in my mind. The supporting repellor ray, I had been told, became molecular in character at what was called a logarithmic level of five (below that it was a purely electronic 'flow' or pulsation between the source of the 'carrier' and the average mass of the earth).

Below that level, if I could project my explosive bullet into this stream where it began to carry material substance upward, might it not rise with the air column, gathering speed and hitting the ship with enough impact to carry it through the shell? It was worth trying anyhow. Wilma became greatly excited, too, when she grasped the nature of my inspiration.

Feverishly I looked around for some formation of branches against which I could rest the pistol, for I had to aim most carefully. At last I found one. Patiently I sighted on the hulk of the ship far above us, aiming at the far side of it, at such an angle as would, so far as I could estimate, bring my bullet path through the forward repellor beam. At last the sights wavered across the point I sought and I pressed the button gently.

For a moment we gazed breathlessly.

Suddenly the ship swung bow down, as on a pivot, and swayed like a pendulum. Wilma screamed in her excitement.

"Oh Tony, you hit it! You hit it! Do it again! Bring it down!"

We had only one more rocket of extreme range between us, and we dropped it three times in our excitement in inserting it in my gun. Then, forcing myself to be calm by sheer will power, while Wilma stuffed her little fist into her mouth to keep from shrieking, I sighted carefully again and fired.

The elapsed time of the rocket's invisible flight seemed an age.

Then we saw the ship falling. It seemed to plunge lazily, but actually it fell with terrific acceleration, turning end over end, its disintegrator rays, out of control, casting vast, wild arcs, and once cutting a gash through the forest less than two hundred feet from where we stood.

The crash with which the heavy craft hit the ground reverberated from the hills — the momentum of eighteen or twenty thousand tons, in a sheer drop of seven thousand feet. A mangled mass of metal, it buried itself in the ground.

Then far down the hillside, a single figure leaped exultantly above the foliage screen. And in the distance another, and another.

In a moment the sky was punctured by signal rockets. One after another the little red puffs became drifting clouds.

"Scatter! Scatter!" Wilma exclaimed. "In half an hour there'll be an entire Han fleet here from Nu-Yok, and another from Bah-Flo. They'll get this instantly on their recordographs and location finders. They'll blast the whole valley and the country for miles beyond."

Over the ridge we went, in long leaps towards the east, the country of the Delawares.

From time to time signal rockets puffed in the sky. Most of them were the 'red warnings', the 'scatter' signals. But from certain of the others, which Wilma identified as Wyoming rockets, she gathered that whoever was in command (we did not know whether the Boss was alive or not) was ordering an ultimate rally toward the south, and so we changed our course.

We travelled far before nightfall overtook us, trying only to put as much distance as possible between ourselves and the valley.

When gathering dusk made jumping too dangerous, we sought a comfortable spot beneath the trees and consumed part of our emergency rations. It was the first time I had tasted the stuff – a highly nutritive synthetic substance called 'concentro', which was, however, a bit bitter and unpalatable. But as only a mouthful or so was needed, it did not matter.

In the morning we found the practical problem facing us was great. Wilma felt that the Wyoming plan must be to rally in the Susquanna territory, but she had her doubts about the wisdom of this plan. In my elation at my success in bringing down the Han ship, and my newly found interest in my charming companion, I had forgotten the ominous fact that the Han ship I had destroyed must have known the exact location of the Wyoming Works.

But at any rate it was clearly our business to get in touch with the other fugitives as quickly as possible, so in spite of muscles that were sore from the excessive leaping of the day before, we continued on our way.

We travelled for only a couple of hours when we saw a multi-coloured rocket in the sky, some ten miles ahead of us.

"Bear to the left, Tony," Wilma said, "and listen for the whistle."

"Why?" I asked.

"Haven't they given you the rocket code yet?" she replied. "That's what the green, followed by yellow and purple means: to concentrate five miles east of the rocket position. You know the rocket position itself might draw a play of dis rays."

It did not take us long to reach the neighbourhood of the indicated rallying, though we were now travelling beneath the trees, with but an occasional leap to a top branch to see if any more rocket smoke was floating above. And soon we heard a distant whistle.

We found about half the gang already there, in a spot where the trees met high above a little stream. The Big Boss and Raid Bosses were busy reorganizing the remnants.

"You two stick close to me," he said, adding grimly, "I'm going back to the valley at once with a hundred picked men, and I'll need you."

Inside of fifteen minutes we were on our way. A certain amount of caution was sacrificed for the sake of speed, and the men leaped away either across the forest top, or over open spaces of ground, but concentration was forbidden. The Big Boss named the spot on the hillside as the rallying point.

"We'll have to take a chance on being seen, so long as we don't group," he declared, "at least until within five miles of the rallying spot. From then on I want every man to disappear from sight and to travel under cover. And keep your ultrophones open, and turned on ten-four-seven-six."

Wilma and I had received our battle equipment from the Gear Boss. It consisted of a long-gun, a hand-gun, with a special case of ammunition constructed of inertron, which made the load weigh but a few ounces, and a short sword. This gear we strapped over each other's shoulders, on top of our jumping belts. In addition, we each received an ultrophone, and a light inertron blanket rolled into a cylinder about six inches long by two or three in diameter. This fabric was exceedingly thin and but it had considerable warmth, because of the mixture of inertron in its composition.

"This looks like business," Wilma remarked to me with sparkling eyes.

Hart was about to call us on our phones when we looked up. As soon as we did so, he leaped away, waving us to follow closely.

He was a powerful man, and he darted ahead in long, swift, low leaps up the banks of the stream, which followed a fairly straight course at this point. By extending ourselves, however, Wilma and I were able to catch up to him.

As we gradually synchronized our leaps with his, he outlined to us, between the grunts that accompanied each leap, his plan of action.

"We have to start the big business — unh — sooner or later," he said. "And if — unh — the Hans have found any way of locating

our positions – unh – it's time to start now, although the Council of Bosses – unh – had intended waiting a few years until enough rocket ships have been – unh – built. But no matter what the sacrifice – unh – we can't afford to let them get us on the run – unh – We'll set a trap in the – unh – valley if they come back for their wreckage – unh – and if they don't, we'll go rocketing for some of their liners – unh – on the Nu-yok, Glee-lan, Sikaga course. We can use – unh – that idea of yours of shooting up the repellor – unh – beams. Want you to give us a demonstration."

With further orders to follow him closely, he increased his pace, and Wilma and I were taxed to our utmost to keep up.

We slept in greater comfort that night, under our inertron blankets, and were off with the dawn, leaping cautiously to the top of the ridge overlooking the valley which Wilma and I had left.

The Boss scanned the sky with his ultroscope, patiently taking some fifteen minutes to the task, and then swung his phone into use, calling the roll and giving the men their instructions.

His first order was for us all to slip our ear and chest discs into permanent position. The Boss' set was triple powered, so that his orders would cut in on any local conversations, which were indulged in, however, with great restraint, and only for the purpose of maintaining contacts.

I marvelled at the efficiency of this modern method of battle communication in contrast to the clumsy signalling devices of more ancient times; and also at other military contrasts in which the 20th and 25th century methods were the reverse of each other in efficiency. And until my recent flash of inspiration, no one among them, apparently, had ever thought of the scheme of shooting a rocket into a repellor beam and letting the beam itself hurl it upward into the most vital part of the Han ship.

Hart patiently placed his men, first giving his instructions to the campmasters, and then remaining silent, while they placed the individuals.

In the end, the hundred men were ringed about the valley, on the hillsides and tops, each in a position from which he had a good view of the wreckage of the Han ship.

The Boss explained to me that it was his idea that he, Wilma and I should investigate the wreck. If Han ships should appear in the sky, we would leap for the hillsides.

I suggested to him to have the men set up their long-guns trained on an imaginary circle surrounding the wreck. He busied himself with this after the three of us leaped down to the Han ship, serving as a target himself, while he called on the men individually to aim their pieces and lock them in position.

In the meantime Wilma and I climbed into the wreckage, but did not find much. Practically all of the instruments and machinery had been twisted out of an recognizable shape, or utterly destroyed by the ship's disintegrator rays which apparently had continued to operate in the midst of its warped remains for some moments after the crash.

I did not have time to study the ship and its contents as carefully as I would have liked, however. Time pressed, and it was our business to discover some clue to the deadly accuracy with which the ship had spotted the Wyoming Works.

The Boss had hardly finished his arrangements for the ring barrage, when one of the scouts on an eminence to the north,

announced the approach of seven Han ships spread out in a great
semicircle.

Hart leaped for the hillside, calling to us to do likewise, but
Wilma and I had raised the flaps of our helmets and switched off
our 'speakers' for conversation between ourselves, and by the
time we discovered what had happened, the ships were clearly
visible, so fast were they approaching.

"Jump!" we heard the Boss order, "Deering to the north.
Rogers to the east."

But Wilma looked at me meaningfully and pointed to where
the twisted plates of the ship projecting from the ground offered

a shelter.

"Too late, Boss," she said. "They'd see us. Besides I think there's something here we ought to look at. It's probably their magnetic graph."

"You're signing your death warrant," Hart warned.

"We'll risk it," said Wilma and I together.

"Good for you," replied the Boss. "Take command then, Rogers, for the present. Do you all know his voice, boys?"

A chorus of assent rang in our ears, and I began to do some fast thinking as the girl and I ducked into the twisted mass of metal.

"Wilma, hunt for that record," I said, knowing that by the simple process of talking I could keep the entire command continuously informed as to the situation. "On the hillsides, keep your guns trained on the circles and stand by. On the hilltops, how many of you are there? Speak in rotation from Bald Knob around to the east, north, west."

In turn the men called their names. There were twenty of them.

I assigned them by name to cover the various Han ships, numbering the latter from left to right.

"Train our rockets on their repellor rays about three quarters of the way up, between ships and ground. Aim is more important than elevation. Follow those rays with your aim continuously. Shoot when I tell you, not before. The Hans probably have not seen us, or at least think there are only two of us in the valley, since they're settling without opening up disintegrators. Any opinions?"

My ear discs remained silent.

"Deering and I will remain here until they land and debark. Stand by and keep alert."

Rapidly and easily, the largest of the Han ships settled to the earth. Three scouted sharply to the south, rising to a higher level. The others floated motionless about a thousand feet above.

Peeping through a small fissure between two plates, we saw the vast hulk of the ship come to rest full on the line of our prospective ring barrage. A door clanged open a couple of feet from the ground, and one by one the crew emerged.

"They're coming out of the ship." I spoke quietly with my hand over my mouth, for fear they might hear me. "One-two-three-four-five-six-seven-eight-nine. That seems to be all. Who knows how many men a ship like that is likely to carry?"

"About ten, if there are no passengers," replied one of my men, probably one of those on the hillside.

"How are they armed?" I asked.

"Just knives," came the reply. "They never permit hand rays on the ship. Afraid of accidents. Have a ruling against it."

"Leave them to us then," I said, for I had a plan in mind. "You, on the hillsides, take the ships above. Abandon the ring target. Divide up in training on those repellor rays. You on the hilltops, all train on the repellors of the ships to the south. Shoot at the word, but not before.

"Wilma, crawl over to your left where you can make a straight leap for the door in that ship. These men are all walking around the wreck in a bunch. When they're on the far side, I'll give the word and you leap through that door in one bound. I'll follow. Maybe we won't be seen. We'll overpower the guard inside, but don't shoot. We may escape being seen by both

this crew and the ships above. They can't see over this wreck."

It was so easy that it seemed too good to be true. The Hans who had emerged from the ship walked round the wreckage lazily, talking in guttural tones, keenly interested in the wreck, but quite unsuspicious.

At last they were on the far side. In a moment they would be picking their way into the wreck.

"Wilma, leap!" I almost whispered the order.

The distance between Wilma's hiding place and the door in the side of the Han ship was not more than fifteen feet. She was already crouched with her feet braced against a metal beam. Taking the lift of the inertron belt into her calculation, she dove head foremost, like a projectile, through the door. I followed in a split second, more clumsily, but no less speedily, bruising my shoulder painfully as I ricocheted from the edge of the opening and brought up sliding against the unconscious girl; for she evidently had hit her head against the partition within the ship into which she had crashed.

We had made some noise within the ship. Shuffling footsteps were approaching down a well-lit gangway.

"Any signs we have been observed?" I asked my men on the hillsides.

"Not yet," I heard the Boss reply. "Ships overhead still standing. No beams have been broken out. Men on ground absorbed in wreck. Most of them have crawled into it out of sight."

"Good," I said quickly. "Deering hit her head. Knocked out. One or more members of the crew approaching. We're not discovered yet. I'll take care of them. Stand a bit longer, but be ready."

I think my last words must have been heard by the man who was approaching, for he stopped suddenly.

I crouched at the far side of the compartment, motionless. I would not draw my sword if there were only one of them.

Apparently reassured at the absence of any further sound, a man came around a sort of bulkhead – and I leaped.

I swung my legs up in front of me as I did so, catching him full in the stomach and knocked him cold.

I ran forward along the keel gangway, searching for the control room. I found it well up in the nose of the ship. And it was deserted. What could I do to jam the controls of the ship that would not register on the recording instruments of the other ships? I gazed at the mass of controls. Levers and wheels galore. In the centre of the compartment, on a massively braced universal joint mounting, was what I took for the repellor generator. A dial on it glowed and a faint hum came from within its shielding metallic case. But I had no time to study it.

Above all else, I was afraid that some automatic apparatus existed in the room, through which I might be heard on the other ships. The risk of trying to jam the controls was too great. I abandoned the idea and withdrew softly. I would have to take a chance that there was no other member of the crew aboard.

I ran back to the entrance compartment. Wilma still lay where she had slumped down. I heard the voices of the Hans approaching. It was time to act. The next few seconds would tell whether the ships in the air would try or be able to melt us into nothingness.

"Are you boys all ready?" I asked, creeping to a position

opposite the door and drawing my handgun.

Again there was a chorus of assent.

"Then on the count of three, shoot up those rep rays – all of them – and for God's sake, don't miss." I was beginning to think in the terms the others used generally – 'dis' for disintegrator, 'rep' for repellor. And I counted.

I think my 'three' was a bit weak. I know it took all the courage I had to utter it.

For an agonizing instant nothing happened, except that the landing party from the ship strolled into my range of vision.

Then, startled, they turned their eyes upward. For an instant they stood frozen with horror at whatever they saw.

One hurled his knife at me. It grazed my cheek. Then a couple of them made a break for the doorway. The rest followed. But I fired pointblank with my hand-gun, pressing the button as fast as I could and aiming at their feet to make sure my explosive rockets would make contact and do their work.

The detonations of my rockets were deafening. The spot on which the Hans stood flashed into a blinding glare. Then there was nothing there except their torn and mutilated corpses. They had been fairly bunched and I got them all.

I ran to the door, expecting any instant to be hurled into infinity by the sweep of a dis ray.

Some eighth of a mile away I saw one of the ships crash to the earth. A dis ray came into my line of vision, wavered uncertainly for a moment and then began to sweep directly toward the ship in which I stood. But it never reached it. Suddenly, like a light switched off, it shot to one side, and a moment later another vast hulk crashed to earth. I looked out, then stepped out on the ground.

The only Han ships in the sky were two of the scouts to the south which were hanging perpendicularly, and sagging slowly down. The others must have crashed down while I was deafened by the sound of the explosion of my own rockets.

Somebody hit the other rep ray of one of the two remaining ships and it fell out of sight beyond a hilltop. The other, farther away, drifted down diagonally, its dis ray playing viciously over the ground below it.

I shouted with exultation and relief.

"Take back the command, Boss!" I yelled.

His commands, sending out jumpers in pursuit of the descending ship, rang in my ears, but I paid no attention to them. I leaped back into the compartment of the Han ship and knelt beside my Wilma. Her padded helmet had absorbed much of the blow, I thought; otherwise, her skull might have been fractured.

"Oh, my head!" she groaned, coming to as I lifted her gently in my arms and strode out in the open with her. "We must have won, dearest, did we?"

"We most certainly did," I reassured her. "All but one crashed and that one is drifting down toward the south. We've captured this one we're in intact. There was only one member of the crew aboard when we dove in."

Less than an hour afterward the Big Boss ordered the outfit to tune in ultrophones on three-twenty-three to pick up a translated broadcast of the Han intelligence office in Nu-Yok from the Susquanna station. It was in the form of a public warning and news item.

"This is Public Intelligence Office, Nu-Yok, broadcasting warning to navigators of private ships, and news public interest. The squadron of seven ships which left Nu-Yok this morning to investigate the recent destruction of the GK-984 in the Wyoming Valley, has been destroyed by a series of mysterious explosions similar to those which wrecked the GK-984.

"The phones, viewplates, and all other signalling devices of five of the seven ships ceased operating suddenly at approximately the same moment, about seven-four-nine.

"The Intelligence Office has no indication of the kind of disaster which overtook the squadron except certain evidences of the explosive phenomena similar to those in the case of the GK-984, which recently went dead while beaming the valley in a systematic effort to wipe out the works and camps of the tribesmen. The Office considers as obvious the deduction that the tribesmen have developed a new, and as yet undetermined, technique of attack on airships, and has recommended to the Heaven-Born that immediate and unlimited authority to be given the Navigation Intelligence Division to make a investigation of this technique and develop a defence against it.

"In the meantime it urges that private navigators avoid this territory in particular, and in general hold as closely as possible to the official inter-city routes, which now are being patrolled by the entire force of the Military Office, which is beaming the routes generously to a width of ten miles. The Military Office reports that it is at present considering no retaliatory raids against the tribesmen."

The message ended with a repetition of the warning to other airmen to avoid the valley.

BATTLING THE MORLOCK

1895 FROM THE TIME MACHINE

H G WELLS

The Time Traveller has arrived in the year 802,701 AD, next to a large statue of a sphinx. He meets the Eloi, a race of peaceful human-like creatures. He has rescued one of them, Weena, who now travels with him as he seaches for his time machine. In the darkness, he encounters the Morlocks, a subterranean humanoid race who rise to the surface at night to feed on the Eloi.

WE EMERGED FROM THE PALACE while the sun was still in part above the horizon. I was determined to reach the White Sphinx early the next morning, and ere the dusk I purposed pushing through the woods that had stopped me on the previous journey. My plan was to go as far as possible that night, and then, building a fire, to sleep in the protection of its

glare. Accordingly, as we went along I gathered sticks or dried grass I saw, and presently had my arms full of such litter. Our progress was slower than I had anticipated, and besides Weena was tired. I began to suffer from sleepiness too; so that it was full night before we reached the wood. Upon the shrubby hill of its edge Weena would have stopped, fearing the darkness before us; but a sense of impending calamity, that should indeed have served me as a warning, drove me onward. I had been without

sleep for a night and two days, and I was feverish and irritable.
I felt sleep coming upon me, and the Morlocks with it.

While we hesitated, among the black bushes behind us, I saw
three crouching figures. There was scrub and long grass all about
us, and I did not feel safe from their insidious approach. The
forest, I calculated, was rather less than a mile across. If we
could get through it to the bare hillside, there, as it seemed to
me, was an altogether safer resting place; I thought that with my
matches and my camphor I could contrive to keep my path
illuminated through the woods. Yet it was evident that if I was to
flourish matches with my hands I should have to abandon my
firewood; so, rather reluctantly, I put it down. And then it came
into my head that I would amaze our friends behind by lighting
it. I was to discover the atrocious folly of this proceeding, but it
came to my mind as an ingenious move for covering our retreat.

I don't know if you have ever thought what a rare thing flame
must be in the absence of man and in a temperate climate. The
sun's heat is rarely strong enough to burn, even when it is
focused by dewdrops. Lightning may blast and blacken, but it
rarely gives rise to widespread fire. Decaying vegetation may
smoulder with the heat of its fermentation, but this rarely results
in flame. In this decadence, too, the art of fire-making had been
forgotten on the earth. The red tongues that went licking up my
heap of wood were a new and strange thing to Weena.

She wanted to run to it and play with it. But I caught her up,
and in spite of her struggles, plunged boldly before me into the
wood. For a little way the glare of my fire lit the path. Looking
back presently, I could see, through the crowded stems, that
from my heap of sticks the blaze had spread to some bushes

adjacent, and a curved line of fire was creeping up the grass of the hill. I laughed at that, and turned again to the dark trees before me. It was very black, and Weena clung to me convulsively, but there was still, as my eyes grew accustomed to the darkness, sufficient light for me to avoid the stems. Overhead it was simply black, except where a gap of remote blue sky shone down upon us here and there. I struck none of my matches because I had no hand free. Upon my left arm I carried my little one, in my right hand I had my iron bar.

For some way I heard nothing but the crackling twigs under my feet, the faint rustle of the breeze above, and my own breathing and the throb of the blood vessels in my ears. Then I seemed to know of a pattering about me. I pushed on grimly. The pattering grew more distinct, and then I caught the same queer sound and voices I had heard in the Underworld. There were evidently several of the Morlocks, and they were closing in upon me. Indeed, in another minute I felt a tug at my coat, then something at my arm. And Weena shivered violently, and became quite still.

It was time for a match. But to get one I must put her down. I did so, and, as I fumbled with my pocket, a struggle began in the darkness about my knees, perfectly silent on her part and with the same peculiar cooing sounds from the Morlocks. Soft little hands, too, were creeping over my coat and back, touching even my neck. Then the match scratched and fizzed. I held it flaring, and saw the white backs of the Morlocks in flight amid the trees. I hastily took a lump of camphor from my pocket, and prepared to light it as soon as the match should wane. Then I looked at Weena. She was lying clutching my feet and quite

motionless, with her face to the ground. With a sudden fright I stooped to her. She seemed scarcely to breathe. I lit the block of camphor and flung it to the ground, and as it split and flared up and drove back the Morlocks and the shadows, I knelt down and lifted her. The wood behind seemed full of the stir and murmur of a great company!

She seemed to have fainted. I put her carefully upon my shoulder and rose to push on, and then there came a horrible realization. In manoeuvring with my matches and Weena, I had turned myself about several times, and now I had not the faintest idea in what direction lay my path. For all I knew, I might be facing back towards the Palace of Green Porcelain. I found myself in a cold sweat. I had to think rapidly what to do. I determined to build a fire and encamp where we were. I put Weena, still motionless, down upon a turfy bole, and very hastily, as my first lump of camphor waned, I began collecting sticks and leaves. Here and there out of the darkness round me the Morlocks' eyes shone like carbuncles.

The camphor flickered and went out. I lit a match, and as I did so, two white forms that had been approaching Weena dashed hastily away. One was so blinded by the light that he came straight for me, and I felt his bones grind under the blow of my fist. He gave a whoop of dismay, staggered a little way, and fell down. I lit another piece of camphor, and went on gathering my bonfire. Presently I noticed how dry was some of the foliage above me, for since my arrival on the Time Machine, a matter of a week, no rain had fallen. So, instead of casting about among the trees for fallen twigs, I began leaping up and dragging down branches. Very soon I had a choking smoky fire of green wood and dry sticks, and could economize my camphor. Then I turned to where Weena lay beside my iron mace. I tried what I could to revive her, but she lay like one dead. I could not even satisfy myself whether or not she breathed.

Now, the smoke of the fire beat over towards me, and it must have made me heavy of a sudden. Moreover, the vapour of camphor was in the air. My fire would not need replenishing for an hour or so. I felt very weary after my exertion, and sat down. The wood, too, was full of a slumbrous murmur that I did not understand. I seemed just to nod and open my eyes. But all was dark, and the Morlocks had their hands upon me. Flinging off their clinging fingers I hastily felt in my pocket for the matchbox, and – it had gone! Then they gripped and closed with me again. In a moment I knew what had happened. I had slept, and my fire had gone out, and the bitterness of death came over my soul. The forest seemed full of the smell of burning wood. I was caught by the neck, by the hair, by the arms, and pulled down. It was indescribably horrible in the darkness to feel all these soft creatures heaped upon me. I felt as if I was in a monstrous spider's web. I was overpowered, and went down. I felt little teeth nipping at my neck. I rolled over, and as I did so my hand came against my iron lever. It gave me strength. I struggled up, shaking the human rats from me, and, holding the bar short, I thrust where I judged their faces might be. I could feel the succulent giving of flesh and bone under my blows, and for a moment I was free.

The strange exultation that so often seems to accompany hard fighting came upon me. I knew that both I and Weena were lost, but I determined to make the Morlocks pay for their meat.

I stood with my back to a tree, swinging the iron bar before me. The whole wood was full of the stir and cries of them. A minute passed. Their voices seemed to rise to a higher pitch of excitement, and their movements grew faster. Yet none came within reach. I stood glaring at the blackness. Then suddenly came hope. What if the Morlocks were afraid? And close on the heels of that came a strange thing. The darkness seemed to grow luminous. Very dimly I began to see the Morlocks about me — three battered at my feet — and then I recognized, with incredulous surprise, that the others were running, in an incessant stream, as it seemed, from behind me, and away through the wood in front. And their backs seemed no longer white, but reddish. As I stood agape, I saw a little red spark go drifting across a gap of starlight between the branches, and vanish. And at that I understood the smell of burning wood, the slumbrous murmur that was growing now into a gusty roar, the red glow, and the Morlocks' flight.

Stepping out from behind my tree and looking back, I saw, through the black pillars of the nearer trees, the flames of the burning forest. It was my first fire coming after me. With that I looked for Weena, but she was gone. The hissing and crackling behind me, the explosive thud as each fresh tree burst into flame, left little time for reflection. My iron bar still gripped, I followed in the Morlocks' path. It was a close race. Once the flames crept forward so swiftly on my right as I ran that I was outflanked and had to strike off to the left. But at last I emerged upon a small open space, and as I did so, a Morlock came blundering towards me, and past me, and went on straight into the fire!

And now I was to see the most weird and horrible thing, I think, of all that I beheld in that future age. This whole space was as bright as day with the reflection of the fire. In the centre was a hillock or tumulus, surmounted by a scorched hawthorn. Beyond this was another arm of the burning forest, with yellow tongues already writhing from it, completely encircling the

space with a fence of fire. Upon the hillside were some thirty or forty Morlocks, dazzled by the light and heat, and blundering hither and thither against each other in their bewilderment. At first I did not realize their blindness, and struck furiously at them with my bar in a frenzy of fear, as they approached me, killing one and crippling several more. But when I had watched

the gestures of one of them groping under the hawthorn against the red sky, and heard their moans, I was assured of their absolute helplessness and misery in the glare, and I struck no more of them.

Yet every now and then one would come straight towards me, setting loose a quivering horror that made me quick to elude him. At one time the flames died down somewhat, and I feared the foul creatures would be able to see me. I was thinking of beginning the fight by killing some of them before this should happen; but the fire burst out again brightly, and I stayed my hand. I walked about the hill among them and avoided them, looking for some trace of Weena. But Weena was gone.

At last I sat down on the summit of the hillock, and watched this strange incredible company of blind things groping to and fro, and making uncanny noises to each other, as the glare of the fire beat on them. The coiling uprush of smoke streamed across the sky, and through the rare tatters of that red canopy, remote as though they belonged to another universe, shone the little stars. Two or three Morlocks came blundering into me, and I drove them off with blows of my fists, trembling as I did so.

For the most part of that night I was persuaded it was a nightmare. I bit myself and screamed in a passionate desire to awake. I beat the ground with my hands, and got up and sat down again, and wandered here and there, and again sat down. Then I would fall to rubbing my eyes and calling upon God to let me awake. Thrice I saw Morlocks put their heads down in a kind of agony and rush into the flames. But, at last, above the subsiding red of the fire, above the streaming masses of black smoke and the whitening and blackening tree stumps, and the diminishing numbers of these dim creatures, came the white light of the day.

I searched again for traces of Weena, but there were none. It was plain that they had left her poor little body in the forest. I cannot describe how it relieved me to think that it had escaped the awful fate to which it seemed destined. As I thought of that, I was almost moved to begin a massacre of the helpless abominations about me, but I contained myself. The hillock, as I have said, was a kind of island in the forest. From its summit I could now make out through a haze of smoke the Palace of Green Porcelain, and from that I could get my bearings for the White Sphinx. And so, leaving the remnant of these damned souls still going hither and thither and moaning, as the day grew clearer, I tied some grass about my feet and limped on across smoking ashes and among black stems, that still pulsated internally with fire, towards the hiding place of the Time Machine. I walked slowly, for I was almost exhausted, as well as lame, and I felt the intensest wretchedness for the horrible death of little Weena. It seemed an overwhelming calamity. Now, in this old familiar room, it is more like the sorrow of a dream than an actual loss. But that morning it left me absolutely lonely again – terribly alone. I began to think of this house of mine, of this fireside, of some of you, and with such thoughts came a longing that was pain.

MELLONTA TAUTA

1849

EDGAR ALLAN POE

To the Editor of the Lady's Book,

I have the honour of sending you, for your magazine, an article which I hope you will be able to comprehend rather more distinctly than I do myself. It is a translation, by my friend Martin Van Buren Mavis, of an odd-looking MS, which I found, about a year ago, tightly corked up in a jug floating in the Mare Tenebrarum — a sea well described by the Nubian geographer, but seldom visited nowadays.

Very truly,

Edgar A Poe

On board balloon 'Skylark'
April 1, 2848

NOW, **MY DEAR FRIEND** — now, for your sins, you are to suffer the infliction of a long gossiping letter. I tell you distinctly that I am going to punish you for all your impertinences by being as tedious, and as unsatisfactory as possible. Besides, here I am, cooped up in a balloon, with some one or two hundred, all bound on a *pleasure* excursion (what a funny idea some people have of pleasure!), and I have no prospect of touching *terra firma* for a month at least. Nobody to talk to. Nothing to do. When one has nothing to do, then is the time to correspond with one's friends. You perceive, then, why it is that I write you this letter — it is on account of my boredom and your sins.

Get ready your spectacles and make up your mind to be annoyed. I mean to write at you every day during this odious voyage.

Hi-ho! Are we forever to be doomed to the thousand inconveniences of the balloon? Will *nobody* contrive a more expeditious mode of progress? This jog-trot movement, to my thinking, is little less than positive torture. Upon my word we have not made more than a hundred miles an hour since leaving home! The very birds beat us – at least some of them. I assure you that I do not exaggerate at all. Our motion, no doubt, seems slower than it actually is – this on account of our having no objects about us by which to estimate our velocity, and on account of our going with the wind. To be sure, whenever we meet a balloon we have a chance of perceiving our rate, and then, I admit, things do not appear so very bad. Accustomed as I am to this mode of travelling, I cannot get over a kind of giddiness whenever a balloon passes in a current directly overhead. It always seems to me like an immense bird of prey about to pounce upon us and carry us off in its claws. One went over us this morning about sunrise, and so nearly overhead that its drag rope brushed the net-work suspending our carriage, and caused us very serious apprehension. Our captain said that if the material of the bag had been the trumpery varnished 'silk' of five hundred or a thousand years ago, we should inevitably have been damaged. This silk, as he explained it to me, was a fabric composed of the entrails of a species of earthworm. The worm was carefully fed on mulberries – a kind of fruit resembling a watermelon – and, when sufficiently fat, was crushed in a mill. The paste thus arising was called 'papyrus' in its primary state, and went through a variety of processes until it finally became silk. Singular to relate, it was once much admired as an article of female dress! Balloons were also generally constructed from it.

Talking of drag ropes – our own, it seems, has this moment knocked a man overboard from one of the small magnetic propellers that swarm in ocean below us – a boat of about six thousand tons, and, from all accounts, shamefully crowded. The man, of course, was not permitted to get on board again, and was soon out of sight, he and his life-preserver. I rejoice, my dear friend, that we live in an age so enlightened that no such a thing as an individual is supposed to exist. It is the mass for which the true Humanity cares.

April 2nd – Spoke today to the magnetic cutter in charge of the middle section of the floating telegraph wires. I learn that when this species of telegraph was first put into operation by Horse, it was considered quite impossible to convey the wires over sea; but now we are at a loss to comprehend where the difficulty lay! What would we do without the Atlantic telegraph? (Pundit says Atlantic was the ancient adjective). We lay to a few minutes to ask the cutter some questions, and learned, among other glorious news, that civil war is raging in Africia, while the plague is doing its good work beautifully both in Yurope and Ayesher. Is it not truly remarkable that, before the magnificent light shed upon philosophy by Humanity, the world was accustomed to regard war and pestilence as calamities? Do you know that prayers were actually offered up in the ancient temples to the end that these *evils* (!) might not be visited upon mankind? Is it not really difficult to comprehend upon what principle of interest our forefathers acted? Were they so blind as not to perceive that the destruction of individuals is only so much positive advantage to the mass!

April 3rd – It is really a very fine amusement to ascend the rope ladder leading to the summit of the balloon-bag and from there survey the surrounding world. From the car below, you know, the prospect is not so comprehensive – you can see little vertically. But seated here (where I write this) in the luxuriously cushioned open piazza of the summit, one can see everything that is going on in all directions. Just now there is quite a crowd of balloons in sight, and they present a very animated appearance, while the air is resonant with the hum of so many millions of human voices. I have heard it asserted that when the first aeronaut, maintained the practicability of traversing the atmosphere in all directions, by merely ascending or descending until a favourable current was attained, he was scarcely listened to at all by his contemporaries, who looked upon him as merely an ingenious sort of madman, because the philosophers (!) of the day declared the thing impossible.

April 4th – The new gas is doing wonders. How very safe, commodious, manageable, and in every respect convenient are our modern balloons! Here is an immense one approaching us at the rate of at least a hundred and fifty miles an hour. It seems to be crowded with people – perhaps there are three or four hundred passengers – and yet it soars to an elevation of nearly a mile, looking down upon poor us with sovereign contempt. Still a hundred or even two hundred miles an hour is slow travelling, after all. Do you remember our flight on the railroad across the Kanadaw continent? – fully three hundred miles an hour – *that* was travelling. Nothing to be seen though – nothing to be done but flirt, feast and dance in the magnificent saloons. Do you

remember what an odd sensation was experienced when, by chance, we caught a glimpse of external objects while the cars were in full flight? Everything seemed unique – in one mass. For my part, I cannot say but that I preferred the travelling by the slow train of a hundred miles an hour. Here we were permitted to have glass windows – even to have them open – and something like a distinct view of the country was attainable.

Pundit says that the route for the great Kanadaw railroad must have been in some measure marked out about nine hundred years ago! In fact, he goes so far as to assert that actual traces of a road are still discernible – traces referable to a period quite as remote as that mentioned. The track, it appears, was double only; ours, you know, has twelve paths; and three or four new ones are in preparation. The ancient rails were very slight, and placed so close together as to be, according to modern notions, quite frivolous, if not dangerous in the extreme. The present width of track – fifty feet – is considered, indeed, scarcely secure enough. For my part, I make no doubt that a track of some sort must have existed in very remote times, as Pundit asserts; for nothing can be clearer, to my mind, than that, at some period – not less than seven centuries ago, certainly – the Northern and Southern Kanadaw continents were united; the Kanawdians, then, would have been driven, by necessity, to a great railroad across the continent.

April 5th – Pundit is the only conversible person on board; and he, poor soul, can speak of nothing but antiquities. He has been occupied all the day in the attempt to convince me that the ancient Amriccans *governed themselves*! Did ever anybody hear of

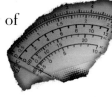

such an absurdity? That they existed in a sort of every-man-for-himself confederacy, after the fashion of the 'prairie dogs' that we read of in fable. He says that they started with the queerest idea conceivable, viz: that all men are born free and equal — this in the very teeth of the laws of gradation so visibly impressed upon all things both in the moral and physical universe. Every man 'voted', as they called it — that is to say, meddled with public affairs — until, at length, it was discovered that what is everybody's business is nobody's, and that the 'Republic' (so the absurd thing was called) was without a government at all. It is related, however, that the first circumstance which disturbed, very particularly, the philosophers who constructed this Republic, was the startling discovery that universal voting gave opportunity for fraudulent schemes, by means of which any desired number of votes might at any time be polled, without the possibility of prevention or even detection, by any party which should be merely villainous enough not to be ashamed of the fraud. A little reflection upon this discovery sufficed to render evident the consequences, which were that rascality *must* predominate — in a word, that a republican government could never be anything but a rascally one.

While the philosophers, however, were busied in blushing at their stupidity in not having foreseen these inevitable evils, and intent upon the invention of new theories, the matter was put to an abrupt issue by a fellow by the name of Mob, who took every thing into his own hands and set up a despotism. This Mob (a foreigner, by the by) is said to have been the most odious of all men that ever encumbered the earth. He was a giant in stature — insolent, rapacious, filthy; had the gall of a bullock with the heart of an hyena and the brains of a peacock. He died, at length, by way of his own energies, which exhausted him. Nevertheless, he had his uses, as everything has, however vile, and taught mankind a lesson which to this day it is in no danger of forgetting – never to run directly contrary to the natural analogies. As for Republicanism, no analogy could be found for it upon the face of the earth – unless we except the case of the 'prairie dogs', an exception which seems to demonstrate, if anything, that democracy is a very admirable form of government – for dogs.

April 6th – Last night had a fine view of Alpha Lyræ, whose disc, through our captain's spyglass, subtends an angle of half a degree, looking very much as our sun does to the naked eye on a misty day. Alpha Lyræ, although so very much larger than our sun, by the by, resembles him closely as regards its spots, its atmosphere, and in many other particulars. It is only within the last century, Pundit tells me, that the binary relation existing between these two orbs began even to be suspected. The evident motion of our system in the heavens was (strange to say!) referred to an orbit about a star in the centre of the galaxy. About this star, or at all events in the centre of gravity common to all the globes of the Milky Way and supposed to be near Alcyone in the Pleiades, every one of these globes was declared to be revolving, our own performing the circuit in a period of 117,000,000 years! We, with our present lights, our vast telescopic improvements, and so forth, of course find it difficult to comprehend the ground of an idea such as this.

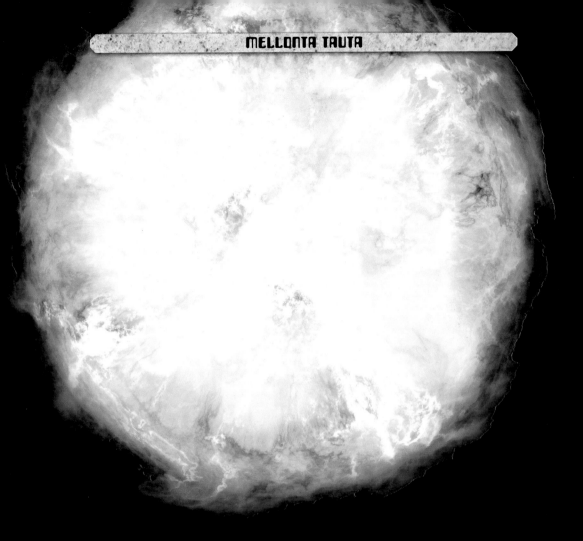

April 7th — Continued last night our astronomical amusements. Had a fine view of the five Neptunian asteroids, and watched with much interest the putting up of a huge impost on a couple of lintels in the new temple at Daphnis in the moon. It was amusing to think that creatures so diminutive as the lunarians, and bearing so little resemblance to Humanity, yet evinced a mechanical ingenuity so much superior to our own. One finds it difficult, too, to conceive the vast masses, which these people handle so easily, to be as light as our reason tells us they are.

April 8th – Eureka! Pundit is in his glory. A balloon from
Kanadaw spoke to us today and threw on board several late
papers; they contain some exceedingly curious information
relative to Kanawdian or rather Amriccan antiquities. You know, I
presume, that labourers have for some months been employed in
preparing the ground for a new fountain at Paradise, the
Emperor's principal pleasure garden. Paradise, it appears, has
been, literally speaking, an island time out of mind – that is to
say, its northern boundary was always (as far back as any records
extend) a rivulet, or rather a very narrow arm of the sea. This
arm was gradually widened until it attained its present breadth –
a mile. The whole length of the island is nine miles; the breadth
varies materially. The entire area (so Pundit says) was, about
eight hundred years ago, densely packed with houses, some of
them twenty stories high; land (for some most unaccountable
reason) being considered as especially precious just in this
vicinity. The disastrous earthquake, however, of the year 2050, so
totally uprooted and overwhelmed the town (for it was almost
too large to be called a village) that the most indefatigable of our
antiquarians have never yet been able to obtain from the site any
sufficient date (in the shape of coins, medals or inscriptions)
wherewith to build up even the ghost of a theory concerning the
manners, customs, and so on, of the aboriginal inhabitants.
Nearly all that we know of them is, that they were a portion of
the Knickerbocker tribe of savages infesting the continent at its
first discovery by Recorder Riker, a knight of the Golden Fleece.
They were by no means uncivilized, however, but cultivated
various arts and even sciences after a fashion of their own. It is
related of them that they were acute in many respects, but were

oddly afflicted with an obsession for building what, in the ancient Amriccan, was denominated 'churches' – a kind of pagoda instituted for the worship of two idols that went by the names of Wealth and Fashion. In the end, it is said, the island became, nine tenths of it, church. The women, too, it appears, were oddly deformed by a natural protuberance of the region just below the small of the back – although, most unaccountably, this deformity was looked upon altogether in the light of beauty. One or two pictures of these singular women have, in fact, been miraculously preserved. They look very odd, *very* – like something between a turkey and a camel.

Well, these few details are nearly all that have descended to us respecting the ancient Knickerbockers. It seems, however, that while digging in the centre of the Emperor's garden (which, you know, covers the whole island), some of the workmen unearthed a cubical and evidently chiselled block of granite, weighing several hundred pounds. It was in good preservation, having received, apparently, little injury from the convulsion which entombed it. On one of its surfaces was a marble slab with (only think of it) an inscription – a legible inscription. Pundit is in ecstasies. Upon detaching the slab, a cavity appeared, containing a leaden box filled with various coins, a long scroll of names, several documents which appear to resemble newspapers, with other matters of intense interest to the antiquarian! There can be no doubt that all these are genuine Amriccan relics belonging to the tribe called Knickerbocker. The papers thrown on board our balloon are filled with facsimiles of the coins, MSS, typography, etcetera. I copy for your amusement the Knickerbocker inscription on the marble slab:

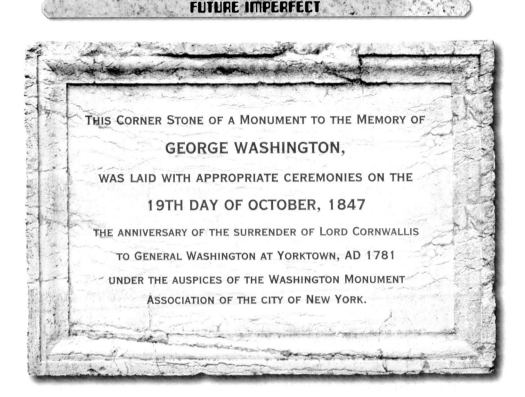

THIS CORNER STONE OF A MONUMENT TO THE MEMORY OF

GEORGE WASHINGTON,

WAS LAID WITH APPROPRIATE CEREMONIES ON THE

19TH DAY OF OCTOBER, 1847

THE ANNIVERSARY OF THE SURRENDER OF LORD CORNWALLIS

TO GENERAL WASHINGTON AT YORKTOWN, AD 1781

UNDER THE AUSPICES OF THE WASHINGTON MONUMENT

ASSOCIATION OF THE CITY OF NEW YORK.

This, as I give it, is a translation done by Pundit himself, so there *can* be no mistake about it. From the few words thus preserved, we glean several important items of knowledge. Not the least interesting of which is the fact that a thousand years ago *actual* monuments had fallen into disuse — as was all very proper — the people contenting themselves, as we do now, with a mere indication of the design to erect a monument at some future time; a cornerstone being cautiously laid by itself 'solitary and alone' (excuse me for quoting the great Amriccan poet Benton!) as a guarantee of the generous intention. We ascertain, too, very distinctly, from this admirable inscription, the how, as well as the where and the what, of the great surrender in question. As to the *where*, it was Yorktown (wherever that was), and as to the *what*, it was General Cornwallis (no doubt some wealthy dealer in corn). He was surrendered. The inscription commemorates the surrender of – what? – why, 'of Lord Cornwallis'. The only question is, what could the savages wish him surrendered for. But when we remember that these savages were undoubtedly cannibals, we are led to the conclusion that they intended him for sausage. As to the *how* of the surrender, no language could be more explicit. Lord Cornwallis was surrendered (for sausage) 'under the auspices of the Washington Monument Association' – no doubt a charitable institution for the depositing of cornerstones. But, Heaven bless me! What is the matter? Ah, I see – the balloon has collapsed, and we shall have a tumble into the sea. I have, therefore, only time enough to add that, from a hasty inspection of facsimiles of newspapers, I find that the great men in those days among the Amriccans were one John, a smith, and one Zacchary, a tailor.

Goodbye, until I see you again. Whether you ever get this letter or not is a point of little importance, as I write altogether for my own amusement. I shall cork the letter up in a bottle, however, and throw it into the sea.

Yours everlastingly,
Pundita

IN A THOUSAND YEARS

1852

HANS CHRISTIAN ANDERSEN

YES, in a thousand years people will fly on the wings of
steam through the air, over the ocean! The young
inhabitants of America will become visitors of old Europe. They
will come over to see the monuments and the great cities, which
will then be in ruins, just as we in our time make pilgrimages to
the tottering splendours of Southern Asia. In a thousand years
they will come!

The Thames, the Danube, and the Rhine still roll their
course, Mont Blanc stands firm with its snowcapped summit,
and the Northern Lights gleam over the lands of the North. But
generation after generation has become dust, whole rows of the
mighty of the moment are forgotten, like those who already
slumber under the hill on which the rich trader whose ground it

is has built a bench, on which he can sit and look out across his waving cornfields.

"To Europe!" cry the young sons of America; "to the land of our ancestors, the glorious land of monuments and fancy – to Europe!'

The ship of the air comes. It is crowded with passengers, for the transit is quicker than by sea. The electro-magnetic wire under the ocean has already telegraphed the number of the aerial caravan. Europe is in sight: it is the coast of Ireland that they see, but the passengers are still asleep; they will not be called till they are exactly over England. There they will first step on European shore, in the land of Shakespeare as the educated call it; in the land of politics, the land of machines, as it is called by others.

Here they stay a whole day. That is all the time the busy race can devote to the whole of England and Scotland. Then the journey is continued through the tunnel under the English Channel, to France, the land of Charlemagne and Napoleon. Molière is named; the learned men talk of the classic school of remote antiquity; there is

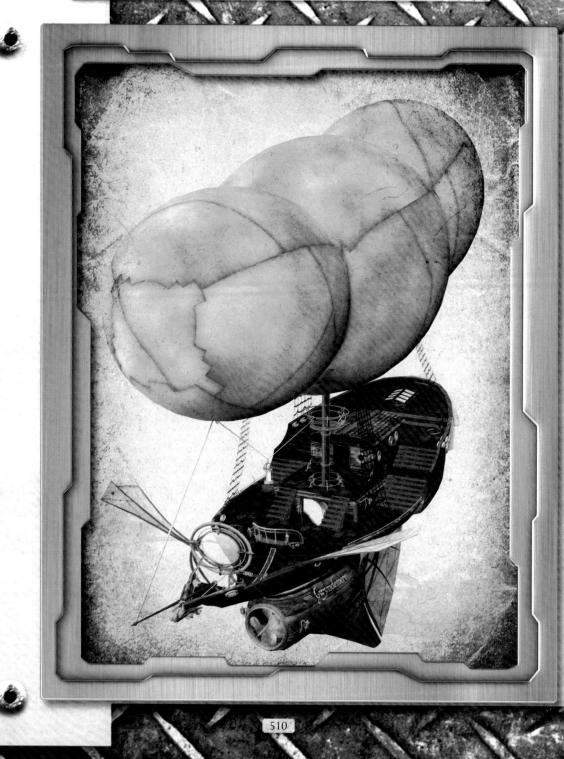

rejoicing and shouting for the names of heroes, poets, and men of science, whom our time does not know, but who will be born after our time in Paris, the centre of Europe, and elsewhere.

The air steamboat flies over the country whence Columbus went forth, where Cortez was born, and where Calderon sang dramas in sounding verse. Beautiful dark-eyed women live still in the blooming valleys, and the oldest songs speak of the Cid and the Alhambra.

Then through the air, over the sea, to Italy, where once lay old, everlasting Rome. It has vanished! The Campagna lies desert: a single ruined wall is shown as the remains of St. Peter's, but there is a doubt if this ruin be genuine.

Next to Greece, to sleep a night in the grand hotel at the top of Mount Olympus, to say that they have been there; and the journey is continued to the Bosphorus, to rest there a few hours, and see the place where Byzantium lay; and where the legend tells that the harem stood in the time of the Turks, poor fishermen are now spreading their nets.

Over the remains of mighty cities on the broad Danube, cities which we in our time know not, the travellers pass; but here and there, on the rich sites of those that time shall bring forth, the caravan sometimes descends, and departs thence again.

Down below lies Germany, that was once covered with a close net of railways and canals, the region where Luther spoke, where Goethe sang, and Mozart once held the sceptre of harmony. Great names shine there, in science and in art, names that are unknown to us. One day devoted to seeing Germany, and one for the North, the country of Oersted and Linnaeus, and for Norway, the land of the old heroes and the young

Normans. Iceland is visited on the journey home: the geysers burn no more, Hecla is an extinct volcano, but the rocky island is still fixed in the midst of the foaming sea, a continual monument of legend and poetry.

"There is really a great deal to be seen in Europe," says the young American, "and we have seen it in a week, according to the directions of the great traveller" (and here he mentions the name of one of his contemporaries) "in his celebrated work, *How to See all Europe in a Week.*"